CALLING IT SAFE

LO EVERETT

DEDICATION

To the dreamers of the world, don't settle for love or friendship that doesn't amplify your worth. Bad bitches reject less.

FOUND FAMILY TREE

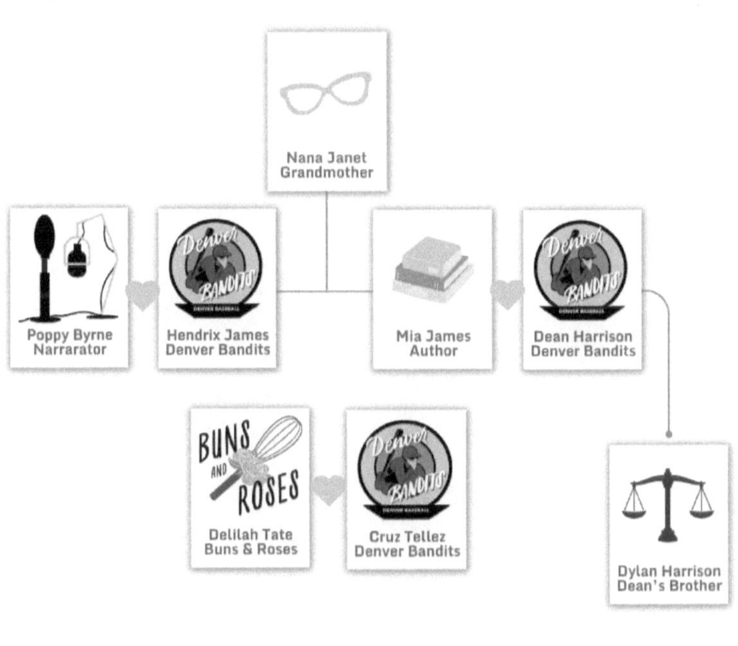

PROLOGUE

MIA

1 MONTH EARLIER

My fingers brush cool metal as I grapple for the door handle behind me. I press my lips into a tight smile, making my cheeks ache—afraid the scream I'm holding back might slip out of my mouth.

All the while, my sweet agent continues her stream of questions and praise. "Girl, you're brilliant! If anyone can top a manuscript this swoony, it's you! Will you bring your laptop along on vacation? Of course, you will. You're Mia James. Nobody works harder than you." Gianna's words press down on me like physical copies of my backlist being stacked on my shoulders. Each compliment is heavier than the last.

That's what happens when you work tirelessly—people come to expect it.

Once the door handle is firmly in my grip, I let my lungs expand with a deep yoga breath, willing my body to relax even as my skin itches with the need to be out of this building.

Gianna's been by my side since I was a fledgling author.

Normally, her passion is energizing, but lately it has me feeling like I'm on the brink of letting everyone down. Then I spiral into guilt because she's become a friend and those are scarce. It's a vicious cycle.

"As always, it was a joy, but I've gotta go. If I miss my flight, my brother will never let me live it down." I give her the most genuine smile I can muster.

"Of course. Sorry to keep you. Enjoy the beach!"

The heavy door to her office seals behind me and, for the first time in four years, I leave work behind. By the time I'm in the elevator, my hands are trembling at my side, and I'm fighting with everything in me to keep the tears that are burning in my eyes from falling. At least until I get to the car waiting to take me to the airport, where I can fall apart in private.

This vacation with my brother and our friends is the cure I'm counting on for the severe workover I've developed. It's like a hangover, but less fun to get, although it still comes with the same wonderful side effects.

At first I thought I was just overwhelmed, but after consulting Urban Dictionary, it turns out I'm not the only one suffering. Symptoms to watch for include work-induced headaches, poor sleep, irritability, and just plain old anxiety. *Lucky me*, I have all of them.

My remedy is a trip to St. John's—without my laptop—much to Gianna's disappointment, but she'll have to deal. Things need to change, or my career is going to be novella-length. Once I get back, I'll put up more boundaries, I swear. I just need to finish my current projects first.

The tension in my shoulders eases when I spill out of the revolving door and onto the sidewalk to find the sleek black town car waiting to take me to the airport. Heat from the car collides with the chill in the late October breeze, as I pull open the door, making me glad that I'm about to escape the cold for a while before winter really settles in.

For the first time all day, it's blissfully silent as the driver maneuvers through traffic. I lean my head back, closing my eyes and soaking it in.

But the respite is short-lived. Boisterous noises from inside the private plane we're taking to the Caribbean reach me as soon as I step out of the car. Since my brother was traded to the Bandits and started dating Poppy, this group has welcomed me into the fold. I can already pick out some voices as I climb the stairs to the plane. The girls, Delilah, Indie, and Poppy, are chatting excitedly over the sound of my brother and his teammates, Cruz, Dom, and Dean, whose deeper voices blend in the background.

Hendrix is the first to greet me with a bear hug tight enough to crack a rib.

"Geez. Put your sister down before she runs screaming in the other direction," Poppy chides as she steps forward and wraps me in a soothing embrace that calms any lingering anxiety.

"Hey, Pops. Are you ready to spend the next week surrounded by all this chaos?" I ask as she releases me.

"We're the best kind of chaos!" Indie, her childhood best friend, shouts from the back of the plane where she's sprawled across a small couch. Her long legs dangle over the end, and ebony curls cascade over her opposite arm, making her look like a freaking goddess. The two of them are a package deal, even though Indie lives in Chicago. She swings her legs down to the floor sitting up. "I saved you the best seat, Mia."

Dom opens his mouth to say something, but before he can, an elbow to the stomach from Dean causes him to double over dramatically.

The plane erupts with laughter, including Indie, who blows the dark-haired baseball player a kiss for saving her from what was sure to be an obnoxious comment from the team clown. If it wasn't for the twitch of his mouth, I wouldn't think Dean noticed. But Indie seems unfazed by his surly demeanor. Whether because they know each other, or she just gives zero fucks, I'm not sure.

The pair of Bandits causing the circus are well-known for their antics on and off the field. Dom, the life of every party, has a new girl on his arm at each event. He's unapologetic about his playboy behavior or his zest for—well, everything. Dean is never far behind him, always hovering at the edges, not as brazen about flaunting his lifestyle, but no less interesting.

Maybe it's the writer in me, but something about Denver's mysterious first baseman has me curious about his story. Since my brother joined the team last season, I've picked up tidbits about Dean here and there. But seeing him in person . . . he lives up to all the hype and I'm pleased to confirm that he's even more attractive than his team picture gives him credit for.

Without the black hat he wears on the field pulled low over his eyes, I can see how intense he really is. His squared jaw frames the poutiest lips I've ever seen on a man. Which somehow makes him look grumpier. Short, nearly black hair is styled in a way that looks just a little messy, but would also be respectable in one of the many country clubs that I'm sure he was a member of growing up, considering he's part of one of Boston's wealthiest families. The man is the kind of rich that loans out his family plane so we can all fly to a tropical oasis.

Like a pinball, I'm passed around for more hugs, making me push pause on my daydream about the tall, dark, and broody baseball player.

My brother's friend and partner in the outfield, Cruz, lets me go, passing me onto his sweet girlfriend, Lilah, who squeezes me with a squeal.

Over her shoulder, I find Dean's mossy green eyes focused on me from the seat he settled into. Most people would look away once they were caught staring, but he doesn't, and the attention throws me off balance.

The man is impossible to read. Judging by the crossed arms that only accentuate the bulge of his biceps, I'd guess he's bored with all the chaos. Then there's the way his gaze holds mine like he doesn't care if me, or anyone else, catches him looking, with a mix of—is that disdain or interest? The set of his jaw has me thinking it's the former, but there's a gleam in his eyes that makes me believe he's as intrigued by me as I am by him.

CHAPTER 1

MIA

"You're a personal trainer. That must be rewarding."

It's our first date and I hate small talk, but Indie and I made a pact on vacation.

I would date, get out, meet some new people, and get my groove back.

And she'd deal with her shit. Whatever that means.

This entire night is Indie's fault, and with post vacation blues and work stress hitting me harder than ever, my patience is nonexistent. If this date gets any worse, it may prematurely end our budding friendship. She'll be hearing from me as soon as I can extract myself from this situation. The two of us bonded as the only single girls on the trip to St. John's last month, and the pact was born one rum-fueled night towards the end of the trip.

While the couples were off doing romantic things, everyone else headed to a local bar we adopted as our own because of its proximity to our villa. Indie and I sipped our drinks and watched as women flocked to the guys— each of them flirting shamelessly all night.

One off-handed comment about wishing dating was as effortless for me, and the plan was hatched. It had so much promise with the coconut-infused glow of rum clouding reality.

Right there, in the middle of the tiki-style bar, Indie snatched my phone from my palm and downloaded three different dating apps—setting up profiles that would attract the "right type" of guy. There were some glaring plot holes in this plan. Mainly the fact that the profile she crafted, while mostly factual, gives off *her* adventurous vibes, where I'm much more of a homebody.

So, here I sit, in a poorly lit Italian restaurant on a date with Caleb, the twenty-four-year-old personal trainer from Jersey who can't keep his eyes off my tits long enough to make decent conversation.

"Sure, what's not to love? The gym access is great, and it's got certain perks," he says, his eyes openly roaming down my body again.

In a blind panic about what to wear, I FaceTimed Indie, and she picked my shirt. Another mistake. The low-cut, black tank is nothing special, considering I'm the founder of the itty-bitty-titty committee; yet, somehow she talked me into losing the bra I was planning to pair with it.

I'm not convinced he's worth it. Whether he picked this place for a discount or the clout is unclear, but he dragged me across town to his buddy's restaurant.

He should tell his friend to turn down the fan blasting above us. One wrong move and my nipples will slice through the thin fabric.

"My job's boring. Tell me about yours. What kind of books do you write?" Caleb drags his gaze from my body just long enough to signal the waiter. As the teen approaches us, my date downs his light beer in one gulp. His cheeks puff up and I think for a second he's about to belch. Instead, he swipes the back of his hand across his upper lip, wiping away the droplets that were clinging to his beard.

"Mostly romance, but I've written everything from poetry to thrillers for fun over the years."

"But your profile said you weren't looking for anything serious." Dirty nails scratch at the scruff on the side of his face. It has me fighting a full body shiver. Some people can't stand loud chewers, or too much body hair, but my personal ick is dirt under a guy's nails. I'll take your chip crunchers and yeti's as long as they scrub those fingers clean before a date.

"I'm not. It's been a while since I've dated. My career keeps me busy. I thought this would be a fun way to meet new people. Get out and have some new experiences along the way."

A romance author that's not looking for a husband sounds ludicrous, right?

Would I like to get married and have a family one day? Absolutely. But I have my doubts that today is that day. Maybe someday a guy that has the potential to stay will come around, but I'm not holding my breath.

If life has taught me anything, it's that people who stay—like really stay—through all of life's unexpected trials are rare. And if I'm going to settle down, it's going to be with someone who chooses me every day.

"Cool. My ex used to read romance books. The kinky ones. Is that what you write?"

What the actual fuck.

I blink, hoping I imagined that, but the smarmy smirk on Caleb's suddenly unattractive face tells me this is all too real.

"My books are open door, so there's sex on the page, if that's what you mean." I grit my teeth, hoping he can't see it through the polite smile I've plastered on my face to match my diplomatic answer.

"I'm down to help you with some new material anytime, babydoll." The wink he offers has me repressing a shudder.

It's the second time he's creeped me out in a matter of minutes and I'm ready to flag the server down to ask for the check when my phone buzzes in my purse. Typically, I wouldn't answer, but right now I'm hoping this call will get me out of here. I cover my grin with my napkin and flash my phone at him so he can see the word Nana lighting up the screen. "Sorry, it's my grandmother. She's frail and old. I need to take this."

Frail is not a word I would use to describe my Nana Janet, but desperate times and all that.

I've never been a believable liar, so I bolt before he can sniff out the truth. Without looking back, I duck into an alcove near the bathroom before answering. "You just gave me an excuse to leave the worst date ever. Please tell me you need something so I can leave this god-awful man behind without lying about it." I huff before my grandmother even says hello.

"I was calling to nail down Thanksgiving plans. Very dire indeed. It could take all night. This type of thing can be very stressful in my old age."

This woman has had my back since the day I was born. My mother couldn't be bothered to raise my brother and I—leaving us behind and taking off for good.

She and my brother have been the only constants in my life. At five, when I got my appendix out in emergency surgery, she calmly sang to me until I finally let go of her hand so they could take me back. She bought me my first book and taught me to use tampons; then how to stay safe when I became sexually active. It's no surprise she's a willing accomplice to this.

"For the record, there's never a time when you need an excuse to leave a situation that you aren't comfortable with, but if you need to deflect some of that guilt, I'll happily take that on for you, Gumdrop." Her voice is soft with love as she uses the childhood nickname.

"Let me extract myself from the creeper, and I'll call you back in ten minutes."

"Make it five and we've got a deal. Don't give him another second of your time if he hasn't earned it."

"Five." Her spunk has me pulling my shoulders back and preparing myself to tell Caleb that our date is over.

Three minutes later, I'm popping my earbuds in as I wait for my Uber to take me back to my Manhattan hotel. I'm in the city for business. My job has me here so often that I should probably get an apartment, but I'm stubborn. I settled in Charlotte after going to college nearby, determined to prove myself. And I did, but it no longer feels like home. Maybe it never did, and I was just too driven to notice. But with my grandmother spending more time in Denver, near my brother, and friends spread across the country, I find myself lonely more often than not.

"That was quick," my grandmother comments as the call connects.

"The strongest woman I know reminded me that my time is more valuable than some man-child's ego."

The car pulls up to the curb and I slide inside, nodding to the driver that I'm ready, while my grandmother laughs at my predicament on the other end of the call.

"I'm glad you're dating. If anyone deserves to have some fun, it's you. Don't take this the wrong way, but why are you dating overgrown fuck boys?"

"It's silly. Work has been so crazy lately. I've been feeling a little restless." The bright city lights look like starbursts through the tinted window as the car makes its way uptown. It's colorful and bustling with excitement, the exact opposite of how I feel. "My life feels like it's passing me by in grayscale. I wanted to do something fun and new. I'd hoped it would help reignite the spark that's gone out inside me." What I don't tell her—what I'm *afraid* to tell her—is that nothing I'm writing right now is working either.

Everything feels like the recycled versions of stories I've already written. My readers deserve more and I'm terrified I'm too boring to give them the stories they deserve. Life has me so busy I barely have time to breathe, let alone try new things and meet new people.

"Maybe it's time for a break. You've released five books this year. I'm worried you'll run yourself ragged and suck the fun out of this beautiful career that used to give you so much joy."

"It's barely been a month since I got home from vacation," I remind her, wishing I could click my heels together and go back to the island. Not because of the beautiful turquoise ocean, or the salty breeze that would ruffle the sheer curtains each morning, but because of the people. For the first time since college, I felt like I belonged with Hendrix and his friends.

"You've been pushing yourself to the limit since you were a teen. And now you're traveling all over the country with no roots, all the people you care about are clear across the country. When we visit your brother for Thanksgiving, maybe you should stay in Colorado for a while."

When I think about home, it's not a place that comes to mind. It's people—my brother, Poppy, and Nana. Even Indie and Lilah. Spending some extra time over the holidays in Denver doesn't sound like the worst idea. My work can be done anywhere. It's not like she's suggesting I move there.

That I'm not ready for. Hendrix has a whole life there. One that's all his and I would feel like I was latching on if I moved there. This rut I'm in can't be solved by inserting myself into his life. I still need to find my own way, even if it's no longer in Charlotte.

"Maybe. I don't want to bother them. Those two need their space." And I need mine. Since they reconciled, they're nauseatingly happy. I love that for them, but I don't need to be immersed in it.

"Just think about it. I'm going to stay for a few weeks." The worry in her voice morphs into a wistful tone.

I can read between the lines. She misses her special friend, Marv. The two of them have been quietly seeing each other since they met last year, when she was visiting my brother in Denver. It was a meet-cute worthy of a later-in-life romance novel. If my grandmother would get out of her own way, the relationship would be serious. He's head over heels, lord help him. The feeling is mutual, but she hasn't been serious with anyone since my grandfather passed away four decades ago.

"I'll consider it," I promise, and I mean it.

In fact, days later, I still can't get the idea out of my head.

CHAPTER 2

DEAN

Mixing with the hum of the treadmill, my phone dings with a text. I don't even need to look at it to know it's going to be another plea to do the one thing I've been dreading this trip to Boston: Go home.

Between my mom and sister, they've been incessant in their efforts to get me to come to Sunday dinner while I'm here for an endorsement deal. My feet slow to a walk and I drag my discarded shirt over my face, dropping it over my shoulder. Preparing myself for a guilt trip, I pluck the phone from the cup holder to see which one it is this time. The name I find has my fingers denting the padding encased handrail.

GRANDFATHER:

You might duck everyone else, but I can tell by the plane manifest that you're still in Boston.
I expect to see you at supper tonight.

Maternal nagging I can deal with, but demands from my grandfather are the fastest way to trigger defiance. It's a juvenile reaction—one that I've honed and have yet to shake since he decimated our relationship my junior year of high school.

Uncomfortable tightness settles in my shoulders, I'm going to need a massage to work the knots loose all over one stupid text. I could lie to get out of it, tell him I took a commercial flight home. But that would only hurt the people I actually care about. So, like always, I do what needs to be done, even if it makes me want to punch something. Preferably him.

DEAN:

I'll be there.

Cranking the treadmill back up to a breakneck speed, I channel my irritation into the one thing that's always been a surefire way to piss off the old man: I work on my craft. My choice to pursue a career playing baseball instead of going to law school and practicing at his firm is only one way I've disappointed him. But it's given me the freedom to get out from under his thumb after a childhood of being groomed to be something I fight daily not to be.

Him.

I'll never be him, and thank fuck for that. For all his talk about family, he's destroyed ours. The moment I realized baseball was my way out, I committed to making sure I was the best, and it worked.

Seven miles later, my legs are shaking and I'm dripping with sweat. Although, that doesn't stop the blonde on the bike across the gym, who's been eye-fucking me for the last thirty minutes, from slowing her pedals and sauntering over to my machine.

"That was quite a show you put on. You look like you're running away from your problems. Maybe I can help," she says, pulling her foot to her ass in a quad stretch. It's a strategic maneuver that pushes her tits up and out. Unnecessary, considering the barely-there sports bra she's wearing was enough to catch my eye.

Too bad for her, I have a strict policy when it comes to women. I don't fuck where I work or where I live. Technically, I don't live in Boston anymore, but it's still too close for comfort.

The last name Harrison is synonymous with power in this city. Something about the hungry way she bites her lip tells me she already knows who I am. If she was using me for the clout of sleeping with Dean Harrison, MLB player, I might entertain a quickie to ease some of my tension. But if she thinks sleeping with me is the fastest way to secure a lifetime membership to the Boston elite, she'll only be disappointed. And that's not my style either. Say what you will about my away game hookups, but every woman I fuck on the road knows the score.

Happily ever after doesn't exist, at least not for me.

"I wish I could, but I have plans." I flash her my best smile. It's the same one I used with our nanny when I was a child to get out of trouble. As I got older, I found it worked just as well to get me into trouble.

Her lips quirk down before she can mask her disappointment. "Another time then."

And there it is. I might be an asshole, but I won't use a woman just to get my dick wet if she's not onboard with that plan. "I'm heading home tomorrow. By the time I'm back in Boston, someone else will have scooped you up. But it was nice to meet you."

"Of course, you too," she says to my back as I head for the locker room, trying to make a clean getaway.

♥

A cryptic message from my grandfather tells me to be in front of the hotel at five for supper. I assume he sent a car to pick me up as extra insurance that I'll show up. Part of growing up a Harrison was having the importance of timeliness ingrained in us from birth, and no one's time is worth more than his. At ten to five, I'm waiting at the curb when a Suburban stops in front of me.

The door to a blacked out SUV swings open and I'm almost toppled over when two teen girls barrel out of the car, their matching blonde hair bouncing around their shoulders as they bury their adorable faces in my shirt.

"My favorite little twisters. This is unexpected, and much better than the crypt keeper hobbling out of the car." Ruffling my nieces' hair, I find my sister stepping out of the car behind them.

The universe pulled a copy and paste on my sister when she had these two. Right down to their piercing blue eyes and tenacious personalities. Which is a blast for me, not so much for her. Hence the nickname the twin tornadoes earned before they could even walk.

"You better be careful. The geezer has ears everywhere. Do you really want to endure a lecture on your only night home for months?" my sister, Natalie, asks, wrapping me in her slender arms, sandwiching the girls between us.

"That doesn't sound like any fun, but you know what does?" My question is drowned out by high-pitched protests.

"Absolutely not!" Chloe shrieks, trying to wiggle free of our hold.

Next to her, Camille whips her head side-to-side. "You promised no more sandwiches once we turned thirteen. That was two years ago. We had a verbal agreement."

I raise an eyebrow at my sister, who responds with an eye roll and a silent, "Shut it."

"I've never really followed the rules, and twin sandwiches are my favorite," I tease, snatching her arm from where it's waving dramatically between her mother and me. Camille's eyes widen as I lift her forearm toward my mouth and lick my lips. Like a hungry wolf, I pretend to devour it.

"Did you hear that Chloe? My stomach is growling. I'm famished," my sister adds. The girls try to cover their laughter with indignant protests. My grandfather would have a coronary if he saw us acting like fools in front of one of the swankiest hotels in Boston. Knowing that warms my heart almost as much as seeing these three.

Once the girls fight their way free with a couple of well-placed elbows, I wrap my sister up and murmur a thank you into her blonde hair.

"Anytime. I would never send grandfather to pick you up. If I did that, you might never come home, and the girls would miss you." Her hand comes up to give me a condescending pat on the face that only she can get away with.

"Uncle DeDe, get in. Grandma made your favorite, chocolate pie for dessert. If we don't hurry, Uncle Dylan will get there first and eat it all," Chloe says, her head popping out of the waiting car.

"Don't you worry Chloe girl, little Uncle Dilly is afraid of me," I quip back, holding the door for my sister as she slips back into the car.

With the girls in the third row, absorbed in their phones, my older sister gives me *the look* from the seat next to me.

"Is this when the interrogation portion of the evening starts?"

"I'm appalled you think I would do something like that," she teases. "But I'd love to hear your explanation for the entertainment factor alone. I'm sure that conversation with grandfather was fun." Light from her screen glows in the dark car as she turns her phone to me—the picture I'm all too familiar with front and center.

The morning after it was taken, I woke up at dawn to the sound of the devil himself barking through the phone. Such a rare *treat* for him to actually call. He went on for nearly ten minutes about what an embarrassment I was to my family and how lucky I was that his team buried it before the media released it. The best thing about living across the country is my ability to hang up the phone when I've been pushed to my limit. Which I did when he started in on the woman pictured with me.

The grainy photo shows me sitting on a couch in the VIP section of a club with a stunning raven-haired woman straddling my lap. The way her hand wraps around the base of my skull and her plump maroon lips graze my ear looks incriminating as hell. What makes it worse is the fact that not only is my hand disappearing up the back of her skirt, but my head is thrown back as she whispers the dirtiest promises about where the night could go. But that's not what had my grandfather's blood pressure dangerously high. It's the way my best friend stands, casting a shadow over both of us, a possessive hand curving around her waist as he pushes her hair to the side and nips at her neck.

The picture makes us look like a throuple with a PDA problem. Which isn't exactly the case, even if I let my grandfather's imagination run wild. Thankfully, the shadow and shitty lighting hid her face.

My grandfather is a piece of work, but *she's* the most terrifying woman I've ever met. The filthy picture she painted was indeed blowing my mind. Had it not been crystal clear that I would've been a pawn in her ploy to make my teammate, and best friend, jealous, the night would have ended differently.

Instead, when we left the club, the two of them barely made it out of the car with their clothes on. The only thing I got that night was a hot as fuck make-out session, and a raging hard on from the whimpers Indie failed to hide while Dom made sure she knew who she belonged to during the drive to drop them off.

"Would you believe me if I told you it's not what it looks like?" I ask my sister, not really wanting to rehash all the details with her.

"Sure, I've caught enough of your hook-ups sneaking out in the middle of the night to know Dom's not your type. The girl, though—I want to meet her."

"Then it's really not what you think, and don't let Dom hear you say that. His pretty boy ego is fragile," I joke, hoping to distract her.

"But I'm not the one you have to worry about. Grandfather was wild when the team found the picture. You know that vein on his forehead? It got so big I was nervous he would float away like a hot-air balloon."

"Would that really be the worst thing?"

My big sister's lips are pressed into a thin line. She's trying to use her scary lawyer face on me, but it's a battle she's losing. I hold my breath, filling my cheeks and swivel my head in an S pattern, like a helium balloon disappearing into the clouds. I win. She doubles over in her seat clutching her stomach as giggles burst free.

Ready for a change of topic, I turn toward the back and level the girls with a serious look. "We need a game plan. How are we going to make sure Dylan doesn't gobble down all of our pie?"

"Tickle attacks!" Chloe and Camille declare, simultaneously wiggling their fingers in the air, phones forgotten.

"And do you pledge your loyalty to Team DeDe?" Only my very favorite people get to use my nickname, all because my younger brother couldn't pronounce Dean until he was almost six.

My teammates sure as fuck don't know about it or I'd never hear the end of it.

"I'm easily motivated by bribes, so I can't say for sure," Chloe says with a matter-of-fact shrug.

"No scruples!" Camille declares, giving her sister a disapproving look. "You can count on me. I thrive on order."

"You're in so much trouble," I whisper to my sister out of the corner of my mouth.

"Don't I know it. I blame Gavin." A lovesick smile graces her face at the mention of her husband, and high school sweetheart. My sister has fared much better than I have at the hands of my grandfather—I made sure of that. She's the oldest and the first to follow in his, and my mother's, footsteps by joining his law firm as a future successor when he finally calls it quits.

The driver slows the car next to the Beacon Hill brownstone we grew up in. At the top of the front stairs, the double doors part, revealing my mom and her beaming smile as she waits for the four of us. Even at home, she's always put together. Today she's got on a knee-length black and white patterned dress with her chestnut hair swept into a twist. She's free from any jewelry aside from her wedding ring. It's her uniform for days when she's in court.

"Trial day?" I ask when my sister joins me on the sidewalk.

"Yep. It was a big one, and it went well, so maybe he won't be as foul."

Chloe and Camille take the stairs two at a time dashing in front of us, only stopping for a quick hug before they race up the sweeping staircase to disappear until supper time.

"Get your butt up here and give me a hug. Both of you." Crinkles appear at the corners of my mom's eyes as she gives us both a warm smile.

"But you just saw me." Natalie lets my mom squeeze her tight, anyway.

"You know I don't play favorites with my kids. Everyone gets hugs no matter how old, or how often, I see them."

"Ouch. That felt personal." I step into her open arms—the rich smell of chocolate clings to her hair. "They all know you're lying about being unbiased when you make my favorite dessert every time I come home."

"It's your brother's favorite, too." She drops her arms, but I keep mine draped over her shoulder as we head into the house.

"Is he here yet? I've gotta make sure I get the first piece," I ask about my brother.

"He'll be here soon. When I left, he and one of the legal interns had their heads together doing research. But he knows better than to be late," my mom says, leading me into the kitchen. "What if I told you I made an extra? Just for you."

"I'd keep your secret and not tell the others that I really am your favorite," I tease as she pulls not one but two chocolate pies out of the fridge. "I figured you might need it. Just do me a favor and try to keep the peace. I hate it when the men I love argue."

She doesn't need to elaborate, it's always the same three—my dad, my grandfather, and I. Everyone knows there's tension, only we know the reason. That's just one more part of the web of lies my life has become and another secret I'll keep to protect the people I love the most.

"Shall we?" she asks, with a poignant look.

"May as well get it over with." My hand tugs on the back of my neck, not looking forward to sitting through whatever tongue-lashing he's got in store for me today. Speaking of the devil, we find my grandfather in the living room with my sister. He's seated in the large armchair at the head of the room.

It's a well-thought-out power move, sure to piss my dad off if he ever leaves his office to join us. A reminder that this may be my father's house, but my grandfather is the puppet master of this family.

My sister gives me a sly smile, continuing her animated debrief of her current case. When she asks for the crotchety old man's opinion on the matter, I make a note to buy her an extra Christmas present. She keeps him plied with work talk until my brother shows up and it's time to eat.

I catch Dylan by the elbow on the way to the formal dining room, tugging him into a hug. "You've got lipstick on your collar. Better go change before one of them notices and realizes you and the legal clerk are doing more than just research."

"Fuck." He groans. "I'll run upstairs. Cover for me?"

"Make it quick or I tell the twins you're taking a dump so they tease you about being stinky all night," I tell him as he takes the stairs two at a time.

"You know they're fourteen, not six, right?" he hollers over his shoulder, almost crashing into the wall.

"Fifteen, dipshit," I remind him before he disappears around the corner.

I make it through the meal mostly unscathed. Dear ole Dad takes a few well-placed jabs from my grandfather, much to my mom's annoyance. It's dysfunction at its finest. The only thing the geezer and I agree on is that she deserves better than what my dad gives her.

My mother loves him endlessly. It's written all over her face as she gazes at him, their hands woven together atop the dining room table. The comments by my grandfather barely bruise Dad's ego anymore. The only people they hurt are my mom, sister, and nieces. When I've finally taken as much as I can handle, I push back from the table, without being excused, because I'm a full-grown man.

"Girls want to help me cut the pie? We can make sure Uncle Dilly's piece is extra small. He told me he had a tasty snack at the office and isn't that hungry." The comment catches my brother off guard, and his napkin flies to his mouth to stop the wine from spraying everywhere.

This is what I miss about coming home—being part of this family. But that all went up in flames when I learned things I never wanted to know, and was too young to handle, about my dad and grandfather.

"Mom, can you help me find the dessert plates? I can't remember where they are."

"Of course, dear. I'll show you."

I'm the master of diversions and keeping the peace. My mom says it's the middle child in me, but that's bullshit. It's a product of the turmoil the men in this family have caused.

Everyone I care about is gathered around the large island when Camille hands my brother the world's thinnest slice of pie. The girl took her job seriously. "Here's your dessert, Uncle Dilly. Was your snack at work sweet or salty? I don't want you to get a stomachache." This time it's me who's trying not to choke, coughing around the bite of pie I just swallowed.

"Especially after that big poop you took upstairs," Chloe adds as she passes me a quarter of the pie.

My brother levels me with a glare, but this is all her. "It wasn't me." I hold my hands out in front of my chest as Camille chimes in with her logic.

"Everyone knows you only go upstairs if you have to poop and don't want anyone to know."

"So what was it, little brother? Did you gorge yourself on your snack and end up with a bellyache?"

He scratches the side of his head with his middle finger before smiling at Camille. "Something like that. But I'm feeling much better now."

"I bet you are," I mumble under my breath as the girls join my mom and sister on the other side of the island to dig into their treat.

"Just wait until you bring someone home. I'm going to get you back for that," he threatens.

"Never gonna happen. So, which legal clerk was it?"

My brother's eyes shift to where my sister sits. His forehead creases before he looks back at his plate. "Ava."

I almost ask him to repeat himself because there's no way he's reckless enough to hook up with the other half of the Harrison & Crawford legacy. "Ava Crawford? As in Gregory's barely legal granddaughter?" I hiss through my teeth.

"Lower your fucking voice. She's twenty-one, but I stopped it before it went further. You're not the only idiot in this family. Apparently it comes with the male genes."

I shake my head. "You win the prize there. I don't mess around with anyone that has the potential to complicate my life. Hooking up with one of your boss's granddaughters is the biggest fucking complication of all."

CHAPTER 3

MIA

Open-mouth snoring on an airplane should be illegal.

Although, this guy next to me doesn't seem to think so and even my noise canceling headphones can't drown this out. It's like a freight train barreling down the tracks while I'm trying to write a blow job scene.

Until this moment I was confident in my ability to write spice anywhere, under any condition, but I've been proven wrong. I know hundreds of ways to describe a climax, and right now, all I can focus on is the grating wheeze coming from the passenger next to me. The seven thousand words I need to write today aren't going to write themselves, and this flight was my longest block of time before the calls I have scheduled later.

After the longest flight ever recorded from Laguardia to Charlotte, I grab an Uber back to my condo just in time for a call with my editor.

"How was your flight?" she asks as I take a sip of peppermint tea to ward off the restless feeling that's been plaguing me more often than not these last few months.

"It was fine," I lie, not ready to admit that a snoring stranger was enough to put me behind on my word count. I'm only half-listening as she drones on about how much she loves the plotting I've done for my next release.

Maybe my grandmother is right, and I need a break. When I told Poppy and Lilah how I was struggling last summer they mentioned a cabin in the mountains that Dean owns. At the time, I dismissed it, but when I close my eyes and imagine myself writing with the snow-covered mountains in the background, it feels like maybe they're onto something.

Even though I caught him with his eyes on me more times than I could count on vacation, other than stolen glances, he acted like I didn't exist. There's no way I can stay at his place, but that doesn't mean I can't find one like it to rent after Friendsgiving.

"Let's talk about character development."

Oh shit, that's my cue to focus.

After an hour of taking notes I leave the call ready to retire at the ripe age of twenty-seven.

Before I overthink it, flights to Denver are pulled up on my laptop. All I really want right now is a hug and a girlfriend to cry over a glass of wine with. I need a few days to recover from this last trip, but find a one-way flight for later this week and hit purchase on my one-way ticket to Denver. The knot in my chest loosens for the first time in weeks.

As hard as I tried to stay engaged during my meeting, all I could think of was the chilly mountain air on my face and writing by a fire in a remote cabin. It has nothing to do with the Bandit that owns the cabin.

Now that I've made the decision to go, I should probably make sure I have a place to stay. Especially since I'm flying out earlier than planned. Ideally I want to stay someplace where I don't have to wear earplugs to bed to keep me from hearing traumatizing sounds coming from my brother and Poppy's room.

Scrolling through my messages, I pull up the thread with Poppy, Indie, and Lilah.

NAUGHTY SLIDERS & TACO SLUTS

MIA:

Work is chewing me up and spitting me out.
I need my people, so I'm flying out a few weeks
before Friendsgiving.

POPPY:

A few weeks before is like now. Not that I'm
complaining, but didn't you just get home?

INDIE:

That sounds like complaining to me. You know you
can come stay in Chicago with me. I don't complain.

MIA:

I'll take you up on that soon.
But something about mountain air is
inspiring at the moment.

INDIE:

Well shit, I can't help with that.

POPPY:

The guest room is ready for you whenever
you get here. And there is always that cabin
in Telluride I mentioned a while back 🤭

MIA:

About that . . . I fly in on Friday and
you know I love you but . . .

POPPY:

For fuck's sake. Lilah ruined it, didn't
she? You'll never stay here again.

LILAH:

I ruined nothing. Blame your boyfriend and his kitchen sex fetish for that one.

INDIE:

Chicago looks better with each message.

MIA:

They're doing the work for you.

LILAH:

Wait . . . we have mountains and my place is still open. Fully furnished and no brotherly noises.

MIA:

 *You're the best.*

INDIE:

Dammit. So close.

It's settled. I'll fly to Denver for Friendsgiving and stay at Lilah's for a couple weeks until I find a place in the mountains for the winter.

♥

"That's it. I'm done. No more dates," I rant to Indie through the phone as my heels clack along the Charlotte sidewalk. It's dark and chilly, but I can barely feel the cool fall air through my faux leather jacket. The rage boiling in my veins is more than enough to keep me toasty.

"Was it really that bad?" she asks, but I don't let her get any further.

"There's no excuse for the atrocities I witnessed tonight. He brought a nail clipper to the movies. Clippers, Indie! Because 'they're already sweeping,' so yeah, fucking horrendous," I hiss as I stalk past a crowd of people lined up outside a trendy restaurant. The date was painful enough without strangers being privy to my humiliation.

"He was so cute, too. I had high hopes for that one. Maybe you'll have better luck in Denver?"

"I'm not dating while I'm there. I need a break from all of it—the terrible dates *and* work stress. The whole point of going out there early is to decompress with my people. I *need* this."

"I know, babe. You work so hard and I didn't mean to add to your stress. I was going to keep it a surprise, but you seem like you could use a pick-me-up. Guess who's flying out for Friendsgiving?" she sing-songs.

"No way! Really!"

"I booked my flight today. It's only the weekend, but I can't wait to see you all." Her voice softens, something I've noticed only happens when she's talking about her girls or her parents.

"That's amazing! I have so many questions. Does Poppy know yet? Are you staying at Delilah's with me so I can keep you out of trouble? Or more accurately, keep trouble out of you?"

"Slow your roll. She knows and I'll be staying with you so that you can keep me from falling off the wagon just like you did on vacation."

"I'm like the anti-wing woman, saving you from falling vag first onto sascrotch himself."

"It's a noble cause, athletes are my weakness. Especially ones with pretty faces and big dicks."

I shoulder through the door to my condo and collapse into the couch cushions. In the solitude of my living room, the floodgates open and all the uncertainty I feel about my writing comes gushing out. How nothing feels fresh, and that I'm a fraud. My fear of disappointing my readers. To everyone else, Indie comes off as fearless, but I know her secret: she's a big softy. She doesn't diminish the way I feel, or placate me with insincere reassurance. She listens with the patience of a saint until I sag into the maroon fabric, letting it swallow me up with all my insecurities exposed.

"So, what are you going to do about it?" The spark of defiance in her voice dares me to keep whining without offering a solution. The universe gave me a new friend in this woman when I needed it the most. So, I give credence to the plan that's been forming in my head.

"After Friendsgiving, I'm going to rent a cabin, invest in some snowshoes. Who knows, maybe find a mountain man to rail me while I'm at it. Someone who can properly toss me around and knows where to find my clit at a minimum." My declaration sounds more confident than I feel, but it's a step in the right direction.

"Yeah, you fucking are. Sometimes a girl just needs to be turned inside out by a monster meat pickle."

"Never say that again," I beg through laughter.

"What? Seriously. I thought it might inspire you." Somehow, she keeps her tone serious.

"My vocabulary of slang terms for genitalia is not my problem. I know them all and *that* is going right on my list of forbidden phrases, next to milking and cleft." An involuntary shudder makes my body tremble from head to toe.

"Vocabulary lesson over. Now go pack and don't forget to raid the toy chest to keep you busy in case those backcountry nights get lonely."

Spreading my suitcase out on the bed I repack, leaving all my city clothes from my last trip behind. I opt for flannels, leggings, and warm sweaters that will be cozy for writing by the fire. I'm about to zip the bag shut when Indies' voice echoes in my subconscious and I pull open the nightstand drawer. Before I can second guess it, I pick my favorite battery-operated boyfriend and do a double take to grab one more—the long and girthy one I rarely use. It's the perfect replacement if I fail on my mission to find some real-life inspiration.

CHAPTER 4

DEAN

"I still can't believe Poppy and Lilah talked you into hosting a Friendsgiving dinner party," Dom says as he cracks open a beer next to me while the caterer works in the other room. I don't mind hosting, especially because there's one guest in particular that makes opening up my place to everyone a little less painful.

Hendrix's sister has been in town for weeks, but I have yet to see her. Knowing she would be here tonight was extra incentive.

Until recently, it's just been the guys who hang out here, and even that was rare. No one gets it, but this is the last place I want to be.

My grandfather gifted the penthouse to me when I was called up from the minors. They all see the luxury and shine, but no one understands how this place sucks the soul out of me. Not that I blame them. I've worked for years to hide this part of my life. This penthouse is another reminder of how fucked my family life is. Most people would probably sell it, but I'm stuck, which I deserve. If I sold it, my mom would have questions. The answers to those questions would only hurt her. I'd be lying if I said I wasn't also afraid of her reaction to learning that I've been keeping secrets for my father and grandfather all these years. So here I sit, stewing, in this fucking cavernous reminder of the ways I've been failed, and the way I fail every damn day.

"Don't get used to it. Just because I fell for that fluttery thing they do with their eyelashes this time doesn't mean it's going to be a regular thing." The only people who hold that kind of power over me are back home in Boston, enjoying their annual Black Friday shopping trip. Chloe sent me a selfie of my four favorite girls packed into the back of a limo surrounded by shopping bags. It was the highlight of my day.

Or it was, until the door to the penthouse swings open, and a majority of our teammates and friends pile through the door at once—stripping out of their jackets and stacking them in Hendrix's outstretched arms.

At the back of the pack is my own personal, walking, talking form of divine torture. I didn't know I was a masochist until I spent an entire vacation trying not to stare at my teammate's sister and failing spectacularly. Mia James is off-limits, and not because of some sense of loyalty I have to her brother, but because she's everything I'm not, and I know, without a doubt, that I would ruin her.

Her piercing gray-blue eyes meet mine as she sweeps her wavy dark hair behind her ear, granting me a small smile. It's the same little twitch in the corner of her mouth that she treated me to every time she caught me looking her way when we were in St. John's. I've cataloged and collected each of them. From the moment she changed into the sinfully tiny bikini on the plane and found me gawking, to when she checked me out over a pair of oversized shades as we deplaned in Denver.

Keeping my distance puts my willpower to the test. Not only is Mia gorgeous, but she's wicked smart and undeniably kind. And from everything Hen's told me, that's just scratching the surface. You don't get to be a best-selling author in your twenties without being dedicated and passionate.

All those things turn me the fuck on, but getting involved with Mia would be complicated. Not only is she my teammate's sister, but I'm not interested in getting serious, *ever*.

So, unless I'm willing to trash my friendship and team morale for a one-night stand, she's untouchable.

This career gave me the freedom to carve out my place in the world, and that's not worth giving up, no matter how badly I want to get to know every inch of her.

As if she can see the filthy images I'm conjuring in my mind, she runs her tongue along her deep red lips. Hendrix holds out his hand for his sister's coat, pulling her eyes from mine and down to the buttons on her long beige coat. She works the buttons free and peels the thick fabric from her body.

I should look away, but I can't. Not when I see the thigh-high boots that leave a strip of skin on display. The dress she's wearing is like nothing I've seen before, it's soft like a sweater but sexy as fuck. Snug without being skintight and it's got this one shoulder thing going on that shows off the tan line she earned strutting around in her turquoise bikini on the beach. Just the memory of it has me dragging my hands down my face.

Fuck me. This is going to be harder than I thought.

My dick agrees, stirring in my pants.

Dom slides up next to me, clearing his throat right next to my ear. When I glance over, he's offering me a fancy napkin that Lilah picked out. "Here you go, boss. Looks like you need this."

"Pretty cocky for a guy with his own secrets," I remind him under my breath as another off-limits, dark-haired beauty saunters over.

"Looking good, Dean. Thanks for hosting this little soirée and letting me crash." Indie pushes up on her toes to kiss my cheek and I'm pretty sure I hear Dom's molars crack beside me.

"Same to you, and it's not really crashing if you're welcome." I take her hand and step back to take a look at Indie. Her long legs are encased in skin-tight jeans and the top she's wearing looks suspiciously like lingerie, with a long, cozy cardigan to keep her warm. With her hand still in mine, Indie's dark eyes shift to where Dom is silently seething next to me.

"Hey Domino, are you feeling alright? Your face is all . . ." Her hand waves around in front of him before shrugging and walking away, completely unfazed.

"Looks like maybe we're both fucked, kid." I give his shoulder a squeeze and follow our friends into the game room, leaving the caterer to finish preparing the food.

The girls have started a game of shuffleboard that has me wishing away a boner as I watch Mia wiggle her ass in the air. She's bent over the table to get eye level with her weight before she sends it gliding down the table. With a *clunk*, one of Lilah's red weights goes careening into the gutter and wins the game for them.

"Don't get too excited. Dean and I are about to take over the title," Dom says, stepping up next to me.

The fuck we are. My goal for the night is to keep a healthy distance from temptation.

Dom nudges me with his elbow when I don't immediately respond and I grumble, unable to think of a decent reason to decline.

"Fine," I agree, sounding every bit the surly asshole I have the reputation for being.

CHAPTER 5

MIA

Jeepers, you'd think Dom asked for a kidney, not a match of shuffleboard.

Dean pisses and moans, his eyebrows drawing together causing a divot in his forehead that sticks around while he and Dom reset the table. He's a walking contradiction. The guy looks at me like I'm a puzzle he can't quite solve, but anytime he's forced to interact with me, he withdraws. He's given off those moody vibes since the first time we met.

Not to make this personal, but I'm starting to see a correlation between me and his testy behavior. Trying to figure him out only confuses me more because I have no clue what I did to set him off. Thankfully, I found an adorable, tiny, rustic cabin nestled into the mountainside that was available for a long-term rental this winter. Maybe now Poppy will stop suggesting I crash at his place, since he clearly doesn't want me around.

Tonight, I'm celebrating and I won't let this giant, broody, grumpopotamus bring me down. His piercing eyes drill into me as I toy with the blue weight in my hand. Twirling it absentmindedly I study him. His broad shoulders have his forest green sweater molding to the swell of his muscles. My gaze drifts down to where he's got the sleeves pushed up, revealing powerful forearms. Perfectly veiny. The one that's setting the last red weight in place has dark ink scrawled across it. I've noticed it before, but never gotten close enough to get a clear look. As I'm trying to make out the words, his deep voice slashes through my musings.

"You ready over there, Dreamer?" Dean juts his chin to where my hand is still spinning the red weight.

An uncomfortable tingle creeps up the back of my neck, making me want to flee. The man caught me, not only staring, but in the middle of a full-blown daydream about all the ways he ticks my boxes. Despite the smug look on his face as he calls me out, he keeps his voice low, like it was just for us. Probably because my brother is within range.

My palms are clammy, but I have nowhere to wipe them in this dress. With no other option, I shake them at my side. "Let's go, Indie. They look ready to get their asses kicked." Pushing my shoulders back I square up to the table. Pretending is basically my job, so I throw on all my armor, not willing to let Mr. Tall Dark and Broody affect me.

"This should be good," my brother's deep voice says from behind me. His hand lands on my shoulder giving me a shake. "What are the chances the two most determined women I know and the cockiest fucks on the team can play each other without any bloodshed?"

"I can handle my own. Big egos don't scare me. I grew up living with one. You just have to coddle them until they're nice and comfortable. Then, when they least expect it, you crush them," I say, my eyes trained on his teammates across the table. Dean's white teeth dig into his pouty bottom lip, holding back a smile, but those earthy eyes shimmer like the devil. I wait for one of them to spout off, but our opponents stay quiet.

Maybe I was a little too bold in my earlier statement. The guys use the same focus they have on the baseball field to chip away at our early lead until they pull ahead. All the smack talk we threw around earlier has ceased. This is one of those times when actions speak louder than words, and when

I glance up from where I'm preparing to take the game-winning shot, I find Dean looming at the other end of the table.

His wide-legged stance screams detached confidence, with his shoulders pressed back, and his powerful arms crossed over his chest. He looks down at me with an intensity that should unnerve me. Narrowing my eyes, I focus on my shot. There's no way in hell I'm missing this, so he can throw that little insulting nickname from earlier around again.

So what? He caught me with my head in the clouds. He couldn't have possibly known I was thinking of him. Right now, the only thing I'm dreaming about is wiping the floor with him and Dom. The little red weight skates effortlessly down the table, bumping a blue one right into the gutter before gliding to a stop right over the three-point line, securing our win. Everything in me wants to leap into the air—give them an in-your-face celebration. But with all my metaphorical armor weighing me down, I opt for mimicking Dean's posture from just a moment ago. I look up from the table to find those piercing eyes and say, "What a shot. I couldn't have *dreamed* of a better way to end that game."

Next to me, Indie holds her hand out for a discrete high-five under the edge of the table. "I could use a refill before dinner." My girl knows how to read the room. "Thanks for playing. Always fun to face off against the *both* of you." The last barb hits its intended target as the tips of Dom's ears flare red. She turns on her heels, grabs my hand, and leads me over to the bar.

"Are you gonna tell me what that little jab you threw over there was about?" I ask, knowing it's unlikely my guarded friend will tell me.

"Just riling Dom up. It's my favorite pastime. And so easy," Indie says, grabbing a can of ginger beer and vodka. "I'll build, you garnish," she says, nodding to the cutting board with limes.

The knife is suspended precariously over the lime when a shadow falls over the cutting board. My eyes skate up, the figure towering over me from across the bar. It's unfair that I'm in the midst of a dry spell and a quarter-life crisis when I'm suddenly thrust into situations where I'm forced to engage with Mr. Prickly himself.

He's all my weaknesses rolled into one. Brooding? Check. Uninterested in me? Double-check. A known playboy that's sure to break my heart? Triple check. Combined with the fact that he's my brother's teammate and friend? Run that red flag right up the pole.

And because this is just the state of my life at the moment, as I'm about to slice off another lime wedge, he does the one thing that's sure to make this little daydream I'm trapped in go full spice. He lays those flawless forearms, the kind I write about in my books, across the bar top, giving me the view I've been waiting for. Perfectly corded with that swirl of dark ink that I still can't quite make out.

"Shit." The sting of lime juice in the fresh cut sears from the tip of my finger all the way up my arm. I roll my lips inward, cursing myself for letting a man's arms throw me so far-off balance that I sliced my finger.

I guess I've officially earned that stupid nickname.

My head spins, only easing slightly when strong hands latch onto my wrist.

"I don't do blood. Just tell me if I should panic before I do something silly, like faint," I say quickly, but Dean doesn't let my rambling slow him down, pulling me around the bar and wrapping my finger in a towel.

"It's not bad." The reassuring smile he gives me softens his face in a way I didn't expect, easing some of my worry. Under different circumstances, that look would unravel me, but the pulse beating in my fingertip has me focusing on just staying conscious. With a quick glance over my shoulder, I find Indie still standing at the bar, one hand on her hip and an amused look on her face. Probably because my hand is clutched against his chest as he sneaks us out of the game room. "Really. It's probably more the sting of the lime juice than the cut itself. I'm just gonna clean it and find you a Band-Aid. No fainting required."

"Then why is it wrapped in a towel?" I ask, not convinced.

"Consider it extra insurance. I can't have you conking out on me. There's a first-aid kit in here." He pulls me through a dimly lit bedroom. The woodsy scent of pine and juniper surrounds me as he leads me to the most impressive bathroom I've ever seen.

The walk-in shower has a bench running along the length of the back with dual rainfall shower heads.

The things you could do in that shower.

I memorize the details, because it is most certainly going to make an appearance in one of my books.

Dean lowers me to sit on the edge of the tub and drops to one knee, gingerly unwrapping my hand. When the fabric is peeled back, he looks up to find my eyes still locked on the shower. One side of his mouth lifts as he realizes where my attention is. "See something you like?"

"Just avoiding embarrassing myself further," I lie, keeping my focus just past him. Reaching across me he wets the towel and carefully cleans off my hand. For how frosty he normally is around me, I don't know what to think about his attentiveness. He uses the same care I would expect from someone warmer. It's almost like he's invested in my well-being, as he continues to cradle my hand.

There's no escaping how close we are with his gentle fingers repositioning my hand in my lap to bandage it. I look for the first time, seeing how small the cut truly is. His thumb settles over my pulse point, circling and easing any mortification I had. I can't take my eyes off the way he works, his brow scrunched as he concentrates on getting it just right.

Everything I thought I knew about the stand-offish man kneeling in front of me vanishes because I think I just got a glimpse at who he is under the indifferent personality. I'm afraid if I see much more of it, I might do something really stupid, like open myself up to a whole world of hurt just to see a little more of what makes him tick.

CHAPTER 6

DEAN

The clang of metal gives way to the sound of merry humming coming from Dom as he squats on the rack next to me. It might be the off-season, but the guys and I still get together at the Bandits facility to lift weights every few days. After all the stuffing and pie we ate at Friendsgiving last week, our bodies need a reminder that we are professional athletes, not couch potatoes.

At least for the next few weeks.

Once the snow starts flying, I'll head to the only place besides the baseball diamond where I feel at home: my cabin in Telluride. It's nothing but mountain views and much-needed peace and quiet after the chaos of the 162-game season.

Out of the corner of my eye, I see Hendrix duck into the trainer's office with his phone pressed to his ear. I turn down the volume on my AirPods and watch him pace the small office, dragging his hand down his face.

"What's going on there?" I rack my weights and grab my discarded shirt to wipe my sweat from my brow.

Dom does the same and loops his arms over the bar, stretching as he watches our friend through the office window. "Not sure, but something's got a bee in his bonnet."

I raise a questioning eyebrow at my best friend.

"You know that shit just pours out of me after bingo night." You'd never know it from the image he lets everyone see. But he spends his free time playing Bingo at a community center for seniors.

"There are worse habits you could pick up."

"Just wait until Janet moves here and joins Bingo. My language is sure to get much more colorful," he says of Hendrix's grandma.

As far as I know, Hendrix and his girlfriend Poppy haven't convinced Janet to move here, yet.

"I've heard the truly disgusting things that come out of your mouth when you're properly motivated. Janet's got nothing on you." His penchant for jealousy-fueled dirty talk is something I didn't need to know. Where Dom is okay with an audience, I'm the opposite. Or I would be if I had ever cared about someone enough. The noises she makes and the way she looks would be just for me. An image of a certain off-limits brunette sitting in my bathroom comes to mind before my friend quickly chases it away.

"Don't pretend you've never benefited from my linguistic abilities. The chicks fucking love it and you've reaped those rewards plenty of times." The playboy smirk that gets him anything he wants tilts his lips. "Is he okay in there?" Dom asks, tracking Hendrix as he lets his forehead hit the wall.

The door to the trainer's office opens. Most people would pretend that they hadn't spent the last few minutes watching his private conversation and speculating about it, but not us. Hendrix looks up as he pockets his phone, finding the two of us waiting for an explanation.

"Is it break time? You two are worse than the girls. You're practically salivating out here, waiting for gossip. If the *Golden Girls* are almost done with their gab session, I'm ready to grab some brunch. Heavy on the Bloody Mary," Hendrix announces to the group, pushing his hand through his hair and turning to look at me.

He's let it grow since the season ended. In an unfortunate turn of events, I overheard Poppy telling Lilah that she threatened to hold out on him if he cut it because she loves tugging on it when he visits her lady cave. My buddy has no clue that I'm privy to that information, but I'd prefer to keep it that way and fly under the radar like I usually do.

"Sure, I can be done after this set. Everything okay?"

"Yeah. Just some drama with Mia. Actually, I could use your help with it. Finish up and we'll talk." The mention of his sister's name immediately has alarm bells going off.

Adding an extra thirty pounds to the bar, I push through my last set of squats, going harder than necessary. He probably just wants advice because he knows I have a sister.

A half an hour later we are all seated around a high-top table at Draft, our regular hangout during the season because of its proximity to the ballpark.

The server drops off our drinks before Cruz finally asks, "Are you going to tell us why we cut our workout short to day drink?" He's just as serious about his commitment to the sport as I am. It's part of the reason our group gels so well together, we all want to be the best. My hand wraps around my cool glass bringing it to my mouth to soothe my dry throat.

"Mia's been running herself ragged for years and it's catching up to her. The vacation was a great start, but she came back to more of the same— demanding deadlines and new projects. She's stuck on this idea that she needs a change of scenery and found a cabin rental in Telluride for the winter. For the first time in a while, she was excited about writing—"

"That's perfect. Dean can keep an eye on her when he's up there," Cruz cuts in, offering me up. Which is a problem because she makes me want to break all my rules and I have no right getting entangled with her.

"It would have been, except the property owner just canceled on her and it's too late to find something else. All the long-term rentals are gone."

"What's her plan?" I ask without really intending to. Coming face to face with her again at Friendsgiving and witnessing her feisty side coming out during shuffleboard, then subsequently softening when she cut her finger, only heightened my need to get to know her. I should take those things for the warning signs they are and back away slowly.

"There isn't one. She says she's working on it, but it doesn't sound promising." Hendrix taps his fingers against the tabletop, his frustration building.

"Lilah's place is open as long as she needs it," Cruz chimes in, trying to help.

"She's always needed to do things on her own; I just want to make things easier for her. Seeing her struggle like this sucks, especially with her being all the way on the East Coast. She should be here where she has support."

His words hit me square in the gut. Writing is Mia's baseball. The two of them didn't have the easiest start to life, if writing brings her joy and peace, I want her to hang on to that. If it were my sister, I'd do anything to make sure she had whatever she needed, but I'm not sure how I can help. His blue eyes lock on mine and it's unsettling. He's looking at me like I'm the answer.

"She looked at other places. Breckenridge and Crested Butte, but she'd be alone, in a secluded cabin, with no one around to check-in. If she stays in Telluride, you'd be able to watch out for her."

"I thought you said the long-term rentals were full?" The picture of what he's asking starts crystalling in front of me.

"They are, and I know your place isn't huge, but it's big enough for two. Besides, you're not there all winter." He's reaching and he knows it. I'm there as much as possible and don't want the key to her happiness in my unworthy hands.

I'm about to open my mouth to tell him hell no. But he cuts me off. "Just think about it before you say no. It's a big ask. I get that. That cabin is your peace, but you spend most of your time out there snowboarding and doing lumberjack shit. You'd hardly see each other."

The real kicker is that when I look at his eyes, although not as gray, they're an awful lot like the pair I spent so much time looking into when I bandaged her hand last week. And I know if it comes down to it I won't be able to say no to helping her.

CHAPTER 7

MIA

"Hendrix, tell me you didn't!" I whisper-yell at my brother, trying not to let our conversation carry through the apartment. Poppy's recording and I don't want to disrupt her while I try not to pummel my idiot brother in their living room.

"It's really not that big of a deal. I couldn't just stand by and do nothing," my clueless, sweet brother says.

The last thing I want to deal with is trying to undo the damage he's unwittingly caused. I can't possibly stay with Dean—if he even says yes. The whole point of renting a secluded cabin was to create at my own pace without the outside world and pressure creeping in. It was going to be serene—just me and the snow-covered pines, while I find the joy in life again.

And maybe that mountain man to fuck me senseless at the end of the day.

Something I can't do with a grumpy baseball player lurking.

Being around Dean is the exact opposite of serene. But how do I explain that to my brother without telling him that his hot teammate rattles me to my core? Especially when he was just trying to look out for me.

I pinch the bridge of my nose. I'm on my way out to meet a guy I've been chatting online with for the last two weeks. Indie and I tweaked my profile after Friendsgiving—another wine-fueled decision led me to agree to this date. I really have to stop swiping and drinking. The only reason I'm going through with it is the slim chance it helps me forget about the way someone else gets under my skin.

"Just undo it," I say, hoping he'll read between the lines and see that this is *not* the brilliant idea he thinks it is.

"Really? His cabin is exactly what you were looking for. It's secluded and not at all like his penthouse—it's peaceful and cozy. There's two bedrooms so you'll have your own space and he's really not there that much. He could still say no." His shoulder lifts like he hasn't just completely fucked my whole winter.

"You don't even believe that. He's going to help if he can. You're his teammate and you guys are like a family." At least my brother has the decency to look sheepish. "I've got to go, before I'm late."

"Sorry, Mia. I was trying to help." The remorse in his voice cools my anger, but only slightly.

"If he says yes, you can figure out how to explain that I'm not taking him up on his offer." My brother scratches at his jaw like that's not a job he really wants. Not my problem. He made this mess. He can clean it up.

I type out an angry message to my Nana because, even though I'm a grown-ass woman, sometimes I just can't help tattling on my brother when he's made an absolute ass of himself.

MIA:
Your grandson is an asshat.

NANA:

And how did he earn this title?

MIA:

*He asked one of his teammates
if I could stay with him this winter.*

NANA:

Which one?

MIA:

Dean. Not that it should matter.

NANA:

*Oh, it matters. You could do so much worse
than being locked in a secluded cabin
with that hunk of a man all winter.*

MIA:

You're supposed to be on my side.

NANA:

*I'm on your side. Let that man ring your
bell. God knows the guys you're meeting on
the interwebs aren't hitting the mark.*

MIA:

Just no . . .

NANA:

You came to the wrong person if you wanted pity.

An hour later, I've almost managed to forget about my brother and Dean because I'm on a pleasant date with an attractive, gainfully employed man who's been nothing but attentive. Maybe after a month of awful dates, things are turning around.

After the bill is paid, Floyd holds out his hand for mine. I feel petty for thinking it, but the only downside to the night is his name. I just can't imagine throwing it around casually. "Floyd, can you open this jar for me," or even worse, "Yes! Harder Floyd." But, given my track record, I'm willing to overlook it.

"Can I walk you home?"

The giddy, romantic part of me squeals at the request, but I keep my cool. "I'd like that. Thanks."

He slips my jacket over my shoulders and offers me his arm as we step out onto the sidewalk. The cool air hits and I burrow in closer, not used to the fall temperatures in Denver. Our seasons in Charlotte are much milder.

"You're cold." Floyd's brows draw together as he drapes his arm around me. "Snuggling always helps."

"Much better, thanks." I look up at him to find his eyes on me—not quite the rich green I've become so accustomed to having on me. They're more of a muddy hazel, but he's sweet and clearly interested. Not having to question what he's thinking has been really refreshing.

"Let's get you home, where it's warm," he says, breaking the spell.

We continue our small talk from dinner for the next few blocks as we make our way back to Lilah's. There are no big revelations, but our conversation flows easily as he talks about his job and asks me about my plans for the rest of my time in Colorado.

My palms are damp with nerves and the ding of the elevator when the doors slide open has me almost jumping out of my skin. I'm positive he's going to kiss me and I'm here for it.

Let's kick start the end of this miserable dry spell.

"Which one are you?" he asks, dropping his arm from my shoulder and threading his fingers through mine.

"This way," I tell him, leading him down the hall to the left. My little author's heart stutters in my chest when he props his forearm against the doorframe above my head and leans in close.

"Maybe I should play it cool and not tell you this, but that was the best first date I've had in a long time." His eyes search mine and I can't hold back my smile.

"Me too. It's a jungle out there, but I really enjoyed dinner." I let my head rest against the wall, tilting my chin up to look at him. His eyes drop to my mouth, lingering there.

"Would it be okay if I kissed you?" He steps in closer, and my heart flutters wildly in response.

"I think I'd like that."

He leans in, dusting a gentle kiss on the corner of my mouth. A move that always makes me go a little weak in the knees. His hand finds my jaw, stroking his thumb over my bottom lip, and then his mouth is there, kissing me gently. The easy way his lips move against mine, the swipe of his tongue as he silently asks for more . . . this kiss exceeds my low expectations. He pulls back and I follow, chasing his touch.

"Normally, I wouldn't say this until the second date, but, *wow*!" Floyd says with a chuckle against the shell of my ear.

There's an internal fight raging as I try to decide if I should invite him in. Indie flew home almost a week ago, so the apartment is all mine. It's been so long since anything in my life has felt this organic. I hum in agreement waiting for him to continue—my hand twisting in the blonde hair at the base of his skull.

"Come back to my place with me. My wife and I . . . we've been looking for someone we vibe with, and I know she'd like you as much as I do."

I rear back, bouncing my head off the sharp edge of the door frame painfully, but the throbbing bump that's forming there is the least of my worries.

"Excuse me?" I must've knocked myself silly, because I swear I just hallucinated him propositioning me for a threesome with his wife. It *would* be a real cosmic kick-in-the-crotch for the universe to pull the rug out from under me in such a cruel way when this date felt so right.

Don't I deserve just a little joy? The simple pleasure of a date gone right?

He smooths my hair back from my face and smiles down at me sweetly, but I bat his hand away. "I promise we'll make it good for you. Before you rush to answer, just think about it. My wife is just as gorgeous as you. Want to see a picture?" Then he pulls out his damn phone like this whole encounter isn't completely bonkers.

Listen, I'm not a prude. In theory, the idea of a threesome has always been kind of hot if you're knowingly signing up to be the third party. But being ambushed after I was lulled into a false sense of security—that part has my body flushing with a different heat. My hand shoots to the doorknob, twisting the lock aggressively.

"It's going to be a hard pass from me. In the future, maybe be up front with your *dates* instead of taking a bait-and-switch approach. You never know what I might have said."

Floyd stands there, glancing around the hallway like he's looking for a clue to where things went oh so wrong. "*So . . . that's a no then?*"

"It's a big fucking no. See you never, Floyd," I say, slipping through the door and locking the deadbolt behind me before I slide to the floor and pull out my phone to text Indie.

MIA*:*

No more online dating. EVER! For real this time.

INDIE*:*

That seems drastic but okay.

MIA*:*

*Trust me when I tell you this was
the worst date in the history of dating.*

Indie calls, but I send her to voicemail. I'm too keyed up to talk, too keyed up to sleep, and definitely not in the right frame of mind to write. When my phone rings again, my finger hovers over the decline button when I see it's my agent calling. My lips roll together, plenty of excuses on the tip of my tongue for why I can't answer before I give in. I really need some professional boundaries.

"Hey, Gianna," I say, letting my head rest against the door.

"How's my favorite author?" she croons.

It's well past the time she would normally call me—she's buttering me up for something.

"You say that to all your authors. Quit brownnosing. We both know it's beneath you," I say, uncharacteristically grouchy, but I've got no fucks left to give tonight. Consider this the start of my journey to have more life-work-balance.

"*Okay, then.* I'll get to the point." She drags out the first two words.

"Sorry, Gi. You wouldn't believe the night I've had," I say, sounding as beat down as I feel. My friend takes pity and gets right to business.

"There's this small-town anthology coming out, and an author dropped out. Anthologies aren't your bread and butter, but this would be the opportunity you've been looking for to stir things up."

Normally my writing skews open-door sweet, but lately it's all felt dull. My readers are still loving it, but I know I'm capable of more. My creative muse is begging me to push the envelope, give my readers something filled with angst and spice that leaves you panting for more. "You've got my attention."

"These are novella-length stories, heavy on the kinks—age gap, morally gray, toys, why choose. You get the picture. Adding your name to the collection is unexpected and would pull in new readers for everyone. You included. It's perfect, right?"

"Yeah, it is. And I appreciate you bringing it to me. What's the deadline? Would it impact my work-in-progress?" I mull it all over, this sounds like the opposite of slowing down. Instead, I'd be stepping on the pedal and going full-speed, but at least it has me trying something new. But maybe there's a way . . .

"I need thirty to forty thousand words by the end of January. That means overlap with your work in progress, but the novella would come out first. It could be the perfect way to introduce your readers to another side of your writing before your next release."

My head drops to my knees. "When do you need an answer?" I can't believe I'm considering this. The timing is all wrong. But this kind of opportunity doesn't wait.

"Soon. If we don't get them a response by next week, we could lose the spot."

Well shit. Can I really squander this chance?

"Okay, let me think about it. Just so we are on the same page, this doesn't change the fact that I plan to spend the winter in Colorado. If I do this, I do it on my terms, from here—with fewer commitments and events in the meantime." My readers might deserve more, but so do I.

"That won't be a problem."

Well, at least this gives me something to think about besides my awful night.

I push off my spot on the floor, turning back to the door after I hang up with Gianna. My hand covers the knob before I stop, checking the peephole to make sure Floyd is gone. I've had enough surprises for one night. I think best with a milkshake in my hand and there just happens to be a creamery nearby with a to-die-for cookie dough milkshake.

CHAPTER 8

DEAN

"A small cookie dough shake, please," the brunette in front of me says, her voice caressing my skin.

Even with melancholy coloring her normally cheerful voice, I know it's her. If the lifeless, drawn-out words hadn't given away the fact that she's having a crappy night, the slump of her shoulders would have. I've gotten good at pretending to be unaffected by Mia, but seeing her like this, with the sparkle that makes her shine so brightly snuffed out, I'm not sure I can hold myself back.

My mind races through all my options. I could turn and make a run for it like a coward—in the long run, I might be doing us both a favor. Still, it doesn't settle right when it's so obvious she needs a friend. Leaning in from over her shoulder I whisper, "Cookie dough? Huh. You seem like the type that would get jimmies in her shake, Dreamer."

She whips around, spinning right into me, while her chestnut hair swishes around her shoulders and delicate hands brace against my chest. Reflexes have my hands going to her hips to steady her. On contact a startled gasp leaves that perfect Cupid's bow mouth.

"Dean! You scared the bejesus out of me." Her almond-shaped eyes widen, the color of stormy seas looking up at me. With our bodies connected, and the way she's looking at me—like I'm the best thing to happen to her tonight—it's a recipe for making terrible decisions.

"A mint brownie shake with whipped cream. Please," I say over the top of her head.

The teen working behind the register wears a shell-shocked look of recognition.

"You're Dean Harrison. First baseman for the Denver Bandits. Holy shit— oh crap. I'm not supposed to say that. My boss has a strict no swearing policy. Please don't tell anyone. It's just, my teammates won't believe it."

Mia turns back towards the counter, taking in the scene before she smirks over her shoulder at me. With his eyes still glued to me, he starts making our order, all the while wearing a look like he wants to ask me something.

"Your secret is safe with me, bud." I pull out my wallet and hand him my card when he finishes. He looks around, even though he seems to be the only employee here.

"Do you think you could sign my hat? You know—so my buddies believe me. You're the best at first since The Machine. I have it here. The boss won't let me wear it when I work," he grumbles, already stepping back as he thumbs toward the door.

"After high praise like that, of course. Go grab it. Albert Pujols is the G.O.A.T."

He disappears in the back, and I reach across the counter to grab a napkin and jot down the email for the ticketing manager. He skids to a stop in front of me and thrusts the Bandits hat into my hands.

"Thanks so much, Mr. Harrison. I can't wait to show the guys on my team. They are going to lose it." He's bouncing on his heels as I hand the hat back and grab the shakes.

He's still gawking at where my name is scrawled across the brim when I slide the napkin across the counter. "Email Debbie in the Ticket office and she'll hook you up with seats to our home opener." I didn't think it was possible, but his eyes go wider yet and I think I might have broken the kid. It's the same look I got the first time I met my favorite player.

Mia's hand brushes mine and I look down to find her looking up at me like she's seeing something brand new in me—something she didn't expect. Her jaw slack and her eyes crinkled at the corners. "Mr. Tall Dark and Broody has a soft side. Don't worry, I won't tell anyone." She takes her shake and turns toward a booth in the back corner of the small shop.

Hypnotized by the sway of her hips I follow her to the table, watching as her cherry-red lips wrap around the straw. Mia always looks stunning, but the only time I've seen her wear lipstick is at Friendsgiving and the nights we went out as a group on vacation. It's never the same shade, but it always gives me the filthiest ideas about what those plump lips would look like stretched around my cock as I thrust into her mouth.

And that's exactly the reason I've kept my distance. I can't be trusted to do the right thing when it comes to her.

Now that it's just us, my eyes sweep over the rest of her. The soft sweater she's wearing is begging to be touched. I know from having a sister that the waves in her dark locks, which are slightly messy, take a fuck-ton of effort. She looks nice—too nice for lounging around. It's none of my business, but I ask anyway.

"You look nice. Did you have plans tonight?" Safe. Friendly. Maybe I can do this without screwing it all up. At least that's what I tell myself as I drop into the seat across from her.

She looks down, assessing herself, her forehead creasing. My fingers flex against the table to keep from reaching out to smooth it away. "I had a date. Well, maybe an ambush would be more accurate."

"That doesn't sound promising." Somehow my voice remains calm even as envy stirs in my guts.

"He and his wife were in the market for a third party to join them."

The rapid intake of breath has a piece of brownie ricocheting off the back of my throat. Pounding my fist against my sternum, I cough. "Christ, warn a guy. Please tell me I didn't hear that right."

"I wish that were the case. I was mortified." She lays her head on her forearms, her shoulders shake. For a second, panic wells up in my chest at the idea of her crying. "The worst part is I thought it was going so well. He walked me home like a gentleman." She peers up at me, one arched eyebrow raised. "I let him kiss me and even *that* was good." Her head drops again and her shoulders lift with a deep sigh. But I can't get past the irrational jealousy brought on by knowing someone else got a taste of her tonight. Someone who wasn't me and who certainly didn't deserve her.

"Hold on. How did you even meet this guy?" I ask tersely.

"Indie, set me up with an online dating profile after we got home from the island." Her cheeks flame, matching the bright shade of her lipstick.

Why does she need dating apps when she could walk up to any man she wanted and he'd jump at the chance to date her?

"And he wanted you to hook up with his wife?"

"We didn't exactly get into specifics, but I got the impression that he planned to be an active participant. A heads-up might have been nice—at any point when we were messaging back and forth. 'By the way, this date is a scouting mission for another woman to join my harem.' Is it a harem if there are only two women?"

I think the question is rhetorical but Mia seems to be on a roll, and I don't want her to stop talking. Every new thing I learn about her only makes me want to know more. So, I play the role of the friend she needs. "Sounds like more of a throuple to me."

She snaps her fingers. "Yep, that's it. But I didn't get the vibe that this was a 'why choose' situation. They had no plans to keep me. It seemed like a temporary way to spice things up."

The questions swirling in my head would push us over the boundaries of friendship. Like, do you want to be kept? Did the idea turn you on? Instead of asking, I sip from my shake hoping it will quell the possessiveness I feel over her. "Your date sucked, and this is your consolation prize?" I ask, pointing to her half-full cup.

"The date definitely sucked, but this is to help me think. My head always feels clearer after something sweet—or tea. But tonight called for indulgence."

From there, the words pour out of her as she fills me in on the call from her agent and the offer for a new project. I get the impression, from the thoughtful way she chooses her words, that while the decision seems clear cut, there's more to the story. And I can't blame her for being vague with me. Until tonight, the only glimpse she got of the unguarded version of me was the few minutes we spent together when I bandaged her finger.

Hearing the discontent in her voice, and her downcast eyes as she told me about her night, weakens my resolve to where I'm about to do the one thing I promised myself I wouldn't do.

I push my hand through my hair, debating. I can either stand by and watch her plans slip away, or I can offer a solution that puts her directly in my path.

"Your brother told me about your plans for the winter, and how they got canceled."

"*Dean*, if you're about to offer your cabin out of pity, please don't. I won't survive any more humiliation tonight." She punctuates her plea with a heavy breath, all the humor she found in the situation earlier, gone.

She glances down at the table and I reach across it, lifting her chin. "You're too strong to let this drag you down. You didn't get where you are without having an unshakable drive. Not only that, but you're fearless. Not many people go after what they want right out of college. From what I gather, you did it without hesitation."

"Some would call that delusional." She snorts, her chin still trapped between my fingers.

"Not me. You found the thing that stokes your fire, and you went after it. Don't tell me you're willing to give that up. You and I aren't so different where our careers are concerned. I don't pity you. I want to see you soar, because your wings are too stunning, too powerful to be clipped by whatever is holding you back right now."

As we talk, I can see the luminosity return. She straightens her spine and nibbles on her lips as she listens to my words. Her eyes flick back and forth over my face, looking for any sign that I'm lying—that I'm masking my pity with words.

I've never feared being found inadequate more than I do with her eyes assessing my every move. I don't have much to offer her, but if I can make her see just a little sliver of her worth, I'll do it every single time. "So, what do you say, Dreamer? Are you going to soar?"

CHAPTER 9

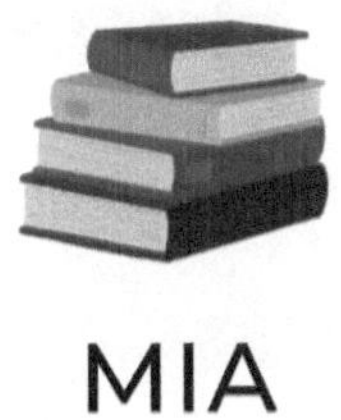

MIA

NAUGHTY SLIDERS & TACO SLUTS CHAT

MIA:

I think I just did something monumentally stupid.

POPPY:

Tell me more. I love it when I'm not the one making poor decisions.

INDIE:

As the queen of questionable decisions, I couldn't agree more.

LILAH:

It can't be worse than the time Poppy sent a vibrator to my "lady cave" and Cruz found it.

POPPY:

The word you're looking for is "thanks."

LILAH:

Nope, that's not the one. Tell us how we can help.

MIA:

To be fair, I was under the influence of the worst date EVER and a cookie dough shake. But I think I agreed to live with Dean this winter.

LILAH:

That was unexpected, but I like this for you.

INDIE:

Are we talking you out of it, or into it?

MIA:

This is why I love you guys.

POPPY:

I totally support this. He could use a little sunshine in his life, and you need the escape.

MIA:

I do. Give me blind courage.
What's the worst that could happen?

I should really know better than to throw that kind of energy around with the way the universe has laughed in my face lately. Dean won over the idealist in me by showing me how much he believes in me, even though we barely know each other. It was like he could see through the outward mess and recognize something in my soul. The girls don't have to try hard to talk me into it.

I'm hauling my suitcase down the hallway when the buzzer drones through the apartment, causing me to yelp. He's not supposed to be here for another fifteen minutes. After we ran into each other last weekend, we exchanged numbers and started texting about the logistics of our cohabitation plans. I triple checked our conversation just this morning in an anxiety fueled effort to make sure I was ready.

Frantically, my hands work to loosen the heatless curler adorning my head like a jumpy unicorn. Freeing myself, I toss it into my open tote bag before hollering, "Just a second." I come skidding to a stop at the door and shake my fingers through my hair, hoping this is one of those times my curls don't take on that deranged look.

When I yank the handle, I double down on my silent prayers because Dean is leaning against the opposite side of the hallway, looking like he just stepped out of an ad for woodsy cologne. Of all the looks I've seen on this man, this one is my favorite.

Even better than tan and covered in a sheen of sweat as he goofs around on the beach with Dom. Right now, with green and navy flannel sleeves pushed up a few inches, I feel like I'm getting a glimpse of him that most people never see. With one ankle crossed over the other in a pair of well-worn jeans and boots that look more functional than fashionable, he looks at ease, which is rare for him. Even on the diamond, he's got an edge to him.

"Sorry, I'm early. I was eager to get on the road and thought I could load up the car while you finish getting ready." He pushes off the wall and crosses the hallway in one easy stride. "Sound okay?" The corner of his mouth ticks as I stand there silently gawking at him.

"Yeah, *of course*." My voice does that weird, high-pitched thing at my insistence that everything is cool. "I just have a few things to do and then I'll be ready."

Eager for some space I step back to allow him inside. As he passes, his hand comes up and he wraps a stray curl around his finger, like it's the most natural thing. He shifts it out of my face and tucks it behind my ear—leaving me feeling dumbstruck.

"No need to rush," he says, grabbing the handle of my suitcase. "Is this ready?"

"Yeah. I should be finished when you come back up. Then we can get going." Suppressing the urge to fan myself, I twist away. He looks too damn good, *and* he touched me. It's giving me ideas that I have no business thinking about—like how it would feel if he slid his fingers into my hair and tugged me towards those pouty lips.

"Perfect. It's a long drive and I have a few things to do around the property when we get there to get it ready—cutting some firewood, getting the wood stove going, those kinds of things," he says, seemingly not the least bit affected by my insanity.

Once the elevator doors slide closed behind him, I race to the bathroom to collect the last of my things. Miraculously, my hair looks fresh from a blowout, except for the one misplaced strand he pushed behind my ear. I shift it to the other side of my head, where it belongs, and grab my toiletries. I narrowly miss stubbing my toe on the bed frame as I race through the bedroom one last time, looking for anything I left behind. After opening his cabin up to me, the last thing I want is to be a passenger princess for our six-hour drive, so I lock the door and hurry to where he's loading the car up.

"Coffee?" Dean asks when I settle in my seat after dropping my tote into the back. When I turn he's holding out two cups. "I remembered you liked the iced coffee with lavender syrup in St. John's, but I grabbed a honey-lavender latte just in case you wanted something warm. I'll drink either."

Plenty of people have bought me coffee over the years—assistants, friends, even boyfriends, but no one's ever paid enough attention to know my order, unless it was their job. What I can't figure out is why this seemingly surly baseball player cares enough to bring me not one but *two* choices. It makes my pulse flutter as I glance between him and the cups.

My fingers wrap around the cold plastic. "Once we're in the mountains, I'll switch to the hot stuff. Anything below thirty degrees, and I need it to warm me from the inside," I explain, bringing the straw to my lips for that first sip. The sharp bite of cinnamon and the honey flavor work in perfect harmony. "Is this from Buns & Roses?"

"At this point I'm so addicted I won't get my coffee anywhere else," he jokes. "But I get it, my sister is the same way. She switches between iced and hot based on the temperature outside. But her order is much more complicated." Crinkles appear at the corners of his eyes tempering his normally serious expression.

"Is it just you and your sister?"

I know a little about Dean's background from our mutual friends. He comes from an affluent east coast family. Lawyers, I think. Reflecting on all the times I've interacted with him, I've never heard him talk about family much, which is odd because his whole demeanor shifted when his sister came up.

"No. My sister has twin girls, Chloe and Camille. I also have a younger brother that I'm close to. My mom is the best. She's wicked smart, like you. Maternal as hell, even though her career is demanding, she tried to keep it from impacting how hands-on she was with us. And then there's my dad and grandpa . . ."

The set of his jaw tightens, ticking when he mentions the latter. It appears the warmth he feels for the rest of his family doesn't extend to them. My curiosity has me wanting to keep digging, but his body language is telling me it's not up for discussion, and I'm enjoying the lighter version of Dean too much to ruin it.

"Is there anything I can help with when we get to the cabin? You said you had some things to take care of. Put me to work, make me earn that room and board. Anything you need."

Out of the corner of my eye, I notice Dean's knuckles turn white on the leather steering wheel—his hands twisting as my words replay in my mind. *Wow, that sounded an awful lot like me propositioning him.* The heat that crawls up my neck tells me I'm turning a splotchy shade of pink.

Most girls blush and look adorable, but not me. I get bright spots that cover my neck, like a brightly lit billboard advertising my feelings.

"I just meant if you need help with your wood or something. *The* wood. Not yours." For some ungodly reason, my hands start gesturing towards his lap. I get them under control by shoving them under my thighs. Oh god. *Shut up*, Mia. Words. You get paid for your words and *this* is what you come up with under duress?

Next to me, Dean barks out a laugh. "Jesus." He merges on the highway as we head out of the city. Now I'm truly trapped as we leave the skyline behind. Just me and my mouth to get into trouble. And a baseball player that scrambles my brain. What could go wrong? "I'm sure we can find something to keep you busy." Glancing over at me, those striking eyes glitter playfully and, for a second, he looks almost boyish.

Huh. That carefree look on his face is something I need more of and I'm going to make it my goal over the next few months to find less embarrassing ways to coax it out of him.

Maybe I'm not the only one that needs this escape.

"Do you miss baseball in the off-season?" My question is a blatant attempt to change the subject and gather intel. If I know what makes him tick, it'll only be easier to get him to lose the moody exterior.

"Not as much as I used to. Baseball has always been an escape for me. My siblings always knew their path in the world was to join my grandfather's law firm. That hasn't been an option for me for a long time. When I was traded to Denver, I bought the cabin with my signing bonus and it got easier to enjoy the downtime. Like baseball, it's just mine. I earned it."

His answer catches me off guard. It's no secret that Dean's family is loaded, but I guess I expected that he would've used money from a trust fund to buy this place. Possibly even take the opportunity he has to play baseball for granted because life has always been easy for him.

It's also possible I've misjudged him and we have more in common than I realized.

"Writing's the same for me—minus the legacy law firm, obviously. Hen gravitated towards baseball. Everyone could see it was his calling from a young age. Figuring out where I fit took longer. I was a decent softball player, but that's not really a career path like baseball. In seventh-grade my English teacher encouraged me to submit a short story I wrote for a contest. It won, and I threw myself into writing, head first, because it was the only thing that felt like it was all mine. Everything just fell into place from there."

"Don't sell yourself short. You worked hard to get where you are, just like Hen and I. Don't let fate take credit for your hard work." His voice doesn't leave room for argument as his eyes drill into me for a moment before they return to the road. *Why was that so hot?*

"Don't take this the wrong way, but how can you be so certain about that? For all you know, I could have just gotten really lucky."

A shiver runs down my back at the hardened expression on his face. The bossy look aimed at me—at this proximity really packs a punch. If I endure it much longer, there will be nothing left of me but a pile of ash staining his expensive leather seats. I wonder if he would use that same tactic in the bedroom to keep me in line.

Nope. Don't go there.

The wake up call has warning bells going off in my head, reminding me that nothing can happen between us. I'm here to work on myself and my writing, nothing else. He's graciously let me take up space in his oasis.

"Luck has nothing to do with your success. Your brother is your biggest fan. He makes sure the whole team knows when your release dates are and how your books are ranking. The man brags about you endlessly—how proud he is of everything you've accomplished and that you do it on your own terms."

"Well, that's a little embarrassing. Please tell me he doesn't make you all read them book club style." The image of Hendrix and his teammates sitting around the locker room reading one of my romance novels, wine glasses dangling from their fingers, has me laughing out loud while Dean looks on like I've lost it.

"What's going through your head, Dreamer?"

"Sorry, just the visual of you guys, huddled up in the locker room, reading my newest release." I glance out the window before continuing. "You know the first time you called me *that* I thought you were belittling me?"

"Dreamer?" His forehead creases where his brows pull together. "Why would you think that?"

I tilt my head to the side, thinking back to Friendsgiving. I'm not about to admit I was daydreaming about him and how good he looked when in those dark jeans, so I kept it vague—safe. "You caught me lost in my thoughts and called me out on it. Not sure if you're aware, but you can be a little . . . intimidating. I wasn't sure how to take it."

CHAPTER 10

DEAN

The upside to Mia thinking the worst when I called her "Dreamer" at Friends-giving is that she's clueless to how badly I want her, but it doesn't sit right with me. Admitting that her optimism and creativity drew me to her wouldn't be smart. She's a spark of joy in a world often lacking. If I confess I envy her ability to indulge her whims, it could send the wrong message—that there's more here than just a mutual friend helping her out. And that can't happen.

"Not at all. Mia, don't let my grumpy ass yuck your yum." My self-depre-cating joke has her puffing out an unexpected giggle, which she quickly traps with her hand over her mouth.

Reaching across the console, Mia plucks her phone from the cupholder and then twists in the seat, rummaging through her giant tote bag in the back, giving me a very distracting view of her round ass in a pair of tight black leggings. I bite down on my knuckle, forcing my eyes from the rearview mirror so we don't wreck.

After I'm sure we aren't going to drive off the road, I allow myself one last glance. I'm only human.

With a triumphant hum, she bounces back down into her seat. "Do you mind?" She plugs her phone in and cues up her music app.

Normally I would, Mia seems the type of girl who has a playlist full of upbeat pop music. I hear enough of that shit when it's Dom's turn to choose music in the weight room. But if it's going to make her smile light up like it is right now, I can endure it.

"Go for it. The same goes for the cabin. Make yourself at home. If you're tiptoeing around, it's just going to stress me out. You don't need to ask to grab food out of the fridge, or to play your music. I'll give you the code to the gym in the garage and the hot tub is free range as well."

Judging by the way she bites her lip and nods uncertainly, this is not the last time we are going to have this conversation.

She crosses her legs, getting swallowed up by the large captain's seat, and opens her laptop. "Thanks, I write better with music, and I accepted that new project that was offered to me. I could use the extra inspiration. If you hate it, tell me, and I'll dig out my earbuds."

"It's fine, Mia," I tell her, a little more sternly than I intended.

I swear I hear a quick intake of breath over the music.

Mia stays busy with work as the mountains close in around us. Captivated by all the little facial expressions she makes, I sneak glances at her more often than I should. When she giggles out of nowhere, I have the urge to ask her what's got her laughing. The next time I look, her nose is scrunched, and she treats me to a little shake of her head before skipping a slow, sad song for something more upbeat. The electric beats and sensual words of *A Little Bit Dangerous* by CRMNL fill the car.

"Not the vibe you were looking for?" Outside of my teammates, I can't remember the last time I put in this much effort to get to know someone new. This girl just draws me in. Every new thing I learn only makes me want more. Even if it's as simple as small talk about what she's working on.

"Not exactly. This project is different. It's stretching me and requires something a little more . . . provocative." The way she drags it out, letting the four, loaded syllables float in the air while pink crawls up her neck, has me hanging on her every word.

"What's so different about this project? Aren't all your books at least a little provocative?" I put the same emphasis on the word and watch her shift in the seat, lowering the screen of her laptop.

"Have you read any of my books?" she challenges, with a raised eyebrow.

"No, but I have an English lit minor from Northwestern, so I'm familiar with the genre."

She cocks her head back like my admission is the most unexpected thing she's ever heard.

"Sounds like you're more than familiar. I never would have guessed. Most of Hendrix's teammates in college were sports management or kinesiology majors."

"When you're young and impulsive, sometimes you pick the major that's most likely to piss off your bitter grandfather as a form of juvenile payback. A lit major is about as far away from pre-law as I could get. My goal in life, back then, was to stick it to him."

"That's one way to do it," she quips. "Rapid fire question. Who's your favorite author from the Victorian period?"

I don't even consider acting macho. The answer just spills out of my mouth like so many other things around this woman. She has a way of putting me at ease. We can do this, be friends, co-exist, whatever this is, without crossing a line.

"Wilde. Equally, because he pushed the envelope to make people uncomfortable in his personal life, and because of his written work. Now that I've admitted that, it's probably worth mentioning to a therapist." My shoulders shake with silent laughter.

"That tracks with the dual personalities. You let people think you're closed-off, but I've seen you with our friends, and then with that fan when we got shakes. You're not as grumpy as you seem."

"I bet I can guess yours," I tell her, steering the conversation away from me.

"That seems presumptuous." The side of her mouth quirks up as she sets her laptop aside and turns in her seat so her back is pressed against the door.

"Bronte." She opens her mouth to tell me I'm wrong. "But not the sister most people would think. I bet you loved *The Tenant of Wildfell Hall*."

Like a fish out of water, her mouth opens and closes wordlessly. Finally, she finds her voice. "That's a fun party trick."

"I've yet to pull it out at a party, but never say never. It's all those people watching skills. Plus, you would've related to Helen as a main character. She's strong like you—an artist, rising from the ashes of life's unfairness. Determined not to let it stop her." My hands steer us into a gas station. Mia is frozen, watching me like she's not sure how to respond to my assessment, so I save her the trouble. "I'll pump gas, you grab snacks." Peeling a couple of bills out of my wallet I hand them across the console to her. She looks down at her hand frowning, but doesn't fight me on it before she steps out of the now parked car.

"What kind of snacks?" she asks when she meets me at the back of the car breathing into her hands to warm them up. As we've gotten further from the city the temperature has dropped, and in a few more miles, everything will be covered in snow.

"Surprise me. I guessed your author, you can guess my road trip snacks."

"This feels like a trap," she huffs out.

"Nah. You're an observer of the universe. I believe in you." I tug on a strand of mocha hair, loving the way the silky strands slip through my fingers before she turns away and heads into the building.

Mia comes back to the car with a skip in her step, and she presents me with a bag before pulling each item out individually.

"Andes because you obviously love mint and chocolate, so that seemed like a safe bet. Peanut Butter M&M's if you wanted something different but still a little fun with your chocolate. They're also my favorite so it seemed practical. Cherry Twizzlers because we always had those on road trips growing up and they're superior to strawberry. Lastly, in case you weren't feeling like something sweet, Chili-Lime chips because you strike me as the type of guy who embraces a little spice."

"First, this is an impressive spread. You did good. And I love everything here, but when I'm craving something spicy I'll go with a jalapeno cheddar beef stick if I can find it. I know for a fact that this gas station doesn't carry them because I look every time I stop."

"I did good?" She looks up at me hopefully.

"You did so good, Dreamer." I grab the Andes from the pile of snacks, unwrap it, and pop one into my mouth.

Mia falls right back into her work when we're on the road again. Her fingers fly across the keys as we make our way around the mountain and head off the main road to the one-lane stretch leading to the cabin. My library at the penthouse is filled with books from all genres and periods, but there's not a single book in the massive collection that I want to read more than whatever Mia is creating right now.

Her face is relaxed, a slight curve to her lips as she works, and I hope this isn't the last time I get to see her in her element this winter. Most of the reluctance I felt about sharing my space has dissipated. In its place is the desire to give Mia anything to make sure her winter is everything she needs.

There's a stunned gasp from the passenger seat as we slowly round the corner and the cabin comes into view. It's not a hovel, but my mountain escape contrasts the penthouse in almost every way. I spent the entire season in the cavernous space back in Denver and it's never felt as much like home as this little cabin.

One place I splurged on was fixing up the garage to add a heated workout space so I can be here as much as possible in the off season. Between the gym, snowboarding, and snowshoe running, it's enough to keep me fit. If I need to get in some batting, I'll go into town and use the high school facility. There's also a new hot tub, because I just really wanted to bask in the moonlight, enjoying this space I carved out for myself.

"Dean, this view is incredible," she says when she joins me, stretching her hands above her head, causing the cropped sweatshirt she's wearing to lift, showing off the little gem dangling from her belly button.

"It really fucking is." I force my eyes from her body and take in the tall, snow-capped mountains in the distance before she catches me. It wouldn't be the first time, and she always lets me get away with it, but I should probably get it under control if we're going to be spending the next three months together.

She glances up at me, her cheeks pink from the cool air. "I can get this unloaded. Why don't you go warm up inside. Just give me a minute and I'll get the wood burner going and turn on the water."

"I meant what I said when I offered to help. Put me to work. It'll be faster with both of us."

"Are you trying to tell me you want to help me with my wood?" My resolve to keep this platonic crumbles like the snow in an avalanche. But the look on her face makes it worth it.

She blinks back at me shocked and it's too fucking cute, but it's cold out and if I let her stand there gawking much longer it's going to get awkward. "Grab your bag from the backseat and I'll grab the groceries. You can start putting those away while I get the car unloaded."

Mia turns on her heels as I follow her to the door, setting the cooler down and reaching around her to unlock the deadbolt. Her sweet scent surrounds me. Somehow, after a six-hour drive, she still smells like peach cobbler-laden heaven.

Silky brown strands swish around her shoulder as she spins on her toes, arms spread wide. The tote on her shoulder slips down her arm to the entry-way floor with a light thud. My chest puffs with pride as her gaze sweeps over all the details of my favorite place like it's a castle instead of a simple two-bedroom cabin. "This place . . . wow. I can't believe I get to stay here for the whole winter."

"I'll give you the full tour once we get unloaded," I say gruffly, the warm and fuzzy feeling I just had overshadowed as I realize how little space this is for two people, and how much her warmth creeps into every corner already. There's no escaping her in this small space.

"Right, I'll get the cooler unloaded while you take care of the other stuff." Her eyes flick over me and I can't help but remember the way her cheeks flushed pink when she offered to help me earlier. Being near her makes me feel like a yo-yo. One second I'm dragging across the floor, and the next second she tugs my string and I'm winding right back up into the palm of her hand.

"If you finish up quickly, come outside and I'll show you exactly how I like my wood handled," I say over my shoulder as I move the cooler to the kitchen. My reward is watching Mia's jaw become unhinged as she stands frozen in the middle of the space, trying to figure out what to do with that. "You have to stack it just right, or it ends up wet from the snow that melts off the roof." I roll my lips to keep from laughing as she rips open the cooler and buries her face inside it, pretending to work.

Her sweet voice turns husky, stopping me in my tracks. "Who would have thought playboy Dean Harrison was afraid to get his wood wet?"

Touche.

I'm dying to tell her just how wrong she is but I stop myself before I take this from innocent flirting to showing her all the different ways I want to prove her wrong.

Manual labor and icy mountain air are exactly what I need to get my head on straight after being spun around in circles by the cheerful brunette inside. Except, with every swing of the ax, as I chop wood, I catch sight of her inside, flitting around the cabin, through the floor-to-ceiling windows. She's settled right into my space and instead of finding myself annoyed with her presence, I can't take my eyes off her as she dances through the kitchen putting away groceries.

When I went in earlier to check on her, after unloading the car, I found her humming along with the music playing through the speaker on her phone as she fluffed pillows and pulled blankets out of storage. I hadn't even had a chance to give her the tour before she dove in. And of course, she wouldn't hear it when I told her she didn't need to make the bed and set out towels.

I shake my head, watching her disappear back into the bedroom before I pull the ax back over my head and bring it down, splitting the wood and letting it clatter to the ground. Surveying the piles of split logs, I swipe the back of my hand across my forehead. We have enough to get us through the first few days.

Bending down to clean up my mess, I hear a blood-curdling scream from inside. The ax hits the snow with a thud as I take off towards the cabin in a sprint. I whip the door open so fast I'm surprised it doesn't come right off the hinges. I've got one foot inside the cabin when a blur of limbs collides with my chest, knocking the air right out of my lungs.

My arms wrap around Mia, to keep her from tumbling backward. It probably makes me an asshole, but the first thing I notice is that she's shed the sweatshirt she had on earlier. Her cropped long-sleeve shirt leaves nothing between my hand on her hip and the other splayed across her back. And fuck me, her heated skin is smooth under my rough hands. It feels too damn good.

I drop my hands like they've been seared.

"Are you okay? What happened?" I pull my shit together because now that I'm looking at her face, I see her trembling lip, reminding me of what led me here in the first place.

"Mouse," she huffs out, her chest rising and falling rapidly as she points towards the open closet door.

"Jesus, that's all? There are some traps in the shed." I'm doing a shitty job of hiding my annoyance, but based on her screams, I thought she was hurt. My heart still hasn't returned to its normal rhythm from the adrenaline.

Her jaw ticks as she shakes her head, her gaze hardening. "Mice. A whole family. I pulled out the towels and there they were." She rolls her lips together to keep them from quivering. "The poor things."

Wait. "So, no traps?" I ask carefully, my aggravation lifting when I realize what she's telling me.

"No traps." Her voice shakes. "Can you just clean it up? I don't think I can do it."

All the instincts I had before that made me let go of her disappear and pull her back against me—letting her bury her head in my chest. It's the least I can do after being so cold.

"They were just babies. Something must have happened to Mom."

She's trying to hold it together and my arms flex, holding her tighter, hoping that's enough to keep her from falling apart in front of me. I'm not equipped for this. My family dynamics are dysfunctional at best and Mia is the opposite of me in every way—soft and caring where I'm hardened and callous. But I'd do anything to calm the way she trembles against my chest.

"Yeah, I'll take care of it." I make a note to look for Mom because I don't think I can stand to see her like this again if she stumbles on another mouse's gravesite.

CHAPTER 11

MIA

With wet hair dripping down my back, I towel off in front of the fogged mirror, feeling more like myself. Dean, to his credit, cleaned the mess up right away and did a sweep of the bathroom, throwing all the remaining towels in the wash, before grabbing me a hot tub towel. It's the second time I've witnessed the softer side of him—where he drops his guard and does everything in his power to make sure I'm taken care of.

Now that the shower eased any of the blues his embrace couldn't chase away, my concern is that, in my scramble to wash the morbid discovery away, I forgot to grab clean clothes. I eye up the pile of clothes I shed like they were on fire the second the bathroom door clicked shut. My body shakes with a shudder at the thought of putting them back on.

My ear is pressed against the door, listening for movement, but I'm met with silence. Seizing my chance, I twist the knob and step into the hallway. Head down, I turn toward my room and run straight into a very familiar wall of muscle, one that smells like the pines outside. Twice in one day, I find his hands unexpectedly on my skin and both times I can't ignore the sizzling sensation that zings through me.

"Better?" The one word is hoarse as the hand on my shoulder wraps around the back of my neck, tilting my head up. Everything about him is so intense, the way his eyes search mine, looking for any sign that I'm still fraying from finding the baby mice. The hold he has on me feels more intimate than anything I've experienced recently, which says volumes about my dating life.

"Mhmm." My head tilts into his hand, and I clutch the towel to my chest. All at once it's like he realizes the state we are in, me, in nothing but a tiny towel, and him, holding me like I'm the most precious thing in the world. He drops his hands, stepping back abruptly just like earlier. All the heat that was coursing through me turns to ice at his change in demeanor.

"Sorry, I forgot my clothes. I'm just going to go . . ." His retreat has me feeling more naked than I did with his hands on me just a moment ago.

"I started supper. It should be ready soon. Could you listen for the buzzer while I run out to stack the wood?"

"Of course. Thanks for earlier," I tell him, nodding towards the closet door.

His lips press into a line like he's holding himself back. His head ducks in a curt nod before he shoves his feet back into his boots and pushes through the door.

"I guess the grumpopotamus is back," I whisper to the empty cabin as I swing my door shut and rifle through my suitcase. My bra falls to the ground and I swiftly toss it back in with the rest of my clothes. *Not today, Satan.* I slip my arms into a well-loved henley before pulling on a pair of cozy joggers. Showing up at the dinner table in my slinky pajama set seems like a surefire way to make Dean short-circuit after that hot and cold interaction in the hallway, but there's also no way in hell I'm putting on real clothes.

I'm about to gather my things up and move out to the kitchen to work when the vibrations of my phone on the nightstand catch my attention. Flipping the phone over in my palm my grandmother's face comes into view— all sleek silver hair and bright pink lipstick.

"Hello, Gumdrop." The sound of her voice through the phone has my heart warming immediately.

"Hey, Nana," I respond, taking a seat at the end of the bed.

"I take it you survived the long drive with the handsome baseball player?"

"Handsome, huh? I hadn't noticed." *Lie.* I noticed so many times today. Especially when he had me wrapped in his arms.

Her loud cackle has me pulling the phone from my ear. "I'm old, not senile. And you'd have to be blind not to think that man is handsome. He might be my favorite Bandit. I've got a thing for that hot, cranky look."

"And how would your grandson feel about that?" I ask, scrunching my damp hair in my hands, hoping to infuse some life into it without actually styling it.

"Hen knows I still have a very active love life. Why? Did Dean ask about me?"

Her question doesn't even shock me. This is how she is, and I love her for it, but the last thing I need right now is a reminder that my grandmother has a better sex life than I do. "You might be disappointed. He's not as grouchy as he wants everyone to think." The way he took care of me earlier with the mice is a stark contrast to the scowling man I first met.

"Oh. I see how it is," she says with a laugh.

"You see nothing. In fact, I think you're overdue for an eye exam. Maybe old age *is* affecting you more than you realize."

"We'll see about that. All winter locked up with him . . ." She hums thoughtfully. "You're a stronger woman than me. I'd have already engineered a naked hallway run."

There's no chance in hell I'm sharing that with her now. "Enough of that. Thanks for checking on me." The conversation has gotten too far out of hand to save and I still have work to do. We talk for another minute before I get off the phone and collect my things.

Making myself at home, I spread my laptop and notebooks out on the kitchen island, and the butt end of my pen taps against the paper. I stare at the same sentence I typed fifteen minutes ago—jumping when buzzer rips me out of my thoughts. At this point, it's a blessing because I was headed down a dark rabbit hole filled with doubt.

My hands pull one heavy wood drawer open after another, searching for an oven mitt when a large palm lands on my hip, nudging me out of the way.

"They're down here," Dean says, bending in front of the oven. The worn fabric of his jeans stretch against his ass, doing nothing to hide the toned muscles beneath them.

I've been around athletes my whole life. Hell, I was an all-state softball player in high school and our coach had us in the weight room all the time. But the way this man fills out his jeans is really doing something for me. I can already imagine what those perfectly proportioned buns would look like in a pair of tight black boxer briefs. High and round, with the perfect amount of shelf.

Words swirl around in my head and I do my best not to skip at the first sign of my muse hitting me. Like a lady, I speed walk back around the counter to where my laptop is open before I lose them. My lip stings from my teeth pressing into it. I feel guilty over the fact that I'm using Dean like this. The keys clack under my fingers as I write an aggressive ass grab into the kissing scene I was working on when it stalled out earlier.

Brown sugar and garlic waft around the small kitchen and my stomach rumbles to life begging for something other than the road trip fare I fed it all day. Dean stands to his full height turning with a steaming foiled covered pan in his hand and I slam the laptop shut.

My cheeks flame like he can see every word I typed and knows exactly where I found my inspiration. One dark eyebrow arches at me in question and I can't help it—the words just pour out, taking my guilt with them.

"I think your ass is my muse."

Well, there's no taking it back, so I just own it—doing my best to look unaffected by my confession.

A strangled choking sound rumbles out of Dean's chest as he looks around the kitchen to find the hot pad he grabbed earlier and sets the hot pan down on the opposite side of the island. "Come again, Dreamer?"

Taking a peek through where I've buried my face in hands, I see him rounding the island to the stool next to me. "It's a really nice backside. Can you blame me?"

"I can't argue with that, but I'm still not sure what we're talking about. You're going to have to fill me in, from the beginning."

Grasping at straws because I'm suddenly feeling in over my head with him sitting this close, I point to the pan. "Dinner smells delicious. We don't want it to get cold."

"The chicken is resting and I'm very interested in hearing more about how much you love my ass," he says, never letting those forest-green eyes stray from me.

"I don't think that's exactly what I said. It was more of a general appreciation for it."

"All I hear is that my squats are paying off. What exactly did my bent-over backside inspire?" He waits, propping his elbow on the counter.

I blink once, twice, three times.

"The oven door is reflective, and you do this thing where you tilt your head to the side when you're thinking. I noticed it in the car when you were writing and just now when I caught you checking me out. You know what I think?"

I'm afraid to ask because this feels a little like flirting and it's going to hurt if I'm wrong. "That you're grateful you could provide me with such a service, and now you're ready to eat?"

"Cute, but no. I think you should let me read what you wrote. It's only fair since I did two-thirds of the work."

"What kind of guy-math is that?" Oh, it's definitely flirting. He's being ridiculous on purpose to ease my embarrassment, and it's working.

"Was it one butt cheek? Or their combined efforts that inspired the furious typing I heard while I was finishing up supper?"

"I can't believe we're really having this conversation." I laugh but pull my laptop closer, like he might snatch it away from me.

This new project is so far out of my comfort zone that I'm not eager to share it with anyone. The idea of watching him read any of it, let alone *this* scene, is unnerving. It's not particularly spicy, but it's the scene where my heroine realizes she wants her boss *and* his best friend.

"If you don't tell me, I'll just let my imagination run wild. And I guarantee you it will be so much worse than anything you wrote. It's the Wild West up here." He taps two thick fingers on the side of his head where his beanie still covers his ears from working outside earlier. "I can come up with all sorts of creative scenarios."

"I bet you can." My voice comes out huskier than I expect as I envision all the dirty things I could have written but didn't. He's right, it could be so much worse. "You can read it." He lunges for the laptop, but I pull it tight to my chest. "After we eat," I amend with a *tsk*. With Dean making our plates, I set the computer aside and grab two glasses of ice water before rejoining him at the island.

"Who taught you to cook like this?" I ask around the juiciest bite of chicken I've ever had.

"My mom. We had a nanny who helped during the week when she was working, but every Sunday, without fail, my mom cooked breakfast and supper. The three of us had to rotate helping her. She claimed it was bonding time, and it was, but I think, secretly, she was afraid we would all end up as complete disasters with no life skills, given the upbringing we had. So she made sure we had the basics down."

"That sounds nice, it seems like you and your mom are close."

"She's the best. No matter how hard she worked, we always came first. I know it wasn't easy balancing it all, but she's never complained. Even now, with more responsibility at the firm than ever, she still goes to every hockey game and dance competition for my nieces. Did you and Hen have any traditions like that with Janet?" he asks, seeming genuinely interested.

"Every Sunday we had donuts in the park. We'd walk to this ma-and-pop coffee shop that sold the best long johns, and then we would sit on a bench and talk about our week. She always made us tell her three things. It was different each week, and we never knew what she would ask," I say with a chuckle, remembering some of the off-the-wall questions.

"I can only imagine the questions she would have asked," he says with a deep laugh.

The memory of those Sunday mornings has an airy nostalgic feeling surrounding me. "They were the most random questions. One time she asked us, 'What sitcom scenario would you like to see play out in real life?'"

"Okay, now you have to tell me what you picked. Let me see inside that pretty head, Mia."

Heat blossoms on my cheeks, but thankfully not a full, splotchy blush, "It's silly but it reminded me of our weird little family and it sounded like something we would do. You know the episode of *FRIENDS* when Joey adopts a chick for Chandler?"

"Sure, it's iconic." He pushes some chicken around his plate frowning at it before spearing the piece with his fork. "My sister loves *FRIENDS*; she always made me, and my younger brother, Dylan, watch it with her."

"That was my pick. Maybe it was the way Chandler couldn't give up the chick when he learned what would happen to it, or that he doubled down and brought home a duck too." My shoulders lift in a shrug. "It just always stayed with me. I begged for a pet duck for weeks after I saw that episode."

"Did you ever get one?"

"No." The most unladylike snort comes out of me. "Thank God. I can't imagine ducks actually make great pets, and Nana had enough to deal with raising the two of us."

"I think she did okay with you, Dreamer. Now tell me about this story you're writing." The ceramic plate scrapes across the cream-colored marble countertop as he pushes it away, done with his dinner, and turns his attention to me expectantly.

"You're annoying. You've spent too much time with my brother," I tell him, grabbing his plate and stacking it on top of mine.

"And you're stalling. It only makes me more curious to see what kind of butt stuff I inspired." He sounds far too innocent for the look on his face.

I force out a confident laugh. "If that's the bar, you are going to be very disappointed. It's way too early for butt stuff." I know my ploy works when I glance over my shoulder from where I'm rinsing the dishes at the sink to find his Adam's apple bobbing roughly.

By the time I'm done, the plates are cleaner than the day they left the store and my fingers are soggy prunes. I'm about to start drying and putting away the dishes when Dean's hand comes down on mine.

"Leave them. The only reason I let you get this far is because you looked like you needed a minute." It irks me that this man can see right through my bravado. "I'll finish later. In the future, we do the dishes together or you leave them for me. You're not here to clean up after me. Now, quit stalling before you wash the finish right off."

He tugs me away from the sink, grabbing my laptop as we cut through the kitchen, heading for the living room where the fire is crackling.

"This is for the new project that you said was pushing you outside your comfort zone?"

God must be a man because, just as I've accepted my fate, Dean joins me on the couch, settling next to me, his long legs stretched out in front of him. My pulse jumps when his arm loops over the back of the couch, brushing my shoulders. He grabs a pair of dark-rimmed glasses from the coffee table and slips them on. I swear I feel my ovaries twitch as they release an egg begging to be fertilized. There's no way I can keep it together under these conditions.

CHAPTER 12

DEAN

Mia licks her pouty lips. Her eyes trained on the dancing flames instead of me as her head inclines away from me—giving her reluctance away. I know there's more to the story and I think it has everything to do with why she's here, crashing in my cabin this winter.

"It's not only this project, I'm burned out from years of hustling to make it this far. Everything I write feels stale, but no one else sees it." She snorts out a laugh. "Honestly, I wish my editor would tell me that my latest draft is garbage. It would make it easier because nothing I write feels genuine. It's like I'm letting everyone down and they're all just too nice to tell me." Her shoulders deflate at the admission. "I've been wanting to write something a little different, stretch myself for a while and this project just kind of fell in my lap, but it's picante and I'm mild. If I can't even write something fresh in my typical tropes, how am I supposed to write something spectacular in a new one?"

Platitudes seem like the last thing she needs. The way she sees it, everyone in her life is telling her what she wants to hear. Tough love is something I can give her. "Maybe you're just not ready for it. Read what you wrote earlier.

We can put my degree to use and I can tell you how bad it is." Opening the laptop I tap the spacebar bringing it to life before I set it in her lap and wait.

"I've never done this." Wide, blue eyes stare back at me, wild with nerves. "Not *like* this, I mean. One-on-one, with someone outside of my team."

"Would it be better if I read it out loud?" I cock my eyebrow reaching for the computer.

"No!" she practically screams, snatching it back, and I can't hold back the smile.

"Ready when you are, Dreamer." That earns me an eye-roll and fuck does sassy look good on her.

"Benji's hand finds the back of my neck. He's wearing a smirk that should come with a flood warning. The glint it lends to his dark eyes is enough to cause a deluge, soaking my panties until they're entirely useless. I tilt my chin up looking right into those magnetic orbs, not letting my mask slip. He can't know the hold he has on me or the way it affects me when his eyes flick to my lips. That's more power than I'm ready to give him. If I forget, even for a moment, that I'm a game to him, I lose all my power. And I refuse to be that girl again."

Her eyes find mine, and she clears her throat before continuing with a shaky voice.

"'Are you still playing hard to get? Or are you ready to admit to how badly you want me? What's it going to be, Tenley?' He steps in closer, tugging me towards him at the same time until we are chest to chest. I offer a silent prayer that the sweater I'm wearing is thick enough that he can't feel the way my nipples bead against the hard planes of his torso. 'All I've heard so far is a lot of talk. For someone that's so well-known for being ruthless in the board- room, I expected a little more action. I'm beginning to think you're all bark and no bite.' I'm goading him and I know it, but I need him to be the first to make the move. His mouth crashes into mine, hard. It's bruising and beautiful the way he works my mouth open, nipping at my bottom lip before he invades my mouth, taking it without hesitation."

Jesus. I'm not sure what I expected, but it wasn't this. Forget the cutesy covers. This is raw and has an edge to it that makes me shift in my seat. "Damn, I knew it was a great ass, but I didn't know it was capable of *that*."

She nibbles her lip, looking up at me through dark lashes. "That part was finished, but I was struggling with what comes next."

"By all means, continue." I sweep my hand out toward her.

"I can't stop the moan that slips into his mouth when his hard length nudges my stomach. The grip he has on my hip tightens, and my eyes drift open just in time to see a shadow glide through the dark office. I track the movement as Benji's stubble burns a trail down my neck. Vance. I'd know those broad shoulders anywhere. My boss's best friend spends just as much time here as I do. And I've spent more hours than I care to admit tracing the long lines of muscle through his tailored dress shirts."

A rough breath shudders out of Mia before she moves on. And fuck me if this is going where I think it is, changing into gray sweats after eating was the wrong move.

"My eyes stay glued to Vance, who's perched against the desk, watching with those denim blue eyes as his friend's hand slips under my skirt, cursing when he realizes there's nothing but an impossibly wet scrap of lace there.

'If I'd have known this is what you were hiding under those flowy skirts all this time, I would have bent you over my desk and fucked you months ago.'

I open my mouth to tell him we have an audience. But I'm silenced by Vance pushing off the desk and holding one long finger to his lips. Instead I ask, 'Who says I would have let you? I'm still not convinced you're worth the trouble.' His rough grip bites into my ass as he kneads the flesh roughly. 'You're not what I'm craving, but you know who might be?' I'm playing with fire, but I want the heat. No, I need it.

The way Vance's eyes rake over us, the bulge making itself known in his pants, tells me he's enjoying this. Benji's head lifts from where I'm sure he's left a mark on my neck to find his friend sliding behind me, letting one hand fall to my waist and the other grabbing my face and tilting it up towards his. 'You sure you know what you're asking for, Trouble?'"

"I've never been more impressed with my ass. That was some heavy lifting." It's meant to sound playful, but my voice is filled with gravel. If that scene had gone any further, I'd be grabbing a throw pillow to hide my boner—haven't had to do that since middle school.

"Don't give yourself too much credit. It's not like your ass grew fingers and typed it out." Her whole demeanor has shifted. Instead of tension marking her features, Mia looks at ease. Joyful, even.

"Let me get this straight. Me, squatting in front of you, made you think about grabbing a mitt full."

She closes her laptop and gives her shoulders a little shrug. "You wear that meat suit well."

Across the couch, her eyes crinkle in the corners with amusement as my whole body quakes with laughter. "At the risk of sounding like a douche, I've been called every version of hot, including some interesting ones I had to google, but no one has ever complimented me quite like that. You are one of a kind."

"Thank you, I think?" Crimson dots her neck as she busies her hand by tracing the pattern on the couch.

My fists squeeze into balls at my side to keep myself from reaching out to rub my thumbs over one of those rose-colored marks to see if my touch soothes it or makes it spread across the rest of her chest which is exposed by her unbuttoned Henley.

"Let me ease your doubts. That was a compliment. Few women keep my attention for long. But you would be hard to overlook with that witty tongue and miles of ambition. The way those stunning blue eyes take in the world around you like every detail is the most fascinating story just begging for you to unravel it and give it a voice. We'd all be better people if we took a page out of your book, Dreamer."

You know that line in the sand, where I keep things strictly friendly?

I just barreled right over that fucker, and I can't even bring myself to regret it. Not with how she flushes from her chest straight to the tips of her ears.

"And here I thought you were going to play critic for me." Folding her legs under her she sets her laptop on the coffee table, resting her arm across the back of the couch. All it would take is me extending my arm out to wrap my fingers around her wrist and pull her closer. But that would be reckless, and I've done enough of that already. "So much for putting that degree to use."

"Just because I said a few nice things about you doesn't make me any less of a bastard. You want to know what I think?"

Out of the corner of my eyes, I see her knuckles turn white as her fingers tighten around the back of the couch. "Don't sugarcoat it."

"I promise never to sugarcoat anything with you. People don't give you enough credit for your resilience. There's not much you can count on me for, but the truth is one thing I can give you every single time." Her eyes flick over my face before she finally nods. "The actual writing isn't your issue. Your lack of confidence in it is. It's what's kept you from trying something new. You're afraid you're going to fail. And now you've taken the leap, but how can you convince people to believe in you if you can't even do it yourself? You either need to tackle your fears or stay complacent."

She leans in, crossing the invisible barrier between us, and skims her fingertips up my arm. Such a light touch shouldn't feel so charged, but it sends a jolt of desire up my arm. Her palm stops on my forearm. "You get it. How do you understand me better than my team?"

"You and I are the same. You pour your heart into writing, the same way I bury myself in baseball. It's an escape, or it used to be, in your case. Now it's not giving you that same spark of life because you're afraid."

"How I wish that were the whole truth, but it's not just writing. My whole life feels like one big rut. All I do is work." The more she talks, the faster her words come, like they are desperate to be free. "The only friends I have are people who are paid to spend time with me, or live across the country. Don't even get me started on the dating pool. Either it's a shallow puddle of stagnant rainwater, or I just picked a pond full of fuck boys to drown in. How can I expect to write anything interesting when my life is a hamster wheel of dull?" When she finally stops, her fingers have tightened around my forearm like I'm the only thing keeping her from spiraling entirely off her axis.

"That's your fear talking. *You* are anything but dull. Get out of your own way and the words will come."

I look at where her fingers are gripping me, realizing I'm so screwed. Part of me is begging to be the reason she stays upright. To give her what she's aching for, make her feel something. When I look up and find her hopeful eyes waiting, I remember I can't give her what she needs. Not only would it be way too fucking complicated to untangle ourselves without any lasting awkwardness, but I would be taking advantage of the situation.

There's no way I can do that to her or Hendrix. He's not the type of brother who would try to warn me off his sister because of some false sense of preserving her innocence. If I hurt her, he wouldn't hesitate to come after me, which is inevitable given my outlook on relationships and the examples I've had. I let my hand drop into my lap, breaking our connection.

The loss of her touch rattles more than it should.

CHAPTER 13

MIA

"Alone again, just me and you," I mumble to my laptop, dropping into the cushy new chair that's become my dedicated writing space over the last few days. The day after we got here, I found Dean surrounded by pieces of wood in the garage. Buried in the back of the SUV were the materials for a small writing desk. He spent the day building it for me and even had the perfect spot picked out in the corner. Now I have a gorgeous view of the mountains and an adorable bird feeder painted in Bandits colors that I suspect he also made.

Oddly enough, other than when he moved the small desk into my room and assured me it wasn't his way of banishing me, I've barely seen him. No, that's not true. I've seen plenty of him. Every day I get an eyeful of him doing anything that ensures he's nowhere near me.

Somehow, even keeping his distance, the man still makes me want him. The views of the mountains are breathtaking, but it's nothing compared to the brawny baseball player donning a worn-out flannel and chopping wood in the late afternoon sun. Or his bare chest glistening yesterday in the gym. I got more than an eyeful that time. In my hurry to escape the flurries and cold, I burst through the door, running right into his solid chest, his heated skin burning my fingertips as my hands glided up his chest, gripping his shoulder so I didn't land on my ass. His rough hands spanned the bare skin of my waist, locking us together before releasing me like a hot potato and sulking off with a grumbled remark about enjoying my workout. Which I spent fantasizing about the feel of him beneath my palms.

Like some sort of *Beetlejuice*-esque magic, the man himself appears outside my window. Even from here, I can see the way the long muscles of his back flex under the thermal top he's wearing as he runs through the snow, heading for a clearing in the snowy tree line. He's already worked out today. Now he's just running from his problems. Although I'm pretty sure there's only one, me.

When I agreed to stay here, my biggest concern was that we were going to be tripping over each other. It seems it was for nothing because, other than societal required greetings, he's kept things very surface level when we are in the same room.

If he thinks he's going to crawl inside his own asshole to dodge me all winter, he's going to be disappointed. The part that pisses me off the most is that he pushed me to step outside my comfort zone and now he's acting like I did something wrong.

No, sir, we aren't playing these games.

Lord knows I have enough of my own issues right now. Like the fact that being in the mountains hasn't been the magical solution I'd hoped for where my writing is concerned. I'm still struggling with finding my authentic voice for both my projects.

That's where my focus needs to be.

He doesn't know it yet, but it ends tonight because it's messing with my ability to write and that's the reason I'm here.

After shutting myself away all afternoon, I needed to escape the four walls of the guest bedroom. Earlier, I heard Dean come back from his run, only to take the world's fastest shower and disappear again, this time in his truck. There's no telling when he'll be back, or where he ran off to this time, but I've been parked in this kitchen for the last hour and I'm not leaving until we clear the air.

We have two weeks before we get a break from each other when we head home for Christmas, not to mention all of January and some of February together after that. It's going to be a long cold winter if we can't figure out how to coexist in this little cabin.

Steam rises from the large pot, making the spicy scent of the chicken chili even stronger with each pass of the spoon. Simmering right here on the stove is my plan to get him to talk to me. As prickly as Dean pretends to be, he's never straight-up rude. My theory is that, despite his silver spoon upbringing, he's a pretty humble guy, and from the stories he's shared with me, his mom is to thank for that.

Even when he's avoiding me, the man is blatantly thoughtful. I returned to the cabin after my workout yesterday to find coffee with a note that said, "Morning, Dreamer. Hope your words come easy today." And today, a pathway to the gym was freshly shoveled. I've watched him hop through the snowdrifts doing a ridiculous version of high knees enough times to know it's not something he does for himself.

Twisting the knob, I lower the heat on the stove while I wait. There's no way he'll be able to walk through the kitchen and ignore me. His hidden, affable side will force him to stop and enjoy a bowl, whether or not he wants to. That's when I plan to spring into action and force him to talk to me.

But for now, I pick up my book to do some research. Plopping onto the plush green couch, which makes the rustic cabin look straight off a Pinterest board, I crack open my paperback. I'm so engrossed in a spicy scene that has my whole body flushing with heat, I don't even register the sound of the front door opening until it slams shut, making me leap off the couch.

In a recovery worthy of an Olympic medal, I manage a smile that feels genuine as I square up to face the king of the disappearing act.

"Wow, what smells amazing?" Dean asks, scratching his jaw where he let his stubble grow since we've been here. He still trims it, but it's not the clean shaven look I'm used to seeing him sport on TV during the season. He looks back and forth between the stove and me, his mouth slackening. "You didn't need to cook."

That's my signal.

With sure strides, I make my way to the stove lifting the top off the pot to stir the chili. "Didn't I? We've hardly seen each other in the last few days. It's almost like you're finding excuses to be anywhere but here." There's no point in beating around the bush. My confidence slips when I turn back with two full bowls and find the normally cocksure man looking anywhere but at me. Pushing my shoulders back I carry the bowls to the island. "And I want to know why."

His eyes lift from where he's brushing a piece of imaginary lint off his shirt. "Ouch, going right for the kill." He sighs, heading for the fridge and pulling out two beers. With an impressive flick of his wrist, that shouldn't be so attractive, he's got both caps off. "I suppose I deserve it."

The stool next to me scrapes across the floor as Dean pulls it out and offers me one of the cold beers.

"Care to share where you've been?"

Dean brings the bottle to his lips before tilting his head side to side. "Honestly, a little bit of everywhere." The chuckle that echoes between us is self-deprecating. "Yesterday, I did some backcountry snowboarding. Today, I wasted time at the hardware store before I came back and tinkered around with the snowmobile and then went for a completely unnecessary run. Oh, and I've chopped more wood than we'll be able to burn all winter." His mossy eyes soften when they look at me.

"I don't want to chase you out of your own space. If this isn't working for you, I'll figure something else out. This winter was supposed to be about me finding the peace I needed to write. Thank you for opening up your home to me, but worrying about whether you're annoyed that I'm in your space isn't exactly fostering creativity."

His hand hovers midway to his mouth. With a shake of head, he lets the spoon drop into the bowl with a clatter. He turns on his stool to face me before saying, "God, I've really fucked this up. You haven't done anything. As always, I'm the problem."

There's a lot to unpack there, but I'm going to start with the obvious. "Then why have you been avoiding me?"

"You aren't going to drop this, are you?" His lips press in a hard line.

"Doesn't really seem like it, considering I made dinner just to trap you into talking to me." My arm sweeps out to where the chili sits in the pot. "I don't want to leave, but I don't want to spend the winter feeling like an unwanted guest, either." My palms break out in a sweat at the thought of him sending me packing because, when he's not avoiding me, things are really good.

"I'm afraid I'm only going to make things worse for you. You're here trying to figure out your life and I don't want to muddy that for you." He pushes a hand through his hair in frustration, looking anywhere but at me now.

"I'm not sure that's possible." This weird limbo we're in is worse than being back in Charlotte.

"Fuck." His whispered curse is pained. When his gaze settles back on me, I see the regret in his eyes. "You're not unwanted, and that's the problem. I'm avoiding you because no matter how hard I've tried, I can't stop myself from wanting you—even knowing that it would end in disaster for both of us. I'm not the kind of guy you need. At best, I would be a temporary distraction from the reason you're here."

My pulse flutters in my neck as I try to wrap my head around the fact that this gorgeous man thinks I'm so tempting that I've driven him out of his own home. I choke out a laugh.

"Dreamer, you're really smashing my ego here." Dean takes a long drink from his beer. His brow wrinkles while he waits for me to calm down.

"Sorry," I say, reigning myself in. "I'm not laughing at you. It's just that the guys I've dated lately have been horrendous. One tried to convince me to partake in a sweat lodge to help stimulate my creativity. Another kept telling 'your mom' jokes, after I'd shared that my mom abandoned me. And don't even get me started on the movie theater toenail clipper." Dean stares back at me, all stunning green eyes and a five o'clock shadow that only makes him look more rugged. "I just find it a little hard to believe that the same girl is sitting here with you in this perfect mountain cabin while you tell me I've got you tied up in knots."

Dean leans over flipping my hand up on the island and taking it in his—making my whole arm break out in goosebumps when he traces circles in my palm.

"First off, Indie must have set up the worst dating profile in history. Second, don't doubt for one second that you aren't a catch. Fuck Mia, you're stunning and brilliant. I've thought so from the first time I met you. Do you know how hard it was to pretend not to notice you when we were on vacation? Now you're in my space and I can't escape you even when I'm not here." He shoves his hand through his thick strands again. They're wild now from the way he keeps tugging on them.

I know the *but* is coming before he even says it.

He's waved his red flag around like a race marshall signaling danger ahead and I'm the reckless driver approaching too fast. I save him the trouble because I'm not sure I can take the brush off. If he tells me it's too complicated and I deserve better, I might just scream. I've looked for better and what I've found is not that.

Threading my fingers through his, I connect our hands because, even knowing I'm about to put up a boundary that hopefully spares both of us from a lot of awkwardness down the road, I'm not ready to let go. "But you and I don't work. You don't date and our lives are far too entangled to do the casual thing. Not to mention at the end of this winter, we will both be busy with our careers in different parts of the country."

"There is that." His large hand squeezes mine. "But don't think it's not because I don't want to. Everything about you makes me weak. That brain, those eyes, everything. So much so that I can't stand the idea of hurting you."

"We can still be friends. Stop running from me, please?"

"No more running," he agrees.

It's what I asked of him, but I hate how easily he agreed.

Friends, a singular word that brings me crashing back down to earth.

Dean can't be the man I need either. The one who chooses *me*.

CHAPTER 14

DEAN

The hollow feeling I get deep inside my chest is a reminder that I'm the one that keeps pushing Mia away. So why do I feel like I want to take it all back and listen to the voice that's screaming at me? Telling me that for her I could be different? Maybe we could be friends and still cross the line without anyone getting hurt.

"Friends," I finally say, but the words taste sour coming out of my mouth. I cover it by lifting her hand to my mouth and brushing my lips across her knuckles before I let go of her hand. New friends don't hold hands, no matter how right it feels.

I can't tear my eyes away from Mia's mouth as she wraps her perfect lips around her spoon. When that first bite hits her tongue, she lets out the sweetest moan. Again, I pretend not to notice because we don't turn our platonic friend's innocent moans into something far dirtier.

Lifting my spoon to my mouth, my eyes roll back in my head the minute the spices hit my tongue. The groan I let out sounds feral compared to the cute little murmur that Mia made. "What is it about chili when it's cold out?

It hits you right here." My hand balls into a fist and I tap it against my sternum twice. "Warming every inch of you. Our nanny always had soup on the stove for us when we came home from school during the first big snowstorm of the winter."

"I can't imagine you as a child. Were you always so serious?" Mia asks, looking me over as if she's trying to picture it now.

I snort out a laugh, but she just continues, "No matter how hard I try, you're just this miniature man-child walking around with that pensive look on your face."

"You make me sound like Mr. Darcy, but believe it or not, I wasn't an asshole until my teen years."

"Those hormones got the best of you?"

Ordinarily someone digging would make me shut down, but with her it's different. "Something like that. My male role models are deeply flawed. Despite my mom and nanny doing their best, some of that was bound to wear off." I play it off like it's not a big deal. In reality, my father's and grandfather's betrayals have shaped me into the man I am today, and not in a good way.

"Sometimes I wonder if the reason I suck at dating is because of my mother. I've never admitted that out loud before, and it makes me feel shitty to even think it, because my Nana tried so hard to make sure we never felt abandoned. She's loved us like her own since before she took us in. But something like that just sticks with you." Her down-turned eyes watch as the spoon scrapes the bowl, moving in a circle, lost in her thoughts. "Sorry, I just felt like I should offer something of mine, so you didn't feel so exposed. No more sad talk. Quick new topic."

She doesn't need to ask me twice. "What are your plans for the rest of this week, *friend*?" I force the last word to sound casual and unaffected when they feel anything but.

"Not much, honestly. I came up here with intentions to explore when I'm not writing, but I haven't even gone into town."

"Wouldn't it be nice if you had someone to teach you how to snowboard? You're supposed to be getting out of your comfort zone. Conquering your fears. Why not learn a new sport?"

The corner of her mouth tilts up in a smile as she considers the idea. "Yeah?" Her reaction is everything I hoped it would be, pink lips tipping up in a wide smile. I'm already so addicted to seeing her look at me like I'm the reason for everything good in the world. I think I'd do just about anything to make sure she never stops.

"Of course, it's not a problem."

"See, we can be good at this friend thing. I'll just pretend you're hideous when you've got your hands on me, teaching me how to shred the pow."

I cringe, but internally I'm focused on the knowledge that she's affected by me, too.

"That bad?" Mia asks, her nose wrinkling. "I thought it might be taking it too far."

"Please never say that again. For a second, I thought you were a fourteen-year-old boy visiting us from 2002." The laugh that fills the space between us is enough of a reward that I almost think I can handle this.

We finish our chili, conversation flowing comfortably between us. And when she goes to clean up, I take the bowls from her. "I've got this. Go read."

"You wash, I'll dry, and then we can relax together," she says, bumping her hip into mine as I reluctantly hand her the towel.

Working side-by-side we settle into a rhythm. Every time I pass her a dish, Mia's eyes find mine. She's as transparent as they come. She chews on the corner of her lip, her eyes darting back to me. "Just say it before you chew a hole through those pretty lips."

"It's none of my business."

"Curiosity is ingrained in you, Dreamer. It makes you the best at what you do. So tell me what's on your mind." I shake the sudsy water from my hands, brace myself against the counter, and wait.

"You're always saying what a terrible person you are. Why do you do that? I'll be the first to admit that you can be a touch unapproachable, but you're not an asshole. I wouldn't be here if you were."

"Do you always see the best in people?" A ladle passes between us, but neither of us is paying much attention to the work anymore.

"I try to. Are you avoiding my question?" One hand is propped on her cocked hip as she looks up at me with a challenge in her eyes.

"Other than my teammates and my family, I don't let many people in. I'm not good at sharing. I learned a long time ago the one guarantee in life is that people will let you down. And that includes me. So don't put me up on a pedestal, just because I did one nice thing for you."

"That's where you're mistaken. This grumpy front you put on . . ." She waves the dish towel in front of me dramatically. "I see right through it. Dean Harrison is a secret softy and I have receipts."

I level her with a glare that's intended to set her straight, but it doesn't have any venom behind it.

Mia just chuckles, holding up her hand, fingers in the air.

"You light up when you talk about your mom, sister, and nieces." She folds her thumb into her palm, ticking it off her list. "You can't be a momma's boy and an asshole. That's just science. I don't make the rules."

My mouth opens so I can call her out on her bullshit, but she's undeterred.

"Then there's the coffee with a sweet note." Her pointer finger joins the thumb.

"And don't forget about the desk. I feel like that deserves two fingers." She's down to just her pinky now and looking more smug by the second.

"Oh, and this morning, I made it to the gym with warm, dry feet. Are you going to try to convince me that the perfectly edged path through the fresh snow was some sort of natural phenomenon?"

"Seems like it would be pointless." I pass her the last of the dishes to dry and let the water drain from the sink.

"You're like a marshmallow someone left over the fire too long, charring you to a crusty exterior. But if you're brave enough to take a bite, there's a perfect gooey center. Who burned you, Dean?"

"Are we just going to skate past the fact that you just called me crusty?" Mia leans against the counter, not even justifying my nonsense with a response. Avoiding her eyes I tell her, "My dad and my grandpa. They were my idols growing up, but neither of them turned out to be the men I thought they were. They were selfish and forced me to carry a load too heavy for my young shoulders. It changed who I am as a person." I leave it at that.

It's more than most people know, but Mia just coaxes it out of me. Every single time. That should probably annoy me with how closely I've guarded that part of my life, but I feel lighter having told her. Not only that, but I may as well be a fucking peacock with the way I feel like strutting around after she called me perfect. I'm far from it, but warmth spreads across my chest at the way she sees me.

When the dishes are done and Mia retreats to her room to get some more writing done for the night, I take my phone off the charger to find a string of texts from the guys.

BLANCHE'S BATTERS

DOM:

Hello … Earth to Dean.

CRUZ:

Are you alive up there, Dean? Or has little James gotten sick of your attitude and buried you in the back forty already?

HENDRIX:

You're overestimating my sister's willingness to do the dirty work. She would have flown home and clocked me over the head for setting this whole thing in motion.

XAVIER:

Can I have your penthouse if she off'd your grumpy ass? You don't even like it.

DEAN:

No one is getting off'd. How unpleasant do you think I really am?

DOM:

I'm not sure you want us to answer that.

DEAN:

I'm a fucking joy and a pleasure to be around.

HENDRIX:

Name one time where that was true.

CRUZ:

And Friendsgiving doesn't count because it wasn't your idea.

DEAN:

. . .

XAVIER:

He can't even think of one. Now I feel sorry for our cranky old man.

DOM:

Let the record show that wasn't me.

DEAN:

I'm not old, you asshat. I'm teaching her how to snowboard this week. That's pleasant.

HENDRIX:

Good luck with that one.

CHAPTER 15

MIA

"You promise you won't let go?" My voice shakes as I look down the hill. It's so big and there are people everywhere. Each one looks like a death-defying obstacle in front of me. He didn't warn me about this part earlier in the week when I agreed to this. Yet, here they are, just waiting to be mowed over. Someone should tell them I have no clue what I'm doing.

"Assuming you don't break my fingers, I'll be here helping the whole way down. It's the bunny slope, Mia, I promise you can do it." He squeezes my hands and I swear I see his lips twitch. But I could be wrong because I'm too terrified to focus on anything other than all the child-shaped speed bumps littering the run.

"Remind me again how to turn."

He drops my hands and panic lances through me at the loss of stability he was providing.

"What are you doing?" I screech, practically hyperventilating. "You promised."

"Calm down, Dreamer. I'm taking my board off so we can go over turns again." My head swivels as he walks behind me. I almost lose my balance and my arms windmill as I fight gravity.

Dean's hands land on my hips. Even through the layers, I can feel the heat of him wrapping around me. "Do you trust me?" He leans in close over my shoulder. Having him this close helps me push away my fear.

"I do. Don't make me regret it." The tremble in my legs now is just adrenaline. I know in my gut he won't let anything happen to me.

With one hand on my waist—which I'm pretty sure is more to keep me mentally stable than physically—the other trails from my bicep down to my wrist and lifts it so my arm is level with my shoulder. He does the same on the other side, so I form a human "T." If he's trying to distract me from my nerves by being hands on, it's working.

One big palm comes to rest between my shoulder blades and moves in closer. "You're going to keep this frame strong and point where you want to go with your front hand. Imagine that there's a broomstick running from one arm to another, so they're always moving together." His hand moves across my shoulders, back and down my arm to demonstrate.

"Seems simple enough. And if I want to stop, I just point uphill with my front hand?"

"Make sure your eyes and torso follow that hand and it will help swing your board so it's perpendicular to the hill. And I'll be right behind you, ready if you need me," he reassures me.

"Okay, I can do this!" I shake out my arms, pumping myself up. He squats down in front of me to strap his board back on. In a display that puts most people's coordination to shame, he hops around me using the nose and tail of his board like they are springs. "That wasn't intimidating at all."

His glove-covered hands sneak under my jacket settling on my waist. Not to sound like an ungrateful jerk, because I borrowed them from his sister, but fuck these snow pants. My body craves the feel of his skin against mine. *Traitor.* I haven't been able to stop thinking about it since we held hands in the kitchen during our heart-to-heart. I keep trying to blame the writing I'm doing for my uncontrollable horniness. But that's a bold face lie to distract from how badly I wish there could be more than friendship with Dean.

"Tell me what you're afraid of, Mia," he demands in my ear.

"I'm afraid of falling." I swallow roughly around the loaded truth.

"We do this together. I've got you." When he wiggles us forward, it's not the threat of knocking out my teeth that has my heart pounding hard against my ribs. It's a feeling I can't ignore. A constant hum inside me, begging me not to listen to his warnings about who he is and what he's *not* capable of giving me. Even though I know anything more than friendship would be disastrous, Dean's proving to be a man worthy of that complication I want in my life.

When things were rocky between us, I hated every second of the tension. Being around him now is the easiest thing I've ever done. If friendship is all we can have, then I'm going to enjoy the hell out of it. I've peeled back that crispy shell he wears and found the softest, sweetest center. Dean's loyal beyond compare and kinder than I would have ever expected. He's funny too, which I was wholly unprepared for.

My hands drop to grip onto his wrist when we pick up speed. *Shit, we're moving.*

"Arms up, Dreamer." His tone is commanding and with his fingers curved around my waist, keeping me safe, I obey. "Such a good girl."

Now is not the time for wet panties, so I focus on the hill in front of me, using my body to make big S-turns like he coached me on this morning during the drive over, instead of the way he showers me with praise.

The board skids to a stop when we get to the bottom. My calves burn and my legs shake from the effort. But more than anything, I'm relieved. I let my hands fall to my knees, bracing myself and laughing like a lunatic.

I fucking did it!

Dean swings himself around me in an effortless arc. Then wraps me in a hug, lifting me, board and all. "That's what I'm talking about! How does it feel?" He seems almost more excited than I am. *Almost.*

"Like I'm on top of the world. It's not so scary once you trust yourself and just go." I wonder if it's that simple with my book, like Dean said. If I stopped worrying so much about all the ways I could fail, would the words come?

"Let's go again. This time you're going to do all the work." He lowers me to the ground giving me time to find my balance before he releases me.

Dean pops his foot loose and guides me to the magic carpet. We take our spot in line surrounded by kids in ski school.

"Have you been snowboarding since you were little?" I ask over my shoulder as the black belt pulls us up the gentle slope.

"My grandpa has a place in Whistler. We used to go there a few times every winter. He taught us all to ski as soon as we mastered walking, but I taught myself to snowboard when I was sixteen."

"Why'd you make the switch?" I ask as we crest the top of the hill. When the momentum pushes me off the conveyor, I lift my arms just like Dean taught me and steer myself to the side.

"To piss off the old man," he says gruffly, moving to my front side and helping me out of the way. "Ready?"

Well, I guess that conversation is over. Turns out doing all the work makes getting down the hill upright much more difficult. I spend more time on my butt more than standing, but every single time his hand is there waiting to help me up. True to his word, he's diligent in brushing me off and making sure I'm completely free of powder before he coaches me on where I went wrong.

Add patient and encouraging to the endless list of qualities Dean pretends he doesn't have.

"You know what we need?" he asks when I lean against him at the bottom of the bunny hill. My muscles feel like Jello, and I haven't even left the learning area yet.

"A nap?" I ask, only half-kidding. Letting a professional athlete teach me a sport might not have been the best move. I sit on my ass for a living. Yoga and running didn't prepare me for this.

"Hot chocolate." He stands me up from where I'm propped against him and comes around, one foot still attached to his board. Bending down, he unstraps my feet for me. Thank God, because I don't think I could do it myself.

"With extra 'mallos?" I tease. His hands stop working my feet free and he looks up with faux annoyance on his handsome face. With his goggles propped on top of his helmet, his green eyes stand out against the snowy background.

"Not too tired to give me a hard time," he tosses back teasingly, the prickly tone from our earlier conversation about his grandfather melting away.

My legs wobble when I'm free and I have to grab Dean's shoulder before I go down. With him still on his knee, the position he's in doesn't escape me. Suddenly feeling eager for that drink to soothe my dry throat, I ask, "Aren't you glad I forced you to be my friend?"

"I was never *not* your friend, Mia." He looks up at me with so much genuine adoration that I almost have to look away. The struggle to keep him squarely in the friend zone is already hard enough, but with every new piece of him he shows me, it gets harder. Standing with our boards under his arm, he leads me to the lodge for a break and a much needed sugar rush.

One large mug of perfect hot cocoa later, my spoon scrapes against the bottom of the ceramic mug as I fish out the last of my extra marshmallows. Dean watches in amusement, his drink long gone. Our gear is scattered around the wooden table and I'm toasty warm and dry from the fire crackling behind us.

"That hit of sugar was exactly what I needed. I'm a whole new woman." We gather up everything we stripped off and weave through the tables back toward the bottom of the hill.

"Let's get you on the gondola and down a green run before that sugar crash hits." Reaching out, Dean takes my helmet from my hands. With his gloves off, warm fingers brush my stray hair off my face, easing my helmet over my head before using meticulous care to buckle it. He wears the serious face I was so accustomed to seeing when we first met as his fingers tighten the straps and tests it to make sure it's secure.

"All good?" I ask, feeling useless and loving it. No one besides my family has ever taken this much care with me.

"Gotta protect that brain. It's my favorite thing about you," he says, like it's the most normal thing.

♥

Wispy white clouds stand out against the bluebird sky. The cold snow under me feels heavenly through the layers of gear I'm wearing. My chest rises and falls rapidly as I fight to catch my breath. I'm huffing and puffing so loudly that I barely register the sound of the scraping of a snowboard approaching. The marshmallow sugar high wore off about four runs ago. Turning my head toward the sound I see Dean slide his board out to stop, dragging his fingers on the ground as he circles and comes to rest on his stomach next to me. It's a fancy move, but I'm too tired to worry that he might screw it up and plow into me.

"Just leave me here. I'm one with the mountain now." My heartbeat pounds behind my eardrums. I'm not sure how he still has so much energy left when every ounce has been drained from me. He's hauled me all over this mountain, and strapped my bindings as well as his own every single time, trying to make it easier on me. My muscles are screaming, but it'll be worth not being able to move tomorrow to see the boyish grin on his face.

"Make it back to the lodge without falling and supper is on me," he says, shaking my shoulder playfully.

"What kind of *supper* are we talking about?" My stomach growls right on cue causing Dean to shake with laughter.

"Lady's choice. As long as I can order a cold beer, you pick."

"So, if I told you I wanted the greasiest burger in Telluride, you wouldn't judge me?"

"It might make me like you even more." The lack of oxygen at this elevation must be making me see things because, if I'm not mistaken, there's heat in his eye. But that can't be. We promised to keep things strictly platonic.

"What if you just roll me down the hill?" The thought of getting back up is enough to make my exhausted body protest.

"Come on, let's get you on your feet. I know just the place for dinner. They grill the burgers with a pad of butter on top and season their fries with the perfect amount of salt. If you're lucky, they might even have some of their famous pie left."

"Help me up. I could fuck with some pie."

"That's my girl," he says, lifting to his knees and holding out his hands for me to take.

CHAPTER 16

DEAN

"Oh god, it's so good," Mia moans, putting my dick on high alert. As much as I try to keep him in check, we want what we want, and the boss between my legs is no exception. He wants the brunette who's blissed out on greasy food and beer, and I can't blame him. Not after I spent my day with my hands on her and watching her blossom when she pushed herself. "Dean, I can't take anymore."

It's a small miracle I'm alive. If I'd had food in my mouth I would have choked and died, but man, what a way to go. "You're killing me, Dreamer."

She hides behind her hand, looking remorseful, and I'm sure if I peeled off the turtleneck she's wearing, her chest would be covered in those endearing crimson spots she gets when she's embarrassed. My little fucking dalmatian.

We make it through our meals without any more erotic noises. Once the bill is paid, I lead her out to the truck to find it covered in a layer of fresh snow. Next to me, Mia throws both hands in the air, spinning as she tips her head back. Her smile is brighter than the moon shining against the black sky and the joyful sound that spills out of her warms me from the inside out.

"God, it's so magical. I've never seen snowflakes this big, the way they float through the air, clinging to everything and making it glow." Her nose crinkles as one of those flakes land on the rosy tip.

I'm looking alright, but all I see is her. She's wonder and euphoria. So full of bravery and grit, and a little bit coy. It only makes me want to show her everything she's capable of. The women I usually surround myself with are brazen, but their shine wears off. Not her. She just makes me want more. More of her and more for me. That's something I've never let myself consider before.

"I'm not sure I've ever seen something this perfect before." The ridiculous boots she changed into slip in the fresh powder. Before she can tumble to the ground, I've got my arms around her rib cage, hauling her against me so that she doesn't take us both down.

The pom-pom on the top of her white hat tickles my nose as she shakes against me. Her spirit is contagious. Even if I could stop it, I don't want to. I let the moment consume me, laughing along with her. The powdery flakes stick to the strands of hair that surround her face and she tilts her head up, fighting to catch her breath. The apples of her cheeks are rosy from the cold air or the beer. Either way, she looks so fucking pretty and she's still wrapped tightly in my arms. Neither of us move to separate.

With her gaze on mine, her tongue darts out, swiping a melted snowflake off her lower lip. Those intoxicating gray-blue eyes drop to my lips before they widen. I'm not sure who's to blame, but there's barely room for the snow to fall between us. Her lashes flutter closed and I can't help myself, I've got to taste her. Hollers erupt behind us and the bar door bangs open. As if the universe is trying to keep us from fucking this all up, a boisterous group of tourists spills into the parking lot. Mia's the first to break apart, letting her grip loosen on my jacket, palms flattening and pushing off my chest.

"I'm just going—" Her voice trails off and she skids around my truck in her rush to create space between us. My ego needs a minute to collect the tattered scraps from where it lies at my feet. So I take my time clearing the snow while the remote start warms Mia inside.

The heat hits my chilled skin a few minutes later when I join her. She's already got her favorite playlist pumping through my speakers. Looking cozy, she's ditched her hat and gloves as she scrolls her phone, pink lips moving with the music. She lifts her head and gives me a quick once over before her lips roll together.

"What's so funny?" I ask, a little grumpy—still bruised from her retreat just now.

"Sit still." She leans over the console, her warm hand lifting to cradle the side of my face.

"*Mia.*" The warning is half-hearted.

"Relax." The sassy eye roll she grants me is contrary to her fingers easing up the side of my face. Sneaking under the edge of my hat as her thumb strokes over my eyebrow. "That's better." She shows me where the snow is melting on the tip of her thumb. "Can't have my driver blinded by melting snow."

"Buckle up. It's going to be a slow drive back." I watch as she shifts back in her seat, pulling her seatbelt across her lap. Once it clicks in place, I pull out of the parking spot.

"Thanks for teaching me today. It was the most fun I've had in a while. Even if I won't be able to get out of bed tomorrow."

"With a student like you, it was easy. I'm proud of you for overcoming the nerves you had this morning," I tell her, glancing at her just long enough to see the triumph on her face before I focus back on the road as we weave through the trees, leaving town behind.

"It felt good to challenge myself that way. I realized I'm my own biggest obstacle a lot of times." Her voice softens. "You gave me that, you know. If you hadn't made me feel safe enough to try, I'm not sure I would've kept going."

If I had a mirror, I'm pretty sure I would see my chest actually puff up at her gratitude. There's a lot I can't give Mia, but if she could see herself through my eyes, she'd never doubt herself again. The girl next to me is unstoppable. "That's all you. But if you need me to catch you so that you can get back up and show everyone all the things that you're capable of, I'll pick you up every single time."

"How do you have so much faith in me?" She tilts her head to the side as she looks at me from the passenger seat, those stunning eyes unsure in the moonlight.

"When life gives you lemons, you don't just make lemonade, you have the spunk to say 'I'm going to make the best damn lemonade you've ever had' just to show everyone you can do it. That kind of resolution is rare. I'd never bet against you, Dreamer."

"I'm not sure my stubbornness should be praised." She laughs, twirling a strand of hair. "Can I tell you something else? I'm almost afraid to even say it aloud and jinx it."

"Now I'd be mad if you didn't tell me." The snow slows as we turn down the narrow driveway to the cabin. The tree branches are heavy with fresh fallen snow. It looks like something out of a Christmas movie.

"For the first time in months, the urge to write feels exhilarating. My whole body is vibrating with the need to put pen to paper. Today brought my joy back. Thank you."

"I'm really fucking happy for you." The smile I give her is genuine, but I can't stop the bitter voice in my head reminding me she's going to lock herself in her bedroom and I'll be forced to spend my night without her. A few days ago, that would have made me breathe a sigh of relief, but tonight it fills me with an unexpected loneliness.

CHAPTER 17

MIA

My error is glaringly clear when I try to roll over in bed the next morning only for every muscle in my body to cry out in searing pain. Each movement takes more effort than it should.

Sitting hunched over my computer while I typed into the early hours of the morning might have been just what my soul needed, but it most definitely did not help my body. It's a slow process pulling on a pair of spandex shorts and a sports bra, but the only thing I can think of right now that might help is some yoga.

Leaning on the desk for support I slip my legs into a pair of oversized sweatpants before straightening and gingerly pulling a ratty crewneck on for the walk to the garage. Normally, yoga is a way to clear my head and focus on myself before I start my day. I doubt it's going to be the centered practice that I'm used to, but I'd do just about anything to get relief from the strain snowboarding put on my body yesterday.

Each step reminds me of how beat up I am, but I don't regret any of it. Not the time on the hill with Dean, or the eight-thousand words I wrote well into the early morning. I feel more like myself than I have in recent memory, and it's worth every tender muscle and creaking joint.

The wind howls between the two buildings as I follow the freshly shoveled path to the garage. The snow on the sides is higher than it was yesterday. And, although it's not snowing this morning, the sky is an eerie gray that tells me more is coming.

When the door closes behind me, I lean against it, locking the wind out and closing my eyes. The heat from the wood boiler surrounds me, and I can already feel it loosening the tightness I woke up with. My palms flatten against the door and I push off to strip off my sweats. It's not until I'm reaching for my mat to start stretching, that I find a shirtless Dean with his eyes locked on me from where he's seated on a weight bench. It's unfair that he looks so fresh, sipping from his water, when I feel like I got hit by a truck.

"Morning, Dreamer. Did you get any sleep, or were you up writing all night?" He drops the bottle and picks up a set of dumbbells that look to weigh as much as me. The sheen of sweat coating his body glints under the light.

I center myself on my mat, legs crossed, my upper body twisting. I grimace letting the pose work for a minute before I deepen the twist. "A little. I could have stayed up writing all night, but you wore me out and I crashed hard just after two in the morning."

Twisting in the other direction, I ask, "How'd you spend the rest of your night?"

"Actually, I did a little work, too."

"What kind of work?" I ask, still not firing on all cylinders from my late night and overall exhaustion.

"The non-profit board I sit on needed some attention. We're hiring a new Communications Director and I had to review some resumes." The look on my face must give away my surprise, because Dean's lips tilt up in a wicked smile. "Not just a pretty face."

"That's never been the question. The only time you talk about yourself is to put yourself down. That almost sounds positive. I didn't realize you were that involved in charity work. What organization?"

Hendrix and a lot of the guys have ties to charities outside of what the Bandits require—things close to their hearts. I can't help but be curious about which is the most meaningful to Dean.

"It's a foundation called Double Play. It gives kids the opportunity to be successful as students and athletes. With a focus on literacy as the foundation of the program. The coaching and equipment get them in the door, but they have to spend time with tutors and keep their grades up. The goal is to make sure each kid has the chance they deserve."

"How'd you get involved? Sitting on a board is a serious commitment."

"My nanny. Her son played baseball too and my mom made sure he always had the same equipment and opportunities as me. When I was young, I didn't understand why it was such a big deal. Then I came home from school one day and found our moms embracing, both of them crying. Kim was thanking my mom for the role she played—the burden she took off her shoulders. Until then, it hadn't really occurred to me that he might not have had those opportunities otherwise. Or if he had what kind of sacrifices his family would've had to make."

How this man thinks he's a jerk astounds me, but I'm getting fed up with hearing him talk about himself like he's unworthy. Maybe he just needs someone to show how special he really is. "Did you ever have a swear jar growing up?"

With a light shake of his head, like I've caught him off guard with my random question. "No, we didn't, but now I wish we would have," he says with a self-deprecating laugh. "Sorry, I'm just picturing my grandfather being told to put a quarter in the swear jar. The vein in his forehead would have exploded on the spot."

"Glad to see you still understand the concept, even with that silver spoon dangling out of your mouth. I've got a proposal for you." Moving from my knees to the balls of my feet I push my heels into the ground and can't stop the groan as my muscles slowly lengthen, resisting the urge to uncoil and let the yoga work.

Dean lets the weight drop to the padded floor and moves around the space. Sweat dots my brow as I hold my pose.

"What kind of proposal?" he asks, his feet stopping in front of my mat.

"Like a swear jar, but you're not allowed to call yourself an asshole or anything else demeaning." I drop to my knees, stretching my arms out in front of me, the tips of my fingers reaching for the end of my mat. When I turn my head to the side, Dean is lowering himself to the floor next to me, his long legs running the length of my mat.

"And if I do, are you going to make me put money in the jar?" he challenges as I push back up off the mat realizing that the sound that rumbles out of him is probably because my ass is basically in his face.

"No, I think you need a more creative solution to curb your negativity." I rock my body, shifting my weight from foot to foot. Because why the hell not? Let him look. Heat from his stare seeps into me, warming my muscles all the way to my toes pressing into the mat.

"I bet you do." His voice is rough, like he's hanging onto his composure by a thread.

My body gives out and I drop to the mat, unable to hold myself up any longer. A strong hand wraps around my ankle and works its way upwards. His calloused thumb kneads my calf in a circular motion.

"What are you doing to me?" I don't have it in me to be ashamed of the noise that leaves my mouth. His hand climbs higher working my entire calf until I'm a puddle beneath his fingers. Nothing more than goo on the mat because of his magic hands.

"If it's too much, let me know," he says and then his hands leave my body and I want to cry over the loss of his touch. "I've got a balm I use when I push myself too hard. Hopefully, it's not too cold."

"Not too much. If you stop, I can't be held responsible for my actions." The sounds of his hands rubbing together to warm up the balm has my stomach somersaulting. So damn considerate. The minty smell surrounds us as I melt into the floor. "You've been capable of this sorcery all along and I'm just finding out?"

"We have some of the best trainers on staff and I've picked up a thing or two." He chuckles darkly and maybe it's the state he's got me in, all pliant and serene, but I swear the sound skates over my skin caressing *all* the spots he isn't touching. "What else hurts, Dreamer?"

"Everything." It comes out breathy, causing his hand to pause before he resumes his work on my legs.

"Let me rephrase that. What hurts that I can *safely* touch as your friend?" I can hear the smile in his voice. He thinks he's so clever, but there's nothing *safe* about his hands on me, even as a friend. All it does is stoke the fire inside of me that's begging me to cross that line—to jump headfirst into the inferno with him and burn together.

"Too late for that," I mumble under my breath. When I roll to my side, his brow is creased, and he opens his mouth. With a shake of my head, I lift from my prone position and join him sitting on the floor. "Nothing about you feels safe, and I think I like it that way." My lips graze his cheek in a feather-light kiss before I walk across the gym to where I discarded my clothes, slipping them back on as Dean stays rooted in place.

After our encounter in the gym this morning, I need a little space and perspective. So I took a page out of his book and ran. Only I don't actually go anywhere because my body is falling apart. Instead, I hole up in the bedroom to write until the bright light from my screen makes everything go a little hazy at the edges.

Setting my work aside, I pause my playlist and call Indie. She's the most likely to give me the advice I want to hear without coddling me. It's a bonus that she knows Dean without being overly involved—given she lives in Chicago and her alliance is with me.

"Hello, who's calling?" Indie says in a sugary sweet voice when she picks up.

"Hardy, har, har. Laugh it up," I tell her, plopping down on the bed and stretching my still sore body across it diagonally.

"Is this my long-lost friend Mia? It's been eighty-four years." She does her best impression of an elderly woman and I have to admit it's not bad.

"Shut it, Rose. It hasn't been that long." The laughter that shakes my body doesn't help with my achy muscles, but it soothes my soul in a way only a friend can.

"You've been locked away in a secluded cabin with one of the most gorgeous men I've ever laid eyes on and not a peep. Please tell me you let him paint you like one of his French ladies. Oh, or wait, did you paint *him*?"

"No one is painting anyone, and we've texted. But another note, maybe it's time you watch something other than Titanic." Admittedly our text messages have been very surface level, so she's got a point, but I'm too stubborn to admit that.

"If he hasn't gone all Jack on you, at least tell me *something* has happened. That man could not take his eyes off you at Friendsgiving. Talk *bitch*," she demands, drawing out the last word.

"There's nothing to tell."

That earns me a snorting laugh. "Bullshit! You wouldn't have called me if that were true." It's annoying how she knows me so well. "Did you get him to crack a smile yet? If you think he's devastatingly handsome when he's serious, just wait until he smiles."

"Yeah, I've gotten some smiles." I sound smitten, and my friend is going to latch right onto that. "Especially yesterday. He taught me how to snowboard and Mr. Tall Dark and Broody was nowhere to be found. Did you know he's on the board of a literacy charity?" I'm one dreamy comment away from rolling to my stomach and kicking my feet in the air.

"Oh shit! You like him." She sounds uncharacteristically worried, which throws me off. Indie's a wildcard, always the first to goad you into doing something reckless just for the fun of it. That's why I called her. If I wanted someone more cautious and sensible, I'd have called Lilah. The concern in her voice has me sitting up in bed so quickly that I curse out loud at the sharp pull in my core from the movement.

"Should I not? I know he keeps telling me he's an asshole. Clearly he's got some daddy issues, but there is *so* much more to him than that."

"No that's not it at all. He's great and you're great. Everything is great . . ." The but is coming, I can feel it hanging in the air between us.

Before I can prod, she blurts out, "He's a really good kisser, and you deserve that in your life, but I'm the worst. And I already know that about him. I should have told you before you left because you two would be great together."

I'm stunned by her admission. None of it adds up. "Wait. You've kissed Dean?" The words come out quiet and tinged with hurt.

"It's not what you think. Or maybe it is. It was all very on-brand for me. Let me reassure you I don't have feelings for him. Never have." She's on a roll, barely pausing to breathe. "I only kissed him to drive Dom crazy. It worked, in case you're wondering. But you're not, because I just shit all over whatever was happening between you two."

"*Oh.*" This did not go at all how I expected. My fingers rub small circles on my temple trying to make this all make sense. My feelings for him are confusing enough, but add on this, and it's undoing all the work Dean's hands did earlier, my spine drawing tight like a rubber band.

"Please don't let me ruin this for you. If I could take it back, I would," she says, sounding resigned.

"Don't take this the wrong way, but I doubt that." She's never told me the whole story about what happened between her and Dom. She just said to keep her from listening to her vagina when he's around—claiming his pretty boy face is a weakness she'd screw up her whole life for.

"I would." There's no hesitation in her voice.

"Just one kiss?" I shouldn't need the reassurance. I trust both of them, and I've never once picked up on anything more than friendship between her and Dean.

"It was only once. Do you really want the details? I fully endorse you doing your own research on the subject. It'll be worth it and that's the last I'll say on that."

"Hey, Indie," I whisper.

"Yeah?" It comes out more cautious than anything I've ever heard from her.

"Thanks for telling me." I can practically hear her body relax at my words by the huff of air that comes through the phone.

A few hours after we hang up, the smell of pizza reaches me through the bedroom door. I slide my feet into my well-loved slippers and shuffle through the cabin following my nose. As if on command, my stomach growls, mocking me for skipping lunch like a coward because I needed time to process everything.

Propping my shoulder against the corner of the wall I watch his arm flex as he cuts the pizza. Even seeing him every day, up close and personal, I'm still taken aback by how handsome he is. Tonight he's wearing a pair of low-slung joggers that hug his thick thighs and an old t-shirt that's worn thin and stretched across his broad shoulders.

Knowing that Indie kissed him first doesn't touch how badly I want this man. Not just because of how he looks. He hides behind that off-putting armor like it will protect him from getting too close, but it only makes me want him more. He's got a story inside him and I'm dying to uncover it because from the pieces he's let me see, it's one to treasure.

"There she is. Who's hiding now?" The smile he gives me softens some of the lingering worry over my recent discovery. I've yet to decide if I'm going to bring it up with him. Not sure what the point would be since we've agreed that nothing can happen between us.

"Working, not hiding," I lie and he doesn't call me on it because, contrary to his belief, he's a nice guy like that.

"Come eat pizza with me," he says, wearing a more vulnerable look than I'm used to seeing on him.

Dragging the heavy wood stool closer under the guise of being able to reach the pizza I take the spot next to him at the island. "Thanks for making dinner. You should've come to get me so I could help." My shoulder bumps against his.

"You seemed like you needed the space." His shoulders lift to his ears and fall, but his eyes tell a different story as they search my face, silently asking, *are we okay*?

"I thought I did, but you know what I realized? Space from you never gives me what I think I need."

He nods like he knows exactly what I mean. "How are you feeling now?" he asks, sliding a plate towards me just as my stomach rumbles again. I know he hears it when he tilts his head to the side, eyebrow raising.

"Hungry and a little stiff," I admit sheepishly. "That hot tub is calling my name tonight. Know anyone that might want to join me?"

"The closest neighbor is a mile away, so I guess you'll have to settle for me." His lips wrap around the bottle of his beer and I find myself reaching for my bottle just for the distraction because when he's silly like this it makes me a little irrational.

"I suppose you'll do." There's a lightness to my voice when I really want to scream that I wouldn't be settling, that he's exactly who I want. Yell from the mountain tops that I wasn't running from him earlier. It was everything he made me feel that had me retreating to the safety of my bedroom. I want to tell him that all his warnings are bullshit and even if they aren't, I don't care anymore.

It's not until I've finished my pizza that I realize exactly how screwed I am. My bright blue bikini that I bought for the way it matched the Caribbean hangs from my fingertips as I try to remember what I was thinking when I packed this one instead of a more modest choice.

Seeing as I have no other options, I slip the tiny swimsuit on and continue procrastinating by grabbing the bottle of lotion off my dresser. When I can't think of any more reasons to avoid leaving my room, I pull on an oversized crewneck and swallow back my nerves.

CHAPTER 18

DEAN

Light from the cabin fills in the space behind her illuminating her silhouette in the doorway. From where I sit, submerged in the hot tub across the deck, I have the perfect view. Dark hair falls around her face and her eyes stay locked on the ground. The sweatshirt she's swimming in gives way to gleaming legs and a pair of fuzzy slippers. Not even the beat-up pink bunnies on her feet detract from how captivating she is.

When she turns towards my way, her eyes are slow to find mine. I fucking love the way her gaze lingers on the exposed upper half of my body. But it's fleeting, and she glances back at the cabin like she might disappear into the night.

"What's it going to be, Dreamer? Are you running again?" I ask, urging her to act. She shakes her head, but her feet don't move. If I've learned anything about Mia, it's that she will always rise to a challenge, even when she's scared. The asshole in me uses that to his advantage. "What are you afraid of?"

"Nothing," she declares, pulling her shoulders back as she reaches for the hem of her crewneck and pulls it over her head. And fuck me. She's got that same turquoise bikini that I spent so much time trying not to stare at on vacation this fall. The bottoms are tied in perfect bows that sit high on her hips. Making the legs that I want so badly to touch again look impossibly long. Her waist is highlighted by that gleaming jewel decorating her stomach and I want my hands there too, exploring every inch of her.

Fucking perfect. And I'm not sure how I'm going to make it out of this hot tub alive and with my sanity intact. My impulse control where this woman is concerned is shot to hell and I'm not a strong enough man to walk away. It's too late anyway, because she's sinking into the hot tub across from me, taking the hair tie from her wrist and pulling her hair up into a short ponytail on the top of her head.

There's an internal battle going on in my head. I grip the edge of the hot tub to keep me from dragging her across the steaming water to pull her to the seat next to me. All while I silently beg her to stay as far away as possible, if only for her own good.

My little Dreamer is choosing violence today though, because not only does she slowly glide across the water towards me, but she does it with a crooked smile on her face. She knows exactly what she's doing and welcomes the risk that comes along with it.

"Why did I wait so long to do this?" she asks, sinking into the seat next to me and letting her head fall back, eyes drifting closed.

"Feel better?" She tilts her head towards me, eyes opening just for a second, before she lets them flutter closed again.

"So much better, but you know what's missing?"

"What's that?" I mimic her pose, letting myself slip lower in the water. It only brings us closer, my arm bumping against her under the water.

"Magic hands and beer." She sighs contentedly.

"That's weird, I have both of those things right here." Turning away from her, I reach into the cooler I've stocked and grab her a bottle, twisting off the cap before I hand it to her.

"My hero." She tips the bottle back, taking a long drink from it before shifting in her seat—adjusting herself so the jets are hitting her neck and shoulders.

I do the dumbest thing I can think of. My hand reaches out, wrapping around her wrist under the surface and tugging her out of the seat. Moving her through the water, my other hand finds the curve of her waist and I slide into her seat, taking her spot and settling her between my legs.

"What's happening here?" Her nervous chuckle settles around me and like a cold blanket. But then she wiggles her hips back finding the edge of the seat and rests against me like it's the most natural thing to be between my legs like this.

"Those jets aren't going to cut it between snowboarding and how much you've been writing, your back must be a mess. Let me help." I lean forward, my voice low and bringing my lips to the shell of her ear. The sweet smell of her surrounds me. She always smells like the cobbler my nanny used to make in the summer, fresh peaches and a hint of sugar. "I promise I'll make it feel better."

"Is this the trick you use to get all the cleat chasers?" Her shoulders sag under my touch and her hands drop to my knees, her fingers wrapping around them. The touch burns through me hotter than the water.

"I don't need tricks, and no one else gets my hands like this." My thumb makes deep circles up the side of her neck forcing her head to the side as a tranquil exhale slips from her lips and she sinks into me further. She's all pliant—wet skin against me and it's pure ecstasy.

"No one?" Her question feels like a trap, but there's nothing to hide. No one else has gotten this much of me since high school when my grandfather and dad brought my world as I knew it crashing down.

"Not like this. Everyone else has just been a means to an end and they know it. I give them what they need and they willingly offer what I need. No complications, no commitments." I throw that last part out there as a warning for both of us. We shouldn't even be taking it this far.

"Even Indie?"

My hands freeze on her neck, and she tilts her head back, looking up at me.

"Indie's a friend, nothing more," I respond, not sure how much she knows and unwilling to give away anyone else's secrets.

"Do you kiss all your friends?"

Well fuck. The tone in her voice stays playful, but I can't tell if it's a cover. The last thing I want is for my past to hurt her. It's why I've been so adamant about us being just friends. She half turns in my lap and her molten eyes stare up at me. My palm curves around the back of her neck, cradling it.

"No, I don't." The way she's looking at me, I know that honesty is my best option right now. She's trying to hide it, but there's a vulnerability about the way her eyes flick between mine. "Indie is beautiful. I won't lie to you. When we met, I was attracted to her, but there's nothing there. Never has been." My thumb caresses the side of her face. "Never will be."

Her pupils dilate, any hesitation erased from her stunning face. She turns between my legs so that she's facing me. "What are you afraid of, Dean?" she challenges me in a husky whisper. The dare in her voice breaks me. Fuck the consequences. The brave woman in front of me is worth the risk.

"I'm afraid if I don't kiss you right now, I'll always regret it."

Mia's eyes go wide, like she didn't expect me to give in so easily, but I've been holding back since the moment she walked onto the plane and I'm done resisting. I just hope that she comes out of this thing unscathed because the one thing I would regret is hurting her.

"Because we're friends?" she asks.

"No, because I've never wanted something as bad as I want you."

The moment she leans forward, pushing up towards me, my lips are on hers. The next thing I know, she's scrambling into my lap. Her dull fingernails scrape over my scalp, tugging me to her with the same zeal that courses through me, begging me to hold her tighter, kiss her harder, make her mine. The kiss doesn't just push us over the line; it sends us careening over the cliff. Let's just hope there's a gentle sea below, not pointy rocks.

Wherever we land, there's no going back. I'll never be able to get the taste of her out of my mind or forget the way the soft parts of her fuse to the hard parts of me. When my tongue swipes against the seam of her lips, she opens, matching my urgency as we explore each other. She shivers under my touch when my palm traces down her spine pulling her closer. Our kiss absorbs the moan that falls from her lips when her center settles over my hardening cock. We get lost in each other and when we finally break apart, both of us are breathing heavily and Mia's are glazed over.

My lips find her forehead still holding her close and ask, "What are we doing?"

"Kissing, not running from our fears." She exhales a shaky sigh letting her head fall to my shoulder. "All I know is that I don't regret that kiss and I don't want to stop doing it."

Leaning back I tilt her chin up to look at me so there's no misunderstanding on what this is. "What are you suggesting, Mia?"

"Instead of both of us hiding from what we want, we do what feels good. Make each other feel good. I like you, Dean, but I understand what this can be and what it can't be. No commitments. No complications."

They're my words, but fuck if they don't sting. I've been the one putting up roadblocks every step of the way, and there's no denying that she's right. But I hate that she doesn't see a future for us before we've gotten a proper start. If anyone could make me question my beliefs about relationships, it's her.

"Friends with benefits?" I ignore the twisting in my chest from her dismissal of anything more between us.

"If that's what you want to call it. I'm not stupid enough to think we can do this without any deeper feelings getting involved. We've spent all this time together and we both like each other, but we only have a short time together before life pulls us apart again. You to spring training, and me to my book tour. Hell, even when that's over, we'll be on opposite sides of the country."

"We enjoy everything this winter and part ways as friends." I suppress the desire to pump my fist at the prospect, but my dick doesn't. He twitches against her at the idea.

"If you want to." She looks up at me through wet lashes from melted snowflakes.

My fingers sink into her soft curves and my thumbs slip under the two flimsy straps tying her bottoms together, tugging her down tight against where I'm rock hard from just a kiss. "Is that a real question? It seems pretty clear to me that you're the only thing I want. You did this to me. It's never been a question of *if* I want you. Are you sure it's what *you* want?"

"So sure," she whimpers as she tries to rock her hips but I hold her steady, making a tiny growl tumble out of her. "Why are you stopping me?"

"Because nothing else is happening tonight. If this went further and you woke up with regret . . . I can't do that to either of us. But it's cute how feisty you are when you want me."

"That's not going to—"

My kiss kills the protest before she can voice it. I open, letting her take what she needs and giving it right back to her. My grip on her tightens, and I focus on the kiss, sucking her bottom lip into my mouth before diving back in for more. Fuck, do I want her. My dick is screaming at me to let her grind down and give him the friction he wants.

But I meant what I said. She needs to think this through before we do something we can't take back. Kissing her was enough to tell me that once with her won't even be enough to take the edge off the need thrumming between us. She has to be certain, because once I make her mine, letting her go is going to be impossible. Even now, I can't help myself. I give her one more kiss on the corner of her mouth.

"That was so you don't forget that I want you more than you can imagine." Untangling her legs from me I turn her around so she's sitting in my lap. "You're not getting my dick tonight, so be good."

"Hardly seems like a fair deal if you're not going to give me a good dicking." She huffs in annoyance before leaning back against my chest where she belongs. Her fingers wrap around my wrist, lifting my arm above the water and tracing the letters of the tattoo on my forearm. Her voice is so smoky and low that I almost can't hear it over the jets as she reads the words etched into my skin. "To define is to limit."

I repeat the phrase against her temple as she continues tracing the letters. "Oscar Wilde. It's a reminder not to let my success be contained within the boundaries others have placed on me. To always look beyond for more."

"I'm not sure if that's the most optimistic, or pessimistic, outlook I've ever heard."

"I suppose it really can go either way," I admit with a shrug. "It was definitely the latter when I got it fresh off my eighteenth birthday and full of wrath."

"Do you really believe that anyone who matters would try to cage you and limit the success you can reach?" Her head rests on my chest as she looks up at me over her shoulder.

Yes.

"Not anyone that matters. But I can think of a few people that would rejoice in any misstep I might take. And I never want to give them that opportunity."

"Your Grandfather and Dad," she guesses.

"Mhmmm. Can't get anything past you. Are you sure your major wasn't journalism?" I tease, hoping to keep things light.

"Sorry." Her cheeks flush pink, and she looks out into the darkness.

"Don't apologize. I like your curiosity. I'm just not used to having someone read me as easily as you do. No one else gets close enough."

"I like that you let me get close, even if you are holding out on me," she says, the sass missing now that she's snuggled against me.

"Not holding out. Just trying to do the right thing, for once."

CHAPTER 19

MIA

"Is it ever going to stop snowing?" I ask myself, alone in the cabin. Outside, the mountains are blanketed in a thick layer of snow and it's still coming down. Dean pulls a large sled, piled with wood, towards the cabin. The stack of logs by the fireplace is getting low, too. I'm about to shove my feet in boots and see if he needs help when the front door swings open with a whoosh of cold that sends a shiver down my spine.

"Morning, Dreamer." Dean steps inside and shakes the snow off before he sheds his jacket. His cheeks are rosy from the wind. I imagine if he kissed me right now, they would feel cool against my heated skin.

"Morning. I was working up the courage to come out and help. It's just so toasty in here and it looks so blustery out there."

Small talk is always painful, but with him it's killing me. Even though he said nothing more was happening, I was convinced neither of us would have the willpower for that. I'm trying not to take it personally because he made it seem so easy—walking away and leaving me at the bathroom door with nothing more than a kiss to the forehead before I hopped in the shower to rinse off. When I came out, he was shut away in his room.

"I think I like you here, waiting for me, nice and warm." Eating up all the space between us in a matter of steps, he stalks towards me like I'm his prey. This playful side of him that only I get erases my worry and has me feeling invincible. The logical part of me knows I can't get attached to him or this feeling. But the squealing girl inside of me wants to pretend things will never change between us.

When he reaches me, he drags me against his solid chest. His frosty cheeks brush against mine and it feels even better than I imagined when he kisses the spot right below my ear, sending shivers down my spine for a whole other reason. Gone is the uncertainty, replaced by pure joy that at least nothing changed overnight.

"That's a greeting I could get used to. Did you already workout this morning?" I link my hands together behind his neck, holding him captive.

"No, I wanted to make sure we were set on wood for the snow coming in over the next few days and then I was going to make you breakfast, but you're up early this morning."

"I woke up a little restless and couldn't fall back to sleep."

"Is that so? We'll have to fix that by wearing you out tonight." His lips move across my cheek before brushing a kiss on my mouth. "Now I have an important question for you."

"What's that?" I look up at him and dying for another kiss, reassurance that last night wasn't a dream. Proof that the toe-curling, heart-stopping moment in the hot tub was real, not just a dream.

"Waffles or pancakes?" he asks.

I snort out a laugh because that's not at all what I was expecting. "Um, pancakes."

"Follow up question. Chocolate chips or blueberries?" His voice is low and husky, like we aren't talking about breakfast options. If this is what it's like to have Dean with his charm on full force, I'm not sure I'll survive the winter. The men I've dated recently have not prepared me for someone of his caliber.

"Always chocolate chips. I'm a simple creature. Besides, Nana always told us chocolate chips in pancakes were a sign that the chef cared." I force more confidence than I feel into my response hoping he doesn't notice how off kilter he has me.

"Smart lady, must be where you get it from. Chocolate chips from now on," he says, releasing me from his hold and sauntering across the living room to the kitchen, where he pulls out the ingredients to make breakfast.

"Do you want help?" I ask, still standing where he left me, feeling a little lost.

"Nope. My intention was to surprise you with breakfast. Just because you're up doesn't mean I'm going to forgo the plan."

"Fine, but I demand you let me make us a fresh batch of coffee." I pull down two mugs. "Why are your mugs so heavy? I'm going to get an uneven distribution of muscle drinking out of these things."

"Just switch your designated coffee cradling hand each day. That's what I do." He deadpans. The shirt he's wearing stretches tighter around his biceps as he gives a playful flex.

"Remind me again why you don't date? Funny and makes breakfast in bed? That's gold medal boyfriend material." I laugh at the coffeemaker, giddy that this man who is a walking, talking, sexy-as-sin contradiction is mine.

"You're assuming I was going to bring it to you in bed." He smirks over his shoulders as he combines ingredients.

It's unfair that I have to watch the way his shoulders bulge while he whisks pancakes for me so early in the morning. My vagina and heart are conflicted about the boundaries we set last night when he looks like the definition of domesticity. "Cute, but all I hear is you avoiding my question."

He joins me at the island where the electric griddle is plugged in. "Every example I've had of what it means to be a loving, supportive partner has been a lie. The two men who raised and taught me what it means to be a man are bastards. Just because I make pancakes for you doesn't mean I'd be a good partner. I can't give you that. I don't even know what it looks like."

"We are going to have to agree to disagree on that. I'm terribly sorry you went through that, but I've yet to see you be anything but a gentleman. A little grouchy, sure, but always thoughtful."

He pours the batter in four, large circles as the griddle sizzles filling the small kitchen with the sweet smell of chocolate and cinnamon. "Is that what you want, Mia, a gentleman?" The low tenor of his voice makes my arms breakout in goosebumps.

"There's a time and a place for everything." Those piercing green eyes on me have my palms sweating as I slide his coffee to him.

"And if I want to bend you over this island, do you want me to be a gentleman there?"

"No," I say, now desperately wishing I had iced coffee to cool me down.

"Good, don't forget. I'm not the golden boy who's going to make all your dreams come true. You call me Mr. Tall Dark and Broody for a reason."

"That's the second time you've basically called yourself an asshole without using the word. I better start thinking of punishments at the rate you're racking them up."

"Do your worst. It won't change who I am." His eyebrows turn down and his face frowns, breaking my heart because he truly believes that. It's nearly impossible to reconcile the man he thinks he is with the one standing in front of the griddle flipping the pancakes with a flick of his wrist.

"And that's what you don't seem to understand. I don't want to change who you are. There's nothing wrong with the man I know, and I wish I could get you to see that," I tell him as he plates the pancakes and takes the stool next to me.

There's a break in the snow after breakfast, so we clean up the kitchen together, before I layer up in winter gear and join Dean outside to finish restocking the wood for the cabin. By the third load of wood that I pull to Dean using the sled, I'm sweating enough that I've unzipped my jacket to let out some of the trapped heat.

"I've got it from here," Dean offers as I step beside him to help stack the logs.

"Not going to get rid of me that easily." I grab one and follow the same pattern he's making, working from the opposite end of the row.

"Tell me about playing softball. Did you love it like you love writing?" he asks, catching me off guard. No one ever asks me about softball, not like Hen with baseball.

"I loved the game and my team, but it was never as fulfilling as writing is. Everyone knew Hen would make it a career, and that just wasn't in the cards for me. Honestly, even if there had been a way for me to keep playing, I don't think I would have. I couldn't compete with him and I didn't want to."

"You wanted to have a life separate from his spotlight?"

"Yeah. For so long, I was Hen's little sister, and playing softball always made me feel like an extension of him, instead of my own person. It's part of the reason I moved to North Carolina after school to start my career. Writing gave me something that was mine, and I wanted to prove I could do it all on my own merits. To have something I was really freaking good at. He never made it feel that way—or my grandmother—it was just the comparison game. You know?"

"I think I do," he says, stopping to look at me. "Think you can still hit?"

"I could hold my own," I say, my fist resting on my hip.

"When we fly back for Christmas, we'll have to see how you do in the cage at my penthouse." His lips tip up into a smile and I want to snap a picture of him like this in his element—outdoors, in his favorite place, outside the diamond, looking peaceful and happy.

"After seeing the penthouse and then spending time here, I don't understand why you have that place. You're so much more relaxed here. It seems like something outside the city, with a backyard backing up to the mountains, and a brightly painted bird feeder hanging in the garden would make you so much happier. I can picture you lounging on the back patio in an Adirondack chair enjoying a beer or cutting wood for a firepit."

"That's because it would," he says gruffly, pushing his hand under his hat and ruffling his hair. "I hate that fucking place."

"Why would you stay there? You've got a huge salary from the Bandits. I'm just going to take a leap here and guess that's just the tip of the iceberg."

"It's not about the money. My grandfather bought it for me. Selling it would cause all kinds of problems. The kind I don't want to deal with." The smile he had earlier is gone and his green eyes go murky and hard as he refocuses on the work of stacking logs without another word on the topic.

If he's hoping it's going to push me away, it won't work. Dean's been clear about his boundaries and while I respect them, we agreed to part friends. Friends don't give up when things get uncomfortable. I'll be here to listen when he's ready.

Standing inside the doorway to the cabin I kick off my boots and jacket hanging them on the little moose hook on the wall. My fingers are icy cold against my skin as I cup them near my mouth and exhale into them, trying to warm them.

The door swings open and Dean joins me in the entryway, crowding me with his body and covering my hands with his. "Fuck, Dreamer. You're freezing. Why didn't you say something?"

"I'm fine."

Rather than answering me, he leads me to the living room, his hand clasped over mine. Taking the heavy wool blanket from the back of the couch, he shakes it open and wraps it around my shoulders. "Sit. I'll start a fire and then we can watch a movie. I'll even let you pick if you stop being a little shit and let me take care of you." His lips pull down in that trademark frown, but he can't hide the sweet sentiment behind his scowl.

So bossy.

"Or you could take those boots off, lose the coat, and come warm me up instead." I pat the spot next to me on the couch and flip the TV on, intending to scroll the movie options.

"It's supposed to be cold tonight. Let me get this started and I'll come be your heated blanket." He glances back over his shoulder giving me a crooked smirk before returning to the fire. Once the fire is going, he shucks his boots off, setting them on the hearth. His coat ends up draped over the arm of the couch as he stalks towards me.

I'm not tiny. At five-foot-eight, it's rare that someone makes me feel that way. With his broad upper body hovering over me as he leans over the corner of the couch I'm curled up in, there's no doubt in my mind this man could toss me around in the most rewarding way. *Make me a fucking backpack, sir.*

"What are you do—" My words transform to a squeak as he proves me right, scooping me up and taking my spot on the couch, settling me into his lap. "God that's hot."

"If that's all it takes to impress you, these guys have made this too easy for me." His hand smoothes up my arm, trailing over my shoulder before cupping the side of my neck.

"It's a well-known fact that women go nuts for being manhandled. We're not complicated. Lift us, throw some compliments our way, and feed us. That's basically all it takes to keep us content."

"And here I've spent my entire adult life thinking you all want orgasms and respect."

His hand parts the blanket and slides under my pullover settling on the curve of my waist. The warmth of his touch feels divine, and I want his hands everywhere. "Let's not do anything rash. I've been programmed to expect less from men, but maybe you can help me with that." I loop my hands around his neck pulling him in close so that our noses are brushing. "Show me how good it can be."

I've written about the growly sound that men make when they get possessive, but the noise that comes out of Dean when I nip at his lip is like nothing I've ever heard before, full of raw need and masculinity. If I didn't want him before, I absolutely do now. Wetness pools between my legs begging for him to live up to his words—it's not other guys that have made this easy, it's all him.

Everything about Dean right now emulates the man he keeps warning me about. The dangerous way his eyes rake over me, like I'm about to be his next meal. How his powerful hands grip my hip and cradle my neck, holding me in place so there's no way to focus on anything other than him—not that I'd want to.

"That's what you want? For me to show you everything no one else has been able to for the next few months? Ruin you for every other man when this is over?"

The whimper that passes through my parted lips is a resounding yes.

"Everyone else will be measured against me. When this is over, you'll be so addicted to the way I command your body that you'll never be satisfied with anyone else."

Maybe I'll regret this later, but I can't bring myself to care. Not with the way he makes my heart race when he's got his intensity focused on me.

That realization has me shifting on top of him, centering myself over his lap so that I'm straddling him. Dean brings out a side of me I've never known before. All the crappy dates, loser exes and guys who haven't been more than a passing attraction have all led to this. I've never been desperate for someone the way I am for him. He might act like a broody asshole, but I've seen the man he truly is. The neck rubs when I'm tense from writing, making me dinner when he knows I've been consumed by work and all the other little things he does to make me more comfortable in his space. Even now, there's a softness in his eyes as he threatens to destroy my body. He makes me feel cherished and protected, while turning me all the way on.

"Don't you dare hold back. Do your absolute worst and show me how good it can be." I crash my lips to his in a kiss that feels like it seals my fate. Once I let him in, there's no going back. I'll never be able to forget this man, or the way he makes me feel.

Heat spreads through my body, following the trail his hand blazes up my back as I deepen the kiss that he's letting me lead, but I'm pretty sure it's his way of easing me into this. Giving me a sense of control before he snatches it away.

"Don't worry about that, Dreamer. When I'm done with you, I'll leave you a puddle of bliss on the floor, wrung out and boneless. But right now—this is about you. Work off that chill and use me for what you need." My whole body is on fire for this man as he whispers dirty words into my mouth and pulls me down so I can feel every delicious inch of what he's working with. I deepen the kiss, canting my hips, chasing that high that only he makes me feel.

"How long are you going to let this go on? We both know it's killing you to let me take the reins," I taunt him, wanting to see if I can goad his dark side out to play. His grip on the back of my neck tightens, and he tilts my head back, giving me a glimpse of what I'm asking for when teeth scrape down the side of my neck.

"Make no mistake, the story you're weaving in this fascinating brain of yours won't end the way you think it will. You might be in charge right now, but there hasn't been a single moment where you haven't done exactly what I wanted."

I'm not sure what comes over me. Maybe it's the hardness in his voice, or the way his eyes lose that softness he always has for me, but I break his grip on me and twist out of his lap, sinking to the wood floor between his legs, the movie forgotten. No complaints from me, nothing could stop me from getting my mouth on this man.

"We'll see about that." I try to hide the shake in my hand as it smooths up his thighs before palming his length through his jeans. My gaze is glued to his face, catching the twitch of his jaw when my other hand slips the button of his jeans loose. It's a game of sexual chicken and neither of us is willing to lose.

His knuckles turn white, fists clenched at his side, but he doesn't stop me when I slip my hand into his pants. He's hard and hot. Jesus, the way he fills my hand. I know without even looking I'm in trouble. Unable to hold back any longer, I let my eyes flick down to where I'm gripping him and pull him free.

The crooked grin he gives me when I look back at him wide-eyed and stunned is the first sign of his frosty exterior cracking.

"Oh, wow," I murmur, savoring the velvety feel of him. I'm way out of my depth.

"Not feeling so cocky now, are you?" he challenges, gathering up my hair in his hand. "Fuck, look at you, on your knees for me all doe-eyed while you look at my cock like it's the best, and most terrifying, thing you've ever seen."

He's not wrong, but there's no way I'm going to let him see me waiver. "It doesn't scare me and neither does its owner." Lowering my head I kiss the underside of him. Courage and pride build inside me—along with a deep throbbing between my legs—when he twitches in my hand.

That little move is enough to embolden me, licking up the measure of him before I drop down on him, stretching my mouth wide to accommodate his size.

CHAPTER 20

DEAN

Holy fuck!

Any control I was pretending to have evaporated the minute her knees hit the floor. But it's all a fucking joke. Control doesn't exist where she's concerned. Since she stepped onto that plane, I've tried to hold back, but it's only been a temporary reprieve from the way she strips me of all my composure. Every warning I've given her about the ways I could hurt her . . . they're nothing compared to the damage she could inflict on me.

She looks up, silvery eyes shining with tears that are building in the corners as she brings me to the back of her throat, struggling to take all of me. The need to brush them away overtakes me, but that's what she wants. She's feisty—determined to show me she can handle anything I throw at her. So I brush her hair back, gathering it in my hand. Giving just enough freedom to let her set the pace. Her cheeks hollow and she doubles down, sucking hard and stealing the oxygen right out of my lungs.

"Oh, that's perfect. You feel so fucking good, all warm and wet. Show me how badly you want to make me come apart for you." It takes all my concentration to give her the encouragement I know she craves, my hips fighting to buck up into her mouth. The vibrations as she moans her approval are my reward, making me feel frenzied for her. "You like when I tell you how good you are at sucking my cock? Because fuck me, no one has ever done it better, Dreamer." Like a man possessed, her nickname melds with a growl.

She nods her head, whimpering and squirming between my legs. Before Mia, this would have been solely about me, but she is already so much more. "Slip your hand between your legs and show me what having your lips wrapped around my cock does to you."

Her eyes drift shut as the hand that was braced against my thigh disappears out of sight. I know she's doing as I asked when her grip tightens and her rhythm stutters.

"Let's see it," I demand again as she shifts between my legs, lifting her hand in front of me, the light hitting it so I can see her fingers, slick and coated. "Should I taste you?" I ask, gripping her wrist in my hand and pulling it closer.

A mumbled "yes" comes out as she lets my dick slip free. Taking my time to make sure she watches, I bring her fingers to my mouth and wrap my lips around the soaked digits, licking them clean.

"So fucking perfect." I groan letting her hear how much I love the taste of her. "You're going to be a fucking addiction. I can't wait to get my mouth on every inch of you." The shiver that runs up her spine reignites the urge to take over and fill her mouth.

She opens her mouth to argue, but before she can, I hoist her off the ground and lay her on the couch, settling between her thighs.

"Now it's your turn. Taste yourself, see why I can't wait any longer to get my mouth on you." Her eyes go wide as I take her mouth, licking at the seam of her lips, demanding entrance.

She goes soft underneath me, melting into the couch as we get lost in the kiss. When her leg wraps around my hip, pulling me toward her and seeking more, I slide down her body. Using my shoulder I shove her legs wider for me.

"What are you waiting for?" she huffs out pushing up on her elbows as I toy with the waistband of her leggings. Her cheeks are flushed, her chest rises and drops. Those silky strands disheveled from having my hands in it. She's a perfect mess for me.

"It's not too late to change your mind." I really fucking hope she doesn't because I've never wanted something this badly. We've already crossed every line we set and the most recent ones don't stand a fucking chance.

"Afraid you won't live up to the hype?" She raises a perfectly arched dark eyebrow at me.

"Fucking brat. Next time you talk to me like that with my head between your legs, I'll make sure you don't come for hours."

She licks her lips, eyes flaring in response. She's going to be my undoing, no doubt about it. Ripping her leggings down without warning they fly over my shoulder tangled with her underwear. Leaving her lying there, shocked, with only one sock left.

"Hands stay here." Both of her wrists restrained by my palm, I push them above her head, pinning them to the arm of the couch.

"What if I want to touch you?" she challenges and I push her shirt up so it's gathered around her chest, exposing her black sports bra. The ribbed material is held in place with thin straps, dipping to a "V" in the front that shows just a hint of cleavage. Her tits are on the smaller side, and I've been dying to see them. Not wasting any time, I shove that up, too. My cock twitches at the sight of her under me.

"You had your chance. I don't want your wandering hands distracting me from all the dirty things I'm going to do to this immaculate body." I cup her breast in my hand brushing my thumb over her peaked nipple. Her teeth clamp down on her lip as I pass over it again, this time more roughly.

"Don't hold those noises back. I want to hear it all." Lowering my head I take it in my mouth, making chills erupt over her breast. "That's a start. There's no one out here but me and you. When you come, I want it to echo off the mountains."

There's never been a better incentive than to get her to let go the way I know she can. Switching to the other side I give it equal attention. My mouth distracting her, I grip the back of her leg, draping one over the back of the couch. "Such a pretty picture spread open for me."

Mia arches off the couch pushing her chest into my face.

"I can't wait to spend an entire night worshiping these perfect tits. But I need to taste you again or I'll lose my damn mind. Okay with you?"

She nods wordlessly, collapsing back into the couch. The bright light streaming in through the floor to ceiling windows casts across her body, showcasing every inch of her laid out across my couch like a dirty angel.

I lean back on my heels. "Look at you." My knuckles brush over where she's swollen and pink. It's the lightest touch, but it's enough to tell me she's drenched. "So fucking needy. I'm going to savor every second of this."

"Please, Dean," she begs, her hips wiggling side to side.

"Let me hear it again. Say my name when you beg for my lips right here." I ghost my thumb over her clit on a downward path circling her entrance, toying with her.

"God, Dean. Fuck. I need you," she pants shifting her hips so my thumb slips inside.

"Are you going to ride my fingers while I devour you?"

"Yes!" she cries out as I give her the rest of my thumb, rubbing at the spot inside her, kissing my way up her inner thigh.

"Such a good girl being vocal for me. Keep it up or I'll stop." When she doesn't answer right away, I withdraw my touch.

"Shit, sorry. I'll do anything. Just don't make me wait."

"Can't hear that enough." This time I slide one finger inside her, working it in and out slowly. When my lips seal around her clit, the noise that comes out of her mouth has me grinding my painfully hard cock against the couch. She's squirmy as fuck as she rides my finger, searching for release.

"Tell me what you want. I'll give you anything as long as it makes you feel good," I say against her center.

"I just need more." It comes out whiny. She's right on the edge and I can't wait to push her over the brink.

"That's it, sweetheart, ask for what you need." I pull my finger out to the tip, adding a second and crooking them as I flick my tongue over her.

"Fuck, yes. Just like that—don't stop."

My movement slows just a little, enough to keep her climbing, but not enough to give her body what it's chasing. "You forgot something. Let me hear it."

"Wh—what?" Her head comes off the couch and the fire in her eyes flickers hot enough to burn down the cabin around us.

"You know what to do to get what you need," I remind her, hooking my fingers for good measure.

"Oh fuck, Dean," she groans loudly this time. "Make me come, you cocky fucker."

The unexpected outburst has me chuckling against her clit. There's no way I'm denying her after that. I suck her into my mouth letting my teeth scrape against her. Her core tightens around my fingers. My eyes look up her body to find one hand working her nipple. I swat it away, replacing it with mine.

"Hands, Dreamer. Let go. I'll take care of you. Squeezing me so tight. Give it to me," I pant out and flatten my tongue against her. She rewards me with the most feral noise and her legs shake against my shoulders.

"I'm coming Dean. Fuck—yes."

Yeah, she is. And it's a sight as she shivers, becoming overly sensitive in the aftermath of her release. I crawl up her body, my lips finding the hammering pulse point in her neck before I bring my lips to hers. When our lips meet, she wraps herself around me. I like it more than I should and that scares the shit out of me.

"Let's get you cleaned up." I don't wait for a response. Lifting her from the couch I carry her to the shared bathroom between our rooms. It's as much about taking care of her as it is a distraction to take my mind off the intensity of what we just did. Holding her tight to me with one hand, I grab a towel and lay it on the counter with my free hand, not wanting her to get cold from the stone on her bare skin.

"What are you doing?" Her brow wrinkles as I pull her shirt down from where it's tangled around her shoulders and run the water in the sink until it's warm.

"Grabbing a washcloth so I can take care of this mess we made." I run the gray square under the water and bring it between her legs.

"I can see that, but why are you dressing me?" she huffs, sounding awful grumpy for someone that was just deliriously content in my arms two seconds ago. "What about you?" Her hands reach out and I grab them in one of mine.

"This wasn't about me."

She blinks back at me and it's the first time I've seen her look dumbfounded. She bats the hand between her legs away.

"So you're just going to—what? Walk around with blue balls all day? That's stupid." Shit, this girl. Here I'm trying to administer some aftercare, something that I'm not normally prone to do, and she's giving me a hard time because she didn't get to finish the blowjob she started.

"I'll take care of it," I tell her, leaning in to kiss the corner of her mouth, but she pulls away.

"You'll take care of it?" she repeats back. "I'm not quite sure what to do with that, Dean." She transforms in front of me, muscles going taut. Before I know what's happening, she hops off the counter and storms out of the bathroom, her pert ass bouncing as she stomps away. "I thought this hot and cold shit was over. We agreed to make each other feel good and now you're pulling away, again?"

I look around the bathroom for a nonexistent clue as to how we ended up here. More importantly, how to fix it. Pushing my hand through my hair I toss the towel into the hamper and follow her to her room. When I walk in, she's rooting through her drawer.

"What are you doing?" I ask as she turns around, still naked on the bottom half and clutching an intimidating vibrator in her hand.

I'm more confused than ever. I take a step towards her but stop when she tosses the toy onto the bed and shudders at the way it flops.

Not the time, dickhead.

In the center of the room, Mia whips her shirt off, chucking it at my feet. "Well, what are you waiting for? Go take care of yourself. I'll be in here getting all worked up again knowing you're on the other side of the wall taking your pleasure into your own hands instead of sharing it with me. That's what you were going to do, isn't it?"

Oh, shit. Leave it to me to ruin things this fast. I was trying to take my time and not overwhelm her—and me—mostly me.

"Mia." My arms reach out, banding around her and moving us to the bed before she can break free. "I'm sorry. I didn't mean to upset you." Burying my face in her neck so she can't see the vulnerability there when I admit, "Fuck, sweetheart. I was overwhelmed and assumed you felt the same."

"You don't run from me, not like that. We decided to do this together. If you don't think I'm strong enough for it, we should stop now." And there it fucking is. Of course, she would feel that. She might cover it up well, but she's got her own set of trauma. And like an idiot, I fucking triggered hers. What Mia needs is to feel like she matters, not be left.

"I get it, really, I do. If the situation had been reversed and you ditched me right afterward to get yourself off, it would have driven me crazy. It won't happen again."

"Ugh, I feel like a crazy person." She buries her head in my chest and I pull the blanket she has draped over the bed around her. "I know I don't get all of you, but I want to be selfish with you while I have you."

"No, you're not the one who screwed up. That's on me. I feel the same way about you." I squeeze her tight hoping it reassures her. After a moment, she relaxes into me. "I think I ruined the mood. Want to bring your computer out to the living room and work out there while I make us some lunch?"

"That sounds nice," she mumbles against my chest.

"Now put that toy away before I change my mind and use it on you."

Her cheeks flush pink. "Oh god. I can't believe I did that."

"I fucking loved that you did. Tell me what you need—not just your body, but *you*." I pop a kiss on her nose, nodding towards the veiny monster on the bed. "One of these days, when we have a better handle on our emotions, I'm going to have you show me just how you like to use that. Get dressed, I'll start on lunch."

Turning on my favorite playlist filled with alternative and indie hits from the early 2000s, I grab a couple of thawed chicken breasts from the fridge along with supplies for a salad. I'm dropping the seasoned chicken in the pan when Mia takes a spot at the island opening her laptop.

"Talk about predictable. You were an emo kid in high school." All the awkwardness from earlier is gone with her teasing.

"As emo as a rich kid can be. I went through a rebellious stage when I was a sophomore. The music stuck with me. There's something about working out to angsty music, but I can't handle anything overly ragey."

"Your poor mother," she teases—the smile I chased away with my boneheaded decision, back.

"She thought it was just teenage rebellion and kept me in line accordingly. She wasn't the problem, so I did my best not to turn it on her, but teen boys don't always have the best impulse control. I got my ass handed to me by her more than once when I pushed it too far."

"But it wasn't just everyday hormonal teen stuff."

"Caught that. Huh?" I say, pushing my hand through my hair as I flip the chicken. "No, it was a little more complicated than that."

"There's that word again. Is there a vocabulary test coming up that I don't know about? Or is that just your favorite word?"

"No test. It just seems to be a theme where I'm concerned. Speaking of, are you sure we're okay?"

"We're okay. I can handle you, complications and all."

"Good. I'm not ready for this to be over yet." I turn down the heat on the chicken and start making the salads. "How's the writing coming? Any of my body parts give you inspiration lately."

"Possibly. I guess you'll just have to wait and see if I let you read any more of it. But yeah, I'm feeling good about it."

I hold back my remark about being at her disposal. The ball is in her court with how much that involves me. After my misstep this morning, I want her to know that I'm here for her, not just where her orgasms are concerned, but as a friend too. I get the sense that she might need that even more. "If you're not going to entertain me by reading to me, maybe you could pick out a movie for us to watch after supper."

The smile on her face lights up the cabin and pride swells inside me that just my simple offer to spend time together did that.

CHAPTER 21

MIA

The past week has been a blur of writing and spending all my free time kissing Dean. And hot damn, the man can kiss. On the couch, pressed against the cabin door, and propped on the bathroom counter when we pass each other getting ready for bed. All of them, equally thrilling. They have me practically skipping while I pace in front of the microwave, waiting for my water to finish warming. The wind that Dean brings with him when he steps in from outside whistles through the cabin, pulling me out of my daydream.

I've spent countless hours working in the living room this week, unable to suppress the need to be near my roommate, who's magically more pleasant than he was a few weeks ago. The setup isn't great for my posture, but I enjoy watching Dean be domestic way too much. Rather than hide away, I made the couch into a cozy writing nook and enjoy all the perks that come along with it; from sporadic conversation, to non-stop eye candy, and an occasional foot rub. And kissing, of course.

"Damn, it's freezing out there. I hope the wood boiler can keep up," he says, shaking his hair out when he pulls the black beanie off his head. It's gotten longer on top in the almost three weeks that we've been here. During the season, he rarely sports more than a five o'clock shadow and keeps his dark hair short and styled. Here he wears a more relaxed look and I like that I get to see a side of him most don't.

"You're microwaving water again? What am I going to do with you?" He joins me, grabbing my mug for me when the microwave beeps.

"Shut it, old habits die hard. Besides, it's not like there's some fancy electric kettle lying around even if I decided to change my ways." He hands me the mug, letting my tea bag drop into it with a plop. "Want to watch a movie with me? I was thinking about picking out a Christmas movie to get into the spirit before we fly back home next week."

"You, snuggled up on the couch next to me; I can get onboard with that. Let me get out of these jeans. They smell like smoke. Although, I'm not sure I can trust you to pick one." He gives me a skeptical look.

I can't blame him after I forced him to watch *A Cinderella Story* last week. "Are you really going to complain about anything I pick if I let you feel me up again?" Which is exactly what happened.

"Fair point." His lips press to the top of my head and I get a whiff of smoky pine before he leaves me to change.

Home Alone 2: Lost in New York is ready to go when he emerges from the bedroom wearing nothing more than a pair of gray sweatpants riding low on his hips. Moonlight bathes him in a dim light, but I know better than to think it's the shadows playing off his muscles that make him look like a chiseled god. The man doesn't need the help of lighting tricks.

"Popcorn?" he asks from where he leans against the doorframe, a smirk playing at his lips. His hand coasts over his cut abs, hooking the waistband of joggers and tugging them lower.

"So cocky." I toss a pillow at him, which he catches with ease, his warm laughter kicks my body temperature up a few more degrees. Dropping it on the chair, he moves to the kitchen to make a bag of popcorn—grabbing a bowl for us to share.

"Are you ready to head home for Christmas and see your nieces? It's gotta be fun to have kids around for the holidays," I say when he joins me on the couch, holding out the heaping bowl of buttery goodness.

"It's my favorite time to be in Boston—the only time I enjoy it, really. The girls and I have a tradition. On the twenty-third, I pick them up for the day, take them to lunch, and then we go shopping for presents for their parents. It makes all the other family bullshit worth it; spending the day with them and seeing my sister's face when there's a surprise under the tree for her and Gavin from the girls."

My hands stops an inch from my mouth.

"What?" he asks, giving me a puzzled look.

"You let everyone think you're this cold, detached person when it's the furthest thing from the truth. I just don't get it."

Thick fingers wrap around my wrist, bringing my hand to his mouth and letting his soft lips graze my skin as he steals the kernel out of my hand. "There's more truth to it than you see." He gives me that signature smile, the one that makes my brain go all fuzzy.

"Says, you. I see right through you, Dean Harrison. You're not as much of an ass as you pretend to be. You're sweet and kind—loving, even. But don't worry, I'll keep your secrets. Just keep showing me the real you because the broody side is hot as fuck, but this guy . . ." I lay my hand over his heart. His gaze travels down to where it rests and when he lifts his head to look at me, I tell him the truth that scares the shit out of me. "The one that lives here— he's the one that I can't get enough of."

"What if it isn't enough and everything else that I am hurts you?" The sadness in his eyes cracks my chest open.

"You're worth the risk. Give me some credit. I'm not as breakable as you think."

"Fuck, Mia. I know that." His hand covers mine gently. Even though his words are harsh, they're aimed at himself, not me. "If I thought you couldn't handle what we're doing, I would've never agreed to it."

"Then what are you afraid of?"

"That you'll end up hating me, or I'll end up hating myself more than I already do."

If my heart wasn't already destroyed for anyone but this man, it is now.

"You don't get to talk about my friend like that," I tell him, covering the fear that twists in my gut. Hiding it so he doesn't push me away because of how deeply he affects me. "That earns you a punishment."

"Oh yeah. What are you going to do to me?"

Glad to have his hotshot attitude back, I push play on the movie, ignoring his question. If I tell him my plan now, we will never watch the movie. With a shrug, I cuddle into his side and pop a handful of popcorn into my mouth.

Our legs are tangled, and our hands are roaming freely. The only time we don't have our lips all over each other is during the battle scenes where Kevin has to protect the toy shop. I don't need to look to know that I'm going to have a few hickeys from where he lavished extra attention. Burying my face in his neck I try to cover my yawn.

"That's enough fun for you tonight. Off to bed you go," Dean says when the credits roll, spoiling all our fun. He stands from the couch, and his hand disappears beneath the waistband of his joggers to adjust himself. I bite my lip, but he just shakes his head.

"Soon enough. Up. Bed," he demands, pulling me off the couch and into his arms.

The protest I have ready dies on my lips when my lust-addled brain remembers the punishment he earned tonight. *Off to bed I go.*

I step just inside my room, leaning against the door frame. Dean's got his hands overhead gripping the top of the frame as leans in to kiss me softly. "Sweet dreams, Mia."

"Mhmm . . . I don't think that's going to be a problem tonight," I sing-song, placing one last kiss on his lips before I shut the door, leaving him on the other side.

Stripping out of my leggings and oversized shirt, I dig through my suitcase for my travel tripod. I just need one more thing. Setting everything up the way

I need it I mess up the bedsheets and toss the toy on the bed then strip out of my underwear.

With the timer set on my phone, I strategically position myself on the bed so I get the shot I'm aiming for. With my back arched impossibly high, and my head thrown back, I drape my arm over my breasts and bend my knees, digging a pointed toe into the bed. I let the camera on my phone take a couple of shots, some with me looking, and others where I grip the vibrator I grabbed to up the ante. I take one more set, turning the vibrator on and dragging it down my stomach, letting it disappear between my legs—stopping before I get lost in the hot and heavy need pulsing through me.

The photos turned out even better than I hoped.

I lock the door to the bedroom. This is a punishment, after all. And I'm not sure either of us is strong enough to say no at this point.

I pick my three favorite images and send them. It can't be more than thirty seconds later that I hear the door handle jiggle.

"Fuck me, Dreamer. What are you doing to me?" His voice sounds like it's been raked over hot coals, gravelly and desperate for something to quench his thirst.

"It's a punishment for a reason. You don't get to talk about yourself that way and get rewarded," I tell him through the door. My body's heated from head to toe. The heavy petting during the movie had me on edge. Taking those photos and waiting to see what they would do to him has me hanging on by a thread.

There's a thump against the door before he says, "Oh, I'm going to get my reward because you're going to pick up that toy and fuck yourself while I stand right here pressed against this door telling you exactly what to do."

Holy shit. Um yeah, let's do that.

"Oh, and Mia? I want to hear you scream my name when you come. Loud enough that this door between us rattles and your voice is hoarse tomorrow, because if I were in there, that's exactly what would happen."

"Shit." My fingers wrap around the smooth silicone. His words have an intense ache blooming between my legs. With my eyes closed, I can imagine him leaning against the cool wood, his hand and forehead pressed to it. "Can I turn it on?"

"You must be desperate for a reward of your own, asking me for permission to fuck yourself. Are you a good girl, Mia? Or are you just so wet for me that you'll do anything to get relief?"

Sweat beads on my collarbone and I haven't even touched myself yet. The mouth on this man is like nothing I've ever experienced before. He's broken my brain. "Both. I want to be good for you, but I need this."

There's officially not a feminist bone left in my body and I couldn't care less.

"Jesus," he breathes out. "Making you live up to that promise is going to be the highlight of my life. Do you know all the dirty things I can make you do? I hope you know what you're getting into, giving me that kind of power over your body. We're going to ruin each other, but it's going to be worth it."

"Please, Dean," I beg, my knuckles sore from the grip I have on the toy.

"Not yet. First, I need to get you ready—"

"I am!" my cry comes out sharp, cutting him off.

"Prove it to me. Move the vibrator between your legs. Don't turn it on. You haven't earned that yet—teasing me with those photos and then locking yourself safely behind this door."

"Oh, God!" The first brush of it across my skin sets my nerves on fire.

"That's it. Now lightly glide it over your lips like I would do with my fingers and tell me what you feel."

"It feels like heaven, but I want more."

"You can do better than that. Try again and I'll give you what you need." His voice is husky and broken, like he's struggling to control himself as much as I am. It gives me the confidence to play along with him.

"My pussy is starving for it. The toy is soaked—my hips keep lifting, chasing it with every pass."

"And what are you picturing while you tease that hungry cunt for me?"

Where did he get his master's degree in filth? There's no way he learned to talk like this on his own.

"You. It's you holding my hips down as you explore me with your fingers—using your shoulders to spread me wide," I admit.

"That's because I own your body now. No one else is ever going to make you feel as good as I do. Are you ready for your reward?"

"Yes—fuck. Yes, please."

His dark chuckle hits me hard through the door, dancing over my skin and making me squirm against the toy between my legs. "Start on the lowest setting and keep it away from your clit. Enjoy it now because once I think you're ready, we come together. Think you can handle that?"

"No," I say with a laugh, honestly I'm not sure I can wait until he's there with me. I press the button and gasp when the humming starts against my sensitive core.

"You want to make me proud, screaming my name as you picture me fucking you hard, don't you?"

"Yes, but Dean, I'm so close already. I don't know—oh, God." It's almost too much the way it is. "I don't know if I can hold out."

"Mia, you don't fucking come until I tell you to. Understand? I'll break this door down and take that toy away, leaving that desperate cunt begging to be filled."

"Okay!" I cry out, still unsure if I can do what he's asking, but too far gone to say anything else.

"That's it. You've got the toy nice and wet. It's going to slip inside that perfect pussy so easily. Tell me what you're thinking about and I'll let you do just that. Leave nothing out."

My empty core clenches at the suggestion alone and I squeeze my eyes closed, trying to focus. I don't doubt he's serious about his threat to break down the door. "You've got my legs spread wide and pinned down as your mouth roams over me, sucking and licking the way I like, but you won't give me what I need. You're a tease, taking your time while you taste every inch of me, humming about how sweet I am."

"Now that's something I want to try. Will you let me do that to you?"

"Yes—I'll let you do anything you want." My response is immediate.

"So desperate to please. Fuck, do I love that. You'd better be close, sweetheart, because I'm so damn hard for you. Let me hear you while I fuck my fist pretending it's you."

"Can I?" I ask, on a groan, my head thrashing to the side.

My body shivers and melts into the bed when I finally slide the toy in. There's no finesse in my approach, sliding it into the hilt and twisting my wrist. I almost come off the bed when the blunt head of the vibrator hits the spot inside me that's burning with raw nerve endings. "So good, Dean!" I scream into the darkness. "The only way this would be better is if it were you deep inside me."

"Fuck, I want that. I'm right there with you. It's my voice in your ears, me in your head. Now rub that clit for me and let me hear you soar, Mia."

Shudders rip through me when I guide my other hand between my legs and put pressure where I need it most. The way I moan for him is unhinged. His name flies out of my mouth, along with a string of garbled curses.

And the sound that echoes through the cabin when he slaps the door and roars through his release, panting my name, will live on in my head forever.

For a few minutes, we're both quiet and I think maybe he's left to clean himself up when his lazy voice breaches the barrier between us. "You good in there?"

"Good doesn't even begin to cover it."

"Tell me about it. Give a minute to clean up and then you come out. I'll get the water warm for you and leave a clean washcloth out. My door is going to be locked, Mia. I don't trust myself not to come back for more."

I almost tell him not to lock it, but there's something to this idea of taking it slow. Everything between us has been heightened since we put the brakes on after our misunderstanding the other night. We've gotten closer as friends and physically, every touch feels better than the last. Exhibit A, the way I just orgasmed harder than I thought possible at my own hand. When we finally get together, we might burn the whole cabin down.

Soft footfalls give way to the sound of his door closing a few minutes later. I slip out of bed, not bothering with my clothes, and amble into the bathroom, my body still putty. Lined up on the counter are the aftercare items he promised, along with a lavender-chamomile tea and a note on one of the random Post-it Notes that I leave scattered all over the cabin that simply says, "Sleep tight, Dreamer."

♥

"I'm not sure I could ever get used to this," I say to Dean, who follows me up the stairs of his family's private plane. We went back and forth on what made the most sense. I insisted I could drive myself back to Denver, and he insisted I fly with him on the plane. He's heading back to Massachusetts for Christmas, but the pilot is making a stop in Denver to drop me off.

We'll both be back in Denver for New Year's Eve festivities, so ultimately I gave in because twelve hours in the car, with the potential for snowy mountain roads, didn't sound like that much fun.

Who am I kidding? It really wasn't that hard to convince me.

"With all the travel I do during the season, it's hard to fight this perk of being a Harrison when the alternative is flying commercial during the holidays. Still think I'm not a tool?"

"No one's perfect. If your biggest flaw is that you're a snob about using your grandfather's private jet, I think we'll be okay. It's not like you're greedy about it. You use your powers for good. Like getting us all to St. John's, and didn't you also use it to get Cruz to St. Louis last season?"

He drops into the seat across from me tugging on his neck. "Yeah. But you're giving me too much credit. It's not all altruistic, it eases some of my guilt over using it when it can benefit someone else." He looks back at me from where he's staring out the window. His eyes drop in a slow perusal of my body before they travel all the way back up making me feel overheated.

"Why are you looking at me like that?" I ask, my nose scrunching as the plane taxis on the runway.

"Just thinking about the first time I saw you here—the way you changed into your swimsuit before we even landed. It was fucking adorable. You had me hooked. No one else has ever left me feeling so intrigued. Now I have you alone on this plane and you're mine to touch."

His hand drops to his lap adjusting his seatbelt to accommodate the growing bulge in his pants. We've kept things pretty low-key for the last week. There's been lots of making out, some truly epic dry humping, but we haven't gotten each other off again. My vibrator has gotten a workout, but without his voice in my ear, it's not giving me the release I'm craving.

The build up and connection I feel with him has made it worth the wait. I think if we both hadn't been so busy we would've caved already. He spent a few days this week snowboarding and getting some hitting in at the high school. Back at the cabin, I've been working hard to get ahead of my deadlines so I can focus on enjoying the holidays instead of working.

Knowing that we have to spend the next five days apart has me more melancholy than I expected. And if he wants to distract me from being in my feelings over it, who am I to stop him?

"All because of a swimsuit?" I tease, shifting in my seat under the heat of his stare. The way he's looking at me makes all these boundaries we put on our relationship melt away.

"The swimsuit definitely pulls its weight, but the girl who was wearing it gets all the credit. You're stunning no matter what you're wearing—a swimsuit on my plane or sweats and those tattered bunny slippers." The admission doesn't ease the pout of his lips or the crease in his forehead.

Each foot we climb has my heart rate picking up, and when we reach cruising altitude the click of his seat belt unbuckling echoes through the cabin. His hands are at my waist, undoing mine an instant later. Once I'm free, he's striding to the back of the plane toward the couch and pulling me into his lap without a word.

CHAPTER 22

DEAN

Mia threads her fingers through my hair, tilting my head up so that it rests against the wall of the plane while she straddles my thighs.

"You're extra sulky today. What's going through this handsome head of yours?" Her thumbs smooth over the line on my forehead.

Being back on this plane, where I initially saw her, is doing something to me. The decision to pull back physically wasn't something we talked about after that disastrous first time. It just happened. Getting it right this time is the only thing I'm concerned about, because the idea of letting her down again makes my guts twist. She's under my skin and in my bones in a way that no one else has ever been, and that scares the shit out of me.

The clock is ticking on what we have. At the end of this winter, we both have lives to go back to. Even if I could give her more, I can't even begin to figure out what that would look like for us. Limiting it to hooking up when we're in the same zip code might be worse than being without her. She deserves someone who can give her everything, not bread crumbs.

I've always been a selfish fucker, making decisions that hurt people no matter how good my intentions are. Like now, pulling her into my lap because I'm all twisted up about missing her and dreading having to deal with my baggage when I get home.

"What am I thinking about?" I tap my chin, pretending to think about it, then tug her closer so I can whisper low and dirty into her ear, offering what I can give her. "That I'm sick of waiting to have you again." Her breath hitches and her grip on me tightens. "That I want to get it right this time because I'm about to leave you for five days. How shitty I am to want you the way I do right now, and yet, I can't imagine getting off this plane without seeing you melt into me, happy and sated at my hands."

"There's nothing I want more. But can I ask you something first?" She nibbles on her lip nervously.

"Anything."

"We haven't had this conversation yet because, well, we've been together non-stop. But when you're back in Boston, are you planning on seeing anyone else?" She tilts her chin down looking off to the side.

I wait, letting her find her way back to me in her own time, not saying anything until her eyes find mine again. "Not a chance. You're all I want. As long as we're doing this, there's no one else. Are *you* planning on dusting off those dating apps?" Dread settles in the pit of my stomach at the thought of her with someone else.

"You know, now that you mention it I've really missed toenail clippings and jump scare threesome proposals. I'd have to be an idiot to look elsewhere when I have all this waiting for me." Her heated eyes drift down my body to where we're melded together and back up again.

"So spicy today," I say against her neck, sucking where it curves into her shoulder, knowing it drives her wild.

The rest of the flight is a blur of our lips all over each other as I make her come on my hands twice before she drops to her knees and takes me in her mouth right before we start our descent. It's almost embarrassing how fast she has me exploding down the back of her throat, but she was determined to finish the job this time, and I wasn't strong enough to stop her—not that I wanted to.

I carry her bag off the plane and walk her to the waiting car. Thank fuck she let me order her one instead of having her brother pick her up. We haven't talked about telling anyone what's happening between us, but I don't know if I could have faced him while her lips were still puffy from being stretched around me. With one last kiss, she slips into the car and I watch it head towards the gates before I re-board the plane for Boston.

♥

It's freezing in Massachusetts, but the girls are bundled up and we are ready to tackle one of the busiest shopping days of the year.

"Okay, girls, you know the game plan: fuel first and then we shop until we drop. Or you max out my card."

"Can we get sushi for lunch?" Camille asks, sliding into the front seat, a privilege she won through the age-old tradition of settling sibling beef with rock, paper, scissors.

"Shouldn't I get to pick lunch since she got the front seat?" Chloe whines from the back.

"Or maybe I'll pick lunch if you two can't agree. In five, four, three . . ."

"You know, sushi sounds perfect. I actually love it," Chloe rushes to say.

"That's smart. I was going to pick the oyster bar." Both girls wrinkle their nose at the suggestion.

"The oyster bar stinks. We have plans tonight. I can't show up smelling like the bottom of the bay."

"I guess it's a good thing we remembered how to compromise." I find her blue eyes in the mirror giving me an eye roll identical to the one her mom used to give me growing up.

"She just doesn't want Braxton McCabe to think she smells at his birthday party tonight." Camille snickers, recoiling to dodge Chloe's swat from over the back of her seat.

Sweet Jesus. I love these girls, but now that they are full-blown teenagers there are some things I just wasn't prepared for.

"Millie. Shut up!" Chloe shrieks at her sister.

"Ladies, I'm not sure how to handle this with the two of you, so I'm just going to resort to bribery," I tell them, crossing the Charles as we head towards the shopping district.

"What kind of bribery?" I know this is going to cost me by the eagerness in Camille's question.

"You two are going to be loving sisters and keep the shrieking to a minimum, and I'll let you help me pick out a special gift that I need to buy, but you can't go blabbing about it."

"I'm not sure this deal is worth it," Chloe sings from the back. "Who's the gift for?"

"That's a secret. Make it through lunch first and then I'll tell you."

Camille looks over her shoulder and I see Chloe nod in the rearview mirror. "We'll behave and you don't have to bribe us. We're just happy to spend time with you today," Chloe says, her eyes on me when I check the mirror again.

Suck up.

"I love you both, but we all know that's BS. Now that we've got that out of the way, are you ready to have some fun?" I give Camille's hand a squeeze when she reaches across the console.

"Will you still tell us who you're shopping for, Uncle DeDe?" Her teenage attitude long gone and replaced with a sugary sweetness that might be more alarming.

"Like you would let me get away with it if I didn't," I tease her before I turn into the parking ramp near the sushi restaurant that I know is their favorite.

The three of us sit around the table, our chairs pushed back and looking a tad green after housing the entire chef's special. The girls insisted we could do it, but when a generous helping of sushi showed up—their appetites did not.

"When did you start going by Millie?" I ask hoping a little conversation will settle our stomachs before they drag me all over the shopping district.

"The girl she likes calls her that," Chloe explains matter-of-factly.

"Does she now?"

Camille's cheeks turn pink as she fidgets with the napkin in her lap. I'm trying to play it cool because she looks ready to bolt, but I want to go to her and wrap her in a hug.

"Want to tell me about her?"

"She's nice I guess . . . " Her voice wavers, but when she looks up and finds me waiting patiently, she can't contain the smile that tugs at her lips. "She's so good at sewing, that's how I met her. She helps with our dance costumes. And she's really pretty, like *so pretty*, Uncle DeDe."

"And she likes you too." Chloe hypes up her sister, helping her confidence shine through. Millie squeezes her sister's hand appreciatively.

"I'm happy for you. If it were up to me, I'd tell you that you're both too young to date, but I guess that's not my decision. When you start dating, make sure they treat you like the princesses you are," I tell both girls.

"Now that my secret is out of the way. Are you ready to spill yours?"

The manipulation has me almost choking on the drink of water I'm taking.

"Millie, you told me you were nervous to tell him and wanted help. Then you use it to extort him?" her twin says with a laugh.

"Never change," I tell my niece, impressed by her tenacity.

"I was nervous, but it was silly. Dean's the best uncle ever."

"You don't need to butter me up, I'm going to tell you. And for the record, I'm glad you trusted me, even though it was probably scary."

"Not as scary as telling Mom. I was ready but knew she was going to get emotional, and that seemed like a lot."

"You can't say it like that. People will get the wrong idea. They were happy tears. She was so relieved that she told her instead of hiding it."

"There were still tears. Yuck. You know how uncomfy that makes me."

Me too, Millie, me too.

Once the bill is paid, the girls start on their mission. They find a new leather laptop bag for my sister and talk me into an expensive designer scarf to tie around the handle because Camille says it needs something extra. I pick out a matching portfolio and duffle bag for her, along with a little something extra that I owe her for running interference with our grandfather last time I was home. Then it's a pair of noise canceling headphones for their dad because they feel bad that he lives in such a loud house.

We're recharging with some smoothies when they corner me. They've let me skate by on promises, and I'm shocked that we made it this far.

"Okay Uncle Dean, time's up. Tell us who we're shopping for next," Chloe says before slurping up the last of her *Green Monster* smoothie.

"My friend, Mia. She's been staying with me at the cabin this winter and I wanted to get her a gift for Christmas."

"What does she like? Do you have any ideas?" Millie asks, getting straight down to it.

"That's your question?" Chloe asks, glaring at the side of her sister's face. "You're not going to ask if he likes her?" Her head whips towards me, blond curls sticking out from under her beanie. "Do you like her? Please tell me she's your girlfriend."

"I wouldn't let her stay with me if I didn't like her." It's not enough to deter them.

"So, she's your girlfriend and you live together? Why are we just hearing about this?" Millie only fuels her sister's curiosity.

"Is it true, Uncle DeDe? You have a beautiful girlfriend who lives with you, and we get to help pick out her present?"

"Pump the breaks, twister sisters. She's very pretty, but she's not my girlfriend. We're just friends . . . but I do like her."

"So, you want her to be your girlfriend," Millie says, like it's the most obvious conclusion and fuck if it doesn't send me reeling.

Do I want her to be my girlfriend? I've never wanted that before, but even if I did it's not a good idea; she'd only end up disappointed.

"What does she like, besides you, of course?" Chloe continues, pulling me out of my thoughts with her rapid fire inquisition.

"Mia's a writer, a fantastic one, actually. Sometimes she has a hard time seeing herself the way everyone else does. She likes coffee in the morning, but prefers tea in the afternoon. She's trying to cut back on caffeine, but the tea she drinks is caffeinated. Somehow, she still justifies it as the lesser of the two evils." I chuckle mostly to myself. "Her outlook on life is inspiring, and she always sees the best in people. I've never met anyone more determined. I taught her how to snowboard and, even though she was scared, she never gave up."

"Okay, wow. So you *really* like her," Chloe says with a goofy smile on her face. "Where should we start?"

"I have a few ideas. Let's start at the bookstore."

"Yeah, no. That's not very romantic. We should go to the jewelry store and get her a cute bracelet or a pair of earrings," Millie says, her brow furrowed.

"*Ooh!* How about a ring!" Chloe claps hands together excitedly.

"Not a ring. No jewelry." Their faces fall. "I want to make her life a little easier. Find her a gift she sees every day and reminds her I believe in her. Because she's always doing that for me—telling me I'm more than just a grump."

"I like her already," Chloe says, dropping her empty cup in the recycling container as we walk toward the bookstore. "But are you sure she doesn't want jewelry?"

I'm not sure of anything right now. But rather than tell her that, I hold the door for Millie, who ducks under my arm, still working on her blueberry muffin smoothie.

"She seems really smart and I love your plan," she says, joining her sister on the sidewalk.

By the time I drop them back off with Gavin, the SUV is filled with gifts for Mia, Natalie, and Gavin, and includes extras they talked me into buying for my mom and brother. Gavin and my sister deserve a medal for doing this every day. Teen girls are exhausting. I need a stiff drink and some peace and quiet.

Normally I would head to my hotel, but my mom insists I stay with them during the holidays. Actually, she insists *every* time I visit, but Christmas is the only time I give in. If I'm lucky, there won't be any unexpected visitors tonight, and I'll be able to unwind without a confrontation with my grandfather or dad.

♥

Bringing the tumbler to my lips I let the velvety liquor wash over my tongue and sink back into the plush leather chair. Across the room, the fireplace crackles. The family room is my favorite room in the house—ironic, considering the reason. It's the least formal, which means my grandfather hates sitting in it when he's here, so it's become my own personal sanctuary. Tonight it's peaceful, but glaringly empty. My dad's locked in his study—avoiding interacting with me at all costs, and my mom went to bed about an hour ago. Earlier I was craving solitude, but now a loneliness I'm no longer used to settles into my bones, making me uncomfortable.

Out the window, I see a black SUV pull up to the curb. The headlights dim and moments later the front door opens slowly. My sister slips through, moving straight to the keypad to disarm the alarm. "No need. I haven't set it yet," I say to Natalie's back.

She clutches her chest when she turns around and spots me. "Jesus, why are you sitting in the dark like a creeper?"

"The real question is how you survive those two girls without sitting in a quiet, dark room at the end of every day." I grab a glass and fill it with some of my grandfather's favorite, most expensive, whiskey.

"Pour me a double, really stick it to the old man," she says with a grin. "You can help me wrap Christmas presents and tell me about your day with the girls."

"You're still hiding their gifts here? Aren't they old enough not to look for them now?" I cap the decanter, passing the glass to Natalie when she comes to stand in front of me.

"You tell me. You spent the day with them. Have they lost their sense of curiosity in their teen years?" She brings the crystal glass to her lips, taking a sip of the amber liquid.

"No, they most certainly have not. I'll help you grab everything."

She grimaces, giving me an apologetic look before saying, "They're in dad's study. I don't suppose he's gone to bed yet."

"Nope," I say, setting my whiskey glass on the table. "It's fine. I can be a mature adult for a few minutes."

We creep down the hall, where she lightly knocks on the door before turning the knob and poking her head inside.

"Hey, pumpkin. Son, good to see you." My dad stands from the desk when we step inside, shoving his hands in his pockets. "I assume you're here for the goods." He pulls open the double doors to the closet, which is overflowing with presents.

"Do you two need help? I'm about done here and was going to head to bed, but spending time with the two of you sounds better. We can break into Victor's whiskey."

My sister laughs lightly. "Dean already beat you to it, Dad."

"We've got it. You can go to bed."

His lips tilt down in a frown at my dismal. But he relents, handing Natalie two overflowing totes.

"Do you mind if I talk to your brother for a minute? I'll send him down with the rest and then let you two be."

I fucking mind.

When Natalie turns my way, there's an encouraging smile plastered on her face. Emotional blackmail, just like her daughters. I sigh, resigned to my fate. "I got the rest of it. Be right down."

"Should we sit?" my dad asks, sweeping his hand out towards the same couch he's had in here since I was a teen. I look at it with disdain, wondering how many indiscretions have happened here over the years. Not a fucking chance I'm going near that thing.

"I'll pass." He follows my gaze to the couch.

"I've never . . . this is why I wanted to talk. We've been doing this for years, Son. It's only hurting your mom to see us with this rift between us. But now isn't the time for us to hash it out. She loves the holidays and having you home means so much to her—both of us—but next time you're home, I'd like us to sit down and talk. I miss my son." His voice breaks on his last word and it only stokes the contempt burning inside me.

The rage I expect never comes. I'm too broken and cold inside to even feel it anymore. The hate I carry around for him is still there, but it's duller. Not sharp and fiery like it was when I was younger. I'll never forgive him for what he's done, but I see the toll our severed relationship has caused my mom and sister. Not to mention everything it's still taking from me.

"There's nothing you can say to me that's going to make me forgive you," I tell him, grabbing the last three totes and turning to leave the room.

"Then you have nothing to lose by listening," he asserts, following me to the door. "Let me try, for your mother—even if you never forgive me—I've hurt her enough. If there's a chance that I can make this better for her . . . for you. I have to try. In February, when you're home for your grandfather's birthday party, we'll talk."

"Fine. I'll listen, but I'm doing this for them. Not for you," I say coldly before leaving him standing in the doorway.

"As I make my way back to the family room I find Natalie, surrounded by a pile of gifts, wrapping paper, tape, and scissors. It's like Santa's workshop in here. The cords of *Nsync's *Merry Christmas, Happy Holidays* play softly over her phone. She adopted this as her personal Christmas anthem in middle school and it stuck. At this point, I've heard the song millions of times.

"That's not a jolly face. Everything okay?"

Dropping the totes, I sit next to her on the floor. I've always tried to shield my siblings from the fallout of my relationship with Dad, but they know we've grown apart. Even if I kept *why* a secret. That was part of the deal after all; they can never know what I do. My grandfather made sure of that.

"It's fine. Whose presents are we wrapping first?"

"These are for Gavin." The love for her husband is written all over her glowing face at just the mention of his name.

"You hide his presents too?"

"Are you kidding? He's the *worst*," she says with a laugh. "Where do you think the girls got it from?"

I look at her dumbly.

"Oh, fuck off! I'm not that bad." She adds the last piece of tape to the paper, setting it to the side. "Hand me that one."

"Two words. *Rock Tumbler*." That makes her grin spread. And if I'm honest, it makes me long for a time before my family was split in two.

"Mom still holds that over my head. Every year she brings it up like I found it last Christmas, not twenty-some years ago."

I pass her the gift she's pointing to and grab one of my own holding it up. "Dylan." She nods and I slice through the wrapping paper, cutting a square that a fancy charging station will fit in.

"So, Millie told you about Anabella." Her eyes stay on the gift she's wrapping, but I can see the corners of her lips lift into a small smile.

"She did." I tape the side of the wrapping paper and look up to find her watching me. "I'm so damn proud of her. And honored she trusted me."

My sister swipes at her cheek with the back of her hand. "Me too. You're the best brother and uncle. The girls and I are lucky to have you." Natalie's not overly emotional—she's always been ruled by logic. But she's quick to brush her tears away and refocus. "They also told me about your girlfriend."

"Is nothing sacred? We made a deal over sushi like civilized humans." I set Dylan's present on the finished pile.

"They were so giddy about it. She sounds amazing."

"I hate to burst your bubble, but she's not my girlfriend. She's Hendrix's sister and we're friends. She's staying with me because she needed a quiet place to write this winter."

"Okay, so you're delusional now. That's new." She pulls two more presents off her piles and tosses one to me. "What happened to your rules? Your teammate's sister? Isn't that a little risky considering you don't do relationships?"

"It's not like that. Besides, Mia knows what this is. We talked about it and agreed it would be temporary." The words taste awful coming out of my mouth. They don't even sound convincing to me.

"Chloe and Millie think you're in *love*. They can't wait to stand up in your wedding."

"Of course they do. Look, I like Mia. A lot, actually, but there's no future there." She latches on to the admission like the world class trial lawyer she is.

"What's keeping you two from having a future?" She leans in over the wrapping paper, looking way too intense for this line of questioning. My palms sweat as I try to come up with all the reasons that seemed so logical a few weeks ago.

"Because I'm not built for a relationship. And she deserves better." It's weak, and I'm not even surprised when she rebuttals me.

"So be better. If you really like this woman, take care of whatever bullshit baggage you think you have and just be happy, DeDe." Her shoulders lift in a shrug like it's that simple.

♥

The plane touches down in Denver and all I can think about is that I'm back in the same city as Mia. The conversations with my sister and dad have been swirling through my head non-stop for the past three days.

I don't know what I'm going to do about either of them yet, if anything. There's only one thing I can focus on, and that's Mia. We've texted a few times over the last few days and I know she's lying low to work on her books today. Hendrix and Poppy are taking Nana and Marv to a play tonight as their Christmas gift, giving us the perfect opportunity to see each other without anyone knowing.

CHAPTER 23

MIA

After a week of almost non-stop togetherness with my family, I'm overdue for some time alone to work on my books. All the time at Dean's cabin over the last month has made me used to a laid back, quiet environment. My family is anything but.

For the first time in my adult life, I let work take a back seat to the holidays and soaked up the time with them.

The first draft for my standalone book is almost ready for my editor, and I'm really proud of the way it's turning out. I've left behind some of my usual writing clutches, and amped up the passion and the angst. The only thing left is to cross my fingers that my editor doesn't send it back with a laundry list of changes.

The novella I'm working on still needs a little more finessing, but it's coming along. During my time in Telluride, I've let go of a lot of the hangups and fear that were holding me back. But as much as I'd like to take all the credit, I can't. Without Dean's confidence in me—his gentle pushes to step outside my comfort zone—and the *very* helpful physical inspiration I wouldn't be nearly as far as I am now. Mostly I just care less about what people expect or what I should do. It's freeing to do what I want for once.

Below the table, my knee bounces nervously as I glance up at the clock. I'm answering emails from my team because I'm wound too tight to write any more today. That ship sailed about an hour ago when I realized it was almost time to head over to the penthouse for dinner with Dean.

Closing my laptop I pick up my phone, open up my contacts, and hover over the group chat with the girls. I could really use someone to talk to, but things get complicated with Poppy involved. She would absolutely keep my confidence if I asked her to, but she shouldn't have to, and I don't want to put either of us in that position.

Navigating out of the group chat I pull up Indie's contact and hit call. She picks up almost immediately.

"Hey! It's about time you called to give me an update." Her cheerful voice greets me.

"What makes you so sure that's what I'm calling for?"

That only makes her laugh. "You'd have to be stupid not to see the attraction between the two of you. All the sexual tension in St. John's had me second guessing my ban on sleeping with baseball players. You can't tell me the cabin can contain all that heat without eventually combusting."

"I can't even be mad that you're right, because it's so fucking hot."

"Tell me more. I enjoy being right. In fact, it's pretty much my favorite thing."

"It's like his lips were made to kiss. I thought I'd had good kisses, but they were nothing compared to Dean. Every kiss makes my toes curl," I admit to a chorus of smug humming on the other end of the phone.

"So, is this a thing now?" Indie asks when she's done boasting.

"It's not-not a thing, but it's also not a thing."

She huffs through the line. "That sounds stupid. Explain."

"I guess you could call it friends with benefits, but nothing about that really feels like it fits what we're doing. It feels too unimportant," I hedge, trying to figure out how to explain it. "I like him and we started as friends, but it feels like more than that. More like a relationship with a deadline, where we have to go our separate ways at the end."

"Listen, you know I'm the queen of detachment. If that's what you both want, I fully support this, but why couldn't it be more?" she challenges.

"It's complicated . . . Dean's complicated. We live on opposite sides of the country and even if we didn't, he's been up front about his stance on relationships."

Indie's silent for a moment before she says, "Life isn't easy, and lots of people make long distance work. I'm not saying you should push for more. But I care about both of you, and I'm just saying I don't want to see either of you get hurt when this ends if you're both just too stubborn to make it work."

Confiding in Indie feels good.

Moving on to lighter topics, I show her the outfit I picked out for New Year's Eve and we contemplate what we would do if she was going to be in Denver for the holiday.

The fluttering in my stomach accelerates with each chime of the elevator as it carries me up to the penthouse. Through the parting doors, I catch a glimpse of him waiting for me, with his back leaning against the opposite wall. By the time the door slides open, we're both on the move and I may as well have wings with the way I take off towards him.

"Fuck, Dreamer, I missed you." He buries his nose in my hair, his thick arms wrapping around me as we stand in the hallway outside his penthouse.

"A girl could get used to a welcome like this. I'm glad you didn't make me wait until New Year's Eve to see you. It seems I've grown attached to having you around every day," I admit sheepishly.

When he releases me from the hug, I worry maybe I said too much.

Am I allowed to miss him, given the boundaries we've put in place?

I get my answer in the reverent way the backs of his fingers trail down my cheek before he takes my hand and leads me inside.

The only other time I was here, his place was filled with teammates and caterers, but with just us here, it feels cavernous and lonely. My gut twists knowing he's here all alone during the season, hating every second of it.

"I thought we could order food in. What are you in the mood for?"

You? Is that an acceptable answer?

"Know what I've missed the most while being in the mountains?" I watch as he bends to dig around in the fridge—giving me a view that makes me salivate. This man is even more attractive to me than he was before we left Telluride. Was his ass always that round? I don't remember his shirt fitting so nicely, highlighting each bulge of his arms and shoulders, either.

"It's got to be the variety of conversation you get in the city." When he turns around, he's got two beer bottles in his hand. "Beer? Or I can raid the bar in the game room if you want something else."

"Beer is perfect. And no, it was actually kind of overwhelming being back around other people. It made me realize how much I've thrived in a slower-paced environment. By the end of the day yesterday, I felt like I was crawling out of my skin with the constant buzz of people and the non-stop flurry of activities. But none of that was what I was thinking." I grab the cold beer from his outstretched hand and bring it to my lips. "I miss tacos, Dean. Like at a cellular level. The things I would do for juicy tacos with all the fixings would make you blush."

"The kind with lime wedges and cilantro," he says, stepping into my space and giving me what can only be described as bedroom eyes, the green color shadowed by his half-mast lids. A shiver runs up my spine as he closes the distance between us.

"Yes," I moan and I don't know if it's from the way he's talking about tacos, or the way he's looking at me like I'm everything he wants.

"With Cotija cheese sprinkled over the top."

My back hits the island, his imposing body pressing me against the edge—hips pinning me in place, he brings his hands down on either side of me. I almost lose the grip on my beer when his lips drop to my neck and he sucks the skin.

"Yeah, just like that," I gasp as he gently kisses a path up the side of my neck to my ear.

"And maybe some of that cabbage slaw and fancy chipotle sauce. That's what you miss the most?" he whispers into my ear.

"I miss it so much." My voice is raspy and dripping with lust. I bring my free hand to his chest and run it up the hard planes until it loops around the back of his neck.

"Even more than you missed this?" He takes my beer from my hand and sets it on the counter before pressing his pelvis into me again, letting me feel how hard he is. *Thank God*, I thought I was the only one in the room who was turned on by talking about food.

"Hard to say. It's been too long. I've almost forgotten how good it can be." I have to fight to keep my voice from shaking.

"I guess I'll have to remind you." He gives me one barely there kiss that has me leaning in for more and steps back, while I stand there left wanting. "Tacos it is. I know just the place." He digs his phone out of the front pocket of his pants.

"I take back everything nice I've ever said about you. You are the worst," I say under my breath. He ignores my quip, ordering a smorgasbord of food through a delivery app for us to share, and then takes my hand and leads me out to the living room. My feet stop in front of the enormous windows and I drop his hand, moving closer. The glass wall wraps around the corner of the room, providing sweeping views of the city and snow-capped Rockies with the sunlight giving way to the pinks and orange of dusk. It's breathtaking and heartbreaking at the same time, knowing this place gives him so little comfort.

When I turn back to him, he's standing there, holding a perfectly wrapped present in crisp plaid paper and topped with an expensive-looking velvet bow.

I waver between excitement and dread because I came empty-handed—like an asshole—which he claims to be, but is clearly not. By the wrapping alone, it's easy to see how much care and thought he put into it.

"Before you even start. I know I didn't have to, but I wanted to. It's nothing extravagant, much to my nieces' disappointment. If it were up to them, we would have gone straight to the jewelry store," he says, pulling me down onto the couch next to him when I don't move to sit on my own. "Mia—"

"You went shopping for me with your nieces and told them about me?" His actions are contradictory to everything he's told me about what this is between us. Everything I told Indie on the phone seems so silly now. "Why would you do that?"

He rubs the back of his neck. "It felt right, and I trusted my gut. I'm operating on instinct. The last relationship I was in was with my high school girlfriend. I'm sorry if it was the wrong move."

"No, that's not it at all. It's just I feel like the biggest jerk for coming without a gift. It's not because I didn't think about it. I did—a lot, actually—but I didn't want to overstep and make you uncomfortable. It's not like you're my boyfriend." I hate the words the second they come out of my mouth. They make my chest tighten with discomfort because it feels like a lie.

"Hey, don't spiral on me. I don't need more than what you've already given me. You see something in me I haven't been able to see in myself for a long time. I'm not sure I deserve the faith you've placed in me, but I know I want to try to earn it. Let me start by giving you this?" He sets the present in my lap with a look of sincerity on his face.

My thumb coasts over the luxurious fabric of the bow. "This is fancy. I wouldn't have guessed those gigantic hands were capable of such delicate work."

He huffs out a low laugh. "You know damn well what these hands can do, but I can't take credit. My sister, Natalie, wrapped it for me."

The hope that swells in my heart is dangerous. This isn't supposed to be like this. We've had this discussion, and both agreed to this arrangement.

Even knowing that, I can't deny that I like the idea of there being more between us someday. It would be smart to protect myself—both of us—by remembering that this is nothing more than two friends making each other feel good.

"Did you tell her about me?" I avert my eyes, tugging the navy fabric free of its knot.

"Not the details, but all the important parts. She knows we're friends and that you're staying with me. I told her how much I enjoy your company. Which she told me was clearly bullshit because there weren't any presents in my pile for any of the guys."

Dean is a lot of things. He can be distant and come off as aloof, but he's not shy—not usually. His words are carefully weighed, like he's unsure of the confession.

Look at me, throwing Dean Harrison off his game.

Ever so carefully, I slide my finger under each piece of tape before removing the paper in one piece and carefully folding it.

"You gonna open that present today, Grams?" Dean asks, taking the thick paper from me and setting it on his coffee table.

"I was raised by my grandmother. Where do you think I learned it from?" Wriggling the top loose I stare down at the box. He didn't just get me one thing. There are several small gifts wrapped in tissue paper resting on top of what looks to be a blanket.

"Don't worry, I won't torture you by saving the tissue paper," I tease, ripping into the first gift. It's a beautifully engraved Post-it Note holder. Running my finger over the grooves in the wood I read the words scrawled across it: "Shine so bright that it burns their fucking eyes."

It's so perfect and ridiculous that I don't have time to stop myself from snorting. "I'm not sure what I expected, but this wasn't it."

"Yeah, well, you seem to go through a lot of post-it notes when you're working through an idea. This is to remind you how capable you are, no matter where you're writing." He leaves the real meaning dangling between us. *When I'm not there to tell you.*

"I love it, thank you." Setting it off to the side, I grab the next ball of tissue paper. This one feels breakable and, by its cylindrical shape. I'm pretty sure I know what it is, but he's surprised me more than once and I wouldn't put it past him to do it again.

Once I've freed the gift from its wrappings, I turn the mug over in my hands. It's a tarot card mug that features a pair of mystic looking hands levitating a typewriter. "You got me a girly mug."

"I did, but I'm giving it to you conditionally. It stays at my cabin, so it's there for you to use when you come back to visit."

Someone grab the paper towel and clean up the mess I've made because this man has melted me into a puddle right here on his couch. He's got more disposable income than he knows what to do with. He could have just thrown money at something flashy, yet, these simple, thoughtful gifts mean more to me than something expensive and thoughtless.

The next gift is actually kind of fancy, an electric kettle and a warming coaster for my coffee and tea with smart technology to keep my tea at my preferred temperature.

"No more microwaving your tea," he explains when I open it.

"Maybe I like it that way." I don't. It's a habit that I picked up in college because I was the only girl in my dorm that drank tea. This is something I never would've spent my money on. I stop and look at them every time I'm in a high end department store. It's not that I don't have plenty of my own money, but I'm excessively frugal. I'm always afraid that my readers will find something they like better and abandon me—leaving me with nothing.

At the bottom of the box, is the coziest blanket known to mankind. I lift the plush fabric out of the box to my face nuzzling against it and sighing at how perfect it is.

"This comes back to the cabin, temporarily, at least. You hate my wool blanket."

"I really do."

"It's too scratchy for your flawless skin. Plus, you're like a living, breathing popsicle, and I want you to be comfortable while you're staying with me."

"You might be the best gift giver ever. The guys really missed out," I say, leaning across the pile of goodies scattered across my lap to press my lips to his.

"I think they'll survive," he says, returning my kiss with one of his own. There are too many things in my way to kiss him the way I want. So I pack everything back up with the same care I unwrapped the presents with.

"Will they? Dom can be a wee bit dramatic." I hold my thumb and pointer finger up with only a sliver of space between them. "And my brother would be so pissed to know that I outrank him after a month."

"Speaking of your brother. What have you told him about us?" He takes the box from my lap and moves it to the coffee table, pulling me closer so I'm pressed up against his side.

"Nothing. It's none of his business, and what would be the point?" I turn to face him on the couch, my fingers slipping under the hem of his sleeve where it's stretched around his bicep. This conversation is really dragging down my post-gift high and the only fix is feeling his skin against mine. "What we have is special, even if it's only for now. I don't want to explain that to everyone and justify our decision. Indie knows, I called her today, I needed to tell someone. Hendrix would be worried—about both of us. I'd rather just enjoy the time we have together without everyone else getting in the way."

"I don't want to lie to him. But I won't let anyone fuck with the time we have together, Mia. So if you think it's best not to tell him, I agree."

My forehead drops to his. "Thank you for the gifts, they were perfect. And thank you for letting me handle my brother the way I want."

"You deserve the very best, Mia James. Earlier, when I said I didn't need anything from you, I lied. Let me kiss you. It's been too damn long, and I fucking missed the way you melt into me when my tongue sinks into your mouth."

"You never have to ask," I tell him, kissing along his sharp jawline.

"Never is a long time, Mia." He tangles his fingers in my hair pulling my head back to look at me but I don't want to take it back because no one has ever understood me the way Dean does. He sees me. The things I see as flaws he embraces. It seems impossible that there's anyone out there that's going to encourage me and believe in me more the way he does.

"I said what I said. Take what you want from me."

He groans and flips us both, pressing me into the couch, and then kisses me so hard that my lips are going to be swollen. We barely come up for air. All hands and tongues, grinding against each other like two desperate teens. The doorman has to call twice before we hear the notification that the food is here.

When he leaves me on the couch to go answer the door, he looks like I feel. Wrecked. His dark hair points in every direction and his shirt is a wrinkled mess from the way I fisted it when he started rocking his hips against me. The tent in his pants is obvious and not going anywhere, so he simply pokes his head out the cracked door to grab the delivery.

Closing my eyes I try to pull myself together enough to eat a meal without mauling him. This is how it's been between us for the past few weeks. We kiss and grope—coming together, a mess of mouths and hands. But we still haven't crossed that line and had sex. I'm not sure how much longer I can stand it.

The sound of his soft footsteps has my eyelids fluttering open and I see him standing over me with the bag of food on the coffee table.

"Let's eat out here." My fingers wrap around his outreached hand, and he helps me up from the couch. "Can you grab a blanket out of the closet?" He tilts his head towards it as he shifts the coffee table to the side.

The smell of lime and cilantro fill the living room as Dean unpacks the food while I shake out the blanket, letting it drift to the floor. Containers and plates litter the picnic-like set-up in front of us, our backs resting against the couch as we build my dream tacos.

"Was it good to see everyone after being stuck with just me for the past month?" Dean asks as he scoops a spoonful of barbacoa into his shell.

"It was, but after three days of togetherness, I missed our little bubble." I squeeze a lime over the fish taco on my plate. "Everyone was all coupled up.

Nana and Marv were attached at the geriatric hips. I swear those two have the libidos of horny teens. They put you and I to shame."

"There's an image I won't soon forget. And Dreamer, no one dry humps on a couch better than we do. That kind of dedication takes youthful joints." Some sauce from his taco leaks through the shell and trickles down his thumb. He brings the messy digit to his mouth and wraps his lips around it, sucking it clean.

It's too much. I almost lose my wits and snatch a tortilla off the plate to use as a fan because holy erotica Batman, did it just get hot in here?

With the audacity of a man who knows exactly what he just did, Dean continues, "For the record, I'm just about done taking my time with you."

My vagina may as well be weeping with joy because as much fun as it was to learn all the ways we could get each other hot and bothered, I don't want to waste any more of the winter. February might seem a long way off, but spring training will be here soon, and I don't want to go any longer without knowing what it's like when he finally lets go of the control he's been so carefully exercising.

CHAPTER 24

DEAN

"This fucking guy," Dom says in the worst Boston accent I've ever heard. "Where's the beard, mountain man? I'm disappointed in you. I was hoping you'd go full grizzly and you show up with barely a five o'clock shadow." His hand strokes at imaginary facial hair.

"If I covered all this up, you might forget that I'm so much better looking than you. And we can't let your ego go unchecked like that." I deadpan. "Hey, Xav. How was your Christmas?"

Xav chuckles at my dismissal of Dom. "Good, man. Took my parents and sister on vacation and celebrated in Greece. We just got back last night."

Vivi, the center director for Double Play, breezes through the lobby heading toward her office when she sees us. "Hey, Dean, Dom," she says cheerfully, greeting both of us. I've been dragging Dom here with me since I joined the board, but this is Xavier's first time here to help with a camp. He works more closely with a childhood cancer charity. Today, he'll help us teach the kids drills and work with them to hone their skills on the field. We'll pack as much in as we can over break so these kids don't fall behind their peers who take private lessons all year.

"You must be Xavier Kingsley," she guesses, reaching her hand out to him.

"Always nice to meet a fan," Xavier says doing his best impression of a fuck boy. Dom chokes on his laughter, but I just roll my lips together, waiting for the explosion that I know is coming.

Vivi's all of five-foot-four, with a look that reads innocent, but after working closely on the board with her, I know better. She's the youngest of six—the only girl—and can put the fear of God into teenagers and city council members alike when properly motivated.

She glances at me, the question written all over her face. *Is this guy for real?*

"Dom and Dean, you can head back and join the rest of the guys. Cruz and Hendrix are already back there. Unless, Xavier, do you need one of them to stay back with you to help you complete the paperwork? It seems to me that you're in the middle of an identity crisis and think you're someone far more impressive than you actually are."

Dom's the first to crack when we're out of earshot of the lobby. Through his laughter, he asks, "Do you think she'll marry me?"

"You've really got a type nailed down."

"What can I say? I like them with claws," he remarks proudly as we approach Hendrix and Cruz, who are setting up cones in the center of the gym for a drill.

"What can we do to help before the kids get here?" I ask looking around the space—they have most of the fielding drill ready. "Want us to pull the cage down and set up tees?"

"Yeah. We're almost done here and then it's just setting up for hitting and pulling out the new equipment. The shipment of gear you talked the team into donating made it just in time," Cruz says with a knowing smile, as if he wants to remind me I'm not the asshole I project to the world. He doesn't know that I make a choice to keep secrets every single day—things my family has a right to know, but continue to protect my dad and grandfather from the fallout of their choices. Working with Double Play doesn't erase the truth, but it eases my conscience a bit.

I stalk toward the cage, the compliment grating on my nerves. I don't deserve it, but I'm getting pretty good at taking things I don't deserve. Images flash through my head of pink lips parted in a moan as dark waves fall over her face. Yeah, she's way too good for me, but I couldn't stop the path we're on if I tried.

Four hours later, we're huddled around the kids, closing out the camp with them. We go around the circle, each of them telling us something they learned today that will make them a better player. Ronnie looks at me from across the circle when it's his turn.

He's been coming to Double Play for a few years now. He's a phenomenal athlete, but his attitude isn't always the best. I've worked closely with him and coaxed him out of his shell through bonding over playing first base. We've come a long way, but he's still guarded with the other kids and didn't trust his teammates today. It showed when he got frustrated that his second baseman hesitated and missed an opportunity for an out. I pulled him aside for a chat between drills.

"I'm going to work on controlling what I can and stepping up to help my teammates if they're struggling. If I see one of my teammates is down, the best thing I can do for my team is try to bring them back up."

"You can never have too many leaders out there," Cruz says, giving me a nod. "That's great advice. Dean is one of the greatest first baseman I've ever played with and it's not just because he's an excellent ballplayer, but because he wants every single guy on the field to be just as successful as we are as a team."

With the boys cleared out, we pick up the last of the gear and equipment before heading to Draft for a late lunch. This is the one thing I miss about being in Denver during the off season—getting to see these guys all the time. Not surprisingly, Dom makes sure I don't forget about him by filling our group chat with nonsense at least once a week.

Two hours later, we're all caught up on whatever one another has been up to. Well, mostly. I kept the conversation about my winter very surface level. When we walk out the door an hour later, Dom hangs back by me as we walk toward where we parked.

"Want to meet up for a run tomorrow and you can tell me what's *actually* been going on with you?" he asks, cocking an eyebrow.

"Not sure what you're talking about."

He stops walking letting the other fall further ahead. "And I thought Xavier was going to win the trophy for the biggest idiot today—no, you know what, he still does. But you're a close second."

"Does seven work at Cherry Creek?" I give in, suggesting the trail that he prefers to run on.

♥

Dom's facing a lamppost, his toes elevated against the base, while his heel digs into the pavement, stretching his calf out when I get to the park the next morning. I'm not even surprised to see him in a pair of shorts, despite the fact that it's the middle of winter and it's cold as shit out here.

"You're insane, you know that, right? I hope you freeze your balls off." I flick his ear lobe, which is smartly sticking out from under a beanie.

"I didn't want you to be the only one risking his balls for a good time." I hate the fucking smirk that spreads across his face because if Dom can pick up on the fact that we're hiding something, Hendrix could just as easily figure it out, and Mia didn't want anyone else involved.

"Not sure what you're talking about." Growing impatient with him already, I jog down the trail, heading through the park.

He's right there at my side a moment later, looking at me expectantly. Sometimes it's exhausting, being friends with him. We're polar opposites in so many ways. He's like a golden retriever puppy, eager and carefree. His life has been a cakewalk, and he'd be the first to admit it. People look at me and see the same thing—the upper class family, the lifestyle afforded to me. They can't understand why Dom is Buddy the Elf level cheerful and I'm me.

What I wouldn't give to be more like him. Unburdened by these secrets, by the decisions the adults around me made when I was a teen. Maybe it's why I've clung to our friendship since we both landed here in Denver. I'd give anything to be as carefree as Dom, especially now.

"Fuck, you're impossible," I gripe, picking up the pace.

"Impossible . . . not to love." He sticks right by my side, like he's always done.

"Want to fill me in on what you think I'm doing that would put my dick in jeopardy?" We pass by the partially frozen river on the mostly empty path.

"If I found out one of my teammates was fucking my sister, I'd be waiting in the dark by his bed before he even cracked open his scummy eyeballs to serve him his nuts for breakfast."

"Jesus. That's a truly disturbing visual, but justifiable since your sisters are nineteen and seven."

Do I plan on continuing to skirt the accusation he's making? Abso-fuck-ing-lutely.

"Don't be an idiot. We both know you're probably the smartest guy on the team. Why the hell would you think it's a good idea to go ball deep in your teammates' sister?"

I think the fuck not.

Dom yelps in surprise when I skid on the slick blacktop, gripping the neck of his shirt and pulling him along with me. The shocked look melts off his face morphing into a pleased one—cocky smile front and center.

"Asshole," I grunt, releasing him—pissed that he played me so well. Pacing the trail, I glare at him, knowing he's got me now. "You're a douche, and that was your one get out of jail free card. If you ever talk about Mia like that again, I'll be the one waiting for you in the dark. Your own personal nightmare."

"Shit, Dean. What the hell are you doing?"

"I don't know, but it's not what you think." I tug on the strands on my hair.

"Cool. So you're not respectfully screwing Hendrix's sister into the mattress while she's staying with you?"

"No!" I bark back.

"Disrespectfully, then? I can see tha—"

One swift step later and I'm in his face again. The shithead just chuckles. "Shut the fuck up, Dom."

"Okay, okay. Give me a break. I didn't realize she had you all up in your feels. I'm happy for you, man. You found someone to make your stone heart go pitter patter."

"What?" Now I'm the one laughing in his face. "That's not it."

Except . . . wait. Is he right?

"Lovely, we're in denial now, too. That's fun. It'll go over even better when Hen finds out and you can't even admit your feelings for her."

My pacing becomes more furious as he continues poking at me.

"Wearing a hole in the blacktop might be keeping you warm, buddy, but I'm in shorts. Think you can tell me what's going on with you and Mia while we continue this run? Preferably before my nuts drop out of the bottom of my shorts and roll away, two ice cubes destined to live at the bottom of the river forever?"

"What the fuck is wrong with you?" I ask before I continue down the path. "And we aren't screwing," I start.

"I get it. You're making sweet, oblivious love."

"Do you want me to talk? Or should we just keep letting your nonsense derail us?" Out of the side of my eye, I see him pinch his fingers together and zip them across his lips. *About damn time.* "We haven't had sex."

"Yet . . ."

I glare at him and he rolls his lips inward.

"We're taking it slow because I don't want to fuck this up. You're right, Mia's got me feeling things I've never felt before. Which sucks, by the way.

We agreed to be 'friends with benefits' for the winter, but there's no future beyond that."

"I know this is usually your line, but you're an idiot."

"She doesn't want anyone to know. Besides Indie, you're the only person who does."

His hand goes to his heart. "You went and told my future wife first."

"Now who's risking their balls?"

Dom just shrugs in return. "Totally worth it."

"Indie told her about the kiss a while ago, so Mia confided in her about what's happening with us," I tell him, watching as his shoulder tense up next to me. "But she doesn't know about everything else with Indie. Not yet."

"You should probably tell her the whole story. I know your grandpa buried it, but things like that have a way of coming back to haunt you."

"I know and I will. But I want to talk to Indie first."

"She loves Mia. You saw how tight they got in St. John's, but she'll be here for New Years. Delilah and Poppy were talking about it the other day. Your girl doesn't know. They thought it would be fun to surprise her since it's her birthday."

"Hold the fuck up. It's her birthday?" I practically roar.

"Yep," he says, popping the "P."

Well, she's in so much trouble for keeping that from me, especially since now I can't even acknowledge it without ruining the surprise.

"Oh, I know that look. I think Mia is going to owe me a thank-you card. But you should talk to Indie, then make sure she's cool with you telling Mia about the picture. She'll probably want to be there when you tell her or have the chance to talk to her face-to-face after."

"Yeah, that's a solid idea," I agree as we reach the fork in the trail and go left to loop back to where we started.

♥

My nerves haven't been this frayed since my first major league appearance. I bring the tumbler of whiskey that I'm using to keep my hands and mouth busy to my lips, but my eyes stay trained on the door to Dom's house.

"Waiting on your girl?" Indie asks, pouring a whiskey of her own from the decanter in front of me.

"She kicked me out of Lilah's apartment so she could get ready in peace," I grumble, annoyed we couldn't ride over together and frustrated that she wouldn't let me hang out while she got ready.

"Smart girl. She texted me a picture of what she's wearing tonight. You two wouldn't have made it out of the apartment. It's going to be a long night for you, buddy." She pats me on the shoulder, throwing back her whiskey. "Do me a favor and don't let me do anything stupid tonight."

"He has a name." I deadpan, causing her to snicker. "We should talk before she gets here." I glance around the house. "Patio?"

Indie leads the way to the back of the house and I follow her out the door, draping my jacket over her shoulders when we step outside.

"Thanks." She shrugs, pulling it tighter around her and lifting her long ebony curls free. "Was she mad about the kiss?"

"No. She understood it wasn't anything more. But I haven't told her anything else—about the picture or the ride home. That's your story to tell, and I didn't want to betray your trust, but Indie, I've got to tell her." Her dark eyes soften in the dim light, her head nodding along slightly as I talk. "I'm not good enough for her, and I know that. But if I can keep this from hurting her, I need to do that. And I don't want to come between you two either. I'm just trying to do the right thing."

"I'd like to talk to her, make sure she and I are okay—after you, of course." She turns to leave but stops to look me in the eye when she says, "Don't sell yourself short. You're not as bad as you think, and you're taking good care of our girl." She slides the coat off, handing it back to me before slipping back inside.

Swirling the brown liquid in my glass I spend a minute soaking in the cool air before I turn back toward the apartment to head in. All the air whooshes out of my lungs when I spot Mia standing in the center of the living room, her eyes on me through the glass door, looking like sin wrapped in the sweetest package.

The black, one-piece outfit she's wearing is long sleeve, but that's the only modest thing about it. There's a strip of black fabric that wraps around her neck, the same way I want my hand to later tonight. Below that, the top is split down the center of her chest in a deep V, her small tits barely covered. When she shifts on her feet, light catches the jewelry she's wearing. Only I'm not sure that's the right word for it. I've never seen anything like it. Gold chains lay delicately across the swell of her breasts. My eyes follow the path of the shimmering metal until it disappears under the lush fabric and back down to where the metal meets right over her sternum. The body chain splits turning into thicker curved pieces of metal that cup her breast from below.

Her teeth roll over her bottom lip, and she drops her gaze from mine, looking down for a second before coyly tucking a strand of hair behind her ear. She turns away walking to where Indie is standing on the other end of the room, glancing over her shoulder and giving me a quick smile.

She's living up to her nickname in a whole new way tonight, looking like the most obscene wet dream, and she knows it. My girl is sweet torture.

CHAPTER 25

MIA

There's something about a good looking man in a blazer that makes my thighs clench together on sight. Especially when that man is not *just* run of the mill attractive, but physical perfection. Top that with the fact that he made me orgasm by grinding his muscular thigh between my legs with his fingers gripping my neck just a few hours ago, and I'm weak in the knees for him all over again.

When I spotted Dean on the patio, he was facing away from me, slipping his jacket over his black button-up. I was so distracted by the way his tailored pants fit him that I almost didn't register Indie standing on the other side of the room calling my name. The shock was still fresh when she wrapped her arms around me and whispered "Surprise" in my ear.

"What are you doing here?" I squeal in excitement, squeezing her tight.

"There was no way I could miss your birthday."

My lips pull down into a frown. "I want to know who spilled my secret. There are plenty of other things to celebrate tonight, like New Year's and you being here."

"Unacceptable. There's plenty of joy in this house so we can celebrate *all* the things tonight." She takes my hand and spins me around. "Hot damn, Dean is going to lose his ever-loving mind not being able to touch you all night."

"That's the plan," I say, feeling the smile return to my face.

For better or worse, I'm one of those girls who likes to consult my friends about their outfits for important events. I knew I did good when I revealed it to Indie during our FaceTime call yesterday. The shriek that came through the phone was deafening. I can't deny how sexy I felt slipping it on, knowing it was going to drive him crazy all night long. That alone was enough to bolster my confidence to wear the body chain, which is so far out of my comfort zone it may as well be in another state.

Judging by the way he froze, mouth hanging agape when he saw me from the patio, it's working. Maybe a little too well because when he looks at me like that, it's magic. His gaze, dancing across every bit of my skin like fairy dust, makes me feel all light and glowy. A surprise visitor is just the distraction I need to keep me from giving into our potent connection and going to him tonight after we both agreed to keep this thing between us private.

A short while later, while Indie and I are catching up, the scent of pine and juniper surrounds me and immediately my mind wanders in the middle of a horror story about her boss. When the light graze across my back sends goosebumps scattering across my skin, I know it's a lost cause. I give my friend an apologetic smile, but she just snorts out a laugh and turns to Dean.

"I'm not here to crash your party. I just wanted to say hi and tell you both how gorgeous you look tonight."

Leaning in over my shoulder and grabbing a chip off the counter, he whispers, "So goddamn stunning, Dreamer," before taking a step back and putting unwanted space between us.

"Smooth," Indie mouths, making a deep chuckle rumble out of him, and I glance back just in time to catch an easy grin on his face before he slips away.

"He's good for you," she says matter-of-factly, popping a chip into her mouth.

I'm about to ask what she means when chaos ensues. The front door opens and a large group of people spill into the house. Hendrix and Poppy lead the way, followed by Cruz and Delilah with a woman I don't recognize. The door swings back open before it latches and Xavier files in with a few more teammates that I recognize but can't name.

"Were you surprised?" Poppy asks, once she and Delilah join us, having passed their coats off to their respective partners.

"Very. But I still want to know who told everyone it's my birthday," I say, giving Poppy the most intimidating look I can muster, which isn't much.

"That one is on your brother," she replies. "Take it up with him, but not tonight. We're all together, and Dom is hosting, so we can relax and just enjoy each other."

"What do you say we give ourselves a tour and go find someplace to hang out and catch up?" Indie proposes. "Willa too. I'm sure she doesn't want to get stuck out here alone with all the guys." At the mention of Lilah's friend and employee at Buns & Roses, it dawns on me that she was the unfamiliar woman from earlier. "I'm not so sure about that," Delilah says, glancing over to where her new friend is surrounded by all the guys that came in with Xavier. "But I'll go steal her away, regardless. She has all night to flirt."

Like a line of little ducklings, we follow Indie down a set of stairs to a theater room in the finished basement.

"Is anyone else surprised by Dom's house?" I ask as we drag the oversized bean bags chairs together and pile onto them. "I expected his house to be more frat house and less Martha Stewart Living."

"Don't give him too much credit. He's still one-hundred percent the fuck boy you think he is. I wouldn't be surprised if one of those cleat chasers he's always taking home is an interior designer and decorated the whole place for him," Indie scoffs.

"I don't know. Cruz introduced me to his parents at the Bandits family day last year. They've been together since high school and still walk around with hearts in their eyes. His dad even had his hand tucked into the back pocket of his mom's jeans. From what I gathered, our resident playboy idolizes them," Lilah says with a dreamy look in her eyes.

"Was it like looking in a crystal ball and seeing your future?" Poppy jokes bumping Lilah's shoulder.

"Those sticky buns Cruz loves so much are going to end up covered in vomit if I have to watch those two make out again before the morning rush," Willa adds playfully.

"We get it, you and Poppy are in that disgusting-all-consuming-forever kind of love. It's rough out here ladies, be glad you found your partners when you did. The only thing I'm catching in the dating pool is a major case of the icks," Indie bemoans.

"Amen to that. Please tell me it's better in Telluride?" Willa asks, looking at me. "I could make a weekend trip to a mountain town if it guaranteed I'd get dicked down good."

"Um . . . I couldn't tell you. My dating apps haven't been opened since I've been there," I explain cautiously. These girls are my safe space and I feel the urge to tell them everything, but I don't want to put Poppy in a position where she has to keep a secret from my brother. "I'm focusing on writing and myself."

"You seem different. Must be all the mountain air. I would've bet you were getting railed within an inch of your life on the daily." Poppy waves her hand around in front of my face. "You have that happily-fucked glow about you."

"You really do. Are you looking for some tonight? That body chain, *oh girl*." Willa brings her hand to her mouth in chef's kiss.

"I love this look on you. And not just the outfit, all of it, you deserve to be this happy," Indie adds, wrapping her arm around my shoulder and giving it a squeeze.

There's a rap at the door and Cruz peaks his head in. "Ball drop is in an hour, ladies. Want to come up and join us for a round of flip cup? I'm told it's boys against girls," he says, his brow turning down.

"You know I'll take any opportunity to kick your ass," Lilah says before standing from the beanbag.

"Absolutely. Sounds like a great opportunity to make a dirty bet with Hendrix," Poppy adds, following Lilah.

"Nope!" I shout, covering my ears. "I'll play, but I don't want to hear about any bedroom bets—or kitchen."

Upstairs, the party is full force, with a few more teammates milling around, along with a group of girls that definitely weren't here earlier.

"I'm going to go grab a drink first," I tell Indie, splitting off from the group.

Black pants are pulled tight over an ass I would recognize anywhere, even without being able to see his upper half. Glancing around I find the kitchen empty and sneak up behind Dean, smoothing my hand over his hard, round ass giving it a squeeze.

"I knew you'd come looking for me. Just couldn't keep your hands—"

No. No. No. The words make sense, but the voice is all wrong. Broad shoulders appear first as the body in front of me pulls his head out of the fridge. Not only is he an inch too short, but his hair is several shades too light.

Standing in front of me, slack-jawed, is the look of someone who wasn't expecting me as much as I wasn't expecting him. "Wrong brunette. Mine has fangs, and you belong to someone else." Dom's voice drips with amusement.

"You're not . . ." Coming to my senses, my mouth snaps shut.

Musky cologne that smells nothing like Dean surrounds me and his best friend leans in close. "I'm not who, Mia?" You'd have to be dead not to notice the playful glint in his eyes.

A dark chuckle comes from the doorway behind me, one that was blissfully empty a moment ago.

Of course, he'd walk in right this second.

Over my shoulder, I see him approaching. Dom has yet to step away and, for some reason, my feet haven't moved. With one wall of muscle in front of me, and the other quickly closing in on me, there's nowhere to go.

Dean's hand lands on the countertop beside me, his other coming down on the open refrigerator door. I'm afraid to turn and look at him, and the wide grin on Dom's face gives nothing away.

Behind me, he lowers his head so his lips barely brush against the shell of my ear. "You're playing with fire, Dreamer."

"I thought . . ." Do I really want to admit that I mistook his best friend for him from behind? It's certainly better than him thinking I was hitting on someone else knowingly. "You both have really nice asses. It was all very confusing."

"You like my ass, Mia?" Dom's voice is low as he looks down at me with those amber eyes chock-full of mischief. He loves this and I *hate* him for it.

Shit.

Possessively, the man I'd hoped to find in the kitchen snakes his arm around my waist pulling me in close but not giving Dom enough room to move from where he's trapped. "Careful how you answer that." Hot breath tickles my neck and the hand splayed across my stomach caresses the exposed skin, inching up, until his thumb brushes the cool metal of my body chain.

My lips roll together, sealing my thoughts inside me, knowing my best bet is to say nothing and bide my time. We can't stay locked like this for long with the risk of anyone walking in.

"Smart girl," Dom praises, and dammit his words have me clenching my thighs together. People talk about dying from embarrassment, but can a combination of sexual frustration and embarrassment be fatal? Asking for a friend.

"All those lunges I made you do last season have paid off if my girl is confusing your scrawny ass for mine." It's on the tip of my tongue to tell Dean that there was nothing scrawny about his best friend's ass, but that seems like something that would push him over the edge. I like possessive Dean, but now might not be the best time to provoke him.

Not that his best friend gets that memo. "This was fun. If you ever want to do it again, let me know. Turnabout is fair play."

"I think the fuck not," Dean snarls, stepping forward and sandwiching me between the two men. Dom's laughter vibrates against my chest for a moment before he removes the hand that's blocking his exit and twists away from us.

"Go find someplace private before you two get caught," he says, inclining his head toward the hallway as he waltzes away, completely unaffected by the interaction.

Dean does a quick sweep of the room before his fingers twine with mine and he tugs me through the hallway and into a spare bedroom.

Deft hands make quick work of clicking the lock into place and my back is against the door a second later. "Fuck, Dreamer. Do you know how hard it is to keep my hands off of you? And then I find you touching him. I think you're trying to kill me." He drags his knuckles down my exposed sternum, making my body break out in chills as he follows the path of the body chain one way, and then the other. "Did you wear this for the sole purpose of tempting me?"

"Would I do that?" I ask, weaving my hands around the back of his neck.

"You absolutely would." He touches his forehead to mine, growing serious. "There's something I want to talk to you about while I have you alone. Sit with me for a second." My stomach drops out. All the worst case scenarios start running through my head at his shift in demeanor. What if hiding this from my brother is too much, or he's gotten bored with me, or it's just more than he wanted?

The bed dips when he takes a seat on it, pulling me down next to him.

"I swear I thought he was you." And dammit, my voice wobbles, betraying me.

"Sweetheart, I'm not mad, and this isn't about him." He soothes a thumb gliding over my cheekbone. "It's just something I need to tell you, but I'd really appreciate it if you let me get all the way through before you think too hard about it."

Glancing at him through my lashes, my lips rub together before I relent and nod.

"I mean it, Mia. Please don't let this come between us. That's the last thing I want." He pinches my chin between his fingers tilting my face up to look into my eyes, his filled with steely determination.

"Okay." My response is weak.

"I spoke with Indie first because this isn't my secret to tell. She was okay with me sharing this with you, and the only reason I didn't say something sooner was because I didn't want to break her trust, but you should know the whole story."

"If you don't want me to freak out, you're going to need to cut to the chase. Why are you and Indie keeping secrets from me?"

"Everything I told you about the night Indie and I kissed is true. But someone took a picture of the three of us in the VIP section of the club that night. They were going to sell the photo to the tabloids and it could have been a disaster for all of us. Indie would have taken the worst of it." He takes out his phone and opens up a password protected folder and his frown becomes more pronounced at whatever is on the screen.

It was easy to see why when he turned the phone to me. Under different circumstances, this picture would be hot enough to melt the phone in my hand. But that's my man, with his hand under my friend's skirt. I cover his hand with mine and lock the screen, taking the thick, sticky, jealous haze with it and leaving behind curiosity.

"Somehow, my grandfather's PR team got a hold of it before it could go anywhere and buried it. If it had gotten out, people would have blasted her on gossip sites and social media. We all left the club together, and nothing else happened that you don't already know about," he reiterates, softly cupping the side of my cheek.

From the picture, it looks like Dom and Dean are very comfortable sharing. It doesn't seem like something that should turn me on, but I can't quell the impulse to squeeze my things together. "Have you two done something like this before? Been with the same woman?"

"No, and that's not what happened here either. She was toying with both of us—mostly Dom, to piss him off. She apologized to me and we're fine. Friends, nothing more."

"Is it something you want?" The seconds tick by as anxiety claws at my chest.

Green eyes narrow at me and his hand curves around the side of my neck, his thumb ticking my chin up. "There's no scenario possible where I'd be okay with sharing what's mine. And make no mistake, you are mine. No one else gets what I have with you."

My nipples tighten against the fabric of my shirt. "Yeah, okay," I stutter out.

"I can give you everything you need, and I'm not afraid to get a helping hand from those toys you packed. Although, we'd definitely have to work our way up to that big fucker you packed."

With a nervous laugh, I ask, "Are you trying to distract me by making me horny?"

"Is it working?" His lips brush my forehead and his chest sinks with an exhale, like this was weighing on him.

"Maybe. No more surprises to spring on me?"

"No. There was an awkward car ride home, but I'll let Indie tell you about that." His cheeks turn pink before he asks, "Are we okay?"

"I can't really be that mad about it when you were protecting my friend. Thank you for taking care of her. Indie likes everyone to think she's bullet-proof, but something like that . . . having her dad see those photos. It would have destroyed her," I tell him, leaning forward and planting my lips on the corner of his mouth.

There's a knock on the door and Dean gets up to unlock it. Without another word, he opens it for Indie and slips out. Giving me a longing glance before leaving the two of us alone.

"Do you hate me?" she asks quietly, taking Dean's spot next to me on the bed.

"No, of course not. You did nothing wrong, but you know you can tell me anything, Ind. You don't have to keep it all inside—dealing with it on your own." Placing my hand on hers I squeeze.

"There was never anything between us. I was using him to push Dom's buttons."

"I know that. Can I ask you something?" My voice vibrates with trepidation.

"Anything," she replies immediately.

"Would you have gone through with it? Being with both of them."

She rolls her lips together.

"I'm curious, not judging."

"Probably. I don't exactly know when to quit." Her laugh is self-deprecating. "Dom would have never let that happen. The man is unhinged. Just one more reason I need to stay far away."

"No?"

"Most definitely not. Did Dean tell you what happened when we left the club, after the picture was taken?"

I shake my head. "He just said that it was an awkward car ride home, leaving it up to you to decide if you shared more."

She drops her head into her hands. "Let's just say Dom wanted to make it very clear that I was his and his alone—which, for the record, is not accurate. I'm not his." She punctuates each word. When she turns toward me, I give her a questioning look. "Fine. He made me come all over his lap on the ride home and wasn't discrete about it."

Well, that's not what I was expecting. Maybe I should be mad that he's seen her like that, but all it does is pique my curiosity. Dean and I hadn't even met at that point, so I'd be a hypocrite to hold it against either of them.

"Oh," I say on an exhale.

"Yeah, oh," she agrees, standing from the bed and pulling me into a hug, leading me out back to the party.

Outside the guest room door, the celebration is in full swing. House music vibrates through the speakers and when Indie steps to the side I see everyone gathered around a cake in the kitchen waiting in ambush to make a spectacle of me.

"What was your backup plan if I hadn't taken that news well?" I whisper to Indie when she pauses in the hallway to let me go first. The tall ivory cake is foiled with gold flakes and one sparkler glowing and crackling on the top.

"Kick Dean out and have an impromptu girls' night stuffing our faces with cake and champagne in Dom's basement. It's still an option if that sounds more appealing, all these fools will be singing off-key any second."

On cue, my brother steps forward with the cake, and I second guess my decision not to take Indie up on her offer when the first few bars of *Happy Birthday* starts, getting progressively louder as everyone joins in.

When everyone's full of cake, and the singing and hugs have stopped, Dom's boisterous voice lets everyone know there's a fresh round of flip cup starting. Willa waves me over to where she stands between Xavier and Dean. "I'm sitting this one out. Take my spot."

Yes, please. I'll gladly take any excuse to be near Dean without raising suspicion. The game starts distracting everyone with the extremely competitive race between Hendrix and Delilah to land their cups.

Dean leans in, whispering against the shell of my ear. "Everything good?"

"All good, promise." I link my pinkie with his under the table giving it a reassuring squeeze.

There's only about fifteen minutes before the ball drops and the energy in the room is frenzied and loud as we start the tiebreaker round. We've gone back and forth splitting the rounds.

The smack talk is unparalleled, and you'd be surprised—or not—to learn that it's not coming from the professional athletes. In fact, the wide-eyed panic stricken expression on Xavier's face when he accidentally bumped into Indie mid-flip is going to live rent free in my head for a *very* long time. He's going to be walking around for the rest of the night with one hand cupping his junk after she threatened to "remove his balls from his body without even making him bleed" in her scary, low voice. Every man around the table shivered for that one.

It's down to Lilah and Dom for the win, and the silence cloaks the room as everyone turns to the end of the table to watch. Lilah is the picture of composure, her eyes focused on the red cup as she uses two fingers to gracefully send it tumbling over before setting it back up and trying again. Dom bounces back and forth on the balls of his feet and shakes out his hands before he resets his cup flipping it through the air. There's a collective gasp as it wobbles before tipping. He doesn't even get the chance to set it back up as all our eyes ping-pong back to the other side of the table as Lilah, tongue trapped between her teeth, gives her cup the perfect tap and it flips once, sticking the landing like an Olympic gymnast.

"That's fucking right!" Indie shouts, reaching across the table for a high five as the guys chirp at their teammate for losing the whole thing.

With glasses of champagne in hand, everyone gathers in the living room for the countdown.

Ting, ting, ting.

The sound of a metal tapping against a flute draws all our eyes to the center of the room where Hendrix is standing.

"Okay, wow. That really worked. I thought I was going to have to make Lilah whistle to get you all to shut up. You're probably very confused about why I'm giving this little speech in the middle of Dom's living room. Sorry to steal your thunder, buddy. There are a few things I wanted to say as we close out the year together and welcome in, what I hope, will be an even better one—better because we're all here together. You guys taught me that this year . . . welcoming me to the Bandits and giving it to me straight when I needed it." He tugs at the collar of his shirt, laughing nervously before holding out his hand in Poppy's direction. "This year would have turned out a lot different without the people in this room. It's been a year of lessons and love thanks to this woman."

Once she's within reach, he's taking her hand and tugging her the rest of the way, setting their champagne on the nearby coffee table. My brother's eyes soften and his nerves melt away with her by his side.

It makes my heart seize in my chest. This is what I want, someone to look at me like I'm the center of their world. Chills skate over my skin when I glance to the side and catch Dean's intense gaze on me from where he stands on the other side of the room.

"Poppy captured my attention from the moment I met her. How could she not? She's stunning and charismatic. Without all of you, she might have slipped through my fingers before I even got a chance to really know her. Several of you told me what a dumbass I was, loud and proud, until it finally sunk in that the reason I was miserable without her was that she was my perfect match. It's easy to see now how right you were because Poppy makes me a better man."

Taking both of Poppy's hands in his, he drops to one knee. Around me everyone watches silently as her hand comes to her mouth.

"Poppy Byrne, you are the best thing that's ever happened to me. I'm thankful every single day you gave me a second chance, that you let me be your lover, friend, and family. There's no other way I want to finish this year than by your side as we look to the future—*our* future. Spend the new year with me, planning out the rest of our lives. Let me spend the rest of my life showing you unconditional love. Tell me you'll marry me and make me the luckiest man in the world."

None of the happily ever afters I've written have meant as much as seeing my brother propose. I swipe at the tear rolling down my cheek as Poppy nods excitedly and my brother slips a ring on her finger.

I'm getting a sister! Well "in-law" but same thing.

As soon as the happy couple kisses, chaos breaks out. Starting with Dom whooping in congratulations, making Poppy and Hendrix laugh mid-kiss. With the countdown in full swing now, Indie wraps her arm around my shoulders. Any plans I had for sneaking away to steal a midnight kiss from Dean are dashed by the frenzy around us. There's no way I'll make it out of here unnoticed now.

10 . . . 9 . . . 8 . . .

"I'm sorry you're not getting the kiss you really want, but that man can't take his eyes off you. Dean looks at you the same way your brother looks at Poppy, and Cruz looks at Lilah."

5 . . . 4 . . . 3 . . .

Indie leans over and plants a kiss on my cheek. My eyes find Dean across the room as I return her hug. He watches me intently, his tongue rolling over his bottom lip while time ticks away.

2 . . . 1 . . .

"Happy New Year," my lips move silently as the clock strikes midnight. All around us people pair off, kissing and hugging, but I stay focused on the one person in the room that I want to celebrate with, but can't.

CHAPTER 26

DEAN

Everything around me fades away. My friends, the cheers, all the kissing, it's nothing more than white noise. Ironically, it's Mia's silent whisper into the chaotic room that is the loudest.

A better man would walk across the room and give her everything she's deserving of. A promise of more than just a temporary arrangement, the kiss she should have at midnight, but I'm not that man. Not tonight. Not ever. And I might just be too selfish to care because I want this woman more than I've ever wanted anything else. Spring training gets a little closer every day and I'm done waiting. One way or another, she's coming home with me tonight.

Sharp pain shoots through my ribs, taking me by surprise. "Oof, what was that for?" I grunt out, turning to find Dom with his eyebrows cinched together, not at all remorseful for the elbow he just landed.

"You're looking at her like she's yours. If you want to keep whatever this is a secret . . ." He flaps his hand in Mia's general direction. "Find something else to do with your face."

Ignoring him, my eyes follow Mia, who's practically skipping toward her brother and Poppy, squealing in excitement as she wraps her arms around both of them. In true Dom fashion, he huffs dramatically when I step away from him and walk towards the trio.

"Congratulations." I pat Hendrix on the back. "Poppy, are you aiming for sainthood saying yes to this guy?" Bracing for a second elbow to the gut in a matter of minutes, I add on, "We'll make sure he never forgets how lucky he is to have you."

"Unnecessary. I learned that lesson, and I never intend to forget it," he says, not taking his eyes off his future bride.

"And I plan to remind him every day," Poppy teases, as Mia releases her from the hug.

"I'm sure you two want to get out of here and celebrate." My attention switches from the happy couple to the magnet that drew me over here in the first place. "My driver can give you a ride home if you want to stay a little while longer."

Mia shifts on her feet under my gaze. Her eyes dart to her brother, but he's so wrapped up in his girl that I could kiss his sister right in front of him and he wouldn't notice. *Damn that sounds fun.* "Thanks man," he mumbles, placing a kiss at Poppy's temple before whispering something in her ear.

"Um, yeah. I think we'll be heading out shortly." Whatever he says has her sagging into him, her cheeks staining pink. They say a few rushed goodbyes, never putting space between them before they leave for what I'm sure will be a celebration that goes well into the morning hours.

"That was a pretty smooth move back there. I bet you're pretty proud of yourself." Soft lips brush my ear like she's whispering, but it comes out full volume.

Careful not to let her stray too far on wobbly legs, I hold out her coat and help her into it. "Very proud of myself. It was all designed to get you alone. But judging by the way you're teetering in those *very* sexy boots, and your vocal command, you're too tipsy for what I had in mind." With a guiding hand on her lower back, I lead her through the doorway where the car I hired for the night waits. "It's a shame because now you're going to have to wait for your birthday present." She shivers when my heated breath ghosts her neck.

"You got me a present? But how did you know it was my birthday?" Her plump bottom lip pushes out in an exaggerated pout that makes me laugh. Reaching around her I pull the door open. Ducking into the car, her jacket covers the romper she's wearing. Making it almost look like she's naked underneath and fuck if that doesn't do something to me.

Overcome by my need for her, my hand wraps around the frame of the door, gripping it tightly. I take a step back from the car, before my dick can take control of the situation. If he had a say we'd follow her into the car to lay her across the bench seat. "I didn't, you're just lucky I already have something I know you've been dying for."

Rounding the back of the car I slip in on the other side, immediately deciding it leaves too much space between us. That won't do after having to keep my distance all night. With a click, I hit the red button on her seat belt and reach for her. My hand wraps around the soft curve of her waist, pulling her across the seat and into my side.

"There's no way in hell I'm going to start the new year with space between us. From now, until the moment this ends, you're mine. And I want you right here where I can kiss you the way I should have at midnight." The low timbre of my voice shocks even me, but it shouldn't. This woman makes me feral, out of control, willing to dream about things I've never considered before. If I could change and give her everything she needs, what could our future look like? It's selfish to even think about it because she deserves every-thing. At my very best I'm barely enough for a woman like her.

"Is that a promise?" Notes of peaches and champagne swirl around us, the sweet scent magnifying when she leans in and runs her nose along my jaw.

Teeth clamp down on my earlobe, and I hiss through my teeth. She's feisty when she drinks and I like it, a lot. "Yes, and I'm going to start by taking you back to my place. By the end of winter, you'll be begging to be rid of me."

"Not possible," she hums against me, making my stomach somersault.

God, do I wish that was true. Instead of arguing with her, I do what I've been dying to do since she walked through the door to Dom's house and fuse my lips over hers, stealing the gasp right from her mouth.

The sharp bite of her fingernails digging into my shoulder spurs me on. Twisting toward her, I press her into the seat, tilting her chin up for better access. We kiss like we're claiming each other. It's filled with passion and a promise of what's to come.

The city lights overhead don't even register on my radar, not until the driver breaks and I pull back from the kiss, keeping my forehead connected to hers. Under me, her chest rises and falls rapidly, bumping against mine. The only thing I remember about the drive is the taste of Mia's lips bring me to the brink of madness.

She tries to cover it with her hand, but I see her mouth stretch wide in a yawn when I hold out my hand to help her from the car.

"Looks like someone partied too hard and needs to go to bed," I say as she places her hand in mine and follows me inside the building. The ride up to the penthouse is quiet, with her pressed against my side, her hand resting against my chest. Even in the dull mirrored walls of the elevator, she shines. The heavy eyes and swollen lips only add to appeal because she looks like that for me.

"You're not going to hear me argue. Take me to bed, Dean. Dry humping on the couch like teenagers was the highlight of my year, but I'm ready for the real thing."

I groan letting my head fall against the wall because we have very different ideas of what that means tonight. She's right. We've waited long enough, but a few more hours won't kill us. The elevator doors glide open with a ding and she steps forward, dragging me towards the door.

"So eager for me. I can't get enough of that," I tell her, unlocking the door to my penthouse, only for her to slip inside ahead of me. By the time I've locked up behind us, she's shed her boots and dropped her clutch, leaving a trail of wreckage in her wake.

Those potent gray-blue eyes are clouded with lust and champagne when she finds me over her shoulder as she slips the sleeve of her romper down her arm. The patch of smooth skin she reveals might be more than I can handle. Halfway through the kitchen her steps falter and she spins on her toes.

"Not fair, I had this whole, sexy plan in my head that I concocted on the elevator ride. I was going to strip on the way to your room. It was really going to be something." She looks around, confusion twisting her plump red lips. "But I don't remember the way from when you fixed my finger."

Closing the gap between us, my hand smooths up her arm, sliding the sleeve back over her shoulder. Her mouth gapes open as she stares down at my hand on her shoulder.

"Care to explain why you're trying to keep my clothes on me when I'm trying to seduce you?"

"You've seduced me since the moment we met, so it's hardly necessary. But I'm a weak man and you're the greatest temptation I've ever faced—a drunk temptation—which is a problem."

"Is it though? I'm asking you to take me to bed. I'll beg, I'm not too proud," she says, pouting now.

Jesus this woman, how is it she manages to enchant me even when she's tipsy and ridiculous. "Don't worry, I'm taking you to bed and I'm going to snuggle you so hard." Linking my finger with hers, I lead her through the kitchen, down the hallway and into my bedroom at the end of the hallway.

"I really screwed the pooch when I didn't get naked, you wouldn't be such a gentleman right now."

"Make no mistake, it's killing me to keep you clothed. Especially knowing you put that hot little outfit on for me. But even an asshole like me is capable of not fucking you when you've been drinking."

She stops in front of my bed leaving me in the doorway. The silver tones of her irises almost glow in the moonlight as she looks me up and down.

"I don't remember conceding to wearing this for you. Maybe I just like the way the silk fabric feels against my bare skin," she says, running her hands over her torso. The little minx bites her lip as she cups her breasts through the shimmery material. It's a miracle that I stay upright because there's not a drop of blood that isn't rushing to my dick. "Just because you won't fuck me doesn't mean we can't mess around a little."

If I have any hope of maintaining control of this situation, I need to do something, and quickly. Both her hands move on to the task of sliding the romper down her body, revealing more skin than I can handle in my current state. I'm fucking dying to touch her, taste her, make her mine.

"What are you doing to me, Dreamer? I'm trying to do the right thing here. To be a decent guy, the kind you deserve," I tell her, moving to the dresser and grabbing one of my shirts for her. I set it on the bed next to her. "And you're making it so hard."

"Literally, I hope," she says with a little giggle. "I'm not asking for a saint. I just want you, Dean. All of you. I know what I'm asking for."

Slinky fabric falls to the ground around her feet with a swish, leaving her in front of me in nothing but a black, lace thong that sits high on her hips and the gold body chain cupping her perfect tits. *Maybe the shirt can wait a minute.*

"If you can't help me, I'll just help myself," she taunts, sliding her hands down her body and palming herself over the thin lace.

Stepping into her space I grab her wrist, using one hand, and pin it to the small of her back. My other hand skims up her torso, making her shiver when my knuckles brush over the side of her breast on their way up. My fingers wrap around the side of her neck and my thumb settles under her chin forcing it up.

"If anyone's touching this body tonight, it'll be me. But you'll have to wait to get all of me. The first time I'm inside of you, your mind will be crystal clear so you can remember every single bit of pleasure I draw out of you. If you're going to ruin me, I want you to be fully present when you do it."

"Ruin you?" she repeats, her voice colored with disbelief and her pulse rapidly tapping against my palm. I love the way it jumps when I brush my lips along her temple and force her backwards until her knees hit the bed.

Over the top of her I stare down into her wide eyes and give her the truth. "Fucking destroy me from the inside out. You've already burrowed yourself so far under my skin. Once I have you, you're going to make a permanent mark there."

Under my fingers, her throat bobs as she swallows roughly.

"Tell me you want this. I need to know you understand what the boundaries are tonight, so we don't have any misunderstandings."

"Please, Dean. I need you. Whatever you'll give me, I'll take eagerly."

My thumb brushes across her cheekbone. "Look at you begging for me, just like you said you would. Such a good girl." I release her neck and watch as her hand travels to that place, tracing the skin, her eyes blown with lust. "Don't worry, there's more where that came from."

The moan that comes out of her is borderline unhinged. At least if we're going to go down in flames, we can have fun doing it together.

"Crawl to the middle of the bed, on all fours for me," I tell her. "I'm going to need you to keep your hands to yourself tonight."

"Just tonight?" she asks, looking over her shoulder at me as she does exactly as I ask, putting herself on a stunning display for me. Rounded ass in the air, just waiting.

The bed dips as I join her, kneeling behind her. "Try to keep me away tomorrow. You're all mine and I promise I'm going to fuck you so good that no one else will be able to erase the feeling of me inside you." My hand connects with the creamy skin and she jerks forward with a sharp intake of breath.

"Again," she pleads, her voice frayed.

Which only makes me chuckle. "So fucking surprising. Let's see how much you liked that." Starting at the high point of her hip where the black lace hugs her curves, I run my fingertips along the material, over her tailbone, and along her crack. I press the already soaked fabric against her center. "My sweet Dreamer likes it when I hold that pretty neck in my hands and leave marks on this perfect ass. When I pull this thong to the side, are you going to be a glistening mess for me?"

"Y—yes." Her hips push back, looking for more when I shift the scrap of lace to the side.

"Spread those knees wider for me. I want to watch your pussy drip down your legs when my hand turns your ass red." I wait for her, watching as she lowers her chest to the bed and shifts her legs apart, exposing herself to me just the way I asked. "Fucking stunning," I groan, bringing my hand down on her cheek and watching her as she clenches.

"Patience, I'll give you more." I don't wait for her to respond before I slide a finger inside her.

"Please," she cries out as I add another finger.

"You don't need to beg, sweetheart. You're going to come for me tonight. I'll make sure of it." I slip my other hand around her, sliding it between her legs and making her squeeze my fingers, her body trembling.

"Yes. The way you touch me . . ." Her words mix with a moan as her fingers twist into the comforter. My name tumbles out of her mouth and I can't tear my eyes off her as she comes for me. Mia shudders under me when I pull my fingers free from her heat. With her hair stuck to her face, she's the most beautiful mess I've ever seen.

I kiss up her spine until I reach her shoulder, eclipsing her body with mine. "Lay down and I'll take care of you," I whisper against the slope of her neck, gently helping her lower to the bed before I leave her to grab a washcloth from the bathroom.

After helping clean her up, I help her out of the body chain, and ease the shirt I grabbed earlier over her head. The threadbare, gray fabric barely covers her ass and somehow the sight of her in my clothes makes me even harder.

If my dick got to make decisions, this would end very differently. But this isn't about him. Whether we planned for it or not, the feelings I have for Mia are there. I wasn't bluffing when I told her about my plans to fuck her senseless tomorrow. If I only get her for a short time, I'll be damn sure she never forgets our time together.

"Let's get you to bed. You're going to need sleep for what I've got planned for you tomorrow." I scoop Mia up in my arms and pull down the covers, setting her in the center of my bed.

"Don't threaten me with a good time," she says around a yawn while I strip down to just my black boxer briefs.

The comfort of my bed has never felt better against my skin, but it's got nothing to do with the soft sheets and everything to do with the girl I'm currently wrapping myself around like a big spoon. My lips press to her hair. "I'll make it better than good, Dreamer."

Her body relaxes in my arms as she lets out a contented sigh.

"Oh, fuck," I groan. Through my sleep-addled brain, I piece together the overwhelming feeling of ecstasy before I'm fully awake. There's no telling if it was the fingernails gently scraping down the length of my thighs, the obscene hum coming from Mia, or the warm, wet mouth wrapped around my morning erection that made me stir first.

All I'm certain of is Mia's lips wrapped around me is almost enough to kill me. That's how good she feels—soft and slippery. *Like mine.* Each time she takes me to the back of her throat, my control frays a little more and I simultaneously become more alert. The sleep in my eyes clears enough to give me the full picture of the stunning brunette between my legs with her messy hair flipped to one side, and those mesmerizing eyes shining up at me as she releases me from her mouth.

Her fist wraps around the base of my shaft. "Good Morning," she whispers, her free hand linking with mine.

"And what a way to wake up. What are you doing down there?"

"Seems pretty obvious to me. Taking care of you, the same way you did for me last night. Since you were too much of a gentleman to let anything more happen."

"Is that so?" My question is cut off by a groan as her head dips down so she can run her tongue up the length of me.

"It only seemed fair since I woke up to this massive boner persistently poking at my back. I assumed he wanted some attention."

"I'll have to have a talk with him. How rude of him to wake you."

"Don't you dare. It was the very best way to wake up," she says with a wicked smirk, her thumb circling my tip, smearing the bead of pre-cum that was glistening there.

"I can think of a few ways to make it even better." My grip flips on her hand and I drag her up my body. "I need another taste of you. Get over here and ride my face while you swallow my dick."

Her teeth clamp down on her lip and hesitancy flashes across her face.

"Don't make me ask again. I'm dying to get my mouth on you before I make good on my promises and fuck you right through this mattress."

"When you put it that way." She crawls toward me, those adorable rosy spots on full display and her eyes searching mine. "It's just that I've never— not like that, at least."

Something is wrong with me. I shouldn't want to pound my chest at being the first to have her like this, yet I do. "I'll make it so fucking good for you. But if it's not your thing, say the word and we stop. If you're not into it, I'm not into it. For the next two months, my sole purpose in life is to make you feel good."

Her eyes widen comically. "Ladies and gentlemen, we have an overachiever on our hands. I didn't realize you were so committed to the cause."

"The most committed. Now turn around and straddle my face. You're going to ride my tongue until I'm drowning in you."

She swings a leg over my head and slowly lowers, not giving me what I want.

"That won't do. I'm starving, and you look like breakfast." Gripping hips, I pull her down on my face humming against her center when she settles where I want her.

"That's—Oh wow," she preens. Her praise only makes me work harder. I lap at her, savoring the sweetness that coats my tongue.

Warmth surrounds me as she takes me back inside her mouth. She struggles to keep up, moaning and popping off my dick every time I thrust my tongue deep inside her. It's still the best blow job I've ever had because it's her.

"My face is covered in the mess you're making. Show me how much you like it with my tongue buried inside you and my cock hitting the back of your throat."

Mia's forehead hits my thigh as she trembles above me, her legs tightening around my head as her orgasm hits her. The only downside to the way she's wrapped around me is that it dulls the symphony of moans that mix with my name.

"Such a perfect fucking girl. The next time you scream my name, it's going to be when you come on my cock." My lips graze the inside of her thigh before I lift her off me and move up the bed so my back is against the headboard.

"It's about time you gave me that present you promised," she huffs, turning around to face me. Lust-blown eyes drop to where my cock is stretched up against my stomach. Those nerves from earlier return briefly in the way she nibbles on her lip. Reaching out I grab a condom from my nightstand and hand it to her.

Holding it out between two fingers, I ask, "Would you like to do the honors?"

Mia nods, but instead of taking it from me, her hands reach for the hem of my shirt. The one she is still wearing.

"Leave it on. I want to watch you ride me while you wear my shirt." My thumb swipes across her lower lip. She catches it with her teeth, biting down gently and giving me the most wicked smile.

She replaces my thumb with the foil packet, ripping it open and rolling the condom down my length, her brow pinched in concentration. I've never let anyone else do this for me, and the moment is far more intimate than I expect. Maybe that's because Mia is the first person I've been with in years that I actually trust.

Those endless pools of blue and gray swim with anticipation as she hovers over me—my tip notched at her entrance. The need to thrust up into her is almost painful while I wait for her to make a move.

"What's wrong, Mia?" My thumb strokes her hip bone and my hands grip her.

"Nothing. I'm trying to commit this to memory. The way you look, relaxed and all mine first thing in the morning. The way I feel when I'm with you. Cherished. Whole."

She drops an inch and her mouth falls open, her head tilting back as her hands find my pecs.

"The way you're going to stretch me—so thick. No one's going to fit me better than you will."

Holy fuck.

"Where have you been hiding this mouth? Tell me how it feels when I fill you. While you use me to get off." Too slowly, she lowers, taking another inch of me. The need to be deep inside her is overwhelming. Like I've been waiting for years to find this. And nothing has ever felt better. "Shit, Mia, talk to me before I take over and fuck you hard and fast," I tell her, my control slipping with each inch she sheathes in her warmth.

"It's almost too much. I'm so full already," she groans, her head falling forward—rolling on her shoulders as she lowers a little more.

"Eyes on me. You're almost halfway there. Take me the way you were meant to, sweetheart."

I release my hold on her hips, cupping her cheek and forcing her to look at me. The other hand weaves through her hair, gently gripping the back of her neck.

"Fuck!" she cries out as she takes the rest of me, dropping all the way down and stilling.

"Jesus," I hiss out. "There you go. Such a good fucking girl, letting me fill this perfect cunt. There's only one problem now. I want to see these gorgeous tits while you squeeze my cock."

I gather my shirt, lifting it to reveal perky tits and rosy nipples that are begging for my hands on them as she rocks over me. "Open up," I demand, bringing the bunched up material to her mouth. "Bite, I need my hands free."

Her teeth close over the fabric and she makes the prettiest whimpering noise as my palms cover her breasts, rolling her pebbled nipples between my fingers.

Her hands skate up my chest until her elbows are resting on my shoulders. She uses the leverage to pick up her pace. Circling her hips when she bottoms out, then lifting slowly to take all of me over and over again. She's fucking perfect and I know six more weeks won't be enough time with her.

"Do you know what you look like fucking yourself on my cock with my shirt in your mouth? You're a dream come true. But I'm a greedy fucker and I want more. I want all your moans, this mouth." I lean forward kissing the corner of it where the spit soaked t-shirt isn't covering. Then I strip the shirt from her body leaving her completely naked. Seeing her in various states of undress, and in that bikini, hasn't prepared me for how breathtaking she is like this.

"Dean. I need y—you." Her forehead drops to my shoulder.

"I've got you." Flipping us so she's on the bed under me, I cover her with my body, sealing my lips to hers—swallowing every moan as I make good on my promise to fuck her hard and fast. "Tell me what you need, Mia. I'm not going to be able to hold out much longer. You feel too perfect."

"Fuck me like I'm yours to keep," she grits out, her fingers twisting into my hair.

That should be easy because there's nothing I want more. Pinning her leg over my shoulder I work her clit in tight circles with one hand. She swallows roughly under my palm when the other covers her throat, squeezing just enough that she has to work a little harder.

Mine.

"Love that—don't stop," she chants—the words frayed. Her hips tilt up and the change in angle has her tightening around my cock and me seeing stars.

Mine.

"Dean. Dean. Dean."

Mine, mine, mine.

Heat burns down my spine as I twitch inside her, filling the condom. It's enough to trigger her release and Mia shakes underneath me, her pulse racing where I've loosened my grip on her delicate neck.

My thumb caresses her jaw and I fall to the side of her, pulling her with me and taking care of the condom.

"I hope you don't have anything to do today. Because I'm going to need some more of that very soon."

With a feather light brush of her lips to my chest, she murmurs, "There's no other way I'd want to start the year."

CHAPTER 27

MIA

"Why didn't you tell me yesterday was your birthday?" Dean asks, sounding more curious than angry. He holds up the breakfast burrito he made us from the plate on his lap and I take a bite. My stomach started growling while he was going down on me on his way to giving me my third orgasm of the new year. As far as holiday traditions go, this is one I could get used to.

Chewing slowly, I think about how to answer without totally spoiling the mood.

"Everyone has always tried to make my birthday special. My grandmother. Hendrix. They're actually a little over the top. No matter how hard they try to distract me, it's never far from my mind that my birth, the whole reason for the celebration, is the reason my parents walked away from us."

My fingers wrap around his wrist, pulling the burrito in for another bite, playing off the enormity of what I just admitted with a casual shrug as I hum around the bite. He sits there, stunned, and it makes me cringe internally. This is what I was hoping to avoid, his pity.

After a moment, the blank look on his face is replaced by rage.

Moving on to the anger stage, I can work with that.

"What does that mean?" The sharp, protectiveness in his tone shouldn't turn me on as much as it does, but we are still mostly naked in bed, so it seems fair to blame it on that as well.

"When I came along, it was more than they could handle. I was too much. Two babies under two, for parents that were barely interested in being there for one, was a deal breaker. If I hadn't come along, they might have figured it out—muddled through until Hendrix was older and less work. He could have had a chance at getting to know his parents—a family." It pours out of me and it's more than I planned on telling him. More than I've ever told anyone.

"No. Mia. I'm sorry, but your parents are the only ones responsible for their choices. You are not too much. They weren't enough. Not for your brother, and certainly not for you."

"You don't have to try to make me feel better. Living with my grandmother was the best possible outcome. She was wonderful, and she loved us better than anyone could have. But it's hard to celebrate my birth when it's attached to that baggage. It's always there, in the back of my mind."

"Have I ever been the kind of guy that would coddle you? I've always told you exactly how it is. A family is more than blood. It's the people you choose—the people who choose you. Your brother has that. *You* have that."

He's right, even when he's showing me his sweet side, Dean never says things he doesn't mean.

"I know but this"—I gesture between us—"it was never supposed to be this heavy. We agreed to fun and I think we both know it's gone well beyond just simple fun, but I don't want to spend the little time we have together like this. With me, reliving my past traumas. It's not your job to make this better for me."

"Let me decide what my job is, Mia. We're friends, aren't we? That's how we started and that's how this is going to end." His lips press into a thin line and he pushes a piece of hair behind my ear, his gaze dropping from mine. "I can't fix this for you, but I can be there for you if you want to talk, and I damn well can make sure that you know you're worth celebrating on your birthday, and every other day."

I open my mouth, but he's not done.

"Tell me what would have happened if you hadn't been born, other than the world being a darker place. Because I imagine your brother's life wouldn't even be a fraction of what it is today. Your parents don't strike me as people that would have gone above and beyond the way Janet has." His tone is unyielding, and those green eyes are dark and stormy in the most stunning way. He's furious on my behalf and I don't hate it.

"But he'd still have had the chance to know them," I say, my throat tight with emotion.

"He has that chance now. How hard do you think it would be for him to track them down? Hen knows he's better off without them. And he sure as fuck knows he's better off with you in his life. *I'm* better off with you in my life. *We all are.* Don't second guess that for even a second."

"Okay then." My face flushes with heat from his passionate declaration. "Tell me something about you. Something that no one else knows. I need to feel like I'm not the only one naked, with my baggage hanging out."

He's quiet, running his knuckles along his jaw and when I think he's about to brush me off, he looks back up at me, sad eyes crinkled at the corners.

"My dad wants to rebuild our relationship. He cornered me when I was home for Christmas and asked if we could talk when I came back. But I know I'll never be able to forgive him."

Everything in me is aching to reach out to him to pull him into my arms, but I'm afraid if I move he'll stop. It doesn't matter that we agreed this relationship wasn't supposed to be more than making each other feel good. I can't deny the need to know everything about him.

"He took so much away from me. His actions were callous, selfish, and they changed our family forever. And he's never once apologized for it. Now he just expects to bury the hatchet. Jesus, if it wasn't for him, maybe I could be the kind of guy that deserved a woman like you."

It's heartbreaking how much conviction he has in his steady voice. This time, there's no holding back. I crawl into his lap, needing to give him back every ounce of what he just gave me. I don't know what his dad did, and I no longer care if he shares it with me.

"You already deserve me. Just like I deserve to be celebrated on my birthday. You deserve the life you want. No one gets to take that from you, especially not someone who hurt you."

"It's not that simple. Sure, he hurt me. But I'm no better than him. The fact that you're the first person I've told about this is proof of that."

"No. I refuse to believe that. We agreed to make each other feel good. You do that for me in a way that no one else has ever been able to, inside and out."

"He cheated, and I overheard him and my grandfather arguing about it after the fact," Dean bites out, his hands holding the sides of my face, so I have no choice but to look at him and watch as his eyes turn murky with hatred—for himself, for the men that put him in this position when he was too young to fight back. "A good person would have gone to my mom and told her, not hidden his secret for the last thirteen years. Instead of doing the right thing, I let them convince me it was best that she didn't know. I did that, Mia." His voice breaks.

I turn my head to the side, kissing his palm, trying to infuse everything I'm starting to feel for him without using words that will only make him run. "Just like you believed in me when I couldn't do it myself, I'll do the same for you. Whatever your reasons, Dean, I trust that you made the best decision you could at the time."

"You really shouldn't." The defeat in his voice is so final. The man in front of me is filled with so much self-loathing that it haunts him. This is why he keeps everyone at a distance. Dean doesn't think he's worth it. And it's the reason we can't have a future. All the other bullshit doesn't matter. Not the distance. Not my brother. *This* is our undoing.

"Why? What are you afraid of?" I ask, his fingers tangling in my sex-matted hair.

"I'm terrified that I'm never going to get enough of you and that I'll never *be* enough for you."

"Then I guess you don't have anything to worry about. You already are, and I'll give you anything you want." I don't mention the deadline looming over us. I'm committed to pretending that it doesn't exist—that there is no book tour and spring training. No separate lives tearing us apart at the end of this. Just us. Me, Dean and the way we need each other right now.

That's how we spend the rest of our morning. Acting like a couple that has a long, happy future laid out ahead of us.

But it's a lie. One I know will come back to bite me.

"Up," I groan, pushing on Dean's shoulder. We've been in this bed most of the morning and I need to move.

"No." His arms curl around my waist tugging me against him.

"Dean, I need to do something. I can't just lie around all day." Trying to wriggle my body free from his hold only makes me rub up against all the muscle and bare skin that's kept me in bed all day. I huff out a resigned breath.

"I'll make you a deal. We can leave the bed, but you need to show me your skills."

"What kind of skills?" I'm skeptical as I roll to my back so I can see his face.

"In the batting cage. What did you think I meant?" His eyes crinkle at the corners, his smile the brightest it's been all day.

With a shrug, I roll out of bed. I'm not going to be the one to admit I thought it was just another excuse to have me in a different room. Reaching for the shirt I've been wearing intermittently, I pull it over my head. It's not the same one he had me hold in my mouth while I rode him this morning—so hot, by the way—this is one of his Bandit's warm-ups. I think he might have a kink for me in his clothes. Except, when I move to the dresser to grab a pair of bottoms, his hand covers mine, stopping me.

"Just the shirt."

His tone offers no room for argument, but I can't help the squeak that comes out of me. "What! What if the ball hits me?"

"It won't." Green eyes linger on my bare legs.

"Fine, but you don't get a shirt." It's worth the risk of a ball to the legs if I get to watch him swing shirtless.

He holds out his hand and I'm expecting him to shake on it, but he ducks, pulling me to him and hoisting me over his shoulder. "Off to the batting cage we go."

"What the hell, Dean?" Laughter turns to an indignant screech when his palm lands on my ass with a crack.

"Quit squirming." He clamps down on my thigh, holding me tighter as he navigates through the hallway and enters the gym where he finally sets me down outside the cage.

For a moment my head spins, but once I get my bearings, I'm blown away by what's in front of me. Sure, the techy cage is impressive, but it's the bat and helmet leaning against the netting that has me sucking in a surprised breath.

"What's this?" My thumb runs over the white knob of the brand new softball bat. It's got a gold "15" etched where the length would normally be. "How'd you know my number?"

"Hendrix has a picture of you two from high school in his locker. You're wearing your uniform. The matching numbers were cute," he says, like that explains everything. His fingers move over the controls mounted to the wall, bringing the screen to life. When the simulation loads, it's set up for softball.

"Ladies first." He grabs the white helmet from the ground and spins it on his palm before he eases it over my ears. My insides turn to mush at the care he uses, just like the last time he put one on for me.

We play seven innings like that and I do pretty well, only losing by three. It doesn't feel like losing when, by the third inning, Dean's bare torso is covered in a sheen of sweat and the baseball cap he put on is flipped backwards.

He declared both of us winners, then he chased me down the hallway toward his oasis of a shower. Stripping me of his shirt, he follows me under the dual streams of water where his fingers work their magic in my hair as he washes it. I find myself lulled into daydreaming about lazy days that look like this down the road.

His rough voice cuts in, interrupting the picture perfect alternate reality when he says, "I'm going to miss this."

The reality of our situation comes crashing down around me. Instead of dealing with it, I turn around rinsing the conditioner from my hair. The tile is cool when I drop to my knees and lose myself in him, because we still have time and I refuse to waste any of it.

CHAPTER 28

MIA

"How's the draft of the anthology coming? Will you have something to share soon?" Gianna asks, trying her best to hide her eagerness behind her southern accent.

"Soon," I promise, and I mean it. There's this one scene that's been holding me up. But I have a plan. It'll be fine. I think. The words have been flowing out of me since we got back from Denver last week, but I've gotten stuck on a spicy scene that I can't decide how I want to handle. Don't get me wrong, I know what I want to do, but I just can't get it on paper. Call it imposter syndrome or nerves, but whatever it is, it's blocking my creative flow.

"You know, when you told me you would be gone for the winter, I was skeptical. But you sound more like yourself than you have in the last year. This time away seems like it was just what you needed."

"I feel more like myself than I have in a long time," I admit.

"What's the plan when the winter is over?" she asks casually, not knowing it's the thing that's been plaguing me.

We've been back in Telluride for a week and that question has been a constant dark cloud following me around. It's right there, taunting me, any time Dean isn't melting my brain with his magic dick . . . or fingers, or tongue. *Gah!* The things that man can do with his tongue.

"What if I told you I wasn't sure I wanted to come back to Charlotte?" I ask, almost afraid to give voice to the idea.

"Then don't."

"Really? Just like that?" Her response shocks me. She makes it sound so easy.

Gianna's warm laughter tells me she thinks it is. "You can do this job anywhere. Don't tie yourself to a place where you aren't happiest. You're never here, anyway. And you always come back from visiting Colorado, or St. Louis, happier."

Moving would change everything, and not just for me. As if the universe is listening and needs to remind me of one of the reasons this idea is appealing, Dean pokes his head in my room.

I hold up my finger to tell him I'm almost done. Instead of leaving, he strides into the room kissing my neck gently before lying diagonally across my bed. Not that I've actually slept in it since we've been back. His long body eats up the space, looking more lumberjack and less wealthy baseball player with his worn jeans, flannel, and bare feet.

"Just think about it," Gianna says, reminding me I'm supposed to be on a work call.

"What was that?" I ask, completely flustered by the sinfully beautiful man smirking at me from the bed.

"Distracted much? I would be too if I was living with Dean Harrison. I'll watch for that draft later this month. Give some thought to what I said about slowing down and finding a home that makes you happy," she adds, throwing me a bone.

"I will. Thanks, Gi."

"Of course. And, Mia, maybe that home is your people, not a place."

Gianna's words don't get a chance to take root, because when I turn around after hanging up, I find Dean flipping through the pages of the book I'm reading. My feet move so fast that I'm sailing through the air and landing on the bed next to him with a bounce as the air whooshes out of me.

"Stupid long arms," I grunt out as he holds the book out of reach.

"Dog ears. Really, Mia? I'm disappointed in you."

Please tell me he didn't find the scenes I flagged for research purposes. Who am I kidding? It wouldn't change anything. They were beyond spicy and deserved to be permanently marked with bent corners, so I could always find them for one-handed reading.

"That's market research," I tell him, finally yanking the book free and covertly peeking at where he was, not the smuttiest bits, thank God.

"*Sure,*" he drags out, clearly not believing a word of my bullshit.

"Ready for our adventure? You're supposed to be helping me try new things." Creating a distraction, I walk my fingers up his chest and set the book aside.

"You're off the hook for now because we need to get going so we can beat the snow."

Showing off his athleticism, he rolls over the top of me, gathering me in his arms, without putting his weight on me. My disorientation clears and I realize, somehow, he got me upright with him. Whether it's the way he tosses me around, or the way he takes care of me, I always seem to be off-balance where he's concerned.

Side by side in the mudroom, we get on all our gear for the afternoon he planned out. I'm learning that Dean enjoys surprising people. First with my Christmas gifts, and again this morning when he announced his vague plans over breakfast.

Stepping out into the cold, I follow him to the clearing behind the garage, where he has a snowmobile loaded up and ready to go. I'm about to climb on the back when his arm wraps around my waist from behind.

"Not so fast, Dreamer. You need a helmet." Releasing me, he ducks into the garage and returns with one in each hand. "I didn't want it to get cold sitting out here," he tells me, tugging down my hood and pulling it down over my head with tremendous care. His nose scrunches with concentration as he works the buckle, securing it under my chin. "There. Now you can get on."

No one should be able to make me weak in the knees by putting a helmet on me, yet, here we are.

Dean fires up the machine and then swings his leg over it before securing the remaining one on his head, leaving me standing there looking like a ridiculous statue. Not wanting to be left behind, I scurry on behind him, wrapping my arms around his trim waist.

He turns back to look at me giving me the thumbs up and I nod—jerking backwards slightly when he hits the throttle and takes off into the trees.

Trees zip past as the sound of my squeal echoes in my ears, and my grip tightens around him. Dean kept me in the dark about most of his plans for the day, but judging by the gear strapped to the back, it's more than just the ride. We climb, weaving in and out of the treeline until we come to a clearing. Pulling up to the old shed tucked into the towering evergreen trees, Dean's gloved hand slaps the red button on the handlebar and the sled shudders as the engine cuts out.

With a gracefulness that seems unfair, since my legs feel like jello from the ride, he pops off the machine, holding out his hand to help me, and then pulls off his helmet.

Taking the cue from him, I work the buckle free and remove mine, placing it in his outstretched hand.

"Why'd we stop?" I ask, looking on while he opens the shed door. Ducking inside he stows the helmets and reappears with a set of snowshoes in his hand.

"This is as far as we can take the snowmobile, but there's something I want to show you just over that ridge," he says, pointing to the right side of the clearing.

He rejoins me a moment later and when I look up, I have to stifle a laugh because he looks ridiculous. The pack that was strapped to the back of the snowmobile is now on his back and he has two pairs of ice skates—that I can only guess came from the shed—slung over his shoulders.

"Can I help you carry some of that?" I ask, reaching for a pair of skates. He twists out of my reach just before my fingers can wrap around the laces.

"Nope. Just follow me. The walk isn't long, but the snow can get deep, so stay close to me."

"Am I allowed to ask questions? I'm going to assume, based on the skates, that you have something fun planned? Should I be worried that you're sick of our arrangement and bringing me out here to bury me in a snowdrift? But I don't see a shovel. Where is here, exactly?" I'm rambling but I can't help it. In all the time we've spent together, he's done plenty of thoughtful things, but this almost feels like a date. Based on my history, that makes it dangerous territory. Just when everything was going so well, he had to doom us by planning a sweet date.

Oh god, is he about to reveal a mortifying personality trait?

"I lost count, but I'm pretty sure there were at least three questions buried in there." His glove-clad hand reaches out, taking mine and tugging me forward so I'm walking beside him.

"Sorry about that. You know about my dating history. Just waiting for the other shoe to drop," I admit, as we continue to follow the trees toward the opening in front of us. Beyond the snow-capped trees, I can make out the stunning gray-blue peeks of a mountain range.

Steam puffs up in front of us and his throaty laugh puts me at ease. "Don't worry, this date has a happy ending."

"I didn't mean—I know it's not a date—not like a real one," I huff, stopping and turning towards him. "I'm the other foot this time, aren't I?"

His response is to pull me into his arms, chuckling against my ear. "This is the edge of my property. That's why I had to leave the snowmobile there. When we get to the other side of those trees, we will be in the national forest. It's got the best snow drifts." His tongue pokes the side of his cheek as he looks down at me.

"Oh, you're a funny guy now."

He catches my free hand in his when I go to swat at him. "If you hurt me, it'll ruin our date, our very *real* date. And I don't think you're going to want to miss this." He nods towards the mountain range that's now spread out in front of us. But I'm still stuck on the fact that he called this a date. Maybe he was trying to make me feel better. Friends with benefits don't date, and that's what we agreed to, even if it feels like so much more than that these days.

As far as I can see, the landscape is blanketed in glistening snow and right in the center of it all is the striking, deep blue, alpine lake that is frozen into a slick sheet of glass, perfect for ice skating. The entire scene is framed by those towering peaks, dotted with evergreens.

Dean shifts so he's behind me, wrapping me up in his big body. "No bad surprises today. There's no way I could get sick of you, Dreamer. Today is about making memories."

I try not to focus on the fact that, in just over six weeks, that is all that this will be—a memory of the time that I found the perfect man and had to walk away.

"You can skate?" I didn't expect that.

"I'm from Boston. You don't grow up there without at least playing a few years of hockey."

"Wait, you played hockey. How did that just make you hotter?" My skin warms at the deep laugh that rumbles out of him.

"Let's get you laced up." He leads me over to a rock at the edge of the frozen lake, setting all the gear down on a neighboring rock before getting to work putting on my skates and then doing the same for himself.

"Do you know how to skate?" He grips both my hands and helps me stand on the icy surface.

"My skills are passable. It might be best if you stay close." I flutter my lashes at him, hoping to look sweet instead of crazy. But let's face it, it's probably the latter.

"Is that so? Don't worry, I'll keep you safe." He skates backwards, pulling me with him as my ankles wobble underneath me. After a few strides, everything comes back to me. I start to move my feet and he drops one of my hands. Laughter spills out of me as we circle the frozen lake wind whipping my hair.

"Passable. Seems like that might have been under selling your skills!" Dean yells, chasing after me. Two thick arms band around my waist as he tugs me backwards against his chest. The impact has a puff of breath hanging in the air in front of my face. His cool cheek presses against mine and I can't stop the smile that tilts up my lips.

"Meh. You needed something to make you feel useful. So I played damsel in distress for you. I took ice skating lessons for a few years before I found softball and writing," I tell him, spinning on the blade of the skates, so we are face to face.

"You like role playing, good to know. I can think of a few ways we could make that game even more fun." He licks his lips looking me up and down in a way that has me feeling all too hot given the current temperatures.

Marks from our blades cover almost every surface of the small lake by the time we finally collapse onto the boulder near the shore that Dean has turned into our own personal hot chocolate bar—complete with marshmallows, crushed candy canes, and whipped topping. All of which he had stuffed in the bottom of the pack, along with a blanket to sit on, and the thermos of hot cocoa.

"For someone who doesn't date, you're pretty good at this." The warmth from the cup sinks into my fingers as I raise it to my lips, savoring the decadent flavor of the dark chocolate.

"Only for you. Now get over here and keep me warm," he demands, leaning his back against the sloped part of the boulder and pulling me to sit between his legs.

CHAPTER 29

DEAN

"Someone's in a hurry," Hendrix says with a laugh from behind me as we exit the meeting room at the Bandits facility. Unexpectedly, the team announced the departure of our long-time general manager. Everyone was required to report in for this mandatory meeting, so I arranged for the plane to take me back to Denver.

I look around, expecting to find Cruz rushing past me to get home to Delilah, but find him at Hendrix's side looking equally amused.

"You really fucking suck at this secret relationship thing," Dom says, keeping his voice low as he passes.

"Eat a bag of dicks," I reply, not interested in his shit. One night away from Mia and I feel like the same grumpy asshole I was before she came into my life. I don't like it one bit. In the week since our ice skating date, things have been really good. Too fucking good, because it makes me want things I can't have.

She writes while I work around the cabin or snowboard. We grocery shop and cook together, spend afternoons hiking, watching our favorite childhood movies, and collapsing into bed together at the end of the night, never too exhausted to show each other how we feel.

"Rushing back to my sister. Something you want to tell me?" Hendrix claps me on the back roughly. I fight down the rising panic as I turn to look at him, but he's still wearing the same shit-eating grin.

Discomfort prickles down the back of my neck. I have enough secrets. Lying to my friend and teammate doesn't sit right, but I'm also not willing to break Mia's trust and tell him anything without speaking to her about it first.

At a loss, I open my mouth to say . . . who the hell knows what?

"If you hurt her, I'm going to kick your ass." His smile from earlier fades.

Well, fuck.

"If you didn't want anyone to know, you shouldn't have spent the whole night staring at her from across the room on New Year's Eve," Cruz says, as we push through the door into the parking lot.

"I thought he would be too busy proposing to notice," I grumble in response.

"So, are you going to stick around? Or do you need to rush back to her?" Dom asks, looking up from his phone to chime in.

"She's better company than you three," I shoot back.

"Damn right she is," Hendrix agrees. "But we've hardly seen you all winter."

"It's lonely at night without my wingman," Dom whines and three heads whip his way, mine included.

"What. The. Fuck." Hendrix's words are separated by laughter as he doubles over right there in the middle of the snow-covered parking lot.

Cruz scratches his head under the beanie he's wearing. "You're a brave man to admit that."

"You guys see what I put up with? It's no wonder I need a break in the winter."

"You're heading straight to the airport for sure now, aren't you?" Dom pouts, looking wounded by the idea.

"I'll stay but only—oof." All 225 pounds of my best friend come barreling at me with no warning, almost knocking me on my ass. "Jesus. You're really pushing it today. There are conditions, we do something low-key, no clubs, no ladies."

"Promise," he says way too quickly.

"Seriously, Dom. I'm not in the mood for shenanigans."

He nods eagerly and I know whatever he's planning is going to be a pain in my ass. Still not entirely sure why I agreed to this, I take my phone out to let Mia know about the change in plans.

DEAN:

You should know that what I'm about to tell you is 100 percent your brother's fault.

MIA:

Having known him my entire life, nothing about that shocks me. What'd he do now?

DEAN:

For starters, I'm pretty sure he's figured out our secret. After he called me out for rushing back to you, Dom rallied to guilt me into staying the night.

MIA:

So needy that one.

DEAN:

You have no idea.

MIA:

You're not coming home tonight, are you?

Home. I'm sure she doesn't mean anything by it, but it doesn't change the way my chest warms, starting right over my heart and radiating out from there. Making my whole body tingle in a way I've never felt before.

DEAN:

No, but I'll be on my way first thing in the morning.

MIA:

No one to cuddle with again. What will I do?

DEAN:

*Fuck this. I can probably still
catch the pilot and get home tonight.*

MIA:

*Don't you dare. Neither of us will
ever hear the end of it.*

My eyes are heavy from the late night with the guys the next morning when I board the plane. A giant bottle of water in one hand; a smoothie concoction in the other. Dom was way too cheerful while making it for me on my way out his door this morning.

Much to my surprise, he organized a poker night at his house, instead of dragging us all out to a club, but passed around the tequila early and often. The plus is that I didn't have to spend the night wallowing in my penthouse missing Mia and hating every second of being there without her.

Then there's the picture she texted me, somewhere around the third poker game of her snuggled up in my bed wearing one of my shirts with that damn book she was reading the other day. The extra long bathroom break I took after that was purely coincidental. It had nothing to do with the way my dick turned to stone, knowing she was sleeping in my bed, in my shirt, and nothing else.

This morning, before boarding the plane, I made a pit stop to grab something to bring back for her. Well, for both of us, really. Mia hasn't come out and said it, but I picked up on the clues. The flare in her pupils when she was reading to me, the way her pulse fluttered rapidly with Dom and me in the kitchen. The pages she had dog-eared. So curious. We'll have to work up to what she really craves, but the small package tucked safely in my backpack is just the start.

On the short drive from the airport back to the cabin, my hands twist on the steering wheel. I can't stop my mind from wandering to her and what she's doing there without me. Is she writing? Or out in the gym doing yoga? Maybe relaxing in the hot tub?

The picture the last scenario paints in my head is enough to have me stepping on the gas—her dark locks piled high on top of her head, with a few wavy pieces falling loose, like they always seem to do. The bridge of her nose and apples of her cheeks rosy from the bite of the cold air on her flawless face. Pink lips tilted up in the smile that she grants without fail every time she sees me. Fuck, that glowing smile makes me feel worthy of more than just my baseball stats—something I haven't felt in a long time.

It should be embarrassing how quickly I tear out of my car and leap over the front porch steps when I pull up to the cabin. Key word being, "should be," but I can't bring myself to care. My hand shoots out, stopping the door from banging off the wall when I swing it open a little too eagerly.

Nothing has ever made as much sense as Mia curled up in front of my fireplace—in the place that means so much to me, where I feel most at home.

Her head swivels towards me from the chair she's reading in. "You're back."

There it is, the smile that has my head swimming with emotions that are getting hard to ignore.

Just like I imagined, she's stunning. Stray pieces of hair sway around her face, loose from the ponytail sitting on top of her head. Instead of her cheeks being red from the cold, they're pink with heat. Maybe from the fire, but more likely from the reading she was doing. My eyes drop to her lap, where she sets the closed book. Three cutesy illustrated characters on the cover don't match the handful of sentences I read before she grabbed it away the other day. With eager steps, I cross the small space and place my hands on the arms of the chair so that she's forced to tilt her head back and look up at me.

"I'm back. I see you've spent your time alone getting caught up on reading?"

"Among other things. I've done some work too. It's not all lounging by the fire and reading while you're gone. As a matter of fact, I finished my draft of my book."

"Have I told you lately how damn impressive you are?" I close the space between us and force her further back in the chair.

"Not today." Surprise flits across her face like she can't believe that she's the first thing on my mind after being gone for the last two nights.

"Then let me tell you now." My lips brush against her temple and she melts under me, unfolding her legs and making room for me. "Your intelligence and creativity are unmatched, and it's so sexy how you mold literary masterpieces with this brain."

"I would hardly—"

The press of my lips against hers shut her up. My tongue invades her mouth, kissing her hard before I pull back and continue. "Does your writing make people cry?"

She nods.

"Have you convinced people to give love a chance for a second or third time?"

"Sure—" she starts, but I'm not done.

"Do women everywhere do that thing where they roll onto their stomachs, bury their noses in your book and kick their feet in the air squealing in delight?"

"Well, I'm not sure about that—"

The glare I shoot her has her lips rolling together.

"Like I said."

Kiss.

"Impressive."

Kiss.

"Masterpieces."

"So, you give my brain a five star rating," she says, her voice breathy and sexy as hell.

"Ten." With Mia distracted by the little nips I place along her neck, I'm free to grab the book—the one I suspect caused the pretty pink blush I found her with. "And what's this? Just some little reading for fun, or is this research?"

"Mhhh," she hums, tilting her head side to side as she considers. "Maybe a little of both."

"In that case, I think you'll like the gift I got you." I reach into the backpack I dropped at my feet, pulling out the small box.

Two deep lines crease Mia's forehead, looking from the box to me—turning it over in her hand. "You didn't need to get me anything."

"I really did. You'll understand when you open this. I've told you before I'm a selfish man and this is just as much for me as it is for you."

Her reaction is everything I hoped for, those icy pools almost entirely black now with the way her pupils dilate when she opens the box. Our first time together wasn't sweet and soft, like I suspect Mia is used to. My girl fucking blossomed under me, my hand around her throat holding her down as she begged me to "fuck her like she's mine." I never would have guessed her dirty mouth would rival mine.

Her thumb strokes down the tapered black silicone and a sound I've never heard starts low in my throat. It's a half-whimper, half-shaky exhale, and one hundred percent because of her. My hands squeeze the arms of the chair, rooting me in place while I wait for her to confirm what her body language is telling me.

"You—um. Do you want to use this on me?" Her breathing picks up as she searches my face for an answer.

"The more important question is, do *you* want me to use it on you?" I pluck the toy from the box, taking it between my fingers and trailing it down the side of her neck, along her collarbone and between the valley of her small breast. The plug catches on the fabric of her sweater, pulling down the neck and giving me a peek at what's hiding underneath before I tap the thin end against the book in her lap.

"Tell me you're not curious, I know you, Dreamer. You weave fantasies in that spectacular imagination of yours. And your body gives you away every single time—when you're writing, or reading. But don't do this for me, do it for you." Her eyes fall to the gift in my hand, but then she lifts her eyes to mine—it's stunning. I find nothing but certainty and lust in the expression.

"I can't stop thinking about it. I haven't been able to since . . ." Scarlet marbles cover her collarbone and up her neck. "Since you told me about the night the picture was taken with the three of you." She looks up at me through her lashes with her teeth clamping down on the corner of her lip.

Oh. *Oh.*

"Are you okay? You look stunned. Did I break you?"

Fuck, I think I could love this woman. But I shove that down because it would only lead to disaster, instead I cover my shock with a cocky confidence that I mastered years ago to mask my true feelings.

"You've just managed to astonish me yet again. You are fascinating, Mia James." Her lips vibrate against my neck, the force of her giggles making her squirm in my arms when I scoop her up from the chair unexpectedly and switch places with her. "We should celebrate." With her in my lap, I'm surrounded by the honeyed scent of peaches.

Damn, I missed this.

"What? Why would we do that?"

"Because you wrote a book. A whole damn book. And whether it's your first or your fiftieth, that deserves some recognition."

"Is that part of the celebration?" she asks, tilting her head towards the toy.

"Only if you want it to be," I say, burying my nose in her hair.

My lips latch onto her neck, sucking the skin there, causing the "yes" that comes out of her to be broken and breathy.

That one word has me going from semi to fully hard in an instant. If last night taught me anything, it's that the way I need her is so much more than how well we work together in bed, even if that's how it started.

"Seeing as I can't say no to you. Yes, it is. Wait here. I'll be right back." I stand from the chair, bringing her with me, only to set her back down. A pout that rivals even the most spoiled brat takes over her face. "None of that. Trust me?"

Crossing her arms over her chest she maintains the pout. "Fine."

I'm still laughing to myself as I make the brief trip to grab what I need from my bedroom. Mia's never been guarded with me. Over the last six weeks, getting to know her has been like looking inside the most vivid kaleidoscope. Each turn makes it harder to look away. She's sweet and fearless, clever and unselfish, adventurous but humble. Being around her, when she's so brazenly herself, is changing me and it's getting harder to recognize the man I was when we agreed that this would be temporary.

Finding her waiting for me when I walk back into the living room, icy eyes dark with desire, knocks the wind right out of me.

"What's that look for?" An inky strand of hair falls in front of her face and she tucks it back behind her ear, shifting in the chair.

"You take my breath away, Dreamer." My fist taps twice right over my sternum. "You have no clue what a fucking sight you are. Fucking exquisite. It's unfair, really."

"Is that so?" she asks, tilting her chin up to meet my eyes as I stop in front of her, holding my hand out.

She lays her palm in my waiting hand and stands. A high-pitched squeal comes out of her mouth when I spin her in my arms. With her back against my front, there's no question that she can feel exactly how affected I am by her. Dropping my lips so they hover at the shell of her ear, my voice is harsh and gravely when I say, "No one has a right to look as enchanting as you do when just minutes ago you were practically begging me to fill this tight little hole." I thrust my hips, my dick running the length of her ass.

"I think you like the fact that I'm anything but an angel." She presses back into me as if I need any more proof how badly she wants this.

"Only for me." I've never been particularly possessive, but I've also never considered a woman mine the way I do with Mia. This connection we've built tethers us together in a way I've never expected.

"Just for you." She snakes her arm back gripping the back of my neck, claiming me in the same territorial way.

"Good." I reach for the hem of her shirt, peeling it away, and palming her breast roughly when I find her bare under my oversized crewneck. "You in my clothes is my new favorite thing, but you *naked* under my clothes—nothing has ever gotten me harder. You know I had to sneak off to get myself under control in Dom's guest bathroom after the little stunt you pulled last night with that picture."

She snorts, making her chest shake under my hands. The happy sound is cut off when my fingers find her nipples, pinching sharply, turning her laughter into a throaty moan. "Something funny?"

"It wasn't even that scandalous." Her back arches as I twist and pluck until her nipples form tight peaks.

"Knowing that you were reading that book, in my bed . . . let's just say I'm glad I wore jeans instead of sweatpants or everyone would have had some questions."

She chuckles again, clearly enjoying the predicament I found myself in. "That would have been fun to explain."

"You have no idea." In theory, her brother seems to be handling it well, but that very well may have pushed him over the edge.

My hand slides down Mia's stomach, slipping under the waistband of her leggings. "Drenched. Why am I not surprised? Is it my misery that turns you on? Or the idea of me playing with this sweet ass?"

"The last one." She gasps when I brush my thumb over her clit.

"Good. Bend over and grab the back of the chair," I tell her, stepping back to watch her do just that. Her eyes connect with me over her shoulder waiting for instructions. "That's it, baby. Just like that." My eyes rake over her, noticing the way her back rises and falls as her breathing quickens. I step forward placing my hands on her hips. "We need to get rid of these." My hands peel her leggings and underwear down her legs slowly. By the time they join my sweatshirt, she's squirming, her ass swaying in the air. It's enough to have me struggling to maintain control.

"Dean, please touch me," she whimpers, letting her head hang between her shoulders. And I will, but not until I get my fill of her like this.

"Spread your legs for me. After that tease of a picture last night, I want to see all of you."

Just like last time, she does exactly what I ask, even lowering her back so every glistening inch of her is on display for me. "Fuck yes. Such a good listener."

Closing the distance between us, my hand falls to her ass, massaging one cheek and then the other. Her body cants as she shifts her weight, seeking me out.

"Patience." My thumb circles her hole before flattening against it. "We will get there, but not until I'm sure you can take it. I want to make this good for you. Can you let me to do that?"

She sags against the back of the chair when my hands move away from where she wants me most, tracing the curves of her legs down to her ankles as I drop to my knees behind her.

"Y—yes. I know you will. There's no one else I'd entrust with my body like this." Her words fade into a moan as my hands move back up, this time following the path my mouth creates as I kiss the inside of her knee, the heart-shaped birthmark on the back of her leg, and finally my lips brush against her inner thigh. The sound she makes when I seal my mouth over her center is pure bliss. Not that I need encouragement, the way she tastes, giving her pleasure, it's all the motivation I need. The flat of my tongue works her over and when her legs start shaking, I know she's close.

My dick is heavy and desire clouds my mind as I battle over how I want her to come. The implication that she's never done anything like this before weighing on me. Wetness coats my face when I pull back, replacing my mouth with a finger that slips inside of her easily. Adding another I pump in and out, keeping her right on the edge.

"Soak my face and I'll calm that curious mind. Show you what it feels like to be so full you can't stand it." Wrapping my arm around her hip, my free hand finds her clit, working it as she tightens around my fingers. "That's it. Give me every last drop." My teeth nip at her inner thigh, marking it.

"Oh shit. Do that again. So . . . close."

My lips latch on to the other legs, sucking and nipping as her legs tremble against me. Her knees buckle and my name pours out of her mouth. It's pure, honeyed sweetness, just like her as I lap at her, swapping my fingers for my tongue as she comes undone for me.

The sound of my pulse beats wildly in my ears, the thrill of getting her off ups my need to be inside her. But my dick is going to have to wait because I'm not quite done with her. "I'm a fucking glutton for you. I want to gorge on you, until neither of us can take it anymore."

With a shaky laugh she lets her knees give out, collapsing into the chair a tangle of creamy limbs. "What a way to go. I'd let you eat me alive with a mouth like that." Half-lidded eyes find me over her shoulder, looking deliriously relaxed.

"Don't worry, we are far from done." Her lips part on the softest whimper and her eyes dart to the plug and lube sitting off to the side. The hunger there has me palming my cock in my pants, but it does nothing to relieve the ache. Only she can do that.

"Shirt off." She waves a flop hand in my direction. "Two nights apart was too long. I want this insane body pressed up against mine."

Hours of honing my skills on and off the field have left my body stacked with corded muscle. I'm no stranger to compliments about it, but coming from Mia, it just hits different. It fills me with a sense of pride and makes me hunger for more of her praise. It joins the pile of clothes forgotten on the floor.

"Ass up, sweetheart." It's almost comical the way she clamors to her feet, pushing her round ass back towards me.

"Fuck yes." My calloused palm drags over my jaw before grabbing the small bottle and uncapping it. The snap of the lid has Mia biting down on her lip. "Are you nervous?"

"No." Her eyes fly up to mine and there's no trepidation there. "You've never given me a reason to be."

CHAPTER 30

MIA

"Jesus. You're going to kill me," Dean murmurs as his hand cradles my hip and his hard length bobs between us.

"That would be a shame. You have such a perfect dick," I tell him, an involuntary shiver rattling my spine when the cool lube drips between my cheeks. The joking from earlier evaporates with each roll of the tapered toy against me.

When he presses it against my tight entrance, it has me grappling for a better hold on the back of the chair.

"Relax, for me." He rubs his thumb methodically over my hip bone. It's oddly gentle considering the position he has me in.

"I can't," my whimper is filled with desperation.

"You can." The toy passes over me again, more forcefully this time. Dipping inside me, but only a fraction. Without thinking about it, I'm pushing back into it. "Put your hand between your legs, Mia." His deep voice is calm as he feeds me instructions.

My fingers slip between my legs, brushing over my sensitive clit. Dean uses the distraction to press the toy in further this time. We repeat the pattern a few times. Him pushing, while I circle my clit. Each time leaves me wanting more. My hips push back, chasing the retreating toy, and Dean's dark chuckle taunts me. "I'd say you're ready for more."

"Please. Don't make me wait," I beg, not ashamed of how badly I want it. My legs shake and my release builds, trickling down my spine as he continues to tease me. This time, when he presses the toy against my backside, he doesn't stop. There's a bite of pain as the thickest part breeches the ring of muscle before it slides all the way in and then there's only delicious fullness that has my release doubling down to the point where it's almost unbearable.

"Not yet, Dreamer. I need you to wait for me," Dean grits out over the sound of foil ripping.

"Wh—what?" There's no way I can hold out. I whip my head around to tell him just that, only to have the breath stolen from me when he pushes inside. "Fuuuck," I groan, my head dropping to the back of the chair.

"So tight," Dean growls, pulling his hips back and slamming into me again. "Not going to last."

Thank fuck, because I'm tipping over the edge and with each thrust, the ability to hold on for him slips a little further out of my grasp. With the plug inside me, I can feel every inch of him in a brand new way.

"Dean . . . please I need to—I can't. So full." The string of nonsense coming out of me was so jumbled I couldn't even make sense of it. All I know is if I don't come right now, I might pass out. "It's too much."

"No, it's not. You can take it. Show me how good you can be for me." With each thrust, the toy inside me jostles, making me clench around it.

Dean's hand traces the curve of my spine until it brushes my hair to the side and grips my chin, turning it to look at him as he curls over my back.

"Come for me, sweetheart."

Thank fuck. His permission is all I need to let go of the thin thread of restraint I've been clinging to. His other hand drops to my tailbone and his thumb presses against the end of the toy, making everything go hazy. My vision blurs, and my entire body shudders as my orgasm tears through me.

Dean doesn't give me time to recover. He's lifting me from where I've collapsed against the chair and laying me down on the rug next to the fire, his hand cushioning the back of my head. This time entering me to the hilt as his mouth covers mine.

"Missed you so damn much," he says through clenched teeth as he brings me right back to the edge. "Show me how much you missed me. Give me one more."

Not that he needed to ask. The intensity in his eyes as he hovers over me is enough to get me there on its own.

My fingers find my clit, slipping against my slick skin—finding a rhythm I know will have me there in no time. I feel that familiar buzzing start low in my belly, my whole body tightens like a rubber band stretched to its limits.

"That's my girl. So close." Dean lifts my leg, bringing it to his shoulder and the new angle coaxes a deranged, keening cry out of me.

Just as my orgasm starts, he shocks the hell out of me by sliding the plug out, making me squeeze around the emptiness in the most delicious way possible. It's like nothing I've ever experienced. Dean jolts above me, panting as he swells inside me.

Neither one of us moves for a long while, other than the quick business of taking care of the condom. We stay on the floor in front of the fire while Dean brushes the hair off my face and we both come back down to earth.

I'm the first to speak when I ask him, "What are you afraid of?"

His response is so quiet I'm not sure if I hear him right. "That I won't be able to let you go."

♥

Oh, wow. My footsteps pause in the opening that leads from the bathroom, where I just finished showering. The towel in my hand scrunches my hair and I prop myself against the wall, looking on in awe of the man in front of me. After we tried out the gift he brought home from Denver for me last week, the spicy scene that was causing me so much trouble found some . . . inspiration.

My laptop looks tiny resting on his powerful thighs. Behind black frames, his green eyes scan the screen reading the words I wrote. I wonder how long I can stand here just watching him, memorizing the way his lips quirk as he reads before he catches me. This version of Dean is one of my favorites, but if I'm being honest, I like all of them. Although, now that I think about it, I haven't seen Mr. Tall Dark and Broody make an appearance outside of the bedroom—or hot tub, or gym, or kitchen.

"Are you just going to stand over there staring at me like a creep all morning?" he asks, without looking up from the draft of my finished manuscript.

"It's possible. You, reading, with those glasses, is the best view in Telluride." Slinging the towel over my shoulder I push off the wall and move to the kitchen where he has a plate of bacon and eggs waiting for me.

"If you'd prefer, we can just stay here today while you gaze at me from across the room instead of the day I have planned."

"You're still not going to tell me what we're doing?"

"I could, but I think you like it when I surprise you." His dark eyes track over me, leaving a wake of heat behind before he goes back to reading.

There's no denying that Dean never fails to shock me with the curveballs he throws me. My pulse flutters when I think about last week, when he brought home the unexpected gift from Denver.

"You're sure I don't need to bring anything with me?"

"Just boots and enough layers for a short hike." He closes the laptop, swinging his legs off the couch.

"Are you bringing your swimsuit?" I ask, lifting a forkful of eggs to my mouth. My eyes follow his movement as he closes in on me round the counter. I struggle to swallow the bite without choking when he steps behind me and lays a hand on each side of the counter, dipping his mouth to my neck, crowding me.

"Do you want me to?" He moves along the column of my neck. Scrambling my brains so that all I can do is shake my head. "No?" he asks.

"No," I confirm, finally finding my voice.

"Finish breakfast. We'll leave in twenty minutes." I hold my shiver back until he slips his boots on and disappears outside.

After finishing my breakfast, I spend a few minutes braiding my hair into two braids and throw on my warmest leggings and a base layer top with a pullover. Dean's still outside, tinkering around with the plow on the front of the UTV, while I slip on my boots and grab my hat and gloves.

His face lights up when he sees me approaching. Something about that smile, knowing it's so rarely shared with those outside his circle, has me feeling all warm and fuzzy inside. His gaze drops to my empty hands and his grin turns devilish. "No swimsuit?"

"Nope," I say, popping the "P." "I'm taking my cues from you since you're keeping me in the dark."

"Excellent. I like my decision even more now." He stands from where he's kneeling in the snow, nodding toward the waiting SUV. "Let's do it."

The cabin is just disappearing in the rearview mirror when Dean asks, "Have I told you how brilliant you are today?"

"Not that I can recall."

"The way you've evolved as a writer with this latest book is seriously impressive. I think your readers are going to be blown away by how you've changed things up," he says it so casually that I almost miss the admission buried in his words.

"Don't get me wrong, I love when you praise me. Always. Never stop. But it almost sounds like you've read my backlist."

I turn in my seat to watch as his hand comes up to scratch at his jaw. His eyes shift from the road to me for a moment before he shrugs and says, "I might have downloaded one or two to read when I was back in Denver last week."

"Why would you do that?" My hands fidget in my lap as I wait for his answer. I know my feelings have morphed into more, but we've done such an excellent job of avoiding what happens when we part ways that I don't know where Dean's head is at.

"Is that a real question?" Outside the car, snowy pines give way to rocky walls as we climb higher into the mountains.

"Yes, it just doesn't seem like something you would do for the girl you're sleeping with for the winter." Right now, my guard is up because this man holds all the power to hurt me. We set boundaries, ones that were supposed to keep me safe. But it turns out there is nothing safe about the way I feel about him.

The glare he levels me with is icier than the mountains outside the windows. "You're right, but you know damn well this is so much more than that, even if it's how we started."

"Is it?" As soon as the words leave my mouth, I want to take them back. I don't want to fight with him, not about anything. And certainly not this. Yet, here I am, picking this fight with him when I want to hear these words. Deep in the marrow of my bones, I know it'll only make our end harder. The regret only builds when his eyebrows shoot to his hairline. He's clearly as taken back by my tone as I am. "I'm sorry. I didn't mean it like that. Just forget I said anything."

The damage is already done. I watch Dean shift from soft and playful to that same guarded man I first met. Sulking, I stare out the window as the pines start to reappear along the road. By the time we pull into the turnoff and take a one lane road, leading us further into the middle of nowhere, the atmosphere in the car is glacial.

Gravel crunches under the tires as we pull on to the shoulder. Once we're parked, he reaches around my seat to grab a backpack and gets out without a word, leaving me sitting there surrounded by regret.

Way to go, Mia.

I shake my head, reaching for the door handle when it's pulled open for me. Without a word, he takes my hand, helping me from the car and he doesn't drop it until we get to where the trail narrows to the point where we can no longer walk side by side.

"Are we going to talk about this?" My shorter legs are burning with the effort it takes to keep up with his longer strides as he quickly makes his way through the snow. He says nothing, which only amplifies my frustration, with myself and him. "Hey, you can be pissed. But you don't get to ignore me." I reach out, snagging his arm.

"The only reason I'm ignoring you is because I'm afraid I might say something I can't take back, Mia. And the last thing I want is for my words to hurt you, because I can tell you it fucking sucks."

Ouch. That blow lands like a punch to the gut. Instead of continuing to push him, I give him the space he asked for—trudging along with nothing but an occasional twig snapping or bird chirping to fill the silent void between us.

The few minutes it takes to hike the narrow trail seem to stretch on. When the path widens enough to walk side by side, Dean stops, allowing me to catch up before he takes my glove-covered hand in his and helps me over an outcropping of rocks. Stunning doesn't begin to describe what I see when my feet hit the ground on the other side of the boulders. The snowy landscape of the forest gives way to tranquil hot springs surrounded by majestic evergreens. Steam billows out of the natural pool, a private oasis dropped in the middle of the Rocky Mountains.

"Does this seem something I'd plan for if I was 'just fucking you to pass the time'?" Dean asks calmly.

"No," I choke out, feeling like the biggest asshole.

"I don't care what we said when this started, it's never been just some arrangement so we could get off." He closes the space between us, dropping the backpack at his feet before he's unzipping his jacket and tossing to the side where it lands on a bare tree branch.

When I don't move to do the same, his fingers work my zipper free and slide the coat down my shoulders. With a flick of his wrist, it joins his jacket. His pullover and shirt join the clothes dangling from the tree. Then he's toeing off his boots and stepping out of his pants all while I stand there just watching. I can't tell what he's thinking, and it's hard to work anything out when he's stripping down in front of me. No matter how many times I've seen his body, each inch of muscle he reveals to me has the same appeal it did the first time I saw him like this.

For the second time today, he catches me openly ogling him when he bends to remove his black boxer briefs. "If you like what you see, maybe you should join me in the water, Dreamer."

Dean sinks into the warm water with a groan that sends me into a mad dash to get my clothes off to be as exposed to him as he is to me at this moment. His eyes watch every move I make until I'm standing there in nothing but my light pink thong and matching ribbed bra. The cool air licking at my skin doesn't even register with his heated stare on me.

Glancing over my shoulder to make sure we are still alone, I remove both and drop them on the edge of the springs. I'm not brave enough to leave them by the rest of our clothes in case someone stumbles upon our oasis.

Warm water licks at my skin as I sink into the pool—wading across until I'm within arm's reach of Dean. The sting of rejection burns through me when he doesn't immediately pull me to him. I know my words hurt him.

"I'm scared, Dean. I never meant to feel this much for you. Losing you at the end of this terrifies me."

"Not going to happen. I told you, my life is better with you in it. Even if things change when you go back to North Carolina, I can't imagine a life where you aren't part of it," he says, sinking into the water so he's submerged up to his shoulders.

It's on the tip of my tongue to ask what would happen if I don't move back, but I don't think I could stand it if he hated the idea. "I'm sorry I lashed out and hurt you."

"Come here, Dreamer. I don't want to waste our last three weeks with anything between us. If something is bothering you, talk to me. We can work through it together." He opens his arm for me to swim into his embrace.

"So mature. You're going to make an excellent husband one day, when you realize that you're not as broken as you think. I'll try not to hate her." His arms tighten around me and his warm breath tickles my ear as he laughs.

"Let's not get carried away. Marriage isn't in the cards for me, not after what my dad put my mom through." It shouldn't matter to me because we just solidified that we're parting ways at the end of this, but his words carry a heavy weight that settles right over my heart. Until this wonderful, kind man deals with his past, he won't be able to see past the hurt his family caused.

Yet, I can't stand to break our connection. My legs wrap around his waist clinging to him and what he'll willingly give me. I won't ask him for more. I started my life in a situation where I wasn't enough to be kept and I won't put myself in that situation again by trying to change his mind. That's something only he can do for himself, and for us.

Gripping his damp hair, I tilt his head back and bury my feelings in our kiss. When his tongue invades my mouth and he hardens between us, I embrace it as the distraction I need.

Everything that's happened between us today ratchets up my desire for him. I want to erase the distance I created between us until we are melded into one, even if it's only for a short time—take a part of him to keep with me when this is all over.

"I need you, Dean." I slide my center along the length of him so there's no question what I mean. "Every inch."

He kisses me slow and deep before resting his forehead against mine, his erection pressing against my entrance. "I've never . . ." he starts, and I have to stifle my giggle.

"Look at me, making Dean Harrison stumble over his words."

"Careful. Brats get fucked hard." His teeth nip at my bottom lip playfully as he lowers me down, pressing his tip inside me.

"And bare? I have an IUD and I'm all clear. I want to feel all of you, even if it's just this once."

"You trust me with this?"

Gently my thumb rubs across the two lines etched into his forehead. I think I'd trust him with everything if he'd let me—my body, my heart, my soul—if only he'd let me, but since this is all he's willing to take, I offer the simplest truth I can, "Like no one else, ever."

"I'm clear too. I tested right before we left as part of my team physical." He pulls back out, giving me another chance to change my mind.

My hands grip the sides of his face caressing the strong line of his jaw and I find those jarring beautiful evergreen eyes filled with doubt. Like he's certain I'm going to find him lacking and change my mind.

My grin turns feline, and I lift my shoulder in nonchalance. "I mean, if you don't want to, we don't . . ."

"And everyone thinks you're such a good girl. Do you reserve all this brattiness just for me?" he grits out, his chest collapsing with a relieved exhale.

"Only when I'm promised a hard fuck for my behave—"

He slams into me, not giving me time to adjust to him before he does it again. "Is that what you want? For me to own this pussy?"

"Yes! It's yours!" I cry out, digging my nails into his shoulder as he slams me down on him.

"Damn right it is. You're mine until the second I have to walk away."

I know it's true. I'd bet that even long after we've parted ways, I'll still be his.

"And this is not the last time I'll be inside you like this." Each of his words are punctuated by a thrust that I feel everywhere.

"It's never been this good."

His mouth covers mine, swallowing up my moans as his fingers press into the soft flesh of my ass.

"Nothing else will ever be this good. You're my nirvana," I moan.

His hand wraps around the back of my neck, holding me in place as he continues to fuck up into me. With nothing between us, each pump of his hips drives me closer to bliss.

"You just like fucking me."

My giggle is breathy, and his answering thrust is a punishment for my snark. He's saying too much. It makes my heart swell with a foolish hope.

"No, I like you." My walls squeeze around him like I'm trying to hold him in place.

"Oh, shit." His wheeze is mixed with a laugh. "Unless you're about to come, I suggest you don't do that again."

"Like you'd leave me behind," I huff out, my breath fogging the air.

"Some people use orgasm denial as a punishment," he says darkly.

There's no hiding the thrill that runs through me when I gasp at the suggestion.

"But not today. Can you come like this?"

"Maybe?" I admit truthfully. He feels so good, but in this position, with his hands holding me up, and the water working against us, it's not going to be easy.

"I don't like those odds." He moves us to the edge of the pool, lowering me slowly until my feet find a natural step in the rock. This leaves us so much more exposed to the cool air, and to anyone that might decide to take a dip.

"I need your help to be quick about this," he says, obviously having the same concerns I am. Holding onto my hips to keep me steady as I turn around, Dean sinks back into me from behind. Forcing me to grip the edge of the pool so I don't slip.

"Can you use your other hand to play with your nipples for me, sweetheart?" he asks, covering my back with his. It doesn't allow him to go as deep, but it helps to keep both of us warm.

"Yes." One hand covers my breast, pulling and tweaking the way I like.

Dean keeps one hand glued to my hips, keeping me safe, as his other hand wraps around me, his finger sliding over the spot where we are connected.

"Jesus, I can't believe you let me inside you like this." There's a reverence in his voice that makes me want to turn in his arms and hold him. "I want you like this again when we get home, where I can take my time with you."

"Yes," is the only answer I can formulate when the pads of his fingers find my clit, giving me the pressure he knows my body craves and circles it, never letting his rhythm falter.

It's never taken him long to get me there, but now that he knows my body, he uses all that he's learned, coaxing my body into giving him exactly what he wants.

My legs shake under me as I try not to slip on the slick bottom of the springs.

"Let go. I'll keep you safe."

I couldn't stop if I wanted to when he pinches my clit between his fingers, causing a loud string of obscenities that might be embarrassing if I wasn't coming so damn hard right now. I know he's feeling it too when he swells and continues to fuck me through his release.

Still rooted inside me, Dean pulls me backwards into the warmth of the water wrapping his arms around me and resting his chin against my shoulder. "Are you warm enough?"

All I can do is laugh because my skin is still feverish from my orgasm. "Yeah. All good," I tell him, turning in his arms when he slips free from my body. "I really am sorry about earlier."

"Next time your feelings get the best of you, maybe just tell me. You're not the only one that gets scared sometimes."

Nothing beats the sight of Dean stepping out of the spring, in all his naked glory, to grab my towel and clothes for me, while I bask in the water's warmth.

Sure, the mountains and trees are stunning, but without him it's just another landscape.

CHAPTER 31

DEAN

"You're sure I can't entice you to stay?" her sleepy voice asks before she sits with her back against the headboard.

She's blissfully naked under my bed sheet and I'm fully dressed, looking every bit the Beacon Hill brat I grew up as. My shoulders tense with nerves as I roll the crisp white sleeves of the button-up over a sweater my mother gave me for Christmas. The short scruff lining my jaw is the last piece of my life in Telluride remaining. Well, that and the hickey Mia gave me last night, which is barely visible over the collar of my shirt.

I'm not entirely sure if I kept the facial hair as a big ole fuck you to my grandfather, or because Mia wouldn't quit about how much she loved the feel of it when I was between her legs the other day. Either way, she's now a staunch supporter of it, which means I am as well.

With a whine she drops the sheet, letting it pool around her waist. There's a thump from my duffle bag hitting the floor right before I launch myself at her.

"There's no place I'd rather be than here with you," I remind her. "But my mother would kill me if I missed this party." My lips slot over hers, kissing her until she relaxes underneath me and I'm in danger of missing my window for the pilot to take off.

"I'll see you in a few days," I tell her with one last kiss to her nose before I crawl out of the bed and grab my bag leaving her in my bed. When I get to the front door, I turn around and march back through the cabin stopping in the doorway to my room.

"You came back," she whispers, her eyes half-lidded.

Slipping my phone out of my pocket, I open up the camera and snap a picture of her like that. The sheets cover my favorite parts, but she looked too damn irresistible not to document.

"Did you just take a picture of me?" She shifts in bed so the sheet slips lower, putting more of her creamy skin on display for me.

"Yes," I admit tentatively. If she wants me to delete it, I will, but I really fucking hope she doesn't make me.

"Take another," her sleep filled voice rasps, sliding her hands up to cup her breasts.

"Are you just trying to entice me to stay?" *Click.*

"Is it working?" She rearranges her body on the bed again, giving me another shot, discretely posing herself so there's nothing but skin on display.

Click.

"Almost," I admit, pocketing my phone. "At least I have these to keep me warm at night."

CHAPTER 32

DEAN

It's just like my brother to pick a stuffy ass bar filled with nothing but self-important pricks sipping bourbon that makes them feel better about their life choices. Or maybe that's just my shitty attitude about leaving Mia alone in my bed. To top it all off, he's late and I'm almost out of patience when I see him crossing the bar. "This fucking guy. Twenty minutes late. That's excessive, even for your spoiled ass. Grandfather would be appalled," I say when Dylan drops into the seat next to me. His disheveled appearance has me sliding him my glass of whiskey.

"Thanks. I need that more than I need to get shit on by you."

"Trouble at the office?" I flag down the bartender for another glass.

"Something like that," he murmurs, avoiding eye contact.

"Just let me know when you're ready to talk about Ava. I'll be waiting and ready to listen."

"Oh, yeah. Is there going to be a heavy helping of 'I told you so' with that offer?" Bitterness coats his tone before he drains the glass in front of him.

"Doesn't seem like that's necessary. You're clearly beating yourself up enough." The bartender sets another glass in front of us and fills both of them without having to be asked.

"Does Mom have you doing party prep tomorrow?" Dylan asks, glancing at his phone before he sets it face down on the bar top.

"Of course. I thought about concocting a fake photoshoot to get out of it, but I couldn't do that to her."

"Such a mama's boy," he teases, but it doesn't bother me. I'd be the first to admit how accurate his statement is. I wouldn't have suffered for years keeping secrets if I wasn't.

"Dad wants to talk to me tomorrow. He wants to fix things between us and says it's only hurting Mom and Natalie," I confide—the heaviness of guilt quickly cloaking me. Like the rest of my family, Dylan doesn't know why there's a rift between us. Despite not having plans to tell him, it would be nice to have someone to talk to about it.

Soft and patient, a familiar feminine voice in my head reminds me I have someone I could talk to about it. But Mia doesn't need to deal with my family shit. Especially considering we only have a few weeks together when I get back. That's the last way I want to spend our remaining time together.

"Maybe it's time. The only time I ever see Mom and Dad argue is when you or grandpa come up."

Well fuck, I don't know what to do with that. It still has to be better than knowing her husband's a cheater. But it grates on me that I'd cause her any pain.

"Should we come up with a drinking game for the party to keep it interesting?" he asks, swirling the amber liquor in his cup before he takes a drink.

"Like what? Drink every time a stuffy old man says something condescending to Natalie?" My anxiety builds the more we talk about the party. I know my brother is trying to lighten the mood, but it's not working. My mind is firmly stuck on the impending talk with Dad.

There's too much history, too much resentment. He stripped me of any chance of having a normal, happy relationship before I was even old enough to decide if that's what I'd want. Forcing secrets on me that turned me into this jaded asshole, and now he expects me to forgive him.

Mia doesn't want to end up with someone like me.

Lifting the glass to my lips I swallow down the remaining whiskey and set it on the edge of the bar to be refilled.

♥

"Is this hell? Did I drink so much that I've died and seeing your naked ass first thing in the morning is punishment?" I groan, rolling away from the sight of my brother, cupping his junk as he strolls across the hotel room. Last night is fuzzy, but I vaguely remember him coming up to my room to crash on the pull out after several more rounds at the hotel bar.

"I think you mean Heaven. I'm borrowing this," he says, forcing me to sit up and face the headache blossoming behind my temples.

"Are those my underwear?"

"I'm not going to go into the office in the same ones I wore yesterday." He laughs sliding his legs into a pair of my dress pants.

"So go home and get dressed like a normal person."

"No time. Besides, where's the fun in having a brother that's *almost* the same size"—he adjusts his dick like the moron he is—"if you can't steal their shit. I'll have my tailor let these out in the—"

Reaching behind me, my fist wraps around the corner of the pillow before it sails through the air right at his head. He ducks just in time and it hits the wall with a soft thud before sliding to the ground.

"Crotch," he finishes, smirking.

"Just don't steal the sweater mom got me," I say with a sigh. There's no point in arguing with him. It'll only make my headache worse. "See you tonight," I tell him, slipping out of bed and into the bathroom.

Getting a glimpse of my tired, bloodshot eyes in the mirror I shake my head. Last night, the combination of getting to spend time with my brother, which I haven't done in way too long, the looming talk with my dad, and the party this weekend fueled my decisions. Not my best moment and I'm definitely paying for it today.

"Maybe it's time." Dylan's words come back to me.

Yeah, as much as I hate it, it's time I stop avoiding it. There's a lingering thought rooted deep in my brain that if I could put this behind me, I could be the kind of man that's worthy of a future with Mia. But moving past this might not even be possible, so I push the notion away.

♥

"Can you bring these centerpieces into the ballroom for me?" my mom calls from across the lobby of the country club where she's hosting the birthday party for my grandfather.

Natalie stands next to me, both of us red-faced and looking like we've just finished a marathon. Mom's been running us ragged all afternoon.

I lean in close. "At the risk of sounding like a total jackass, doesn't the country club usually set this all up?"

"You know how she gets. Everything has to be just so. Besides, this event is huge for the firm. It's not just his birthday party. This event brings in the wealthiest players in the Northeast and those people help fund the pro bono program," she whispers back conspiratorially.

"She sent the entire prep staff away, didn't she?"

Natalie just pats my back, knowing I'll do anything my mom needs. The pro bono program she built out of college is her first baby.

"Centerpieces it is," I grumble.

We are about halfway through decorating when my dad shows up, immediately souring my mood and ruining my accomplishment of avoiding him all day. Abandoning the flowers she was rearranging, my sister comes over and greets my dad with a hug. He kisses the top of her head and she beams up at him. To her, he still hangs the moon. "Your mom needs some help at the house. Would you go with her? She's got some photos and awards to pack up and bring over."

"I thought this was a birthday party, not a funeral," I grumble under my breath.

My dad's lips twitch in an almost imperceptible smile. I guess that's something we have in common. Although, disdain for my grandfather hardly seems like enough common ground to rebuild our trashed relationship.

"Be nice," my sister mouths before leaving the two of us. I glance around the ballroom . . . the *empty* ballroom. I get the sinking feeling that this is a trap. I thought we would do this in the privacy of our home, not in public.

"Your mother knows, Dean," my dad says vaguely, passing me a large vase.

"I assumed as much if she sent you over here so we could be alone together. Who's idea was it to do this in public?" It's sneaky. I bet it was hers.

"That's not what I mean. Of course she knows I wanted to speak with you today."

I set the vase down on the table, not at all how my sister showed me, and turn to face him. Waiting for him to continue.

"She knows about Whitney." He glances up at the ceiling before his misty eyes settle on me again. Just the mention of the women he cheated on my mother with all those years ago still makes something in my chest twist painfully. "I didn't expect this to be so hard. Your mom and I made peace with this part of our past a long time ago, but I guess rehashing it now doesn't hurt any less than it did back then."

I've seen my dad cry two other times in my whole life. Once when Natalie was ten and she was hospitalized for a week with pneumonia, and again, thirteen years ago, the last time we talked about this. When he pleaded with me to forgive him and promised me it would never happen again. When he begged me not to tell my mother, promising me it was what was best for everyone.

"The second I sobered up, I scheduled a therapy appointment and told your mother everything. It took a lot of work and years of rebuilding trust, but somehow she forgave me."

"She knows?" I step backward, bumping the table and making the vase wobble.

"At first it was just me doing the therapy, but eventually she joined. I slept in the office for almost a year—sneaking out every morning so you kids never caught on. My back has never been the same, but it was all worth it to have another chance with her."

I'm stunned speechless. She forgave him after everything. And yet I've carried the burden of his secrets with me all this time.

"Last year In Hawaii, we even renewed our vows. It was a special moment, just for us, after everything we've overcome together. She was just as stunning as the first time. Maybe even more so." A smile lights up his face, and for a second, I think he might take out his phone to show me pictures.

"You're the last piece of that time in our life that hasn't been resolved. It hurts her every day to know there's a rift between us and not understand why."

"You haven't told her I know?" His admission is out of character with the man I've come to know. I would have expected him to tell her, if only so that he could ease his own conscience and place the blame for our grudge on me.

"No. At first, it was to protect you kids. The last few years it's become about giving you space to tell her on your own terms. I thought eventually you'd tell her everything you knew. Our relationship was already so damaged I didn't want to risk any chance I had of fixing it."

"Explain to me how any of this protects us." I drop into the chair, overwhelmed by my conflicting emotions, I'm not even sure where to start with processing them.

"We'll get to that. First, what do you remember about that day?" he asks.

Vaguely aware of him taking the seat next to me, I squeeze my eyes shut, pinching the bridge of my nose and tip my head back. The memories of that day in the hallway of my parents' house assault me.

"What the fuck, Victor!" My hand freezes on the doorknob to my dad's office. His voice is unmistakable as he yells at my grandfather. My feet stay glued in place. I was sent home sick from school. He doesn't know I'm here, and it doesn't seem like an ideal time to tell him. Maybe it's best if I just go lie down—

"Don't you start with me, David. You did this to yourself. I told Nora the day you two announced your engagement that you'd break her heart. You were never good enough for her. And you just proved it by cheating on her with some floozy waitress from the club. Tell me, was fucking Whitney worth it?"

I press my fists to my eyes. Backing away slowly until my heels hit the first step of the staircase and I fall backwards. Scrambling to my feet, I run to my room hoping the volume of their voices cover the sounds of my footsteps.

"Mostly, the two of you fighting. It sounded like you were just as angry with him as he was with you." I've spent the last thirteen avoiding this memory. Reliving it now, I feel like that scared teenager all over again. When I finish telling my dad everything, he shakes his head remorse filling his green eyes. Somehow, it makes him look older.

"I'll never forgive myself for putting you through that. I'm so sorry Dean. If I could, I would do it all differently. I should have told you everything then. I thought I was doing the right thing, but I gave Victor too much power."

"I still don't understand. What does he have to do with you cheating on Mom?" I know I'm missing a piece of the puzzle. At the time, I was so consumed by anger that I didn't realize it, but as I've gotten older, it's always bothered me.

The office door slams behind me, startling my father. When he looks up from the whiskey glass he's staring into, his watery eyes are red and blood- shot. Serves him right. I hope he feels as miserable as he looks.

"How could you do this to her?" I bellow, charging towards the desk.

His reaction time is slower than normal. Probably the booze. Maybe I should snatch the glass from him. I bet I could pound it before he could even reach across the desk.

"Dean, what are you doing here? You should be at school." The panic is written across his face, in the shifty way his eyes assess me, trying to figure out what I know. It's a good thing he's not a lawyer—no poker face.

"I was sent home sick," I grit out, my fists balled at my side.

"Oh." He swallows thickly.

"Yeah, I tried to tell you when I got dropped off, but it didn't seem like a great time with Grandpa yelling at you for fucking a waitress half your age."

The blood drains from his stupid face. A face I want to punch. How could he hurt her like that? She loves him so much. My mom would do anything for him and she has no clue he's a cheating pile of shit.

"Y—you can't tell her, Dean. This would destroy her. Destroy all of us." His face twists in pain before he drops his head in his hands, tears streaming down face. *"Please don't. I promise it will never—I'll never do anything to hurt her again."*

Pushing off of the desk, I storm out of the office, leaving my dad behind. I hate him. Grabbing the keys to his Corvette—what's he going to do, ground me—I go to the one person who can help me. My grandfather.

"Your grandfather and I argued about his role in what happened, and then you came down and confronted me. After we fought, I assumed you went to Victor," my dad says.

"Yeah, when I left in the car—"

"*My* car. Don't think I forgot about that." My dad levels me with a glare, one he hasn't dared use on me since before that day. It feels oddly good. He gave up parenting me after everything. It was like he gave up on me.

"Sure did. Man, I miss that car," I say, my arms crossed and a smirk tugging at my lips. It's reminiscent of my teenage self.

"And your conversation with Victor didn't go as planned?" my dad guesses.

"It did not," I admit, my cockiness slipping away.

"Dean, what are you doing here?" my grandpa asks when I walk through the door of his downtown office at Harrison & Crawford. Showing

up unannounced isn't something he allows, but I don't really care right now. My mom will be home from court in a few hours and I don't know what to do.

"This couldn't wait." I drop into the chair opposite his desk and scrub my hands down my face.

"What can I do for you, son? You seem upset." His face in an unreadable mask, this is why he's so good at what he does. But I'm here to see my grandfather, not the world-class litigator whose cool demeanor has my already frayed nerves coming completely undone.

"I was sent home sick and overheard you arguing with Dad."

"And what is it you think you heard?" Another tactic to not give anything away or admit guilt.

"Don't play counselor with me. It won't work on me after years of helping around here. We need to do something. Mom is going to be devastated, have you told her yet?"

"Your mother does not know, and we aren't going to do anything. This is none of your concern."

"None of my concern!" I shout, my temper directed at him as much as my father now. "She's my mother, she has a right to know."

"And you're a child. You will keep your mouth shut and not get involved in adult matters."

My grandfather leans over, steepling his hands on top of the desk. It's a move designed to intimidate. I've seen him do it countless times in and out of the courtroom. The thing about grooming someone to take over your legacy is that they learn from you, and I learned from the best. His opposing counsel might not know him well enough to pick up on it, but I see the way his eye ticks. He's nervous. There's nothing this man hates more than losing.

So I keep my mouth shut and wait. I want answers and the only way I'll get them is if he thinks he has the power. The bumpy vein over his right eye throbs and his face reddens when the heels of my shoes land on the polished surface of his mahogany desk.

"Just who do you think you are?"

Yahtzee! That's right, get angry, old man.

His outburst triggers my dark laughter, which only angers him more. Good. I want him to burn with it the same way I do, and if his rage overrules his logic, maybe he'll slip up and give me answers. Everything about his demeanor and response to me asking for his help screams guilty.

"I could ask you the same thing? Why won't you help me?"

"You ungrateful shit. I've spent years of my life devoting myself to ensure you have the world at your fingertips. All you have to do is get good grades and all of this is yours." His hands sweep wildly in front of him. "I blame your dad. Nora didn't believe me when I told her this would happen. He's not good enough for her. Look where it got her, a cheating husband and brat of a son."

He's leaning over the desk, spit gathering in the corner of his mouth as he berates me. But as soon as he mentions my mom, I shoot to my feet. Even at sixteen, I have two inches on him and at sixty-seven, he's lacking the muscle and speed I've built playing sports.

"So you're just going to do nothing and let him keep hurting my mother?"

"Serves her right. If she would have listened to me, she wouldn't be in this situation to begin with. Your mother chose him, now she gets to live with the consequences."

My fist clench so tightly at my side that I feel the sting when my nails slice open my palms. "No! She deserves to know, and if you won't tell her, I will."

"Sit down, Dean. I've had enough of your insolence." His palm lands on the desk with a sharp crack.

I drop to the chair, exhaustion taking over from the events of this morning, or maybe from the fever that got me sent home in the first place—I can't be sure, but the anger mixes with sadness and pain. It's all overwhelming. Slouching in the chair, my chest heaves as I watch my grandfather round the desk, perching on the edge as he looks down at me.

"You're going to go home and go back to bed. When your mom gets home, you won't say a word to her about this, not today. Not ever."

"Why would I do that?" There's a finality in his tone that tells me this is a battle I'm going to lose.

"Because if you don't, I'll not only make sure you never have a place in Harrison & Crawford, but that Natalie and Dylan never get to follow in your mother's footsteps. This legacy will die with me. I'll leave all of my shares to Gregory."

"You wouldn't."

But I can see it in his face, he would leave the firm to his partner over his family.

Does he hate my mom that much for choosing my dad?

The betrayal makes the ache in my chest intensify to the point where I can barely breathe.

"Test me, Son. You've already underestimated me once today, thinking that you could outsmart me into telling you something that is none of your business. Push me, and you'll find out exactly what I'm capable of."

I blink up at him. This isn't the man I've looked up to for all these years. He's heartless, and I don't want to be anything like him. The future I had planned working in my family's firm slips away with each hateful sentence that he utters.

"Your sister has been studying for her LSATs for a year. Imagine how she'd feel to learn it was all for nothing. No one will hire her knowing she can't even get a job in her family's firm." He knows he's got me. I won't put my siblings' future at risk. Natalie's path is set—she knows what she wants to do. Dylan is not as sure, but I can't take that decision away from him.

Standing, I turn away and walk to the door stopping with my hand on the handle. "Don't worry about saving a spot for me. I'll never set foot in this office again. You're dead to me."

"Why are you rehashing all this? It's not like it'll change anything," I sigh, pushing my hand through my hair. He says he wanted to protect us, but I still don't understand what that means.

He watches me closely, lifting a shaking hand to rub over his jaw. "What I'm about to tell you isn't an attempt to ease my guilt or shift the blame. I was accountable for the decisions I made back then. I'm only telling you this to help you understand the decisions I made afterwards."

I nod, just wanting this conversation to make some sense.

"Your grandfather has hated me since the moment your mom and I met. He didn't want us to get married. And when your mom did it, anyway . . ." He shakes his head, a boyish smile appearing on his face before he clears his throat and continues, "She married me without a prenup just to spite him."

"I didn't know that, but it sounds like something she would do." My mom's always been a spitfire. The thought of her sticking it to the crypt keeper warms my heart.

"When he couldn't keep us apart that way, he paid Whitney to sleep with me." Sadness flashes in my dad's eyes at this mention of the past.

"That's why he didn't want mom to know. It's why he threatened Natalie and Dylan. She would have cut him out of her life permanently if she knew he paid someone to destroy your marriage," I say, quietly putting together the pieces that have been missing all these years.

Shock and anger passes over my dad's face before he adds, "He knew if he told your mom she'd cut him out, and that was the one thing he couldn't stand. You kids were collateral damage in his vendetta against me."

"Why are you telling me now?"

"Victor threatened me the same way he did you. When you hadn't told her, I assumed he talked you out of it somehow, I never expected that he would threaten you the way he did me. You two always had such a connection. For years I wondered what happened, but I couldn't bring myself to ask and then the rift felt too large."

"But you could have shared that blame with him—" I start, seeing him in a different light.

"It only would've hurt her more. Your mother would've lost the only career she'd ever known she worked so hard to make a positive impact on the firm. It's been her purpose, outside our family, for as long as I've known her. And to lose her only remaining parent on top of it . . . Selfishly, I also didn't want to seem like I was making excuses for my behavior. That thrilled my therapist, she encouraged me to tell her for years."

"Thank you for telling me. I don't know what it means for us, but I'm glad I know." I expected this conversion to be a fight, but hearing his side is more cathartic than I expected.

"There's a lot I did wrong, and you paid the biggest price. If I hadn't been such a coward, maybe we wouldn't have lost so much time. I was so afraid to lose your mom that I stopped parenting for a while, especially towards you." His voice is somber and tired. "I meant what I said. If I could change the past, I would. My attempts to protect you only seem to have hurt you more."

"Maybe over time we can rebuild some of what we've lost. But for now, I don't know about you, but I don't really want to decorate for his party."

"What do you say I go see if I can get the staff back in here to finish up? Maybe you and I could go find wherever Dylan is hiding out and get a drink."

That sounds nice. I'm not about to toast the man, but a drink together seems like a good way to get to know each other again.

CHAPTER 33

MIA

MIA:

Just checking in to make sure you're okay.
I hope the conversation with your dad went okay.

DEAN:

It was a lot but we had a good talk.
Enlightening. Everything good there?

MIA:

Sure. Everything is fine.

I stare down at the phone in my hand. I can't put my finger on it. Maybe I'm reading a tone that isn't there. Maybe it's the words that are missing from his text that's bothering me. I type out the words he's not giving me, knowing this trip can't be easy for him.

MIA:

MISS YOU.

Three blinking dots taunt me before they disappear.

Yoga.

That's what I need—a clear mind and a tired body. I step outside to an unshoveled snow drift that has my mind wandering back to Dean in Boston. My stomach churns with doubt. He's probably just distracted, but his brief response has me over-analyzing the entire exchange.

Later that day, I'm soaking in the hot tub and soft flurries start floating down around me. It's about time for the party to start in Boston and I haven't heard from him again. Reaching over the side I grab my phone to snap a selfie. When our conversation for earlier pops up, I nibble on my thumb, debating if I should send it. Before I can think about it too much, I hit the little green arrow.

DEAN:

Thanks, Dreamer. I needed this.

I don't hear from Dean again before I go to bed that night and I hate it.

CHAPTER 34

DEAN

"If I have to hear one more geriatric-past-his-prime lawyer tell me a story about how things were back in the good ole days, I'm going to scream," Natalie says, leaning up against the bar next to where Gavin and I are talking about the upcoming season.

"Let them have it. You've got a wicked mouth. Use it," Gavin says, giving his wife a wink.

On the other side of him, Dylan flinches. "You had to?"

"Nope, but it never gets old, so I keep doing it." He brings his lips to my sister's temple, whispering, "I love your fucking mouth."

Dylan holds up his hand, four fingers in the air, and the bartender brings over shots of tequila.

"I'm not doing this every time someone mansplains something to Nat," I tell Dylan, reaching for the glass.

"Fuck no. We're not doing that, we'd need our stomachs pumped with all the blowhards in this room. This is for Gavin's betrayal," my brother explains, clinking his glass against mine.

"Keep it down, here comes their leader," my brother-in-law whispers, raising his glass to ours and taking his shot. "Dance with me, Wifey."

"Traitor," I mumble under my breath, tipping the citrusy liquor into my mouth, my eyes squeezing closed. When I open them, Gavin is dragging my sister away.

"Sorry, Dilly. You're on your own." I pull my phone out to fake a call and head towards the sitting room.

The door swings shut and I take a seat in one of the cream color high-back chairs. They're pompous, just like everything about this club. Without really thinking about it, I'm flipping through the photos on my phone—six weeks' worth of memories and pictures with Mia.

Holding her at a distance the last two days wasn't my intention, but my head's been all over the place since the conversation with my dad. Weirdly, I've let go of a lot of the anger I was holding onto where he was concerned, but that blackened part of my soul hasn't shrunk.

It's almost worse knowing how my grandfather tried to sabotage my parents, and why he threatened my siblings and I because it was all avoidable. There's no question I'd be a different man if I hadn't been afraid, if I had gone to Mom or even my dad. Perhaps I'd be the guy that could believe in the happily-ever-afters that Mia writes about.

Since I can't change the past, I'll never know. But I need some time to decide what's next. Talking to my mom is an obvious next step—come clean with her about what happened. But I'm not sure if it's the right decision for her and my siblings. Whatever I decide, tonight is not the night to do it. And at this point, I don't even know what I'd say. I need some time to work through it myself first.

My thumb brushes over the picture of Mia in my bed from right before I left. I need to call her tonight—she doesn't deserve the cold shoulder from me.

The creak of the hinges has me looking up to find the one person I don't want to talk to standing in the doorway.

"Surprise, surprise. My most disappointing prodigy hiding from familial responsibility." His voice isn't as strong as it was back then, but it still makes the hair on my neck stand up.

Locking my phone screen I put it back in my pocket before he can see it. Mia and I have almost made it to the end of the winter. There might not be a future for us beyond the next two weeks, but I don't want him tarnishing what we have.

"You don't want to talk to me about family right now." I stand from my seat and head for the door. The stubborn old man doesn't move, blocking the only exit. I entertain the idea of muscling my way around him, but the goal of escaping is to avoid a scene.

"Let me through." I step right up to him, putting us almost chest to chest.

"You and I are long overdue for a chat. Is my money still keeping you warm at night in that penthouse?" A sick grin splits his slimy face.

"Not for long." I make a snap decision, one I'm certain of. "I'm selling it."

"Interesting choice. Your mother will be so upset when she hears that you no longer want to live in the home I gifted you," he says, standing sentry in front of the door. With a sneer on his face that twists his wrinkled skin, I know the threat is coming before he adds, "Don't forget, while your mother may be a partner, she doesn't have the same ownership stake and rights as me. And poor Natalie is a non-equity partner until I decide otherwise. Dylan . . . he doesn't stand a chance as just an associate."

Hearing the mention of my mother and siblings has my blood boiling just below the surface of my skin. "You will not talk to me about them. Not after what you did to our family." It takes all my restraint to keep my voice low so I don't draw attention.

"Still blaming me for your father's indiscretions. You get that from him, I'm afraid."

The audacity of this bastard. "No, the blame for his decisions lies solely on him. The difference is he's made amends and taken responsibility for his actions and the pain they caused. You have not. And you never will."

"David's still feeding you bullshit, I see. Still so impressionable, I thought I taught you to be stronger. The signs were there when you walked out of my office and gave up your place in this family."

"The only thing I gave up on that day was you." It's a lie. I lost so much—my innocence, my entire outlook on life and love. "It's time you find out how that feels. Imagine if Mom found out that you paid a waitress to sleep with her husband."

My sister's head appears as she pushes through the door behind my grandfather. "You're both very lucky it's just me. This is not the place for this long overdue discussion," Natalie hisses pointing at Victor. "You go back out there and pretend like you're enjoying this lavish party that your daughter—whom you don't deserve—threw you at your request, so your fragile ego could feel important." Pride overwhelms me at the effortless way my sister puts him in his place.

Smoothing down his tie, my grandfather turns on his heels and leaves, but not before throwing a disgusted glare in my direction.

"Did you see that? I made his vein pop out," Natalie says with a tired laugh. "Come here and give me a hug. You look like you need it."

"I really fucking do." She steps forward and wraps her arms around my waist. "Why don't you seem surprised?"

"It's my lawyer's face. I knew Dad had been unfaithful, but not about grandfather's involvement. Mom confided in me when the twins were babies. Everything was hard and Gavin and I were struggling. She recommended counseling and told me it saved their marriage. Naturally, I had a lot of questions."

"Naturally," I echo hollowly.

"If you want to sneak out, I can cover for you. Hell, I'll even call the pilot for you if you want to fly home tonight," she offers sweetly.

"Can you tell everyone goodnight for me? I'll stick around for brunch tomorrow. But I can't be here any longer tonight."

"Of course. Get out of here. We'll talk in the morning." She holds the door open so I can slip out.

When I get into the waiting car to take me back to the hotel, I pull up Mia's number, but I'm not in the right headspace to talk to her. And I'm not even sure what I'd say. All I really want right now is to hold her, but that's not fair. We have two weeks left and then we both need to learn how to live without each other.

CHAPTER 35

MIA

From the bedroom, the slamming front door has my whole body stiffening in my desk chair. There's been a feeling of foreboding deep in my bones since our clipped text exchange the other day—an unshakeable notion that the Dean coming back won't be the same one that left for Boston.

Steeling myself to deal with Mr. Tall Dark and Broody for the first time in a while, I push back from my desk and turn to find Dean standing in the doorway, his duffle bag hanging at his side.

"Hey," I say, closing the distance between us but stopping myself before I reach out and touch him. My heart is screaming at me to wrap my arms around his waist and lose myself in him.

"Hey," he says back, letting the bag drop to the floor and stepping into the room and cupping the side of my face.

"You're home and you shaved," I say, my hand coming up to stroke my thumb over his jaw. It shouldn't, but the little change seems ominous.

"Yeah. It was a weird trip," he says, like it explains everything. But what really stings is the way he pulls his hand back and pushes it through his hair.

"Weren't you the one that wanted us to talk about things when our feelings got the best of us. Isn't that what you told me at the hot springs?"

"This isn't about us, Mia," he huffs, clearly frustrated. Whether it's with himself, or with me, I'm not sure. "I'm going to put this away and then check on a few things around the cabin. I need some time to process everything, but we should talk later."

"Sure, whatever," I say, retreating to my desk and busying myself with my to-do list, not wanting him to see how deeply this cuts.

Out of the corner of my eye, I watch as he walks away, wordlessly pleading for him to turn around. He doesn't even give me a parting glance as he leaves me standing there wondering what the hell happened in the last few days. Even when we first met, he wasn't this cold.

When I hear the door to his room shut, I collapse onto the bed, tears burning at the backs of my eyes. *You get five minutes to be in your feelings about this, and then you have shit to do.*

Thirty minutes later, I've pulled myself together enough to work because deadlines don't wait for awkwardness with my friend-turned-roommate-turned-lover. But I don't go back to the desk. I curl up on the bed with my laptop and try to focus on editing, reminding myself that my writing brought me here in the first place.

The words on the screen blend together. Reaching for the tea sitting on the warmer Dean got me, I bring the cup to my lips, finding it empty. I'm going to need more to get through this last round of edits, which means I need to leave this room. Not that I've been hiding—totally hiding. All my efforts to be stealthy are foiled when the hinges creak as I drag the door open.

Dean stands on the other side of the door, hand raised in a silent knock and his eyes narrowed when he catches me peeking around the door.

"Oh sorry, I didn't mean to—Do you have time to talk?" he asks, grabbing the back of his neck.

"Actually, not really. I just need some more tea and then I really should get back to work. Deadlines," I tell him, lifting my shoulders just to drive it home that I'm unbothered. *Lie.* I'm so bothered, but I'm not going to force anyone to choose me.

"Later? Please." The sadness I felt earlier fills his green eyes, and it's almost enough to have me taking back my words. If he's going to go cold on me, I need to protect myself and work is the perfect avoidance technique. Especially since I'm not ready to hear him tell me this is over.

My eyes are gritty when I finally close my computer and I'm mentally exhausted. When I'm editing, it's like I slip into an alternate universe where time doesn't exist. The orange and purple painted skies tell me that the entire day has faded away while I worked.

I'm dreading what's waiting for me outside these four walls, but I need food, so I have no choice but to face it.

He's wearing the fucking glasses, with a hardcover book held in his hand and his long legs kicked out on the couch. *Really, universe?* He's going to break my heart, looking like my very favorite fantasy.

"I was starting to wonder if you would ever come out. There's some supper in the oven for you. I didn't want it to get cold," he says, laying the book across his broad chest.

"Oh. You didn't have to do that."

"I thought we left all this awkwardness back in December."

"I thought so too," I mumble under my breath, grabbing the plate from the oven. "Shit!"

"Fuck, Dreamer, it's hot," he says, rushing to my side. His fingers circle my wrist and he turns us toward the sink. His free hand flips the water on so he can run my hand under the stream. I'm about to tell him it's not that bad, but I let him take care of me, knowing it might be the last time. "What are you going to do without me in a couple of weeks?" The teasing in voice fades as the heaviness of reality sets in weighing down the air around us.

I let my head rest against the hard planes of his chest, my eyes squeezing shut. *Don't cry, Mia.* "I don't know. But I can't have you going hot and cold on me again, Dean. Not now." My hand finds the handle and turns the water off, shaking the excess into the sink before I turn into his chest.

"I'm sorry about earlier. My head's all fucked up, but I'd really like to talk to you about it if you'd let me." Two big hands cover my waist as he lifts me up onto the counter.

"I don't know, Dean." I fail miserably at trying to keep the hurt out of my voice.

"Come on. Eat and then we can talk. All I'm asking for is a few minutes. Just let me explain. I don't want to spend the time we have left like this." His lips brush mine in a tentative kiss that doesn't stretch on nearly as long as it usually does.

We stay like that, me on the counter and him leaning against it mostly quiet as I struggle to get food down with the way my stomach is churning over the looming conversation. Something caused him to shut me out, and it's obvious it was big. But my emotions are all over the place—my concern for him mixing with my anger.

When I'm done eating, he takes my plate from me, setting it in the sink and taking both my hands to help me off the counter. I follow him to the couch, but when I go to sit next to him, he just shakes his head, pulling me into his lap.

"You're mad."

I want to tell him it's fine, but it's not. Not all. "You didn't call, and I could barely get you to respond to a text. Now you're being distant. I'm confused and hurt. I know how this started, but I thought we were closer now. I thought you would choose to confide in me. If something changed for you, just tell me."

"Fuck, sweetheart. I'm sorry. You're important to me, and I never meant to make you think otherwise. This had nothing to do with you. I still want us, just like we talked about. If that's all you hear, know that. *I want you.*"

Well, that's a mind-fuck. I feel so much more for Dean than I ever expected. Two more weeks together isn't enough. Part of me wants to try for more, but the worst feeling in the world is to be the one asking for more when the other person can't or won't give it. And even though he wants me, he didn't choose me these last few days. I won't put myself in that position, but I can't make myself walk away yet either.

"Two more weeks." My voice wavers with the reminder of our looming timeline. "Tell me what happened at home."

"Surprisingly, talking to my dad was the easy part. It was the bomb he dropped about Victor, my grandfather, that really hit me." Holding me closer, he explains the conversation with his dad.

"Nothing about what they put you through was okay." My fingers run over the ink on his forearm, it's a distraction from the pain and rage I feel for the boy Dean was.

He hums thoughtfully. "That doesn't change the fact that it happened."

"Wait, did you still go to the party?"

He winces. "I probably shouldn't have, but my mom worked so hard planning it. I couldn't do that to her. It didn't end well. My sister walked in on Victor and I arguing."

"Ouch. That's a lot to deal with." Looking up, I find his normally vibrant eyes dull with exhaustion. My throat tightens thinking about how heavily this must be weighing on him. I'm still hurt and mad but it's easy to see that he's not in the right frame of mind to take on more.

"It feels like my universe flipped. Suddenly my dad isn't the villain I thought he was. He was wrong to do what he did, but he's done the work with my mom to repair their relationship. Once he told me what happened, I could see it in the way they act with each other. I've missed out on so much the last thirteen years because of my anger towards him."

"You're grieving for the life you could have had," I remark quietly.

"Something like that. Then finding out what Victor did—I'm so angry. His actions created this rift in my family that never had to be there. If I'd known what he did all those years ago, things might have been so different . . . *I* might have been so different."

"You're not so bad. Now that you're not being a grade A prick like this morning. But that's not all you are. You are so much more than the product of their wrongs. You just need to see that. I *need* you to see that." I turn in his lap, wrapping my arms around him to hold him. We stay like that for a while before he leads me to his bedroom. We undress side by side and crawl into bed together, where he holds me close as we drift off to sleep.

CHAPTER 36

DEAN

Sunlight streams through the windows, casting shadows over Mia. Rolling to my side, I watch her sleep, my finger tracing the patterns the shadows create on her bare back.

"That tickles," she mumbles, her voice raspy with sleep.

"If you could see the way you look, you would understand why I can't keep my hands to myself."

"Good thing you don't have to. I mean, we still have two weeks left together." Her hands fidget with a strand of hair and I hate that she needs reassurance from me.

Things might be slightly better with my dad, but it doesn't change the man I am. Damage that was done a long time ago has yet to heal. This arrangement wasn't supposed to hurt either of us, but I already know walking away from her is going to be the hardest thing I've ever done. If she feels for me even a fraction of what I feel for her, maybe getting out now is in her best interest, especially after the way I treated her yesterday. So, I offer her an out. "We do. Are you still okay with this? If you want to end it now, I would understand."

"It's not long enough, but it's all we've got. I want every minute of it," she admits quietly.

My hands snake around her waist pulling her into me. "Good. Me too."

She turns from her stomach so she's facing me on her side. Soft hands gently cup my cheek. "What are you afraid of, Dean Harrison?" Her voice matches the gentle touch like maybe she can coax it out of me, but she doesn't need to.

I laugh because it seems so painfully obvious. As much as I don't want to hurt her, that's not the real issue. Mia's strong—she'll be able to recover from anything I throw at her, but I can't stand the idea of losing her completely. "I'm afraid you're going to end up hating me when this is over."

"Don't worry about that." The forced smile she gives me before she rolls on top of me does nothing to quell that fear. She's still holding back, I can see it in the tense set of her shoulders. *Fuck.* I was so wrapped up in my shit this weekend and I put up a wall between us. One that she's now fortifying. She might be here physically, but mentally she's keeping space between us.

Even with all her smooth skin pressed against mine, we still feel miles apart and I hate it. Maybe it's for the best considering there will literally be thousands of miles between us soon.

When her lips graze my collar bone and start moving south, I flip her under me, making her squeak at the sudden change.

"What are you doing?" she asks, her ribs vibrating under my fingers with her laughter as I kiss my way down her sternum.

"Trying to make up for being an asshole with orgasms." Mornings are really going to suck without her by my side. I trace the curves of her waist trying to memorize the shape of her—how right she feels.

"Don't let me stop you." She giggles, goosebumps erupting over her skin when I blow on her inner thigh.

I *don't* let it stop me. The ticking clock in my head is so loud that I almost can't hear her little whimpers as I devour her. By the time I finally sink inside her, she's begging for me to fuck her.

"Look at us, right back where this all started," Mia says as I slip her helmet over her head, careful not to mess up the adorable braids she's sporting today. She looks cute as fuck, but I selfishly want them to survive the day so I can wrap them around my fist when we get home.

"What does that mean?" Thinking back to the first time we spent the day together here, technically we were still in the friendzone but, for me, it was a turning point. After spending the day together really getting to know each other, I knew there was no way I could walk away from her, regardless of whether it was right or wrong.

Is it wrong that I hope it was the same for her?

Knowing that our end is nearing, I shouldn't want to hear her admit that there are deeper feelings there, but I really fucking do.

Pink sweeps over her cheekbones and I don't think it's from the brisk mountain air. "That day changed everything for me. It was never a question of whether I was attracted to you, but seeing the softer side of you only made me want you more, and not just for your body." She pauses for a second, some of the light fading from her eyes. "I'm glad we decided to do this one more time."

I go from wanting to jump up and down, cheering that this girl wants me, to reeling from her crushing blow. That's how this whole week has gone. Physically, we can't get enough of each other, but the wall that Mia put up to protect herself when I came back from Boston remains firmly in place. And I can't blame her after how I acted. I heard what she said, my happiness is still being held in the hands of others. Until I deal with the shit show that all the secrets caused, I can't be the man I want to be.

A smarter man might back away to save himself the heartache, but the only time she gives me a glimpse at what we had a few weeks ago is when we're physical. It's a decision I might hate myself for next week when we have to leave this bubble and go back to our real lives, but I can't bring myself to not soak up every trace of the girl who's owned me over the last two months.

We spend the morning tackling all the green runs. Mia picks up right where we left off last time, her confidence growing with every run. I'm not sure if it's the fresh air, or the fact that we're doing something that reminds her of how we started, but as the day goes on, she seems to hold back with me a little less.

After lunch we're in line for a gondola that takes guests from one side of the mountain to the other. The line is long, everyone is done eating and trying to get in as much riding as possible, and Mia's leaning against me, her back pressed against my front.

My hand loops around her waist, slipping under her jacket and bibs. My intentions are innocent—I just want to be close to her—but her sharp intake of breath when my hand brushes over the little jewel that dangles from her belly has my whole body heating with the need for more of her.

"You can't make sounds like that," I whisper against her cheek, leaning over her from behind.

"I can and I will. It's not like you have many options to stop me," she taunts, glancing around at all the people to prove her point.

"Don't fucking tempt me, Mia."

She shivers in my arms as the line in front of us moves. I shift my board under my arm so I can pull my glove off with one hand while the other coasts over her warm skin in a circle that gets wider with every sweep.

"What are you doing?" she asks, her words fractured as she sucks a breath in through her teeth.

"This lift takes seven minutes to get to the other peak. Think of all the things I can do to you in that time."

"Very funny." She laughs, but it dies out quickly when my hand dips below the waistband of her joggers.

"I'm so fucking serious," I tell her, shuffling us forward. There's only a few people between us and the front of the line now. "You're going to have to come quickly for me."

She looks over her shoulder at me and her normally light eyes are stormy with lust. "Someone could see us."

"You're crazy if you think I'd let someone else see you that way. This is for me and only me. Just remember what happens to brats."

A huff escapes her when I slip my hand out from under her jacket, and has all my blood going straight to my dick. I stuff my hand back in the glove as the group in front of us prepares to move to the front of the line.

"For the record, being a brat has always paid off," she says, stepping forward in the snow and taking her place next to me at the front of the line.

"Get in and put your board against the back of the gondola," I tell her, my voice low and demanding, but I throw the lift-y a casual smile as we board.

She steps into the lift ahead of me, setting her board against the scuffed up plexiglass blocking the view. When I join her, mine goes next to hers to give us privacy from the group following us up the hill.

She stands there, eyes wide, Before I tug on her hand, pulling her into my lap. With her in this position, my body blocks the view from the car ahead and the rare down-loading group. "Unzip your coat for me. We don't have long and I haven't decided if I'm going to let you come before we get to the top."

Her hand trembles on the zipper and she has to use both hands to work it free.

"Bibs next." My lips move against her neck, and my chilly hand slinks under her turtleneck. She gasps when I roll her already hot, peaked nipples between my cool fingers. "Fuck, sweetheart. Did I get you all worked up in line? All the better to make you come."

"Just cold," she bites out. With my lips still lavishing her neck, I can see her squeeze her eyes shut when my fingers brush her clit.

"Feels pretty warm to me," I groan, fitting my finger inside her and working her slowly. "Think you can come like this?"

"No," she chokes out, her eyes darting to the side at the gondola full of people going down the hill.

"They can't see you."

Her answering whimper sounds disappointed.

Gripping her face I turn her head so she can see me. "No one sees you like this but me. No one." My lips cover hers, kissing her as hard as I can in this position. She moans around my tongue when I thrust another finger into her soaked pussy.

"Fuck, that feels so good," Mia says, sagging into me when I crook my fingers.

"Halfway there. Maybe I'll make you wait until we're right there so everyone at the top knows what we did—hears you scream my name and knows you're mine."

Her heels slip on the floor in her boots as she tries to find leverage to rock against me. I chuckle and it makes the hottest little growl come out of her. "Are you going to be a brat for the rest of the day, or can you be a good girl for me?"

"I'll be good. Just let me come." Her needy pleas fill the air.

"That's what I like to hear. Once we get home, I'll edge you all night, but right now, I need you to come. You have just over a minute before we have to offload."

"Shit—no . . . I'm not—"

The heel of my hand presses into her clit. "Is this what you need?"

"Yes!" she practically screams. This time, her feet find traction and she uses the leverage to shift, grinding herself against my palm.

"Let them hear it, sweetheart."

"Dean." Her raspy voice echoes in the plexiglass lift. The way she rocks against me as she chases her release has me gritting my teeth so I don't come in my pants and ruin the rest of our afternoon.

"Fuck you're tight." Her walls clamp down as her legs shake under the pressure of her orgasm.

We don't have the time for me to let her come down slowly. My fingers ease out of her, zipping her bibs and jacket just as we crest the last of the slope. "You did so good, Dreamer." My lips find hers for a featherlight kiss before I stand, keeping her glued to me as I snag my jacket and shrug it on with my free hand. Once I'm sure she's steady on her feet, I release her just long enough to grab both boards before the doors slide open.

The lift-y raises an eyebrow at me as we exit, making Mia squeak in embarrassment behind me.

"Mine," I whisper, just loud enough for her to hear.

We don't last all that much longer at the resort before both of us are antsy to get home.

CHAPTER 37

MIA

Each morning when I wake up, it gets a little harder to breathe, the weight of what I'm about to lose pressing down. For the last week, I've been up with the sunrise to watch Dean sleep peacefully beside me before he wakes up. Sometimes I stay up the whole time and pretend to be asleep so he doesn't catch me. Other times, I'll drift back to sleep before he wakes me up with his wicked tongue.

This morning I don't go back to sleep. I can't. Tomorrow is our last day in the cabin before we part ways. Since we went snowboarding last week, we've barely come up for air aside from the handful of hours a day that we've set aside to work. Me, finishing all the last minute dates for my book release next week, and proofreading the novella for the anthology. Him, working twice as hard in the gym and kitchen to prepare for spring training.

On top of all that, I still haven't decided what's next. The idea of moving continues to nag at me, but I don't think it's a decision I'm quite ready to make. If Denver ends up being my next chapter, it needs to be for me. Not because of anything else, and it's a decision I want to come to on my own.

Everyone else has biases, Hendrix, my grandmother, my friends. Hell, I think even Indie is secretly rooting for me and Dean to figure this out.

Dean's comforting arms reach out for me as he stirs. He always does this a few minutes before he wakes up, blindly reaching for me and snoozing a few more minutes with me pressed up against him before he wakes.

And I let him tug me closer, wrapping myself around him like a boa constrictor every time. As hard as I tried to distance myself when he came home from Boston, it's been pointless. The idea that I could erect a wall between us and walk away unscathed is laughable. Dean has infiltrated every nook and cranny of my soul. He's part of me, and I'm not sure how I'll move on when that's ripped away.

For a second when he came back, I thought there was a chance that the conversation with his Dad would be the catalyst that made Dean's outlook on commitment and love change, but it seemed to do the exact opposite which is confusing as fuck for my heart because his actions don't match his words. While his attitude towards relationships stayed the same, he's more tender with me than ever. Doting on me every chance he gets. Physically. Emotionally. As a friend.

It's a constant struggle to remind myself that this isn't real. At least it won't be in forty-eight hours. It'll be like a dream that you just woke up from, and no matter how hard you try, when you fall back to sleep, you can't recapture it. You wake up feeling crushing disappointment that it's no more. But it's worse, because I'm pretty sure he's taking my whole heart with him when he leaves for Arizona.

Dean's nose wiggles against my neck as he roots around my hair, currently blanketing his face, as his lips search blindly for that spot below my ear that drives me crazy.

"Morning, Dreamer." His voice sounds sexiest like this. It reminds me of when he's on the edge of his orgasm buried deep inside me. Okay. I lied. *That's* the sexiest. This is a close second and my chest constricts painfully, knowing I only get to hear it one more time.

How am I going to do this?

We take our time waking up, getting wrapped up in each other before we make omelets side by side in the kitchen. After that we go our separate ways, me to work and packing the guest bedroom turned office. And Dean to workout and start closing up the cabin for when we leave tomorrow.

Being alone with my thoughts is almost unbearable. Once I'm done proofreading, each task on my checklist is just a reminder that our time together is almost over. I give packing my things a half-hearted try before I slip on my winter gear and head outside to find Dean.

I tell myself it's to avoid being alone with my thoughts, but I know it's just as much to be with him before it's too late.

"Put me to work. After a winter in the mountains, my wood game is strong," I say, when I find him stacking the pile of logs he cut yesterday along the garage.

"I can vouch for that." He chuckles.

We work side by side making small talk, mostly about our time here or our families. Both of us steer the conversation to avoid anything having to do with what comes next. We don't talk about the start of his season or my book tour.

When the pile is nothing more than pieces of bark lying in the white snow, Dean slings his arm over my shoulder and leads me back toward the cabin but I stop us, soaking it all in, the mountains in the background, the Bandits flag waving on the pole attached to the exterior, the wispy cloud floating overhead. This place and this man have given me so much this winter.

Hours later he's in the bedroom packing and I'm working on a handful of last-minute book release things that always seem to crop up when my phone rings.

It's a real estate agent that I've been playing phone tag with. I glance up at the hallway leading to where Dean is currently packing. My finger hovers over the green button, but I decline the call. This isn't the time to make this decision. I'm far too emotional to have her list my condo. Maybe I'll decide once I've settled back into my routine. I just want to be sure I'm doing it for the right reasons, and right now the only thing I'm sure of is I would give anything for a chance to make this work with Dean if I thought it's what he wanted, and that's clouding my judgment.

"All packed," Dean says, making me look up from the phone still clutched in my hand. Worry crinkles his brow. "Are you okay?"

"Yeah, of course," I reply, trying to keep my cool as I basically hurl my phone at the coffee table. Like that's not a dead giveaway that I'm hiding something.

He frowns looking like he wants to say more, but he just pushes off the door frame coming over to sink down next me on the couch. "Did you get your stuff taken care of?"

"Mostly. I still have a few things to finish in the morning. Let me know what you need help with tomorrow. I'm at your service."

His jaw clenches, the muscle ticking before he simply nods. "I don't want to talk about tomorrow. Are you done here?" he asks, his thick fingers tapping on the top of my laptop.

"Yeah. I am." I shut it and Dean takes it from me, setting it on the coffee table.

His mouth covers mine in the softest kiss. His tongue runs along the seam of my lips, completely unhurried, like we have all the time in the world, but we don't. Fisting his shirt, I pull him to me. I can feel it in his kiss. He's getting ready to say goodbye.

"Don't do this," I plead, my voice breaking and my throat burning with the emotion coursing through me. "Don't kiss me like that. I can't—"

"You're not going to rush me." His voice is soothing, but I can see the pain in his eyes. He's hurting as much as I am. "The day I came home from Denver after the team meeting, I found you right here."

Heat rushes to my face instantly. That's an afternoon I'll never forget. "Mmhmm."

"Dirty girl," he chides softly. "I'm talking about before you begged me to fill your perfect ass up. I walked through that door and found you reading *here*. This place has been my oasis since I bought it. Walking in and finding you in your element felt like the most perfect puzzle pieces clicking into place. Joining together to create the most stunning picture—one I'll never forget."

There's so much more I want him to say, but I know it will only make tomorrow harder. When he opens his mouth like he might continue, I brush my lips over his. Hoping he can feel everything I wish I was brave enough to ask of him. *Take care of yourself* and *come back to me* are the silent pleas as I crawl into his lap kissing him until I'm out of breath.

I relish the brush of his calloused hands as they ghost over my ribs, lifting my sweater over my head, and the way it tickles when he works the clasp of my bra free. No one has ever looked at me with the admiration Dean does, taking his time just like he promised.

He leans back, his gaze flicking from where his hands cover my breasts to my face and back again. Like he can't decide which he wants to watch more. Dipping his head he takes my nipple between his lips, licking and sucking before he switches sides and repeats the process—gradually working me up. When he licks a hot path up my chest to my neck, I'm dying to kiss him.

"Tell me you're mine. I need to hear it," he demands leaving the rest unsaid. *One last time.*

"All yours," I tell him, silently adding an *always* in my head that makes my heart pound impossibly hard. "You next."

"I've only ever been yours." Like a boomerang, those words make me soar and then send me careening back down to earth.

Without warning, he stands from the couch and my legs circle his waist. I think he's taking us to the bedroom, but seconds later, the plush fabric of the blanket he bought me brushes against my back as he lays me out in front of the fireplace. His thumbs hook the waistband of my leggings, taking his sweet time peeling them off me as his lips tenderly sweep down my legs.

"I'm going to kiss every square inch of you," he vows, hovering over me and setting out on his mission. My hands are everywhere, in his hair, nails digging into his shoulders, looping around his neck. I can't stop touching him. The need to feel his skin under my fingers is burning through me hotter than anything I've ever felt before, it's dangerous.

"Definitely want to do that, but first, I want this shirt off." Pushing up on my elbow I run my fingers under the hem, grazing the ridges of his stacked abs. When I feel the coarseness of the spattering of hair there, I tug at the elastic. "These too." I want his skin, every honed muscle, all of him. On display for me. Under my fingers. Weighing down on me. Sinking into me.

It feels like we've been at it for hours when his mouth finds mine and I shudder when the head of his cock nudges my swollen clit through the thin layer of fabric we're both still wearing. It's the one place on me he hasn't touched.

Normally, I'd have been begging for him to give it attention ages ago, but tonight I don't want to come until he does. We seem to be on the same page when he kisses me deeply one more time before his hands settle at my hips, tracing circles with his thumb. His gaze travels over me starting with where his hands rest and not stopping until our eyes meet. "You're fucking perfect."

I lift my hips letting him ease my thong down my legs. His underwear is next, leaving him naked, in all his glory, and I can't tear my gaze away as he kneels over the top of me.

"Ready?" he asks.

"Yes." The word is barely out before his mouth is on mine and he swallows up my moan as he slowly feeds me every glorious inch of him. One hand brackets my hip, tilting it up so that each time he draws back, he drags over the bundle of nerves inside me.

"God, yes," he says through gritted teeth. "I never want to forget how you feel."

Those words are going to haunt me forever, but right now, the only thing I can feel is him. If I let myself feel everything else that is beating down the door trying to get in, I'll crumble. And I refuse to do so.

"It's too good. I'm going to come." Tears form in the corner of my eyes at the overwhelming pressure building at the base of my spine. "I'm not ready," I admit.

"You can let go. I'll hold on and we'll go together on the next one." His hand comes up, wiping the tear that's escaped.

"What if I can't?" My voice shakes as I try to hold back.

"You can. You've always been such a good girl for me." He doesn't leave room for argument and when he thrusts back in, there's no stopping it. My whole body tightens and when he kisses me, my world seems to shift on its axis, revolving only around this feeling of euphoria.

His measured pace drags the feeling out, and I'm not sure it ever totally fades. But he stays true to his word, building me back up. I can count on one hand the number of times we've had sex like this—face to face and never for the whole time. But I can't imagine it any other way tonight.

A bead of sweat forms on Dean's brow and his serious green eyes flick between mine. "You're everything, Mia. All the bests in the world. The sum fucking total." Before I can tell him I feel the same way about him, his lips find mine in a searing kiss that has me tipping over the edge. The last thing I hear before my ears buzz with the power of my orgasm is the sound of my name on his lips as he spills inside me.

Neither of us rush to move. When my hands spear through his hair, dragging his mouth back to mine, he hardens inside me and we start again. It's how we spend the rest of the night—clinging to each other in our sleep, waking in the middle of the night, and slipping back into each other.

CHAPTER 38

DEAN

The whole day has been a whirlwind of activity that's kept Mia and I apart since we showered this morning. Untangling her arms from around my waist, I tiptoed out of bed, leaving her resting peacefully after our long night. The spray of water pounding on the shower tile covered the sound of her bare feet, leaving me unaware until her arms slipped around me from behind and she placed a featherlight kiss on my spine. Together we wordlessly ducked under the stream of water and parted ways with a lingering kiss.

There's a lot to do to prepare the cabin to be closed up for the next few months, including reinforcing the deck rail. My eyes keep drifting away from the power tool in my hand to the wall of windows hoping to catch sight of Mia who's tackling a few things inside because she wouldn't take no for an answer. If I'm not careful, I'll end up with a screw through my hand. All I want to do is sink back into Mia and never come up for air.

Part of me wishes I could lay around relishing the last hours I have with Mia. She's changed me at a cellular level and there's no doubt in my mind that I'll never be the same. Maybe it's better this way. Last night it was on the tip of my tongue to tell her I'd give her more. But it would be a lie, I'm not capable of more, at least not yet.

Now that I know what Victor cost me, leaving her somehow hurts more. Like these last few months were just a tease of what could have been if he hadn't taken that all away by turning me into this apathetic man that keeps secrets from people he loves.

Once I've finished repairing the deck, it's on to the next thing on the list. Only one hour before we have to get on the road so we can get back to Denver before it's too late. Mia's flight to New York, where she's kicking off the series of reader events she's doing to launch her book, leaves mid-morning tomorrow. She's spending the night with Hendrix and Poppy before she leaves.

Another thing I hate, but what was I going to do? Beg her to stay with me at my penthouse? Ask her for one more night? With how we started, it hardly seems fair for me to pull her away from her family because I'm selfish and not ready to say goodbye. I've got a boatload of baggage now with a fresh spin that I have yet to work through.

For fuck's sake, I haven't even had a conversation with Mom about everything that's happened. And with spring training starting, I won't have a chance to see her face-to-face for a while.

I haven't even processed what I'm feeling. What this means for me.

Unexpectedly, I'm angrier now that I know the whole truth. It's like a fresh wound on top of thick scar tissue. No matter how much it felt like I was growing and changing this winter, I still have the same shit holding me back. The only thing I'm certain of is I need to find a way to put it behind me. I'm just not sure what that is.

For now, my only option is to let her go and hope she doesn't end up hating me. Nothing is going to dull the pain, so why drag it out?

I make one last loop around the outbuildings to check that everything is locked up and turned off. When I come back around the front of the house, Mia's hauling our bags out to the truck. My already grouchy mood sours further.

She sees me approaching and gives a weak smile that doesn't come anywhere near reaching her red-rimmed eyes. There's not a damn thing I can do to make her feel better, and that knowledge makes my chest ache. Despite the fact that we are both miserable, I wouldn't take one second of my time with Mia back. Which is exactly why, even though this sucks right now, it's the best thing for her.

"Can you help me with the cooler? It's all packed. I know you probably still want to shower again, but I can finish the last few things while you do that."

"Sure." I try to ignore the sting that her eagerness causes. If getting her out of here is what she needs right now, I'll give it to her. Because I'd *do* almost anything, *give her* almost anything to make a little of the sadness radiating off her go away. Well, anything but do the one thing that's haunting me since we agreed to this temporary arrangement: ask her for more. I won't do that to her no matter how fervidly I wish I could because I'll only cause her more pain in the long run.

She's got this brilliant career and plans. And I'm still the same guy I was when we started this. Mia will move on and find someone who gives her everything she deserves and some day, when I meet him, I'll just have to try very hard not to break his face. My jaw clenches painfully at the thought.

If I thought it hurt watching Mia pack up, it's nothing compared to walking into the cabin and finding it completely void of any evidence of her time here. It's like we never happened and I can't fucking stand it. Marching across the kitchen I pull the cabinet door open looking for the one piece of her that should still be here.

My hand tightens around the wood door. All my mugs are lined up in a perfect row but Mia's dainty little coffee mug is missing from its spot front and center. She took it. Fuck, does that mean she doesn't ever plan on coming back?

My shower doesn't wash away the feeling that's settled over me. It's only gotten worse since I found her packing the car. I have no right to be angry about any of this. My relationship with Mia is coming to an end exactly the way I told her I wanted it to.

♥

This might go down as the longest drive of my life. Neither Mia nor I seem to be in the mood to talk. Six hours feels impossibly long and everything in me screams that this isn't right. After several failed attempts to lighten the mood with small talk, Mia rests her head against the window, pretending to sleep.

When we get close to the city, Mia shifts in her seat and reaches across the counsel to take my hand in hers. My eyes are leaving the road to glance at her more than is probably safe, but I can't stop myself from stealing a glance at her every chance I get.

As the skyline grows closer, I find myself wishing each green would turn red, giving me just a little more time with her. I get lucky and find a spot right by the entrance to her brother's building. I'd have left my car in traffic, not giving a fuck about who I was holding up if it gave me the chance to say goodbye.

"Wait here," I tell Mia when I slip the SUV into park. The eye roll she gives me is the most "us" interaction we've had since this morning. Jogging around the back to grab her bags—setting them off to the side, I stop in front of the passenger door, opening it for her.

"What are you doing?" she squeals as my hands grip her waist hauling her out of the car and into my arms. I don't care who sees. I just need her pressed against me one last time. When her feet hit the pavement, my lips cover hers. She stiffens in my arms before melting into me.

How can a kiss feel this good and this heartbreaking at the same time? Each sweep of my tongue cracks my chest wide open. When Mia pulls back, breaking our connection, there's a tear rolling down her cheek. I catch it on my thumb and press my lips to her forehead, breathing in the scent of peaches and vanilla.

"I'll never forget this winter. Thank you for giving me the gift of time with you. Fuck, Mia . . ." I say, trying to keep it together, but it's nearly impossible to keep the emotion out of my voice and off my face.

Her lips cover mine and her head shakes. "Don't—I can't take it. You promised to let me go at the end of this, unless . . ." Her voice trails off and I think she's going to say more, ask me for more.

Finish what you were going to say, Mia. Ask me to keep you. I might be weak enough right now.

What she says instead will haunt me forever. "Take care of yourself, Dean. Be the man I know. The one who helped me find my voice and changed me for the better. The only one who my heart has ever felt safe with. He's worthy of his own happy ending."

Anything I could tell her would only make this goodbye harder. Maybe someday I will, but Mia deserves better from me and right now I can't give that to her. So I do as she asked, squeezing her tight before I let my arms drop to the side and let her go. She doesn't look back as she grabs her bags and walks into Hendrix's building.

CHAPTER 39

MIA

The ding of the elevator doors closing is my undoing. My bags land at my feet and I slide down the back wall of the elevator. Pulling my knees to my chest, I bury my face as silent sobs make my whole body shake.

The ride isn't long enough to get myself under control. This has been the hardest day of my life and with the way my soul feels flayed open, I don't see that changing soon.

I could see it all over Dean's face out on the sidewalk. He was going to tell me all sorts of wonderful things about our time together, and how much he cares about me, and I couldn't hear it.

My heart was already breaking the same way it has been for the last two weeks. A slow fracture at the foundation of it, weakening with each beat until this moment, just now it crumbled in my chest. The pain steals the air out of my lungs and with it any hope I'd been hanging onto—that some miracle would allow this to work for us.

Not even divine intervention could do that. Our story starts and ends with Dean making a decision that he's not worthy of love. Nothing I can do will make a difference until he opens himself up to more.

Since the night we ran into each other getting shakes he's been reminding me of my worth and building me up. All while tearing himself down. He's already enough, but he refuses to see that and it's time he takes some of his own advice and realizes how much he has to offer to the world. To me.

The doors open and I'm in danger of riding back down if I don't pull myself up off this floor. I swipe my eyes with the back of my hand and take a deep breath.

Standing and gathering my bags, I shuffle towards Hendrix's door. Stopping a few feet from it, I slip my phone out of my pocket with my free hand and open the camera, examining how much damage has been done. My eyes are red and swollen. There's no hiding that I've been crying. Maybe my brother will take pity and not push me.

Adjusting my bags on my shoulder I step forward and knock on the door once. In the past I might have just walked in, but I've learned the hard way you never know what these two are up to and where. Fate must take pity on girls who are falling apart because Poppy answers the door instead of my brother.

When she sees me standing there, looking painfully pathetic, she opens her arms pulling me into her. And I'm crying all over again, soaking her shirt.

CHAPTER 40

DEAN

11 . . . 12 . . . 13 . . . I count off the reps on the leg press machine in my head, *MakeDamnSure* by Taking Back Sunday blares in my ears. It's been my soundtrack for punishing myself in the gym during our first week of practices ahead of spring training games.

A shadow casts over my eyes as Dom comes into view. He doesn't wait until he has my attention—just reaches out and removes my AirPods. He knows I'll blow him off, anyway. They all do. They've all been giving me space this week, especially Hendrix. Not that I blame them. My attitude is foul. If I was grumpy before, now I'm just an asshole—snapping at anyone who dares to ask me if I'm glad to be back, or how my winter was. Dom's the only one stupid enough to approach me.

"That's enough." He removes a weight when I pause my set. "You're going to hurt yourself. If you think you're miserable now, try taking away the only other thing that means anything to you and see how you fare."

The other thing . . . I'm not even sure how true that is right now. My mind is fucked over walking away from Mia, compounded by everything that happened in Boston. In my current state I barely care about baseball. It doesn't give me joy, peace, or anything but a way to wear myself out so that when I fall into bed at the end of the night, my eyes have no other choice than to close.

"I don't need you telling me what to do." He doesn't listen, walking around the machine and removing the weights from that side as well. "Has anyone ever told you that you're like a bad case of the yips?"

"Nope. You'd be the first," he says calmly, like I didn't just compare him to the thing baseball players universally dread.

Behind me, I hear Hendrix laugh dryly. My legs swing over the machine and I swivel towards the sound. Hendrix stands and starts towards me, his fists clenched at his side, but Cruz steps in front of him, putting a hand to his chest and shaking his head. He should step aside and let him do it.

The smile I give him is smug—a taunt. In the six days since I dropped Mia off at his place, he's yet to say a damn thing to me about his sister. But the disappointment is written all over his face when he narrows his eyes at me. Seems I'm really good at two things: baseball and being a disappointment.

"Everyone is fed up with you stomping around like a giant asshole. Maybe you should just call her," Dom offers, stepping back with his hands in the air when my nostrils flare.

"And say what? 'I miss you.'" And I do. So fucking much that she consumes my thoughts most of the time. Unless I'm counting reps, miles, or buckets of balls, she's right there front and center.

"That would probably be a good place to start. And then maybe you could tackle a plan for making this thing work between you two. I have some recommendations if you'd like to hear them."

"You? With the picture perfect family that's offered nothing but support. The guy who's lived a drama free life." I bite out.

See? Asshole with a capital A.

"So, I see we're trying to alienate all of your friends. Cool. Cool. You're going to have to try harder than that if you want to get rid of me. You're also not going to make me feel bad about having had a wholesome AF upbringing.

I know you're not too keen on thinking about anyone but yourself right now. But if you'd pull your head out of your ass for a minute, you'd remember that Hazel and I dated long distance all the way through college. If I were to give any advice on your other problem, it would be to talk to your family. Tell them what you're feeling. The key to my drama-free family life is love and open communication."

I stare at him waiting to see if he's done, because when he gets like this, he's usually not.

"Earth shattering, I know. Are you going to make either of those calls?" He flashes me an annoying fucking smile that usually gets him exactly what he wants. Only it makes me want to deck him right now, but I'm pretty sure that's not what he's hoping for.

"No." I stand from the leg press and walk around him without another word.

♥

NATALIE:

Call me. You don't get to blow up my world with a bomb like you dropped at the party and then ignore my calls for three weeks.

DYLAN:

Call Nat. She's been pacing in front of my desk ranting about you for the only thirty minutes I had for lunch all day. I had plans, asshole.

DAD:

Your mom said you've been extra quiet since you left. She's worried and I'm not interested in lying to her. Call her! Or me.

My knee bounces as I study the three most recent unanswered messages from my family. They are just the latest in a series of messages from them, escalating in concern the more time passes. It's not like I've completely ghosted them. I've just been very short. Pushing them off until I know what the hell to do.

My mom has a right to know what Victor did, and I should be the one to tell her. For years, I've driven a wedge between our family because of his actions, and she's done her best to hold us together like tape and glue. Now she's probably freaking out that I'm distancing myself further and nothing about that is fair. If I hadn't kept these secrets all along, we wouldn't be here.

I tug on my hair, the stress of this decision adding to the weight of missing Mia and the chaos of starting our spring training games in just a few days.

♥

The stadium smells like fresh grass and the popcorn they're giving away for the opening day of spring training. Heat from the midday Phoenix sun beats down on the back of my neck. Ordinarily I would soak it all in, relishing in the start of a new season, but that's not the case this year. I want snow and the smell of pines. Or peaches. Fuck, even a whiff of vanilla.

It's the top fifth inning and we're down by two, all thanks to me. The Vancouver Tridents' big hitter sent one careening towards me in the first, but my foot came off the base in my attempt to make the catch, letting him get on base and subsequently score.

My jaw ticks as I wait for the pitch. I've already let my team down once. I won't do it again. There's two outs, but we are back to the top of the batting order for the Tridents. The fastball sails right over the plate. Thankfully, the batter is behind. I bounce on my toes and tug my hat down low. Our pitcher, Tyson, throws a curveball. Like the schmuck he is, the batter swings. Two strikes. The next pitch is a ball. Between pitches I move around, trying to stay loose before I squat down, getting into fielding position.

Tyson shakes off a few signs from Xavier but sees one he likes, straightening up on the mound. My eyes track the movement of the ball and I see it almost in slow motion as it hits the bat. It's not a solid hit, but it's enough contact to send it down the opposite baseline. Our new third baseman, Braxton Hayes, scoops it up and rockets it across the field. Keeping my foot pushed tight against the base, my other foot slides forward stretching my body out as I reach for the ball. It hits my glove with a thwack in time to get the runner out.

It's the out we need to end the inning, but not enough to repair my bitter mood. My groan as I push up from the splits position in the dirt is a reminder that maybe I should have spent more time working on my flexibility during the off season. That only makes me think of Mia in yoga pants in my gym. A swift slap to my shoulder jars me out of my daydream as I jog towards the dugout.

Picking my head up I find Tyson at my side as we take the stairs side by side into the dugout. "Nice inning man. Thanks for the backup."

Were we playing in different games out there? If anything, he should still be annoyed with me for my screw up earlier, not thanking me.

"Uh, yeah. Just doing my job." It's thickly laced with sarcasm and more gruff than I intend. At this point, I'm not sure I can help it. In the last ten days, this is who I've become.

Cruz appears next to me as Tyson walks away, muttering something under his breath that I'm sure I deserve.

"Listen, I know you're struggling, but you've been a beast to almost every one of your teammates since we got here. I'd tell you to stop taking it out on us and focus that energy on the source of your problems, but I think you've beaten yourself up enough. I'm speaking as your captain, not your friend, when I tell you to get your shit together. You're fucking with the team and if you don't figure it out, I'll have no choice but to talk to Coach about it." He sighs, his palm covering my shoulder. "As your friend, if you need to talk, let me know. We hate seeing you like this." He tilts his head to where Dom, Hendrix, and Xavier are huddled together eyeing me with concern.

"I wouldn't be so sure about that. Hendrix is probably thrilled to see me miserable. And I can't say I blame him," I grumble, dropping to the bench in the dugout.

"He's not thrilled with the way you're handling things, but he doesn't want to see either of you hurting," Cruz says, taking pity on me and keeping Mia's name out of it, probably sensing that it would tip me over the edge I'm so precariously dangling over. With a squeeze of my shoulder he leaves me to stew on his words as he gets ready to bat.

I watch my teammates bat from the dugout, Cruz's warning playing in my head on repeat. The one thing that rings out louder than everything else is that I'm the only one to blame for this. My legs bounce in place as I watch Holden—our newly called up second baseman—connect, sending a line drive between third base for a single. Xavier goes down swinging, but Holden's fast and takes the opportunity to steal second. It's the momentum we need. Cruz steps into the box tracing a "J" and "D" in the dirt like he does every at bat before he drops one right in the gap.

With a runner on second, Hendrix crowds the plate, knowing it throws the pitcher off and sends one right over the third baseman's head. The stadium explodes in cheers, making the air around me vibrate when Holden turns on the gas and scores a run before the side retires leaving us down by one in the top of sixth.

I take the field, anxious to get my chance at the plate in the next inning. One of our relief pitchers, Julio, takes the mound to replace Tyson who maxed out his pitches and headed to the locker room for an ice bath following our conversation. I barely get a chance to settle in at first because he and Xavier are electric tonight, calling and throwing all the right pitches. Their combined efforts end the inning without any runners advancing almost as quickly as it started.

In the bottom of the sixth inning Dom steps up to the plate, sitting on the first two pitches for balls. When the third pitch comes in fast and right over the plate, he reads it and swings big. I know by the crack of the ball off the bat that it's the run we need to tie it up.

I'm there to celebrate with Dom when he crosses home plate. But when he rejoins the guys in the dugout, I'm all too aware, stepping up to the plate, that I have an opportunity to put us ahead and make up for my abysmal play earlier.

My hands twist on the bat as I wait for my pitch. The first three balls are high and outside. I know the next one is going to be a strike, but with the count being in my favor, it needs to be perfect. The ball smacks against the catcher glove and the ump bellows "strike" from behind me. I tell myself it's fine, as my teeth grind together and my cleats dig into the soft dirt as I reset my stance. I didn't want to walk anyways, a walk won't get me any runs scored.

The pitcher gets into his windup and this time I know there's more on the line. I only have two chances left. His pitch is right down the middle. I swing, but the ball drops, hitting the catcher's glove with a slap. The echo of the leather on leather makes me want to break the bat over my knee.

Fuck! I grind my toe into the dent I've made in the dirt. Bringing my bat over my shoulder. The heat and the pressure have sweat gathering on the back of my neck, beading and rolling down my spine.

This is it. I need to make contact. It's a fastball right over the plate. I swing and the ball makes contact, but I know the second I connect that it's garbage. It's caught by the left fielder sending me back to the dugout, rage courses through me as I whip my helmet against the back wall.

"Fuck!" I holler pacing in place.

Cruz starts towards me but he's cut off by Coach Wilson, his face twisted in anger.

"That's enough, Harrison. Grow up or get out of my dugout." His tone is dead calm.

I look around, and find all eyes on me. Walking to the opposite end of the dugout, I take a seat away from everyone else. There's not much I care about right now, but I know that I don't want to lose my spot on this team. It's the only thing I have left, even if it's lost its spark.

The door to my locker slams shut with a clang that echoes through the mostly empty locker room. We lost, and it's all on me. Everyone is avoiding me like the plague and I prefer it that way. I'm sick of Dom trying to cheer me up, or Cruz trying to give me advice to spur me into action. Or Hendrix looking on with a mix of pity and disgust on his face. What I need more than anything is for everyone to just leave me alone.

My shower was longer than necessary, with the goal of steering clear of everyone.

My teammates got the memo. Only those needing treatment are still milling around. Slinging my duffle bag over my shoulder, I push through the locker room door. I keep my eyes on the ground and my hat pulled low over my head, hoping it conveys my state of mind to any stragglers.

"Seriously," I growl under my breath when I look up to find Hendrix casually leaning against the driver's side door of my rental car in the parking lot. "Not in the mood," I bite out as I pop the trunk and drop my bag inside.

"Good, me either." He straightens but doesn't move from where he's standing. I can't exactly run from this conversation with him blocking my getaway vehicle.

Resigning myself to having this conversation with him I sigh, "What do you want?"

"What do I want?" He chuckles and it only grates at my nerves. "For starters it would be fucking fantastic if my sister hadn't shown up at my door with tears in her eyes when you dropped her off."

His words are like a knife, twisting painfully in my gut. I knew Mia was upset. I was too. No. You know what, upset doesn't describe it accurately enough. When she refused to let me tell her how much she meant to me, when she trembled in my arms as she tried to hold it together so I wouldn't see just how deeply I was cutting her, it took everything in me to walk away. But I had to, for her sake. He's got to know that, just look at how I acted today. What kind of man acts the way I have these last ten days.

"It would also be pretty fucking great if my teammate, who I consider one of my closest friends, wasn't lashing out and hurting everyone around him.

You can't keep letting your anger swallow you whole. Coach was right. You need to grow the hell up. If you won't let us help you, at least help yourself."

"Is that all?" I ask, pushing him further away. I can't stand his pity—the way he's still on my side after everything I've done. If someone hurt my sister the way I hurt his, I would drive my fist through their face.

"You know what, I guess so. We can't help you. No one can. Get your shit together." Hendrix steps towards me, his chest bumping mine. "If you even think about reaching out to my sister—even to apologize—before you figure out what the hell you want out of life, our next conversation will end with you eating your teeth."

My fists clench at my side, but it's not Hendrix I'm mad at. I got exactly what I wanted. He's done with me, yet, it doesn't feel the way I thought it would. The loneliness isn't soothing like I expected, it's just empty.

CHAPTER 41

MIA

Another day, another event completed on this book release tour.

When this opportunity to add a signing in Phoenix at the last minute landed in my inbox a week ago, I almost said no. If Gianna had brought it to me the week before, when everything with Dean was still so raw, I definitely wouldn't have agreed. But even now, almost a month after we went our separate ways, it feels like half of my soul is being ripped away just by being in the same city. It's almost unbearable how our proximity has reopened all the wounds. Not even the adorable powder pink aesthetic of the bookstore could lift my mood.

If it hadn't been for the heart-to-heart I had with my grandmother, I wouldn't be here, so close to where the Bandits are playing later today. After Gianna called me, begging me not to turn it down, my grandmother sealed the deal by telling me she'd meet me here—acting like I was the one doing her a favor by giving her an excuse to see both Hendrix and me together for the first time since Christmas.

What I need now is a nap before I have to meet my Nana to head to the game. I amble towards my waiting Uber and drop into the seat, scrolling my phone mindlessly during the drive. As expected, I'm out like a light when my head hits the pillow back at the hotel. An hour later, knocking wakes me and my patient grandma waits while I wipe the drool off my chin and pull myself together to head to the stadium.

With my hand clutched painfully in Nana's we watch as Dean steps up to the plate, his chilly scowl making me shiver. Which is saying something considering I'm roasting in the eighty-five degree weather. Even though he has no idea I'm here it feels like it's aimed at me instead of the Rose City Roasters' pitcher, Jared Pink. The hat and sunglasses I'm wearing are just as much about sun protection as they are about going unnoticed.

The temptation to text him was overwhelming, but I knew it would only end up with me right back where I started when I walked away from him back in Denver—heartbroken and lonely.

I'm still both those things. It's a pain I've begun to live with—one I hope I don't have to live with forever. But that's not really up to me. If I had it my way, Dean would deal with his issues and choose me. That seems unlikely though, since the Dean I've seen out on the field today is a shadow of the man who stole my heart.

Calling him Mr. Tall Dark and Broody right now would seem generous. He looks downright mean. From where we're sitting, I can see that his teammates seem to be noticing the change, too. Only Dom is engaging with him in the dugout, and then the normally cheerful outfielder walks away, looking like he regretted his decision to talk to his best friend.

During the seventh inning stretch I stand up to leave, unwilling to watch him suffer any longer. But the cool metal on my grandmother's ring-clad fingers settle around my wrist, tugging me back down into my seat. "Sit. You're not going to let him take anything else from you."

The thing is, seeing him like this makes me want to do something incredibly stupid. Like go to him and try to take some of his pain away, even if it only means more for me. Or track down his mom and sister to rat him out. I'm pretty sure they are the only two people who could get through to him right now.

At the top of the eighth Dean goes down swinging. He sulks, ducking his teammates as he goes to sit at the far end of the bench alone, where he's been anytime he's not on the field.

"That man is acting like a spoiled brat," Nana harrumphs beside me.

"Please don't," I beg, defensiveness bleeding through in my tone.

I smooth my hands down the Harrison jersey I'm wearing. Right after I bought my flight here I ordered it from the Bandits website. I don't believe our story is over. It was built on friendship and respect. We may not be together right now, but if I'm here, I'll be supporting him because, despite the pain and unfairness of it all, I still care deeply about Dean. Although now, standing here, I feel a little like a creeper wearing it while watching him stomp around the field from behind my oversized sunglasses.

Pushing my own insecurities about how we left things aside, I lean into the pep talk I gave myself at the hotel.

Nibbling on my thumb I stare down at the two jerseys I packed, one with Hendrix's number fifteen stitched on the back, and the new Harrison jersey. I'm certain in my choice to wear number forty-five. I have to believe, for both of us, that our story isn't over. That this is temporary and the relationship we built slowly from friends, morphing to lovers, and then more will get the ending it deserves. I'm choosing to believe that he heard me in Denver, and he'll come back to me when he's ready. That he'll choose us.

Tracing the letters of the last name Harrison adorning the shoulders I pick it up, hoping it will be the only jersey I wear from now on.

Even if nothing goes the way I want, and he never knows I showed up, not wearing it felt wrong.

"Gumdrop, it just kills me to see you like this." Her small hand covers mine and the soft pads of her fingers rub across it reassuringly. Flipping my palm up I give it a gentle squeeze.

"What would you have done if it had been Gramps?" The crack of the bat connecting reverberates through the small stadium.

"Probably exactly what you're doing," she says with an eye roll. "I guess that's why I talked you into coming. You shouldn't stop living your life because of him, but it's okay to hold out hope. He's a good man and I hope he figures it out, for both your sakes. Just promise me you'll let me tell him off if he doesn't get his head out of his ass soon."

"I would never deny you the ability to unleash your brand of fury on anyone who deserved it, but let's give him a little longer to figure it out. He's dealing with over a decade of betrayal and lies. Maybe we can give him more than a month to sort it out." My attention moves to the man sitting with his hat pulled low over his eyes, a glare on his face, and his arms crossed over his broad chest.

At the top of the next inning, when the Bandits are up to bat again, Hendrix makes his way from the on-deck circle to the plate looking right at us and winking. I glance over at Dean, but he's barely focused on the game as he sulks.

The smile my brother has stretched across his face fades as he stares down the pitcher from home plate. The first pitch is right down the center and my brother gets eyes on it. His swing is powerful as he drives the ball out to right field over the fence for a two run, home run.

The bounce of the ball on the green grass sends the kids seated there into a frenzy. They race for the ball. A young girl stands from the pile with her hand in the air, displaying it proudly on the outfield screen. If she sticks around after the game, my brother will be looking for her to sign it. It's his favorite part of spring training, hands down.

Normally I'd wait at the stadium for him, but I'm already too on edge at the idea of running into Dean around the stadium. "I think I'm going to head back to the hotel after this at bat," I tell my grandma as the Roasters take the field.

She frowns and I know she wants to say something, but she doesn't. Instead, she nods. "We'll text Henny and I'll come with you. It's too dang hot out here, anyway."

Bless her heart, I love her to pieces for letting it go without a fight. I didn't have it in me after watching Dean crumble repeatedly throughout the game. The toll it takes is evident in the slump of my shoulders and my yawn as we walk back to the hotel.

"Why don't you come lie by the pool with me for a bit before we meet Hendrix for dinner?" Nana asks before we part ways in the lobby.

I had planned on locking myself in my room to sulk, but this sounds better. "Sure, just don't expect me to be terrific company."

"Who says I need company? I've got a dirty audiobook to listen to from my favorite author." She bumps her hip against mine.

"Not again," I groan. She's listened to it at least twice, and each time I have to listen to her rehash her favorite scenes for me. It's disturbing at best, because her favorites are never sweet moments between my main characters, or funny hijinks with the best friend. Nope. They're the raunchiest sex scenes, every single time. Considering the low-key inspiration for some of those scenes, right now, it's depressing as hell. Still, there's no way in hell I'm admitting why I hate hearing her recaps of my latest book. That's more insight than I want her to have into what Dean and I spent our winter doing.

The worst part is I can't even scratch the itch on my own anymore. We did it too well together and no matter which toy or fantasy I use, nothing comes close. Since I asked him to let me go, it feels like my entire world has dulled back to the grayscale I was trying to escape this fall.

♥

"It makes my heart happy having you both in the same place. I haven't been this happy since—Well, never mind." Nana's cheeks turn the same shade of hot pink as the bikini she strutted down to the pool in. "I'm just really happy to have you both here with me tonight. And a win to celebrate!"

"Please tell me you've been keeping her out of trouble." Hendrix looks at me as he pulls out her chair.

"Have you met her?" I tease, reaching for my chair but my brother beats me to it, pulling mine out as well.

"I'll have you both know. I'm a changed woman." She smiles coyly. Meeting Marv has certainly settled her in many ways, but she's no saint.

My brother and I laugh—loudly, causing the neighboring table to side-eye us.

With her hands propped on her hips she tries her hardest to glare at us. It only makes us double down, gripping our stomachs as we try to pull it together before the whole restaurant is staring at us.

"Fine. I'm not completely reformed, but what fun would that be?" she finally agrees, waving us off as I wipe the tears from the corner of my eyes.

"Oh wow. I really needed that," I admit softly, realizing it's the first time since Dean and I split that I've felt truly happy. My brother frowns at me. "It's okay. You can ask, you know."

"How are you doing?" He watches me carefully, his brow furrowed, like he's not sure I'll give him the whole truth.

My shoulders lift and I smile weakly. "I'll be fine." I nibble on my lip before asking, "Is he okay?"

"You were at the game." He shakes his head. "It's pretty clear, he's not doing well."

Regret sits heavy on my chest and I wish I wouldn't have asked. It just makes me want to fix this for him more, and that's pointless. For the rest of dinner, my grandmother and Hendrix steer the conversation so far away from baseball and Dean that it would be funny if I didn't appreciate it so much. The care they take in ensuring they don't cause me any more pain solidifies the decision I've been considering since Gianna mentioned it for the first time.

I've missed having family close by, so when I get back to the hotel, I'm going to put the plan I've been mapping out in my head for the last two months into action. For me, and no one else. Regardless of what happens with Dean, I know it's time to make this change. With my mind made up, the lightness floating around me is immediate and oddly comforting. In the end,

I want him by my side, but if that doesn't happen, I still have a big beautiful life in front of me.

CHAPTER 42

MIA

"You're squeezing me too hard," Indie complains, squirming in my arms outside the terminal.

"Can't help it. I've missed you so much. Three and a half months is too long to go without seeing each other." I drop my arms, letting her go and open the passenger side door of her car.

"What's the plan for the weekend?" Indie asks, pulling away from the curb.

"Other than you being my fabulous assistant at the book signing tomorrow?"

She insisted that she not only attend, but help with the event. It's cute how excited she is about it.

"Well, duh. That's the most exciting part of the whole weekend." She laughs, merging into Chicago traffic.

Not only did she make that a sticking point of the weekend, but she refused to let me get a hotel. Which is perfect, because I'd much rather stay with her.

"You could help me with some shopping I need to do."

"Nothing's better than spending someone else's money. Or wait, are we shopping for a new man? I fully support that."

"You're never allowed to help me with that again," I tell her seriously. "But I'm not quite ready for that." It's a relief that those words don't carry the same weight they did just a week ago in Phoenix. Nothing's changed between Dean and I, but taking control of my life on other fronts is both a great distraction and empowering. Not to mention I still haven't given up hope, although I'm not sure that Indie will love hearing that.

"That's not fair—"

"Married, threesome, proposition." That's all it takes to shut her up—her lips rolling together as she tries to hold in her laughter.

"You're lucky I can see the humor in that situation now." We continue south, the city coming into view in the distance. "I need to pick out some new furniture and I have no idea what style I want to go with."

"Perfect, I love redecorating," she says, getting off the highway and heading towards her apartment.

"It's not exactly like that, more like . . . *moving.*"

"Shut up! For real?" she practically screeches, her eyes shifting for a split second before going back to the traffic in front of her. "Please tell me you're moving here and not Denver."

"I'd love to, but I don't want to lie to you," I confirm.

Indie holds her hand out across the center console for me to take and I place my palm in hers. "I'm proud of you."

"I am too," I reply simply.

"I don't know how you do it," Indie says the next night, as she slides my drink over to me from where the waitress set it on the table at the Indian restaurant we are refueling at after the book signing. "That was exhausting."

"It can be. But in the very best way." My lips tug up in a smile, thinking of all the new faces I got to meet. Maybe it's being here, with her, or the call I got earlier from the real estate agent that I listed my condo in Charlotte with. Whatever the reason, I feel more optimistic than I have in the last month.

"You seem like you're doing so much better than when I talked to you last week while you were in Arizona," she says, watching me as she pulls her straw between her lips.

"Don't get me wrong, in a lot of ways, I am. Sometimes it physically hurts how much I still miss him. At the beginning, it felt like he wasn't choosing me. Even though, logically, I know that's not true."

"You make it sound so simple. It makes me want to go find him and shake him," Indie says, eyeing the waitress as she walks past. The pretty redhead looks over her shoulder, blushing when she sees Indie watching.

"She's pretty, and I think she likes you."

Indie just waves me off. "I'm not here to pick someone up. No way I'd give up time with you while I've got you for a hookup." She sips from her drink refocusing on me. "You really aren't mad at him?"

"No. I realized we both have some things we need to figure out if we want any chance of a future. Once I started choosing myself, making decisions about my life that had nothing to do with him, things fell into place for me." Bringing my glass to my mouth, I pause, trying to figure out how to articulate my complicated feelings on how we left things. "His decision wasn't about abandoning me, it was about his past. When it came to moving, I took him out of the equation. If I hadn't, I probably wouldn't have made the same decision, because the thought of running into him and facing him if he never came back to me was too much."

"You're so enlightened. I can't say I would have dealt with this with the same grace." She laughs looking over at the waitress again.

"At least get her number." The encouragement makes Indie's smile turn devilish.

"There's no point. Now I'm going to have a whole crew of you trying to get me to move west of the Mississippi."

"Probably. I can think of at least a few people that would be thrilled. One maybe more than others," I sing-song, tapping her foot with mine under the table.

"You're not helping the cause." There's a twinkle in her eye that tells me she doesn't totally hate the idea, even if she wants to.

CHAPTER 43

DEAN

The sun is peeking through the blackout curtains of my hotel room, barely bright enough this early to light the room, when my phone rings next to my bed. I grab it, hope swelling in my chest that Mia's name will flash at me on the screen. It's been five weeks and I haven't heard from her. Not a single text or call. Hope is a tricky bitch. It hurts like hell when it comes crashing down, like it does every time my phone rings lately.

Instead of the one name I really want to see, it's Dylan. I decline the call and roll back over. Before my head has even settled back into the pillow, it's ringing again. I turn over, ready to let my brother have it, when I see it's Natalie's name this time.

"Shit," I grumble to the dimly lit hotel room. I guess they're finally going to get me to pick up. It better be an actual emergency.

The tone in Natalie's voice has me immediately regretting that thought as she frantically says my name.

"Dean, are you there?" She sniffles.

"Yeah, I'm here. What's going on, Nat?"

"It's Mom." Her voice breaks, and it has me shooting up in bed. "The jet is already in the air. Can you get to the airport in an hour?"

"I'll be there, but can you tell me what's going on?"

"She had a heart attack, Dean," Natalie says, her sniffles turning into breathy sobs that make it nearly impossible to understand anything else she tries to tell me.

♥

The tension I carried throughout my body eases a little when I step into the cool, Boston spring to find Dylan waiting for me at the private airfield. I still don't have much information about what's going on with my mom, but seeing him here is reassuring. The only update I got was that she's been moved from serious to fair condition.

My brother pulls me into a hug from across the console when I slide into the passenger seat of his G Wagon. "Natalie just texted me that she's awake and talking."

"Really?" An exhale rushes out of me. It feels like it's the first time I've taken a full breath since I got the call early this morning. "What the hell happened?"

"No one's filled you in?" he says, glancing over at me.

"Natalie was frantic, and the Wi-Fi was out on the plane, so I'm in the dark. The only update I got was a text from Dad," I explain, as he waits for the gate to open to leave the airfield.

"She got really lucky. This conversation might be very different right now if she had slept in and not gone to the gym." I don't want to ask him what he means. I can tell by the look in his eyes that he doesn't want to say it out loud either. The thought of losing her is too painful for both of us. "I should probably warn you, she fell on the pool deck when she passed out. Her face took a brunt of the impact, and she broke her arm. But being someplace where the staff was trained in first aid . . . they were able to determine early that it was likely her heart and get her the help she needed quickly."

I swallow around the lump in my throat, unable to shake the mental image of my mom laying there helpless. "You said she's awake. Does she need surgery?"

"When she came into the hospital, she went straight back to the angio suite to get a stent. They started before any of us even made it there, that's what she was waking up from when Natalie called."

He drops me off at the front door to the hospital while he goes to park, sensing my urgency in needing to see that she's okay with my own eyes.

I don't bother waiting for the elevator, instead jogging up the four floors to the cardiac unit where my mom's room is. Natalie is stepping into the hallway, her head down, wiping tears from her eyes when I turn the corner.

My heart sinks thinking something is wrong. She lifts her head and gives me a weak smile, making the pain in my chest ease slightly. When I stop in front of my sister she throws her arms around me. "I just need a hug," she says sniffling against my chest.

"Dylan said she was doing okay. What's going on, Nat?"

Her eyes find mine through damp lashes. "She's fine. But she scared the shit out of me and I don't really have a handle on my emotions right now." A hollow laugh shakes her body and when I look closer I can see the exhaustion written on her face.

"But she's going to be okay, right?" I ask, trying to figure out what the hell is going on.

"She is." Natalie pauses wavering before she continues, "I wasn't going to tell anyone this, but I'm pregnant. So every time I think that mom might not have gotten to meet this baby, I lose it." Fresh tears roll down her face as her hand goes to her stomach.

I cover it with mine. "Really, my nephew is in there?" That earns me a shove to my chest and a smile.

"You can't say anything yet, the girls don't know," she says, squeezing my hand. "You know, it could be another girl."

"Nieces are pretty cool, too. This is the kind of secret I'm okay keeping." I drop my hand from her stomach right before Dylan comes around the corner.

"How's she doing?" He eyes us warily, zeroing in on Natalie's red face.

"Why don't the two of you go see? I'm going to call Gavin so he can update the girls and grab a round of coffees."

Mom's laying in the bed, facing away from us when we walk in. Her pale arm is looped around Dad's quivering back as he sits next to her, hunched over. It feels like a moment the two of them need together, so I stop Dylan in the doorway.

My brother raises his hand, thumbing over his shoulder in silent agreement. As we are about to leave, Dad lifts his head, his watery green eyes finding us frozen awkwardly in the small entryway. "Look at you two lurking. How many times did I catch you two in similar positions as kids sneaking around?"

"They were always mischievous, weren't they?" My mom's voice is strained as she rolls to her back and gives me my first real look at her.

There are dark circles under her normally vibrant, hazel eyes and her skin is sallow. A purple bruise covers her cheekbone and her arm is in a sling. Even with the warning from Dylan I suck in a breath, shocked by how fragile she looks. It's hard to reconcile with the formidable woman I know—the powerhouse who manages a thriving legal career and raising this family. Her normally smiling face looks tired as she waves us over. "I can't believe you flew all the way across the country for a silly little heart attack."

Across from us, my dad's brows furrow. "Not funny, Nora."

"You're all far too serious. I can't stand you all sitting vigil over me like I'm a ghost. I know this is serious, but I'm okay. I'm going to continue to be okay. Promise," she says, placing her good hand on mine but when I look down, all I see are the wires and sensors.

"Dad is right. Don't downplay this. You could have died," I tell her, my voice breaking.

"If there's anything that can heal my heart, it's seeing the two of you agree on something."

"No need to blackmail us into resolving our differences." My eyes find my dad and he smiles down at her.

"Is that what this is about? Did you do this on purpose to get this one here to finally break his vow of silence?" my dad asks. I know he doesn't mean it to, but the sentiment stings and I have no one to blame but myself.

"Now who's got jokes?" Mom asks with a cough. Dylan's on his feet, grabbing her water before either my dad or I can move.

"I just needed some time. This level of theatrics wasn't necessary. How are you doing?" I change the subject back to the real issue.

"I'm okay. Sore and tired, but I'll be out of here in a few days," she says, handing the water back to Dylan, who is waiting patiently to take it from her. "Don't you have court today?" she asks, eyeing my brother—suddenly looking a little more chipper, like even the idea of work energizes her.

"I do," Dylan says with a sigh.

"What are you still doing here, then?" She raises a brow at him when he doesn't answer right away.

Shoving his hands in his pocket, he shrugs. "Some things are more important."

"Dylan, I'm fine now. You need to be in court. Go."

"I don't—"

"Your mother is right. She needs rest. I'm going to kick all of you out in a little while anyway," Dad says, cutting off his argument.

"Not this one," Mom says tilting her head towards me. "The two of us need to have a talk about his recent behavior, and then he needs to fly back, so he doesn't miss tomorrow's game."

"You're in trouble," Dylan taunts, before leaning over to kiss Mom on her forehead.

"I'll walk you out. I want to check on Natalie," Dad says, standing from his chair, leaning over my mom, and speaking in hushed tones before he kisses her softly. With a parting glance over his shoulder, he follows Dylan out the door.

"Now that I have you alone, why don't you tell me what's going on with you?" my mom says, shifting all her attention to me.

"Mom, it hardly seems—"

"Don't you dare try to get out of this. This conversation is long overdue and not knowing is only going to make me worry more. Which won't help me heal either," she scolds.

"Wow, using your heart attack against me. I didn't know you had it in you," I say jokingly, trying to keep the mood light because, despite what she says, having this conversation isn't ideal. But I know my mom, she's a dog with a bone. "I have conditions." I level her with a serious look I honed from years of watching her work.

"I wouldn't expect any less. You would have made a fantastic lawyer if you hadn't been born a baseball player—although the way you're playing now makes me question that." She shifts on her pillow and places her other hand on top of mine, cupping my palm between hers.

"You listen . . . *quietly*," I add. "And if it gets to be too much, we stop until you're feeling better."

"It won't be, but that seems reasonable," she agrees.

"I wasn't finished. You rest when we are done talking. I'll sit here and watch you sleep if I have to."

"That seems excessive, but okay. Tell me why you've cut everyone off for the last month and a half."

My free hand drags down my face. "It's a really long story." She waits as I figure out where to start. True to her word, she stays quiet and lets me get through the backstory of how the rift between my dad, grandfather and I started. Every so often her mouth opens but she doesn't interrupt. When a silent tear rolls down her cheek at the mention of Whitney and that day in my grandfather's office I almost stop. But she shakes her head, urging me on.

Each confession about the secrets I've been hiding, and how it's impacted me, takes a weight off my shoulders. By the time I get to when I walked out of the firm vowing never to return, I'm questioning why I ever kept all this to myself. It's short-lived, because next my penthouse in Denver comes up—my grandfather's gift to assert his power over me, keep me his puppet for the last four years. An ever-present reminder of all that's at stake by speaking out against him, because he holds the keys to my siblings' futures.

I can't help but remember the moment in the hallway with Natalie, my hand over the baby growing inside of her. Panic races through me that I've made a terrible mistake. I swallow roughly, pausing and looking at my mom, her watchful eyes are filled with so much love. She doesn't break our agreement, but gives my hand a reassuring squeeze. I can't keep living like this, with all these secrets and hate bottled up inside of me.

"What if he makes good on his threats and you all pay the price? Your stake isn't as large as his. He could force you out. And Natalie and Dylan don't have any protection without being equity partners. He could take their careers away." Tightness grips my throat as the panic I've felt every time I think about this rears its ugly head.

She clears her throat and I reach for her water, handing it to her. "I wish you would have told me all of this years ago, Dean, I could have saved you so much pain." Taking another sip of water her voice gets a little stronger. "I've known about Victor's part in your dad's affair for years."

"What?" I blink down at her, not sure I've heard her right. "How?"

"Whitney felt guilty, she came to me earlier this year and admitted everything. Most of it your dad had already told me." There's a hint of annoyance there, but it quickly fades when she clears her throat and starts again. "The part about Victor paying her—that was a fun surprise. He was never a fan of your dad, but to try to break up our marriage and continue to threaten this woman to insure her silence was more deceit than I thought he was capable of." Her explanation makes me feel like all the air has been sucked out of the room. "You've always been such a protector, I should have figured out that this was all tied together. Keeping your siblings safe should have fallen on your father and I, not you."

"If you know, why do you still work with him, allow him in your home?" My mother is wonderful, but not even a saint would have forgiven him for everything he's done. A smile tips up her lips and reminds me that in addition to being my mother, she's wicked smart.

"He can't work forever. And we've all put way too much time into that firm to watch him steal away our legacy. I'm biding my time until he retires or I can force him out. As for allowing him in my home, it seems like the perfect revenge—making him sit at the table while your dad and I hold hands, knowing our relationship is stronger than ever."

"I'm sorry I kept it from you."

Her hand comes up to my face, her knuckles brushing against my cheek. "You don't owe me an apology. I should have forced you to talk to me about this years ago. If I'd have known this was what was causing the rift, I could have helped." Her voice cracks and I'm tempted to stop her.

"I didn't exactly make it easy for you. Even if you had tried to force my hand—I wasn't ready," I admit, not blind to my role in this.

"Your dad and I have discussed this at length in therapy over the years, and he said the same thing. He was afraid it would only push you further away. And insisted he needed to be the one to fix things with you when you were both ready. Year after year, it's gotten harder for both of us to accept this as our reality. He carries so much guilt and loves you so much. We just want to be a family again. After Whitney came forward, I started pushing for him to figure things out with you." A tear rolls down her bruised cheek.

"I want that too," My throat tightens painfully at the truth behind that admission.

"I've watched you change, close yourself off to people. It kills me because you have so much to give—love, friendship, kindness. My loyal son." Her eyes are getting heavy and I know I need to stop her. Force her to get some rest, but something stops me. She needs to say this and I think I need to hear it.

Mia's face is all I see when she starts again. My mom's voice is so soft I need to lean forward to hear her. "I almost lost the love of my life once. It wasn't easy, but we chose each other and fought every single day to rebuild our relationship. Choosing your dad not once, but repeatedly over the course of thirty-seven years was the greatest thing I ever did. I don't want to see you miss out on love because you continue to let this rule your life. Don't let him win," she says, her words fading away as her lashes flutter against her pale cheeks.

Fuck. I've spent years believing that I'm not worthy of love because of him. He turned his back on me when I needed him the most, and the lesson I took away from that shaped who I am today. But I don't want to be that anymore, and I don't have to be.

"I'm done, Mom. He's had all the power for too long, and I'm not going to let him take anything else from us. I'm selling the penthouse. This ends now, I can't keep living like this with my past dictating my future."

I want to be the man that Mia sees in me. I *am* that man. The only question is, will she forgive me for not choosing her? I really fucking hope so, because the last six weeks have been utter hell.

Stepping away from the bed so I don't disturb her, I do what I've been wanting to do since the moment I moved to Denver. Hope fills me as I select contact info for a real estate agent that I saved in my phone two years ago. Easing myself into the chair furthest from the bed to avoid waking my mom I wait for the call to connect and list the penthouse.

My neck aches as my shoulder is gently shaken. Groaning, I wake from a very uncomfortable nap in a chair that's far too small for my frame.

"Rise and shine, sleepyhead." Millie's cheerful voice penetrates my grumpy gaze as she giggles.

"You should see your face. You have sleep lines all over it. They look like prison bars," Chloe adds, laughing quietly on my other side.

"Always a treat being woken up by you two." A chorus of cracks and pops makes Millie blanch as I stretch out my stiff back.

"Gross," Chloe says, wearing a look of teenage disgust.

"At least we don't jump on you anymore," Millie says, her voice growing louder.

I bring my finger to my lips trying to quiet them down and failing.

"Remember that time you kneed him in the crotch—" Chloe starts.

"That's enough girls." My mom's voice is harsh and raw, but there's still so much love there. "Come here and give me a hug. Dean's had a hard day and doesn't need to be terrorized."

They both rush to her side, careful of the cords and sensors surrounding her, wrapping her up in two sets of arms, one on each side of the bed.

"You scared us." Chloe's voice shakes and I hear Millie sniffle next to her.

"Sorry, Mom, they ran ahead and I couldn't keep up," my sister says, her chest heaving with the effort of chasing down two teen girls.

"You okay?" I mouth.

She nods and flashes me the picture in her hand. A small black-and-white image. That instantly brings a smile to both our faces. A happy secret. One I don't have to keep much longer by the look of it.

"Did you girls spill the beans or do I get to do that?" Natalie asks, joining her daughters.

"No, we figured you deserved that since you're doing all the hard stuff," Millie says, making room for her mom next to her. I join Chloe popping a kiss on the top of her head.

"What are you all talking about?" Mom asks, looking around. "No more secrets," she says, exasperated that no one has fessed up yet.

Natalie hands her the picture. "Meet your grandson."

My mom's hazel eyes go wide as she looks from the small photo in her hand and back to my sister.

"Fuck yes, I knew it." I pump my fist dramatically.

And a chorus of "Deans" ring out around me. "Sorry. I was excited. We're finally sharing happy secrets!" My shoulders lift in a shrug, but I'm not really sorry. For the first time in a long time, I feel like a real part of this family and if that means I drop an inappropriate curse word, so be it.

"Does that mean we get to tell grandma about your girlfriend?" Chloe asks, excitedly.

Millie rolls her eyes at her sister. "What if they broke up, and that's why he's been such a shithead?"

"Camille," my sister scolds.

Her daughter just shrugs her off. "I thought it was okay since Dean was doing it."

Little shit.

"Girlfriend?" my mom asks, an eyebrow raised.

"Well, not exactly." My hand grips the back of my neck, looking at the picture in her hand.

"Dean, didn't we just talk about this?" my mom asks and I look at the twins for help, but they both wear the same annoyed expression as the rest of the women in the room. Okay, so no help here.

"I'm going to fix it." They look unimpressed. "As soon as I get back to Denver." Still nothing. "I have a plan. Will you all stop looking at me like I'm an idiot?"

"*Well, are you*?" Chloe asks, the question dripping with sarcasm.

"Yes," I admit. "But I don't want to live without her. If she'll take me back, I'll work really hard to be the man she thinks I am. Because Mia sees the best in me. She makes me better."

"What the heck are you still doing here?" my mom asks.

Four sets of eyes swing to her, taking the attention off me.

"Thanks for coming home for us," Natalie says an hour later when I'm walking her and the twins back outside. "You really have to head back tonight?"

"I'll always be there when you need me. Coach was understanding, but I need to get back for the game tomorrow. I haven't been the best teammate so far this season." Pulling Natalie against my chest, I tell her, "I wish I could stay longer and celebrate. Congratulations, Nat."

"I can't believe we're going to do it all over again." She laughs, it's a little manic, but I can't say I blame her. "You'll come home more now? For your nephew."

"I'll come home more now for me." I open her car door for her and then both the girls who wrap me in tight hugs.

CHAPTER 44

DEAN

Later that evening, my eyes close before my flight to Phoenix even takes off, but nothing about the commercial flight is restful. The perks of flying private are too ingrained in me, only now the thought of using the plane Victor owns, after everything, makes my skin crawl. Fresh start or not, I can't shake the rebellious attitude towards him. Not that he'd care, but deep down, I know I need to cut ties with him completely.

Noise canceling headphones and my hood aren't cutting it. I still wake up every few minutes, no matter what I try. On the plus side, the Wi-Fi is working so I'm able to start putting my plan into action.

There are a lot of pieces that need to fall in place, but all I really care about in the end is telling Mia I'm sorry and asking her to give me another chance. For the first time since my flight landed in Boston early this morning, I look at my notifications.

There's a slew of missed texts from the guys in the group chat.

BLANCHE'S BATTERS

DOM:

Give Mama Harrison a hug from me and tell her to get better soon.

XAVIER:

Thinking of you.

CRUZ:

Let us know if you need anything.

There's nothing from Hendrix and I'm not surprised with how we left things. It's been tense. He's one of the first apologies I need to make. I don't have a lot of time to pull off everything I want to do, especially with the season opener in just over a week. His support would make it easier to win back my girl.

There's dozen's more texts from my agents, Coach Wilson checking in, and a few other teammates that I read through before I see one from Indie. There are no well wishes, just a simple message: "Make me regret this and I'll end you" with a picture attached.

My finger hovers over the picture for a moment before I click it, opening it on my screen. It's just a cream-colored piece of paper with a couple lines of typing across the center of the page—a book dedication.

"To my favorite daydream, you gave me the courage to try new things and the confidence to believe I could succeed simply because of your faith in me. I hope you know, I believe in you too."

I don't need to see the cover, or her name in the byline, to know that message is meant for me. The entire time we were together, I was afraid of hurting her, but I underestimated how strong she was, how good. Now the only thing I'm afraid of is that I won't get the chance to make this right before she moves on.

The man in the seat next to me keeps glaring at me. I'm sure it's annoying with my knee bouncing the entire flight, but I'm ready to get off this plane. When the pilot announces we're making our descent, I can barely sit still.

If I thought it wouldn't piss him off more, I'd go straight to Hendrix's hotel room tonight. But I already owe him several apologies and starting off by waking him up in the middle of the night doesn't seem like the best way to start my apology tour.

♥

My eyes are still gritty, and I look like shit as I stand in front of Hendrix's hotel room door the next morning, a coffee carrier in hand and knock.

It takes a minute before I hear his feet padding towards the door and the lock clicks open. He drags his hand down his face when he sees me. Stepping back and sweeping his arm across his body, he gestures for me to come in. Shoving one hand in my pocket, I step into his room.

"Everything okay with your mom?" he asks, dropping down on the end of the bed. His dark hair is a mess from sleep.

"Yeah, it was scary, but she'll be okay," I tell him, sliding the rolling chair away from his desk to sit in.

"Listen, I'm glad your family is good, but it's early and I'm not really in the mood for your attitude," he warns, the concern he had earlier, slipping away to annoyance with how I've treated him lately.

"Coffee?" I ask, holding out the cold brew I grabbed him.

He eyes me skeptically and I can't say I blame him. I've been an asshole of epic proportions for the last six weeks.

"It's from the coffee shop down the street, not the lobby. Consider it part one of my amends." I hand the cup across the small gap between us.

"Exactly how many acts are there to this thing?" That almost sounds like teasing. Maybe there's hope for me yet.

"How many do you need?" He stares back at me, his lips pressed in a tight line. "Too soon for jokes, got it."

"How about you just tell me why you're here, bringing me coffee, when you've been a complete twatwaffle since you left my sister crying at my door?"

"Yeah." I push my hand through my hair taking a deep breath before I start. "About that. I'm really sorry. I was an idiot and I wish I could do it all over again."

"Which part exactly?" he asks, his expression still stony.

"Both. All of it." This is harder than I thought it would be. I was so focused on the end goal of getting Mia back, I didn't really think about all the damage I'd done to everybody else. "But if I can only pick one, I'd pick another chance with your sister. Every single time."

"Good. She deserves someone who'd pick her." If I think that's the green light I need, I'm mistaken. After he brings his cold brew to his lips for a drink, he levels me with a glare. "But unless you've done the work to figure your shit out, I don't want you anywhere near her."

"I have. Or I am," I tell him, pulling out my phone and finding the listing for the penthouse. Handing it to him. "I'm selling the penthouse."

"Not interested," he says, handing it back with only a passing glance.

"That's not what I meant. I'm done being trapped by my past. I've let it confine me and held onto the anger for too long. That's not who I want to be anymore. Your sister saw more than just the grumpy baseball player. Underneath my crusty exterior, she found someone she thought was worthy of her time and affection, and that's the man I want to be. One she can be proud of. One that she can love. Her marshmallow."

"I have no clue what that last part means." The corner of his mouth ticks and it almost looks like a smile. So I go all in, telling him what I've known for a while even though, until yesterday, I shoved the feeling down anytime it crept in.

"It means I fucking love her, Hen."

"Sounds like you're in the wrong place. She's the one that needs to hear this, not me." The smug smile on his face now is undeniable.

"Just like that?" Why the fuck am I questioning it. I stand from my chair, and then sit again. I thought he would make me jump through hoops for even a glimmer of approval after everything I put her and the team through.

The team. I guess I should start on the rest of my apologies.

"Do you mean it? Not the love part, I've known that since you walked into the locker room looking like a carbon copy of me after I walked away from Poppy. I mean the other stuff about fixing your life, because I don't want your past to hurt her."

"Yeah. My dad and I are talking again. I never want to go back to that bitter place. I'm not saying I won't have bad days, but I want her by my side, helping me through them, and I want to do the same for her."

"Good," he starts, but before he can say more, I continue.

"I've been a shit teammate and I'm sorry that you guys have had to put up with my abuse. The Bandits have been my family when I needed them the most and none of you deserved my childish behavior."

"We're all good, man. I'm just glad you finally pulled your head out of your ass. We just want you to be happy," he says, standing to pull me into a hug.

"Does that mean you'll help me get her back?"

"I guess it's your lucky day. She'll be in Denver next week when we get back."

CHAPTER 45

MIA

Poppy comes out of her office, my brother following close behind. When she sees me coming through the door, she looks guilty.

"Come on! You guys knew I was coming over for brunch. You couldn't wait until I left?" I whine when I notice her messy braid barely hanging on and her swollen lips. They've only been home from spring training for a week, so I shouldn't be shocked that the two of them are making up for all that missed time.

My brother looks up from adjusting his joggers on his waist. His ears turn red when he spots me. "Oh. Hey. Is it ten already?"

"This is why I'm staying in a rental," I remind them. The last time I stayed with them was right after they got back together following a false start. And I'm permanently scarred because of it.

"How could I forget?" he says sarcastically. "Are you ready to head out right away?"

"I don't know. Are you?" I ask, eyeing his joggers and lack of shirt. "I'm sure Poppy doesn't mind, but all the other people trying to enjoy brunch might."

"Doubt it," Poppy murmurs under her breath, eyes moving over my brother's bare torso. It makes my stomach knot uncomfortably remembering when I had the same reflexive reaction to Dean.

God, I miss him.

"Um . . . Yeah. I'll send you a pin for—brunch." He tugs on his neck, glancing to the side at Poppy who's wearing an amused expression as she's against the wall, watching the weird as hell exchange.

"Why did you make me come here if we were just going to drive there separately? Did you guys not finish—Nope. Nevermind. I don't want you to answer that." I glare at Poppy, daring her to open her mouth, but she's too busy trying to hide her laughter. *Thank God.*

"Whatever. I'll see you there. Put some clothes on." I shout over my shoulder as I bolt before I can make things anymore cringeworthy.

Plugging my phone into the charging cord in my car I wait for the robotic voice to dole out directions to—he never even told me the name of the place we are meeting at, just dropped a pin. I'm about to text him when the map appears on my screen. Forget it. I'm not going to chance interrupting anything between those two and having to hear about it.

City highrises turn to a more suburban mix of retails and residential properties as I blindly follow the monotone voice through Denver. Why on earth did he pick a place almost thirty minutes from downtown?

Rolling my eyes, I continue driving towards the mountains. The GPS directions have me pulling off the main road into a subdivision. It's clear after a few minutes of weaving through gorgeous craftsman style houses that I'm not in the right place. Dialing Hendrix, I continue following the map as the phone just rings and rings.

"Oh, for fuck's sake," I grumble, about to turn around when it shows my destination just ahead. There's a familiar black Range Rover in the driveway.

My heart rate picks up at just the sight of it. I blink rapidly, hoping it's not a cruel coincidence.

I suck in a breath and the gasp fills the empty car at the sight of the tall, dark, and oh-so-handsome man sitting on the step of the front porch. Pulling up to the curb, I stop the car, unsure of what to do next because, after almost two months apart, he still has the exact same effect on me.

My heart is begging me to sprint straight into his arms, but my head is warning me to ask a few questions first.

Pain trickles up my arms from my fingers, where I still have my hands wrapped tightly around the steering wheel. I shake them out as Dean stands, his hands shoved in the pockets of his jeans. He looks like the man I remember from Telluride, a thick flannel layered over a Henley, giving him that slightly rugged edge. His gait is easy and relaxed as he moves across the lawn.

Meanwhile my throat gets drier with every step he takes towards the car. He slows as he steps off the curb, looking from me to the house and back again. It's the first time he's looked unsure and I think maybe he's about to flee.

Reaching for the door handle, the seat belt tightens across my chest, yanking me back. *Shit!* My hands go to the buckle hitting the red button and pushing the door open. I almost trip in my rush to get out of the car. If he's about to run away, he's going to have to do it without the car as a barrier.

"Hey, Dreamer." His eyes sweep over me slowly. Forget butterflies, this feels more like a herd of elephants trampling my stomach at being this close to him again. Dean lifts his hand like he wants to reach for me, but stops himself, gripping the top of my car door instead.

"What's happening right now?" I ask, my voice on the edge of panic as I try to let my head take the lead. I've come a long way in the last few weeks. My heart hasn't given up on the idea of a future with this man, but I'm not the wreck I was when we said goodbye almost two months ago.

That isn't to say my feelings for him have diminished. In fact, they are stronger than ever. Our time together at the cabin showed me I was capable of everything I set out to accomplish. His faith in me and encouragement to strive for more in all aspects of my life gave me the courage I needed.

But it wasn't all him. This fall, when I hatched my plan to spend the winter in the mountains, I was struggling to feel at peace in the life I created. Every day was a hustle, and I was drowning in it. There's still more work to do, but I proved to myself that, not only can I have boundaries with my work, but I'm not done growing as an author. I don't have to pick.

It took coming back and packing up my condo to realize that it wasn't a fresh start I wanted, it was my people. And *he* is one of those people. Trying to do it all alone was never the answer. I don't need him. But I want him. *Every single day.* Because even though I can do it on my own, it's better when I share my joy and successes with him. That's what love is. It's that one person that you want to share your joys and sorrows with. Your laughs and new adventures.

Dean Harrison is the man I want my happily ever after with.

Those intense green eyes study me nervously, glancing between me and the house. "Brunch," he finally says. "I made chocolate chip pancakes."

"You made chocolate chip pancakes?" My grandmother's words, that I shared with Dean at the cabin, come back to me, "*Chocolate chips in pancakes are a sign that the chef cares.*"

"I did. Let's go inside and talk."

"Where are we, Dean? I'm so lost and I can't think straight with you standing in front of me. The questions whirling around in my head are too loud." I'm so overwhelmed that I can feel the heat crawling up the back of my neck.

This time when he reaches out, he does take my hand. It instantly calms the noise, but does nothing to ease the flitting sensation in my chest.

"Come on. Let me show you," he urges, shutting my door before guiding me through the yard. My body moves instinctively, following him without hesitation. He's always been talented at commanding my body.

Surreal doesn't even begin to describe that feeling of following him up the steps and through the front door of the beautiful house. Except, once we get inside, it's barely furnished. Still holding my hand, he quickly moves us through the empty house to the kitchen. Unlike the other rooms we've passed, it's fully furnished. And beautiful.

In the center of the room, a long wood table is set for two with a plate of pancakes waiting. The smell of syrup and melted chocolate have my stomach growling loudly.

"Someone's hungry." His shoulders shake as he pulls out my chair for me. "Better feed you. I don't want you hangry for this conversation."

My eyes rise from the empty plate in front of me to the oversized sliding glass door that opens up to the patio and the open backyard. They catalog each piece of the vaguely familiar scene laid out in front of me. Two teal Adirondack chairs sit side-by-side. Off in the distance, a boldly painted birdhouse hangs in the yard, all of it framed by the grandiose Rocky Mountains. It's picturesque.

Turning to Dean, I find him watching me closely with a knowing smile on his face. "Who's house is this?"

"Mine. Pancake?" he responds, holding out the plate like he didn't just tell me he bought the exact house I described him being happy in.

"What about the penthouse?" I ask, sitting there dumbfounded with a platter hanging between us.

He adds a pancake to my plate with a shrug. "I sold it. Well, technically, it's still mine. The sale closes later this month."

"Why would you do that?" My hand wraps around the cup in front of me. The coffee cup. Pausing with the cup halfway to my mouth I look down at it and tears immediately start prickling at the backs of my eyes. It's an identical cup to the one he bought me for Christmas.

"Because I'm trying to fix the biggest mistake I've ever made."

I chuckle because I can't believe this is happening right now. I'm still not totally clued in to exactly what's going on, but I'm trying to keep my heart from getting ahead of itself. All of this feels an awful lot like my dreams coming true. "I'm going to need you to give me a little more than that."

His chair scrapes against the floor as he pushes back from the table. Turning my chair so he can squat in front of me he takes my hands in his. "Letting you walk away from me is my greatest regret. I should have fought for you, but I didn't think I was worthy of the love you have to offer. Or any love, really. You told me you need me to work on myself. But it took losing you, weeks of hating myself, alienating everyone around me, and almost losing my mom for me to realize that I can't keep living like this. And more importantly, I don't want to."

My desire to hear him continue is beat out by concern for him. "Is your mom okay? My brother kept me in the loop, but I wasn't sure if you'd want to hear from me," I explain, his sharp jaw under my thumb as it rubs along the line of it.

"She's going to be fine. I told her everything . . ." He laughs, deep and joyful. It's the sweetest sound. "She's known about what Victor did for years. And I promise to tell you the whole story. None of that is important, but it puts what *is* important into perspective. How I choose to move forward is what matters, and I hope that you never question if I'd want to hear from you again, because the answer is always yes"

"So you bought a house," I say, gesturing to the kitchen and backyard.

"Mhmm. My past is a trap I've lived in for too long. And it's kept me from the best thing I've ever had in my life. You. It's time to be the man I want to be. The one you showed me I could be. If you'll have me, let me show you I can be that man."

"I already know the kind of man you can be. I've always known. You just needed to see it, too. I couldn't force you to see what everyone else already does." I drop my forehead to his, tears clinging to my lashes now.

"I have an appointment with a therapist to help me wade through learning how to rebuild the relationship with my dad and love myself," he adds nervously.

"I love that idea."

"Let me choose you. I promise if you give me a chance, I'll be that man. Not for you, but *because* of you."

"I want that more than anything," I tell him, my hands shaking as I sink my fingers into his hair and brush my lips over his.

"I may need time to figure out all the relationship stuff, like if you prefer roses or tulips. And which kind of toilet paper you prefer—soft or strong."

Snorting at the unexpectedness of this whole morning, I reply, "Wildflowers, actually, and the rippled kind."

"Even though I've never let someone in my life like this before, I've had some of the best examples. I've watched Natalie and Gavin love each other flawlessly for years. And seen my teammates fall in love and grow with their partners. Although I couldn't see it until now, I've got my parents, who've battled back to rebuild a love stronger than the one they started with." He tips his head kissing my forearm sweetly. "I guess what I'm trying to tell you is that I'm really good at loving people. I've done it with my siblings, nieces, and parents. Let me love you the way you deserve to be loved. The way we both deserve."

"Whether or not you had the capacity to love was never a question for me. We spent two months living together, and you showed me every single day that you were capable of love through all the little things you did for me. You just had to realize that you were worthy of it."

"I'll do whatever it takes to keep showing you as we figure this out. But I want to do it together. That's why I sold the penthouse and bought a place that would make me happy. I don't want to punish myself any more. That part of my life is over. This next chapter has yet to be written—"

"You did not." My groan makes his breath skitter across my skin as he laughs.

"I did." His eyes shine with delight, clearly having zero regrets about his corniness.

"I don't think this is going to work. I can't be with someone this cheesy." It almost feels like we haven't lost the last two months together with how we fall back into this easy banter.

"You love it," he claims.

I really fucking do.

"I'm really digging the minimalist vibes."

"I thought we could pick out furniture together."

"You want me to help you decorate your house?"

"I want you to help me decorate *our home.* I know it's a big ask, but I'm tied to a contract here for the next few years and your family is here. If you wanted to go back and forth or do long distance, I'd make it—"

His lips smush together, my finger covering them. Leave it to my brother to help him coordinate this whole grand gesture and not tell him I already made the decision to move here.

"I sold my condo two weeks ago." Before I know it, I'm hoisted up off the chair and into his arms. My favorite place to be.

"Please tell me you haven't found a place yet."

"I haven't, but I think I'm going to need to see more of this one before I make my decision. The kitchen is lovely, but the rest of it could suck."

Please let him have the foresight to at least get a bed. Although the table could work too, or the floor. You know what, I'm not picky. Anywhere will do.

"There is one more room you might be interested in seeing."

His muscles flex underneath me as he moves through the house with my legs wrapped around his waist.

The fact that there's only a mattress on the floor makes it look a little bit like a bachelor pad, but it doesn't stop me from wanting to make use of it. When his feet keep moving past the bed to the closet, my lip juts out.

Like the rest of the house, the massive closet is mostly empty, other than a pair of running shoes and a duffel bag shoved in the corner.

"This is your side." Sliding me down his body, he lowers me to the ground, turning me to see the only thing hanging. His jersey. With the number fifty-five and the name Harrison stitched across the shoulders.

Two large hands loop around my waist from behind, slipping under my shirt to brush against the pebbled skin on my stomach. Looking over my shoulder, I find his soft, green eyes looking down at me filled with so much promise. "Come to opening day tomorrow, wear my jersey and move in with me. Because I love you, Mia James, and I swear I'll choose us every day without hesitation. When things get hard, I'll fight for us because we're both worthy of a once in a lifetime love."

Turning in his arms, my hands travel up his chest and thread together behind his neck. "All I've ever wanted from you was to choose us. I fell for you little by little each day since you let me in. Even when we were apart, that didn't change." I pause, looking back at the jersey. "Actually, I have a little confession to make. This is not my first Harrison jersey. I bought one a few weeks ago to wear to one of your games in Arizona."

"What? You came to Phoenix, and you watched me play? I wish I would have known." There's regret in his eyes that makes me sad because I remember how angry he was that day.

"No, you don't. You were a mess. It killed me to be in those stands watching you fall apart and not go to you. You still needed time. Love isn't something you can do alone, but you were there with me all along. There was love in the way you befriended me, in the way you touched me, in every small thing you did to open yourself up to me. You just needed to stop running from your fears and your past so you could see it. And I needed to know that you'd come back to me. That you wouldn't really leave me."

"I see it now, and I never want to look away." His face softens, letting go of the pain he was holding on to at the memory of those weeks we were apart.

"Good, because I love you too and I don't plan on stopping."

"Does that mean you'll be in the stands for me tomorrow? And that you'll move in?" he asks, looking nervous.

"Yes. There's no place I'd rather be tomorrow, and every day after."

Dean groans, gripping my hips more tightly. "You're telling me I missed the first time you wore my jersey?"

The coarse hair that I've missed running my hands through so much slips through my fingers as I pull him down to me, his lips almost touching mine. "Should we remedy that right now?"

"As long as you promise you'll still wear it to my game tomorrow." He wastes no time peeling my sweater off my body.

"Your wish is my command." My words are punctuated by the sound of the hanger ricocheting off the closet wall.

The light touch of his fingers stroking my bare arms as he dresses me in his name and number has my skin pebbling. "Dangerous choice of words. I've got almost two months to make up for and the list of things I want to do to your body is endless."

"Good thing we have all the time in the world to check each and every one off." Stepping back his hand drags over his mouth as he admires his handy work—leaving me standing there in my leggings with the jersey open down the front revealing a barely there ribbed bra. I grow more impatient for him with each heated pass of his eyes over me.

"You're fucking perfect."

"No, I'm not. But I am yours."

"Damn right you are. Turn around and show me how well you wear my name." His finger points at the ceiling and he makes the universal sign for spin.

I fold like a cheap card table, giving him my back, my whole body willing to give him anything he asks for. The rough noise he makes echoes through the empty space.

He doesn't say a word, but I can feel the heat of his body as he closes in on me from behind. Gathering my hands up in his, he brings them over my head, walking me forward until they are pinned against the wall.

"These stay here while I get reacquainted with your body."

"Always taking away my hands," I tease, although part of me wants to protest. As badly as I want his hands on me, I want to touch him as well, but when he cups my breast through the fabric, all logic goes out the window. His mouth moves along my neck slowly. "That's because I can't think straight when you touch me. And fuck, baby, I want to be sweet and slow with you. Show you just how much I love you, but I don't know if I can." Tugging on my hips so my back is forced to arch, I can feel just how hard he is. "I'm so gone for you, and seeing you with my name on your body has my restraint unraveling."

"Love isn't only soft and sweet. We're building a love to withstand the test of time. It's not fragile. *I'm* not fragile." Shaking my hand free from his grip, I cover the one working my nipple into a tight peak, sliding it down my stomach, continuing until our hands are under the waistband of my leggings. "You feel that?" I ask, guiding his finger through the slickness pooling between my legs. "I like when you don't hold back on me physically, or emotionally. You giving yourself over to the pull between us is hotter than a restrained version of you."

"How did I get so fucking lucky?" He sucks the skin at the base of my neck into his mouth hard and he plunges a finger inside me, causing me to hiss through my teeth at the delicious combination. "Use my hand. Make yourself come while you wear my jersey."

Each time my hips buck, my ass rubs along the hard ridge of him through his pants, multiplying my urgency to come so that I can feel him fill me again. I cry out pushing my hand harder against the wall to gain leverage and reach the spot I need him to touch.

"That's it, sweetheart. Let me hear those pretty whimpers." The deep grunts and the heat of his breath against my neck as he showers me in praise tell me he's right there with me, just as eager for me to find my release. Freeing my hand from his, only to wrap it around my throat, his grip is just tight enough that he's able to gently turn my face up toward him so he can cover my mouth with his. My pulse thrums under his fingers when he deepens the kiss and curls his fingers inside me. The sensation of him so thoroughly possessing me like this is overwhelming, causing my knees to almost give out at the sudden rush of tingles as my orgasm crests.

"Fuck, Mia," he groans, shuddering against my back. His hand slaps against the wall as he folds over me from behind, his dick swelling against my ass.

I can't stop the giggle that burst free. I did that to him, without even touching him.

"This is your fault," he says, his heart still pounding against my back.

"I know. That's why I'm so tickled."

"Just another reason I love you. You're so good at keeping my ego in check."

"Would it make you feel better if I gave you a do-over?" Twisting away from the wall I push up on my toes and press a kiss to his lips. Then take his hand and lead him to the bed, where I pull him down beside me and crawl on top of him. Despite what I said earlier, when I feel his thickness pressing against me for a second time, we take our time. Sweet words of love ghosting over our skin and we slowly bare our souls to each other. And it turns out, we do soft and sweet really well too.

It's not until we're laying there, side by side, wrapped up in the sheet that we pulled clean off the bed when we were rolling around, that I noticed the new ink on his previously bare forearm. Sitting opposite his "To Define is to Limit" tattoo are curved letters spelling out "Somniator."

"It means 'Dreamer' in Latin. It seemed fitting to add a reminder of where I want to go, and that my dreams are worthy of chasing simply because they are my own. Not out of spite or vengeance. I can't change my past, but it's a reminder that there are plenty of reasons not to go back to that place. My future holds so much more than my past ever could."

"It's perfect." The sentiment has my heart melt in a way it's only ever done for him.

He kisses the crown of my head as finger traces the curves of each letter. "I'm glad you approve, considering you were the inspiration for it."

Peace settles over me as I watch Dean warm up on opening day at the Bandit's stadium, flanked by Poppy and Lilah. Five months ago, my life felt like it was coming apart at the seams. Writing was joyless. My favorite people were all halfway across the country, and don't even get me started on my love life.

It's not just the man currently stretching just outside the dugout that has helped me find this sense of contentment. It's the work I've done to put myself first. Things I didn't even realize I was doing at the time, like setting boundaries professionally to allow a better work life balance and putting myself first with the decision to move to Denver. I feel like myself for the first time in a long time.

Over the sound system, the National Anthem plays. When the music fades away, fireworks explode around the stadium and the team takes the field while the Boston Revs prepare to bat. Dean jogs out alongside Dom, slapping their gloves together before they part ways. I watch as he turns away from the field as he nears first base, his eyes scan the crowd, when they land on me, he taps his heart twice and blows me a kiss.

My cheeks heat the way he claims me publicly. It doesn't matter that there is no furniture in our new home, I can't wait to get back there and spend the rest of the night celebrating our love and, hopefully, a Bandits win.

CHAPTER 46

DEAN

There's no better feeling after two months of misery than looking up to find Mia in the stands wearing my jersey. It still feels like a dream. There are so many ways my plan could have gone wrong. Especially since my so-called friends kept me in the dark about her already making the decision to move out here.

After bringing the pancakes to bed, we spent a long time talking. Mostly me reassuring her that I was going to get it right this time and her reiterating that she had no doubt I would. I'm not the only one who spent our time apart working on myself. Mia made some big life decisions and I'm so fucking proud of her for it. Her decision to move out here was grounded in what she wanted, independent of me. And she worked with her team to revise her schedule for the next two years pushing release dates back to give her more time for herself between books—as well as being clear about the types of projects she wants to focus on in the future.

I can't be sure if it was the orgasms or the changes she's made, but Mia was more relaxed than I've ever seen her. Even now, when I look at where she's sitting with Delilah and Poppy in the stands, she looks happy. The final notes of *Take Me Out to the Ball Game* play and I follow my team back out to the field ready to send the Revs back to Boston with their first loss of the season. Just two more innings before my girl will be waiting for me outside the locker room.

"That smile looks good on you," Dom says, clapping my back as he jogs past on his way out to centerfield.

"Get used to it. I don't think it's going anywhere."

He just smiles back, genuinely happy, even if that means he's lost a wingman. Xavier's been spending time with a girl he met at Dom's house on New Year's Eve. It's not serious, but it leaves Dom as the only single Bandit in our group. A fact he continues to complain about.

After a quick detour on my way to first base for a fist-bump with Henry, the fan from the shake shop, I take my spot. We make quick work of the eighth and ninth innings and walk into the locker room riding the high of winning our season opener four to zero. My high is amplified by the fact that when I walk out these doors after my shower, I'll get to walk right into Mia's embrace and there's no place else I'd rather be.

"You and Mia better still be coming to Draft tonight. No ducking out to lock yourself away in that empty house," Dom says, strutting past with his towel draped over his shoulder, bare ass, in nothing but a pair of slides as he meanders towards the showers.

"Yeah, we'll be there." Shockingly, I'd rather just have everyone over for a low-key night. But as Mia pointed out when I suggested it, you need furniture for that.

"Dude, the towel goes around the waist. How many times do we have to tell you?" Xavier tells Dom when he looks up from pulling his socks on to get an eye full of ass cheek.

Last season, I gave Hen and Cruz a hard time for how quickly they shower and get out of the locker room, but I finally get it. My shampoo has barely touched my hair before I'm rinsing it out. I take a little longer with soap, not wanting to leave any post-game funk around for when I finally get Mia alone at home after Draft.

Minutes later, hair still damp, I'm pushing through the locker room door to find someone that's not family waiting for me for the first time since I was in high school. And her reaction doesn't disappoint.

She's launching herself into my arms before the door even shuts.

"Hey, Dreamer."

"Hey, Handsome."

"New nickname?" I ask holding her in the hallway for everyone to see.

"Yeah, I figure since you upgraded to boyfriend, it was time to upgrade that as well. Besides, Mr. Tall Dark and Broody doesn't fit when you're this smiley."

"Can you blame me? We won our home opener and I got you back. Plus, it's hard not to smile when your brother looks at me with that face."

"What's wrong with my face?" Hendrix asks as Poppy snicker beside him.

"You look like you can't decide if you want to hug him for making your sister happy or gag at the PDA," Poppy says, pressing up on her toes to give him a kiss on the jaw.

"Yeah, well. It's weird. Mia's a whole, grown-ass woman and I'm not going to try to dictate what she can and can't do, but I'm not used to seeing her like this, or him this full of glee."

"Get used to it because I spent too much time hiding away. Both in how I feel about him, and being stubborn about not moving here sooner. From now on, if I feel it, you're going to know it."

"Listen, I'm glad you're both happy, but do you plan to carry her to Draft like that? Or is she going to use her legs?"

"I haven't decided yet," I joke before sliding Mia down my body and bending to whisper in her ear. "Just because I let you go doesn't mean I won't kiss the shit out of you as soon as he's not looking."

Her chest rises with her intake of breath, and red splotches cover her chest where my jersey is unbuttoned.

Mia looks over her shoulder to where her brother stands with Poppy, Delilah, and Cruz. "You guys can head over and we'll be right behind you."

Hendrix just shakes his head, laughing, and takes Poppy's hand, pulling her along with him.

"Don't be too long!" Poppy hollers before the door to the player parking lot shuts behind her.

Frowning at the locker room door when I hear some more of my teammates approaching, I take Mia by the hand and lead her to the private room just off the family waiting area.

"What are you doing?" she asks through a laugh.

"Making good on my promise," I explain, pressing her into the closed door.

"Mhmmm. I can't say I hate that idea."

"Fuck, sweetheart. Seeing you in the stands for me tonight made this game better than any other I've ever played in. I spent over a decade feeling like I was dead inside. Never more than the last two months. You burst into my life and lit me up. First from the outside, and then you made your mark on my soul and I remembered what it felt like to really live. I think that's why I slipped so deep into the darkness when I lost you. I finally understood what I was missing."

"I'm not your savior, Dean. Just a girl who loves you, damage and all."

Her arms loop around my neck, pulling me down to her. "I love you too, Mia." Lifting her, she twines her legs around my waist and I kiss her the way I wanted to when I found her waiting outside the locker room for me. We get lost, the kiss turning frantic before I pull back and place a soft kiss on her forehead.

"We should probably get to Draft or they'll give us hell," I tell her, not at all convinced myself.

"After all the shit Poppy and my brother have put me through, they can be patient." She rolls those blue eyes before giving me one more kiss, slow and deep, only to be interpreted by a knock on the door.

"Let's go, love birds." Dom's voice booms from the hallway.

"Such a fuck stick, I'm going to get you back," I tell him, hip checking him into the opposite wall when we join him.

"I rode over with Xavier, but Kristy was whining about going out so he took her home. Can I get a ride with you two?"

"That's a train wreck waiting to happen. I really should make you walk for interrupting us, but yeah, hop in," I tell him, holding the door open for Mia.

"She made him take her home after the home opener. What's her deal?" Mia asks.

"Not sure. She came with one of the rookies to the New Year's Eve party. I get the bad tingles from her, but Xavier doesn't want to hear it," Dom says, visibly shivering. "That girl is looking for a meal ticket and he's pussy blind."

"Dom," I warn, but Mia snickers next to me.

"Is that what you are?" she asks looking up at me.

"Fuck no, our boy here is head-over-heels," Dom says, throwing his arm around Mia as we get to the car.

The ride to Draft, our regular post game spot, is short. Mia and Dom chirp back and forth the whole way. When we step inside the place is packed with fans. With Mia under my arm and Dom flanking her, we slowly make our way to the roped off area where the team hangs out.

"You made it!" Delilah gushes, pulling Mia away from me towards a table where pitchers of beer and our friends wait. I follow Dom to the bar to grab a whiskey.

"You two are good together. I'm really happy for you." His brown eyes flash with sadness as his gaze passes over the girls with their heads tipped back in laughter—Willa, Delilah, Poppy, and Mia.

"Everything okay with you?"

"This winter was kind of lonely. With you up in the mountains, and the other guys coupled up. I don't know man, I'm feeling a little jealous."

"Why didn't you say something sooner? No one is abandoning you. All of us are still here for you."

"No it's not like that. The hooking up, the rookie lifestyle that I've been living for the last few years—I'm just sick of it. I want what my parents have, what you all have. Someone to share post-game highs and lows with. And not just for the night."

"It's not like there's a shortage of women to choose from. If that's what you want you'll find it." I try reassuring him, but he shakes me off.

"If only it were that simple. It's about just finding someone. I want the right one. Someone who looks at me from across the bar like she's looking at you right now." He nods his head to where Mia's standing, her eyes on me as Poppy whispers in her ear.

"Then go after that." I clap him on the back as the server brings over our drinks two whiskeys, neat—a tradition that started on opening day of our first season together. Win or lose, we toast to the upcoming season with the same drink each year.

"Yeah, maybe I will," he says, lifting his whiskey from the bar and holding it between us.

I raise mine to meet his. "To finding happiness on and off the field."

We drain our drinks and he turns his back to the bar, scanning the crowd before he gives me a quick nod and heads over to where some of the older guys are talking with a group of women, some of them WAGs, and some I don't recognize. At least he's staying away from the rookies who have a group of barely legal cleat chasers at their tables.

Not waiting to be away from my girl any longer, I cross the bar and wrap my arms around her from behind.

"Having fun over here?" I ask, inhaling her sweet scent, my nose buried in her hair.

"Always. How was your toast with Dom?"

"We should set him up with someone. Got any ideas."

She considers me over her shoulder, a mixture of amusement and doubt twisting her lips. "I'm not touching that with a ten-foot pole."

"Probably smart," I say, kissing the top of her head. "So, how long do we need to stay before it's acceptable to whisk you away?"

"Just take her to the bathroom like a normal adult," Delilah chimes in from next to me, taking me by surprise.

"And where did you come from?" Poppy asks her from across the table with one side her mouth quirked up.

Everyone at the table turns to look at Lilah, who's rolling her lips together, only for Cruz's silhouette to appear in the hallway that leads to the bathroom behind her.

"Is there a line for it? Or just first come, first serve?" Hendrix asks, through his laughter. Finally stopping when Poppy elbows him in the side as Cruz steps up to the table, taking the empty spot next to Lilah.

Looking around the table, taking in my friends and their significant others I duck my head to Mia's ear. "I loved our winter together in the mountains, but it's good to be back in the city."

"Yeah. It is." Her hand squeezes mine, and she melts into me, a contented sigh leaving her lips.

EPILOGUE

DEAN

THREE MONTHS LATER

"Dreamer, where are you?" I call out pushing through the front door to our house, finding the now-furnished lower level empty of any signs of her.

No answer.

I drop the bags of supplies she had me pick up on the kitchen island as I pass and check the backyard. She's clearly been here—chairs and tables are set up for the party later today, but no Mia.

Taking the stairs two at a time, I call out again, "Where are you hiding?"

"Not hiding, just not so patiently waiting." Her voice echoes through the hallway from our bedroom.

"When you give me a shopping list a mile long, it's going to take me a minute to find every—" My feet stop along with my words when I open the cracked door to find her laying across our king sized bed in the hottest lingerie set I've ever seen.

"What is this?"

"No housewarming party is complete without a little pre-party christening," she explains, pushing up from where she was resting against the obscene pile of throw pillows she insisted we needed and crawling across the bed towards the foot.

"I don't claim to be an expert in hosting traditions, but I've already had you in every room in our house."

"Not today you haven't."

Yeah, I'm not going to argue with that. Not when she's on her knees waiting for me in nothing more than a see-through, baby blue lace set that has her pink nipples poking at the lavender floral pattern.

"How long have you been up here waiting for me?" My thumb brushes over the scrap of lace on her shoulder, toying with it.

"Let's just say if you had kept me waiting any longer, I would have taken matters into my own hands." Her light touch tickles when her fingers ease under the hem of my shirt.

"Show me," I tell her, stepping back and pulling my shirt over my head.

"You don't want to touch me?" she taunts, slipping one hand under the thin lace of her panties.

"I always want to touch you, but first you're going to show me how you make yourself come when I'm on the road, and then I'm going to fuck you so hard our friends are going to wonder why you're walking funny this afternoon."

♥

Mia's rushing around the kitchen an hour later, frantically grabbing dips out of the fridge and pouring chips into bowls when the first car pulls in an hour later.

"They're early. I knew I should have cut you off sooner," Mia groans, looking at me with wide eyes. "I don't have the appetizers all out yet."

"Sweetheart, our friends don't care." Pausing my work filling the coolers I go to the front door letting Poppy, Indie, and Hendrix in.

"Don't freak out, we came to help set up!" Indie shouts lifting her sunglasses to rest on the top of her head.

"And we brought extra ice," Hendrix says from behind her.

The five of us work in tandem finishing the items left on Mia's to-do list just as everyone else pours in. I'm grabbing drinks for some of the guys when my eyes are drawn across the yard to Mia. She's sitting with the girls on Adirondack chairs with their heads together.

"I never would have guessed that you'd willingly invite us all over for two parties in one year, not to mention the post-game get-togethers you've hosted," Cruz says when I hand him his beer. "Are you coming after my captain's spot?"

"No man. You can keep that. There's just something about coming home these days that can't be beat."

"I think it has less to do with the house and more to do with how you've changed. You've come a long way. Are you still going to therapy?" He was the one who recommended I talk to someone during spring training, when I was at my lowest.

"A few times a week. My dad and I are in a much better spot, and there's no amount of therapy that can repair the relationship with my grandfather, but I'm at peace with not having a relationship with him."

Both of us watch as the girls stand from the patio and cross the yard to where we are, Lilah coming to his side and Mia wrapping her arms around my waist.

"You two look like you are up to no good," Cruz says, dropping a kiss on Lilah's head.

"Just wanted to say hi to our two favorite guys."

"Mhmmm. I don't believe that for a second," I tell Mia, whose smile is just a little too wide.

"Well, we were just wondering what's up with the girl Dom brought?" Lilah asks quietly.

"She's sweet. Like really nice," Mia adds, looking between Cruz and I.

"Is that a problem?" I ask.

"What no. Of course not," Mia says a little too quickly.

"It's just unexpected," Lilah adds, looking guilty for the assessment.

"Who did you expect him to show up with?" Both their eyes follow the same path across the yard. Delilah's employee is talking animatedly while Indie hangs on every word.

"Honestly, no one. I thought he'd come alone knowing she would be here." Mia nods towards her head.

"She's had him chasing his tail for months," Lilah continues, glancing over to where Dom has his arm casually slung around his date's shoulder. "Now he's just moved on."

"You almost sound disappointed," Cruz teases.

"I just thought maybe they would both find what we have, and we'd get Indie to move out here in the process." She huffs.

"Come on, Hermosa, let's get you fed and let the two of them figure it out." Cruz keeps Lilah close as he steers her towards the food.

"And then there were two," I say, turning towards my girl so that she's pressed against my front.

"Finally alone. Hosting is hard work. I've hardly seen you since this morning," Mia says resting her head against my chest.

"True, and you know I'll never turn down alone time with you, but it's kind of nice to have everyone here."

"Excuse me, who are you and what have you done with the grump of a man I met last fall?"

"You see, I met this girl who made me see that there was more to this life than my past. She turned me inside out. But don't worry, I can still be bossy and broody when it counts."

"I'm going to need to see proof of that when our friends clear out."

I open my mouth to bark out the order for everyone to leave. When Mia's hand clamps over my mouth.

"Don't you dare. I loved you grumpy and I love you sweet, but I worked way too hard setting this all up today for you to kick everyone out just to drag me to bed."

"How would you feel about hosting Thanksgiving for my family here this year?" It's something I've been considering for a while, especially since my therapy season a few weeks ago, which my dad joined virtually.

"I love that idea." Her arms tighten around my waist. This woman has been patient with me every step of the way. From when I was being difficult about picking out furniture because I wanted everything to be just right, to when I've been cranky after a particularly draining therapy session. Even this party was my idea, and she helped make sure it was perfect, wanting me to have the home I've been missing all these years.

"Your family too."

She turns her face up towards me, eyes soft. "Nothing would make me happier than to have them all here."

"Then that's what we'll do." I probably shouldn't admit this, but I'm completely guilt free when I realize my grandfather will be all alone in Boston, with no family to celebrate with. But as quickly as the thought appears, Mia chases it away with a kiss to my jaw. Maybe that's worth mentioning to my therapist, or maybe that means all the hours I'm paying her for are working.

BONUS EPILOGUE

MIA

ONE MONTH LATER

The warmth of the evening summer sun washes over me through the passenger side window of the Range Rover as Dean navigates through the familiar twists and turns leading us back to Telluride. It's the first time we've been back since the winter. Between the cross-country move and baseball season starting, there's been little down time.

The sense of contentment that I found over the course of the last six months hasn't waned, even with our hectic schedules. There's something about the man I love coming home to me every night that he isn't on the road that balances it all out. Plus, I've continued to prioritize myself, setting work hours, and only committing to projects that nurture my love for writing. The girls and I spend a lot of time together with the baseball season in full swing to help keep the loneliness at bay.

Tomorrow marks the start of the All-Star Break and the crew decided to rent a few cabins in town during the four-day intermission. By some miracle, the last game for the Bandits before the break was a day game, so we were all able to head up right after they finished to make the most of our time together. Behind us is a caravan of vehicles winding through the mountains containing all our closest friends.

In the rear-view mirror, I can see Dom dancing in the driver's seat as Indie looks on annoyed. They are staying with Xavier and this girl Kristy, that's latched on to him like a leech since New Year's Eve. The other couples are each staying in their own cabin at a nearby property.

When we get to a T in the road, we split off from the group, heading to our cabin while they continue on to their own places. We all have plans tomorrow to meet up for a hike before dawn. For the life of me, I can't figure out why we need to be up that early, but Cruz and Delilah planned it and Dean swears the views of the overlook, which is only accessible by foot, will be worth it.

Dean's hand covers my thigh and when I look over at the eyes that drew me to him almost a year ago are studying me. "I wasn't sure you'd ever be back here. I don't know what I would have done if you hadn't given me a chance to prove to you that I could be the man you believed in."

Reaching across to cup the back of his neck I remind him, "You'll never have to know because you've shown me every day since that you're the only man for me." Dean's past is firmly behind him at this point. The only things that remain of the penthouse are his collection of books, some pictures of his family and the batting cage. Everything else was donated, along with the proceeds from the sale.

He used those to fund a new softball facility for Double Play. I'm sure his grandfather was pissed, but we will never know because he's cut off contact with him completely, as has his family. Turns out Victor was quite the villain and his mom had been building a case to get him to retire for years. Once she had recovered from her heart attack, she convinced him to retire peacefully and sign over all his shares to be split evenly between herself and the three kids. Dean gave his shares to his nieces and soon-to-be-born nephew.

"Thank, fuck, because I'm so gone for you Mia James," he huffs, gripping my wrist and threading our fingers together.

As the road narrows and curves, the place that brought us together comes into view. This time, instead of being draped in snow, everything's my favorite shade of green. The same color as the eyes I look into every night before I fall asleep.

Dean parks the SUV and comes around to open my door. "What are you doing?" Laughter bubbles out of me when his fingers grip my hips and lift me out of my seat. I can feel every ridge and valley of the muscles on his chest and torso as he drags me down his body.

"Leave the bags. Right now I just want to make love to you in our place, the one where you changed my life forever by teaching me that I was worthy of someone like you," he whispers against my hair and I follow him inside to spend the rest of the night remembering all the ways he made me fall for him.

♥

"Rise and shine." Soft lips brush over my bare shoulder, the easy sigh I make sounds like it's coming from somewhere off in the distance.

Rubbing my eyes and I turn into the warm body next to me. "Too early."

"Let's make a deal. I'll make the coffee and you can sleep for a few more minutes, Dreamer," he mutters along my jawline.

"Love you so much." My lips part in a lazy yawn, but my eyes stay open just enough to watch him slip out of bed. It's a sight I never get sick of. Bending down, he presses a kiss to the top of my head and pulls the blanket up for me.

There's no going back to sleep once the smell of coffee floats into the bedroom. Besides, without the man I love by my side, the bed doesn't hold the same appeal. My feet drag across the wood floor on my way to find Dean.

The draw to be near him is too strong to deny, my arms wrap around him from behind, he's standing at the coffee machine grabbing one of his mugs. Under my cheek, his back flexes as he reaches up to grab one for me.

"Fuck," he mutters, awe coloring his tone, spinning so quickly that I'm taken off guard by the unexpected movement. His hands are all over me, first steadying me, and then lifting me into his arms and kissing me hard.

My elbows rest on his shoulder and grip his hair as kisses me deeply. "Mhmm. Not that I'm complaining, but what's happening right now?"

"Your mug . . . I thought you took it when you left last winter. But it was pushed to the back. It was there the whole time." How this man was ever cold and detached is unimaginable now because he's the gooiest fucking marshmallow, sweet and soft—his charred exterior completely stripped away.

Except in the bedroom, there's still some darkness there when I ask for it—or when I'm being a brat. Like he did a few nights ago when he edged me until my makeup from our nice dinner out was smeared all over my face from a mix of sweat and tears. Bringing me to the brink and pulling me back again until I was begging for him to let me come.

"I just didn't want it front and center, taunting you when we left—in case it took you longer to figure things out. I always knew I'd be back because I knew who you were in here." My palm covers his thrumming heart.

Coffee forgotten, we opt for something different to wake our bodies up. Although we still make good use of the kitchen with my hands wrapped around the edges of the kitchen island as he shows me both sides of him. The crispy exterior that whispers wicked things against my legs as he drops to his knees behind me, and the melty center that whispers words of love as he covers my back with his body when we finish together.

It's a miracle we aren't late to meet everyone at the trailhead for our sunrise hike.

Although, some of the crew is looking more chipper than others. Xavier stands next to Dom, his arms crossed, looking annoyed. When I glance around at everyone else, I see Kristy is missing.

Indie appears next to me with a headlamp strapped to her forehead. "Please save me," she says, keeping her voice low.

"Already making bad decisions?"

"Not yet, but I might get arrested for assault before the trip is over. Between Dom being—himself—and the early morning drama between Kristy and Xavier, it's only a matter of time before I go off the rails."

"Where is she?"

"Refused to get up. Xav was pissed."

Another car pulls up, the headlights illuminating the dark area. Cruz and Lilah get out first, but then the back of the SUV opens and a man I've never seen before joins them. Next to me, Dean just shrugs when I give him a questioning look.

It seems everyone is just as clueless murmuring to each other as we all migrate to the middle of the open parking lot.

"Thanks for coming this morning. I know it's early, but it means a lot to Cruz and I that you all showed up. This is Thomas. We hired him to come along and take some pictures," Delilah explains, beaming at Cruz more than looking at any of us as she talks.

"Ready?" Dean asks, slapping Cruz on the shoulder and giving him a little shake.

The two share a moment before Cruz slips Delilah's hand into his. "Yeah. I am."

We hike through the forest, the sky growing a little more golden the further we go. Everyone moves fluidly between conversations and small groups talking and laughing. All the while Thomas snaps candid pictures.

It's not a hard hike, and in no time we crest a hill and come into a clearing. Thomas gathers us all in the center of the opening, the sun still low behind the mountains behind us to take a picture. He has us all posed in a semi-circle and then steps back lifting the camera to his face just as he's about to click the shutter Cruz, in the center of the group, clears his throat. "Hey Delilah, this looks like the perfect spot to marry my best friend."

It feels like it all happens in slow motion, everyone turns inward. Dom laughs loudly, Poppy wipes tears from her eyes and I'm totally slack jawed. Dean and Lilah don't look surprised at all. In fact, they both look just as proud of themselves as Cruz does.

"Nothing would make me happier than to marry you in front of all our friends this morning," Delilah says, leaning into Cruz as he beams at her response.

"What about your dress?" Poppy asks, looking around like it's going to appear out of thin air.

Lowering the camera Thomas steps forward. "I think I can help with that."

Retrieving his backpack from where he dropped it at the base of a tree when got here, he calls us over, explaining what he needs from us to help pull this surprise elopement off. Once everyone has a task we divide and conquer. The girls help Delilah get ready using a tarp and rope that he pulled out of his pack to provide privacy. The guys do the same for Cruz, stringing their tarp up on the opposite side of the opening.

"I can't believe this," Poppy says, for at least the third time as she helps Lilah into her dress.

Indie is digging through a small pouch of makeup that was stashed in Lilah's fanny pack. "What made you guys decide to elope instead of doing something after the season?"

"Did he propose?" I blurt out, tacking on my question.

Joyful laughter pours out of Lilah as she slips the straps of her stunning dress over her shoulders. "It definitely wasn't a traditional proposal," she says blushing. "We were in bed."

That causes all of us to break into fits of laughter. "But he did have a ring. I've just been wearing it at home."

"What about your families?" Poppy asks softly.

"They know. We will do something after the season, throw a big party. Neither of us wanted to wait, and Cruz couldn't imagine having a big wedding with groomsmen and bridesmaids . . ." She doesn't need to explain that sadness in her eyes. Getting married with someone other than his brother,

Jarrett, by his side would be too difficult. "This just made sense." Her smile returns as bright as the sun starting to peek over the mountains.

"Is our bride decent back here?" Thomas asks from the other side of the tarp.

"More than decent. She's the most beautiful bride I've ever seen," I reply, in awe that she was not only able to keep this all a secret, but also smuggle a stunning dress up the side of a mountain. Thomas ducks below the impromptu curtain and takes pictures from every angle, making sure to get shots of the open back and the buttons cascading down the fabric that is hugging her curvy backside.

"Can you rearrange her train so it's fanned out by those wildflowers?" he asks Poppy, nodding towards the patch of purple flowers. The shutter to the camera clicks several times. "Everyone squeeze in for a group shot and then it's time to get your girl married."

The bride is passed around each of us pulling her into a hug. Then we all make ourselves scarce as Cruz waits in the center of the opening for her. "She looks breathtaking," I say, keeping my voice low. My favorite set of arms wrap around me from behind.

"She does. Someday that'll be you and me." My breath hitches in my chest and hot tears spring to my eyes. I don't even try to stop them. "Are those happy tears?"

"The happiest," I reply, only loud enough for him to hear.

The golden rays of the sun filter through the pines, playing off the greens of the trees as Delilah and Cruz say their vows. Hendrix stands between the happy couple officiating the whole thing. Part of the boy's duties—get him ordained online.

Dean holds me through the whole ceremony kissing the top of my head and rubbing soothing circles over the back of my hand. This life is even better than I thought possible. All because of the man next to me, and the people surrounding me.

THE END

WHAT'S NEXT?

OTHER BOOKS BY LO EVERETT

MILE-HIGH HEARTS SERIES:

All on the Line - Poppy & Hendrix

All or Nothing - Delilah & Cruz

Calling it Safe - Mia & Dean

Force Play - Coming Soon!

ACKNOWLEDGEMENTS

Each book it gets a little harder to know who to thank because there are so many of you on this journey with me.

To my kids, who've been steadfast in their support and cheerleading since the beginning. I love you guys. Thank you for being patient when I need "just one second" to finish a thought, create a post, or whatever crazy author shit I'm up to. Thank you for being my favorite people to run a game scene by. Your knowledge about the sport as athletes is far superior to mine ninety percent of the time.

To my Alpha Team, who are the actual heroes every single time—telling me when something is too far-fetched or just downright bad. Allison, Kat, Stephanie, Tiffany: I hope you guys enjoyed your break, it's time to get back to work.

To my Beta Readers, who are equally important, impressive, and too many to name because I love you guys so much that I just keep collecting more.

To the hype squad who've stuck with me as I continue to grow and learn. Andi, Amanda, Lark, Devin, Britt, Emily, Dawn, Becca, Cara, and so many more—you all took a chance on me when I had no clue what the hell I was doing. I might have a few more clues, but I haven't quite made my way off the hot mess express yet.

To Ali and Sara, for helping me put my best foot forward when I have no creativity left to give. You guys always make me look good.

To my author friends, new and old, for being a source of support and a sounding board. Especially Ronnie, for always making me laugh, and Jenni for taking me under your puffin wing.

To Cait, my editor, who is literally editing this as I type it in the final hour because that's the way I roll: Your candor and commitment to making sure my books are the best they can be is beyond valuable. You're the best of the best, and I'm forever grateful that my first ARC brought you to me.

Lastly, to my readers, you guys fucking rock and I love you. Many of you have become like friends, and I hope you continue to slide into my DMs until I'm old and gray. Each post, TikTok, reel, and review means the world.

www.ingramcontent.com/pod-product-compliance
Lightning Source LLC
Chambersburg PA
CBHW031841310726
48972CB00005B/1354